# FRONTIER

# FRONTIER

## S. K. SALZER

**PINNACLE BOOKS**
Kensington Publishing Corp.
www.kensingtonbooks.com

PINNACLE BOOKS are published by

Kensington Publishing Corp.
119 West 40th Street
New York, NY 10018

All Kensington titles, imprints, and distributed lines are available at special quantity discounts for bulk purchases for sales promotions, premiums, fund-raising, educational, or institutional use. Special book excerpts or customized printings can also be created to fit specific needs. For details, write or phone the office of the Kensington special sales manager: Kensington Publishing Corp., 119 West 40th Street, New York, NY 10018, attn: Special Sales Department; phone 1-800-221-2647.

PINNACLE BOOKS and the Pinnacle logo are Reg. U.S. Pat. & TM Off.

ISBN-13: 978-0-7860-3625-7
ISBN-10: 0-7860-3625-7

First printing: March 2015

10  9  8  7  6  5  4  3  2  1

Printed in the United States of America

First electronic edition: March 2015

ISBN-13: 978-0-7860-3626-4
ISBN-10: 0-7860-3626-5

*For my much-loved parents,*
*Jean Spicer King, who taught me to love books and history,*
*and in memory of my father,*
*Paul Thomas King Jr., who taught me to love words.*

# Prologue

*Fort Phil Kearny, Dakota Territory*
*December 21, 1866*

Rose heard the wagons before she saw them. She began to shiver as the rattle and clang of the iron wheels grew louder. Sounds moved with deceptive clarity through the thin mountain air, especially after sundown, but the wagons were close, only minutes away.

The other women gathered with their children in one of the officers' cabins but Rose waited with the men by the quartermaster's gate, its heavy plank doors open wide to receive the approaching train. They stood without speaking, eyes fixed on the ribbon of road that trailed off into the gathering darkness. The last of the light clung to the snow-fields atop the Bighorn Mountains, a gleam in the distance.

"Riders on the Bighorn Road!"

The sentry's voice boomed from the blockhouse

moments before Captain Tenodor Ten Eyck and his advance guard emerged on horseback from the gloom followed by foot soldiers lumbering like bears in their heavy greatcoats. As the first wagon rolled through the gate, Rose saw that its bed was filled with naked corpses, stacked head to heel like firewood. Here a stiffened arm protruded, there a leg, white as Italian marble. A second wagon, bearing the same cargo, was close behind.

Colonel Carrington stepped forward, stopping the wagons. "How many, Captain?" he said.

"Forty-nine, sir." Ten Eyck dismounted and walked to Carrington's side. "Including Fetterman and Brown."

"And Grummond? What of him?"

Ten Eyck shook his head. "I don't know, Colonel. It was too dark to continue the search. I fear they've all gone up."

Carrington turned on him, his face contorted with rage. "Dammit, man, you should have taken the road. You might have been there in time, you might have saved them!"

Ten Eyck's one good eye opened wide. "Colonel, I needed the higher ground—surely you see that. My men were on foot, most of them, naturally I was concerned that if I marched them through that defile—"

Carrington raised his hand. "We'll discuss this later. Now is not the time." He pulled himself to his full height of five feet four inches, though in Rose's eyes he had never looked smaller. "Take these men to the hospital. If there isn't enough room, use one of the unfinished buildings. It doesn't matter which."

Ten Eyck gave the order and slowly men came forward to unload the bodies of fellows they had laughed and worked with just hours before in the unusually warm December sun. Rose gasped when she recognized the seal-gray head of Private Thomas Burke sticking from the pile of corpses in the second wagon. Just that morning he had repaired a leak in her cabin roof. Now his eyes were bloody cavities and a stick protruded from his open mouth.

She turned her head and wrapped her woolen shawl more tightly around her shoulders. At that moment there was only one place she wanted to be, only one person she wanted to be with. She ran to the stables where the men who rode with Ten Eyck were tending to the mules and horses. Immediately she saw him, Daniel Dixon, taller than the others, unsaddling his horse in the flickering lamplight.

"Daniel!"

He turned when she called and walked forward to meet her, taking her hands in his. They were warm, despite the frigid night air.

"What happened out there?" she said. "What did you see?"

The surgeon's angular face was half in shadow. "They're dead," he said. "Fetterman and every man who rode with him. Eighty-one men, dead."

Rose shook her head, unwilling to believe this, fearing what it meant for her, for each one of them. She saw her dream of a free, unbound life in the West, a life big as a man's, go all to smash.

"You can't be sure of that," she said. "Grummond and his troop are still out—they might come in yet."

The scout, Gregory, joined them, his cigarette glowing orange in the darkness. "Don't kid yourself, Mrs. Reynolds," he said. "They're dead all right—that or worse." To be taken alive was the greatest fear of every man, woman, and child at the post, the stuff of nightmares. "I'll warrant Red Cloud and his warriors intend to finish us off too, at first light most likely. We'd best be ready."

"How could this happen?" Rose said. Tears stung her windburned face. "How could things go so wrong?"

Dixon laughed bitterly. "It's been nothing but wrong, from the very beginning. Fetterman, Grummond, all those men were doomed from the start, from the day the U.S. Army sent us up here. The army used them, used Carrington, used all of us. Sure, the colonel will take the blame for what happened today, but the die was cast long ago. Tecumseh Sherman and his friends sacrificed those men to the god of railroads and commerce. The world will see that someday."

Gregory grunted and ground his cigarette into the frozen mud with his boot. "Well, I pray you live to see that day, Doc," he said. "But right now I wouldn't lay odds on it."

# Chapter One

*Fort Stephen Watts Kearney, Nebraska*
*May 16, 1866*

Lieutenant General William Tecumseh Sherman arrived in the middle of a windstorm that unsettled the animals, dirtied the freshly cleaned clothes hanging along laundresses' row, and sent the giant garrison flag to snapping like pistol shots. Women in poke bonnets, children in homemade clothing, shopkeepers in aprons, Mexican teamsters, blanket-wrapped Indians, all gathered shoulder to shoulder on the boardwalk to catch a glimpse of the great national hero and commander of all western armies. Sherman's visit was a major event for the soldiers of the Eighteenth U.S. Infantry, many of whom had soldiered with "Uncle Billy'" in Georgia, the Carolinas, and earlier, at Kennesaw Mountain, Peach Tree Creek, and Jonesboro. They loved him as one of their own. No matter how big he got, Bill Sherman never would be too big to sit down with a private and eat a plate of beans at his campfire.

Rose Reynolds tried to find a place in the crowd. Colonel Henry B. Carrington and the post's commanding officer, Lieutenant Colonel Henry Wessells, stood before rows of sweating soldiers under the hard blue sky as Sherman's custom-made Dougherty ambulance rolled through the gate at the head of a column that included an overdue supply train. When it stopped the men shouldered their muskets with a rattling clatter.

A gust of gritty wind grabbed Sherman's hat as he stepped from the vehicle and sent it bouncing along the ground. A junior officer bolted after it.

"Welcome to Fort Stephen Watts Kearney, General," Wessells said, stepping forward. "It's good to see you again."

Sherman returned Wessells's salute without enthusiasm and surveyed his surroundings. A bustling and important place during the gold rush years, Fort Kearney by 1866 had taken on an aspect of decay. The original sod structures listed to one side like drunkards and even the newer wooden buildings were poorly constructed and in need of paint. The surrounding landscape, in all directions and far as the eye could see, was brown and sere, bare of any hint of green other than the rows of transplanted cottonwoods bordering the parade lawn.

"My God, Wessells," Sherman said. "This place hasn't improved any. What a country." He accepted his hat from the breathless junior officer and slapped it against his leg, releasing a cloud of dust.

"It has potential, sir," Wessells said. He was a small man with bushy white hair and a well-trimmed beard. "All it needs is more water and good society."

Sherman laughed without humor. "That's all Hell needs," he said. "Damn place is rotting away. I'm inclined to let it go to the prairie dogs."

Rose could not believe her ears. To her Fort Kearney was a magic place, far better than her native St. Louis with its dirty streets and foul smells. Kearney was the gateway to an exotic new world of beauty and strangeness and danger. New characters arrived every afternoon at two o'clock, when the heavy Concords of the Western Stage Company rumbled in for a team of fresh horses and to discharge passengers connecting with the Holladay lines out of Missouri. Rose entertained herself by inventing histories for weary, rumpled travelers from faraway places like Denver and Salt Lake City as they climbed down from the carriage and stood blinking in the white sun. Men in suits with waistcoats and top hats were card sharps, Indian agents, or felonious bankers absconding with suitcases full of cash; ladies in fitted traveling suits were heiresses fleeing abusive husbands, actresses bound for San Francisco, or women of opportunity returning to their families for a chance at redemption. The fort's dusty streets teemed with Indians, scouts, and malodorous mountain men with hair-raising stories of wild red warriors, giant flesh-eating bears, and arctic cold. Let all this go to the prairie dogs? Surely not.

Sherman moved up the line of men standing at attention, pausing occasionally to greet one he recognized, before he and the high-ranking officers retreated to headquarters for a cool drink and cigars. The ladies of the post hurried back to their quarters to make themselves beautiful for the soiree Wessells would host that evening. It would be a gala occasion, one of the few the families of the Eighteenth Infantry had enjoyed since arriving at Fort Kearney the winter before. The air was charged with excitement, not only because tonight there would be dancing and good food—thanks to an uncharacteristic spasm of generosity from the post sutler—but because Sherman's presence meant the long weeks of waiting finally were coming to an end. Soon their great adventure would get under way.

Officers blacked their boots and unpacked epaulettes, plumed hats, and dress coats while their wives pressed the wrinkles from their finest gowns. Rose took extra care, choosing first an Irish poplin of London smoke, with a mandarin collar and leg-o'-mutton sleeves, then putting it aside in favor of a Nile green silk that she knew showed her blue eyes to advantage. Her auburn hair she carefully arranged in a braided coil at the nape of her neck covered with a snood of sparkling silver thread. She was pleased with the effect despite the dusting of freckles across the bridge of her nose. She hoped Mark would not notice. He was critical of women who "used a hardship posting as an excuse to let themselves go," as he put it, but try as she might there was no escaping the Nebraska sun.

"Our mission must be very important," she said, admiring her husband standing shirtless at his shaving

stand. "Why else would General Sherman come all
this way from St. Louis?"

Mark turned his head to shave his clean jawline.
"It's probably to do with Carrington," he said. "Maybe
he's changed his mind about giving Carrington
the command. One can only hope. Why couldn't he
have chosen Custer? Or Hancock even?"

"You should be careful what you say, Mark. Someone may hear you." Rose could not judge Carrington's
military competence but he seemed to be a kind and
intelligent man, and she liked his wife, Margaret,
very much. You could tell a lot about a man by the
woman he chose.

"Carrington's in completely over his head and
everyone knows it," Mark said, wiping traces of lather
from his face with a hand towel on which Rose had
embroidered his initials. "Someone should have the
courage to say it."

As he finished dressing, Rose sat on their bed
and watched Sam Curry and the regimental band
cross the parade ground to Wessells's quarters, the
shining brasses reflecting the last of the golden
light. Carrington had insisted the band accompany
the regiment on its march up the Bozeman to the
Powder River country, despite the disapproval of his
officers, who called it frivolous and an unnecessary
complication. Carrington said music was good for
morale and would not change his mind.

Only officers and their wives were invited to the
reception. Sherman stood in the parlor greeting
them as they passed by in a line. Rose was a little
disappointed at his appearance. Rail thin with

uncombed red hair, a rumpled suit, and dusty shoes, Sherman looked more like a farmer than one of history's giants.

By the time Rose and Mark neared him, Sherman was showing signs of impatience, shifting his weight from one foot to the other. But when Rose reached him his hawk-like face brightened. He took her hand and raised it to his lips, giving her a roguish smile. Rose was surprised. The Savior of the Union was a flirt.

"General Sherman," Carrington said, "may I present Lieutenant Mark Reynolds? He's with us on detached service from the Second Cavalry. He'll have our boys riding like Tartars before we reach Laramie."

Sherman pulled his eyes away from Rose and returned Mark's salute. "Yes, Reynolds, I've heard good things about you from my brother-in-law, General Ewing. Tom says you were a great help to him in Kansas City with that border business. He says you've got a good head on your shoulders, studied law at the University of Michigan, I understand."

They were interrupted by a howl. Carrington's striker, Seamus O'Reilly, pulled two boys by their ears from their hiding place under the stairs and hot-footed them out the kitchen door. One of the boys was Carrington's older son, Harry, the other his friend Bill Kellogg. The two had stolen into Wessells's house to get a glimpse of Sherman.

Later there was dancing, and Sherman repeatedly sought Rose as a partner. He was not a good dancer and smelled of cigars but Mark was proud of the general's attentions to his young wife and encouraged her to accept his offers. At midnight when the party ended Mark escorted her back to their quarters, then left to join the other officers for cards.

Rose lay in bed, anticipating the grand adventure that lay ahead, too excited to sleep. A bar of silver moonlight fell across the foot of her bed, and a cool night wind played with the calico curtains at the open window. Bored with life in St. Louis, sick to death of needlework, painting flowers on porcelain vases, and other polite ladies' pastimes, she had long dreamed of this. What was waiting for them in the Powder River country? What would a truly wild Indian look like? She had never seen one, only the hang-around-the-forts who struck her as sad and ashamed. How would the mountains be, and the rivers of snowmelt that ran so fast and cold your hands froze when you held the giant fish that swam in them? She had long heard of these things and soon she would know them firsthand. Finally, she thought, her life would truly begin. She was still awake when Mark, smelling of whiskey and cigar smoke, climbed into bed beside her and, to her disappointment, immediately fell asleep. She was still awake when the sentry called the hour at three. At last she drifted off only to be jolted awake by the boom of the morning gun and the sound of breaking glass. Overloaded with powder, it shook the walls and broke her parlor window.

# Chapter Two

Rose's head pounded like a blacksmith's hammer and she burned with fever. She tried to hide her illness from Mark, hoping it would pass. Many officers had disagreed with Sherman's decision to let wives and children accompany the regiment on campaign. A sick wife, she knew, would be a nuisance to her husband, so she stayed in the wagon—an army ambulance refitted and made comfortable for long-distance travel—all morning with a wet cloth over her eyes. When they stopped at midday she told her black serving woman to make her excuses.

"Tell them I'm resting, Jerusha. Tell them I couldn't sleep because of all the noise."

A week had passed since they left Fort Kearney. A pack of wolves had shadowed the column since the Old California Crossing, galloping alongside at a distance by day and fighting ferociously among themselves at night. Then at midnight they were startled by a new sound, a deep, rumbling thunder that seemed to flow from the very earth, rocking the wagons and frightening the horses. Women clutched their children and wide-eyed soldiers stumbled from their tents asking each other what was happening and getting no answers. All was confusion until chief scout Jim Bridger climbed up on a wagon tongue to announce the rumble and thunder were not caused by an earthquake but by stampeding buffalo, miles away. The campers returned to an uneasy sleep.

Rose's misery worsened as the day progressed. Every jolt of the wheels along the washboard road sent a rocket of pain up her spine. In her desperation she discovered the pain was less if she traveled on her hands and knees and Mark found her in this position during a rest stop. He went looking for Sam Horton, the regiment's chief surgeon, and found him eating gingersnaps with Margaret Carrington and her two sons, twelve-year-old Harry and Jimmy, age six.

"Excuse me, Doctor," Mark said, tipping his hat to Margaret, "but I wonder if you might look in on Rose? I think she has a fever."

The plump surgeon got to his feet, brushing crumbs from his immaculate serge trousers. "Of course, Reynolds. I'll fetch my bag."

By the time he got there Margaret was already inside the ambulance sitting by the younger woman's side. Rose lay on her back, a patchwork quilt drawn up to her chin. Despite the day's heat, she was shivering.

"It's nothing," she said, looking at Horton with red-rimmed eyes. "I told Mark not to bother you."

"Shush now." The physician sat on the bed, measured her pulse at the wrist, then placed the smaller end of a belled, wooden stethoscope against her chest and leaned forward, listening with closed eyes.

"Too fast," he said. "When did this start, my dear?"

"This morning."

"Do you have pain? Headache? Stomach? Any bowel complaint?"

"I do have a headache."

Horton took from his bag two glass vials—one blue, the other green—and gave them to Jerusha.

"This is quinine," he said, raising the blue vial. "Give her a teaspoonful every hour. This"—he raised the green—"is laudanum. Of this, four drops every three hours. No more, no less. Keep her comfortable and make sure she takes plenty of water. Do you understand?"

Jerusha nodded and Horton turned back to his patient. "We'll be at Fort Sedgwick this evening," he said. "I can do more for you there."

Margaret insisted on traveling in Rose's ambulance the rest of the afternoon. Despite the difference in their ages, the two women had grown close during the long weeks at Fort Kearney. Rose was intelligent and, like Margaret, fond of reading novels. Most important, she did not try to impress or curry favor with her the way some of the other officers' wives did.

At sundown the column pulled into Fort Sedgwick,

a run-down collection of sod buildings on the South Platte River. Mark carried Rose to the blockhouse, hastily converted by the post quartermaster into a lady's sickroom. Harry Carrington watched the effortless way he carried her, even as he climbed the steps of the blockhouse, as if she weighed no more than a box of groceries. Harry wished he was strong enough to carry her like that.

Semiconscious, Rose was only vaguely aware of being moved, of being placed on a mattress that smelled of fresh hay and pipe tobacco. Her bones ached and her clothes were wet with sweat. She drifted into a troubled sleep, at times struggling for consciousness like a drowning swimmer fighting for the surface. Always she failed, sinking back into the dark and suffocating depths. The fever burned inside her, taking her to a different time and place. She saw her favorite brother, Tim, killed in '61 at Wilson's Creek, Missouri, standing alone on a hillside of glowing autumn colors. She tried to call out to him, to warn him of the Rebel sharpshooter in the tree, but could not make a sound. He jumped when the bullet hit him, then lay crumpled and still on the ground. As his spirit left his body, floating heavenward, she heard the faint and distant sound of a string orchestra, a soothing melody of violins and violoncello, clarinets and flute, French horns and tuba, alternating with a chorus of booming male voices, then the crunch of wheels on gravel.

A gentle hand lifted her head and pressed a cool

cup of water, sweet as wine, to her lips. She opened her eyes expecting to see Mark but instead found herself looking into the eyes of a stranger. They were alone in the red twilight.

"Who are you?" Her voice was raspy and hardly recognizable as her own. "Where is Doctor Horton? Where is my husband?"

She tried to sit, but the stranger pushed her back on the pillow. The room spun and she thought she would be sick.

"You're a strong woman, Mrs. Reynolds," he said. "Stronger than most. I believe you've turned the corner today. You had me worried."

Exhausted, Rose closed her eyes and dreamed of water. She woke to a sunlit room and ravenous hunger. As if on cue, Jerusha appeared carrying an ironstone mug.

"Beef broth," she said, setting the mug on a table beside the bed. "Can you take it?"

Rose nodded and Jerusha helped her sit, packing pillows behind her back. Dizzy and light-headed, Rose sipped the broth slowly till the mug was half-empty. Feeling better, she took stock of her surroundings.

The room was small, with a canvas roof and log walls chinked with plaster. A cannon stood in the center, its muzzle pointed toward a small square window. The wall on either side was pierced with a double row of loopholes, one high and the other low, for standing and kneeling gunmen. Jerusha's straw-tick mattress was on the floor.

The broth was hot and salty and sat heavily in her empty stomach. Still, she forced herself to finish it. Outside, the soldiers began to drill. Rose heard an officer's staccato commands, the rattle of muskets, the rhythmic pounding of boots on the ground.

"Good morning, ladies." A tall man appeared at the open door wearing a surgeon's linen jacket over civilian clothing. "May I come in?"

The door was low and he had to stoop to enter. His face was familiar and strange at the same time, like someone she had met in a dream. He smiled as he walked to her bedside.

"It's good to see you eating," he said. "You're feeling better then?"

"Yes, much better, though there's a dreadful ringing in my ears."

"An effect of the quinine. It will pass."

He had a pleasing voice, deep and resonant, with a barely discernable Southern drawl. Rose found it relaxing and wanted him to keep on talking. Instead he gave her his hand. "We haven't met properly. My name is Daniel Dixon. I'm the post surgeon. I've been looking after you the last few days—with Jerusha's most competent help."

Rose understood he wanted her to know any delicate issues had been addressed by another female.

"You've had dengue fever. Breakbone fever, the men call it. You had an additional complication"—he paused—"which resulted in some blood loss, but this resolved naturally. You shouldn't have any future problems."

Again, she understood what he was saying. "I'm afraid I've been a burden to you," she said. "I'm sorry. Why did Sam Horton fob me off on you? Where is he?"

Dixon dropped his eyes and sat in the chair by her bed. "First things first," he said. "I need to check your pulse." He held a finger to her wrist. "A bit fast yet, but steady and strong. Much better than before."

"Where is Doctor Horton?" she said. "Where is my husband?"

He looked uncomfortable and Rose knew something was wrong. "Lieutenant Reynolds asked me to give you this before he left." Dixon removed an envelope from his jacket pocket and, when she did not take it, put on the table beside the mug. A fat fly crawled along the mug's lip.

"What do you mean, before he left?" Rose said. "What are you talking about?"

"Your husband's regiment moved out two days ago," he said. The words struck her like a blow to the stomach. She closed her eyes, remembering the music she heard at the height of her fever—the strings and the brasses—and realized it was no dream but the regiment's musical farewell to Fort Sedgwick. Mark was gone. He had abandoned her in this savage place.

She could not look at Dixon. She did not want to see the pity in his eyes.

"You need rest," he said. "I'll look in on you later."

Only after he left did Rose reach for Mark's letter, opening it with a shaking hand.

*June 3, 1866*
*Fort Sedgwick, Dakota Territory*

*My dearest Rose,*

*It pains me to leave you in this hole but the regiment moves in the morning and I must go with it. Carrington depends on me and I cannot hang back. Sam Horton assures me you will recover soon, otherwise I would not go.*

*Of course you must come on soon as you can. I've left Spicer behind to assist you. Carrington says a supply train bound for Fort Laramie will arrive at Sedgwick within the week. If you're strong enough— and I trust you will be—you and Spicer must join it. Naturally your little outfit will travel much faster than ours. We should be reunited at Laramie, if not before, as you may well overtake us.*

*Be brave, my darling, and know that I await you with anxious arms.*

> *Your loving husband, Mark*

*P.S. The Indians have been quiet this spring between Sedgwick and Laramie so you need have no concerns on that score.*


She looked up to see Jerusha in the doorway. Rose thought she saw a smile, unpleasant, like a sneer, but immediately Jerusha's face became the usual mask, revealing nothing.

"Please heat some water, Jerusha," Rose said. "I want to wash my hair."

When she was gone Rose gave way to tears. How

could he do this? Surely Colonel Carrington would have allowed Mark to stay if he had requested it. Doubt, like a rat, nibbled a tunnel into her thoughts. She remembered her oldest brother's words on the night she and Mark announced their engagement. "What's the hurry, Rose?" Joe had said. "Get to know him better. If he loves you, he'll wait."

Joe disliked—or distrusted—Mark for some reason Rose did not understand. She sensed it. But nothing Joe could say would have made a difference, for she was determined to marry Mark Reynolds and she would not wait. No man had ever affected her as Mark did. From the moment he walked through the doors of the Blair house that warm June night he had occupied her every thought. Her love for him was like a cavalry guidon, flying full in the wind, or a church bell ringing clear and true. He felt the same—she was sure of it. A woman knows these things. So why had he left her? She must have been disgusting in her illness; sweaty, foul-smelling, not feminine. She should never have let him see her that way. It was her own fault; she should have kept him away.

Jerusha returned with a porcelain basin and a steaming bucket of water. On shaking legs Rose climbed from the bed to the chair, took the empty basin in her lap, and leaned over it as Jerusha poured the hot water over her head. Though her scalp was tender from fever, she did not complain as Jerusha vigorously lathered her hair with a lemon-scented soap, the fragrance Mark liked. Yes, she had been disgusting. The suds floating in the basin were brown in color, as if they had just bathed an animal.

That night Rose lay sleepless in her bed, thoughts churning and boiling inside her skull. She imagined the challenges ahead and knew she had to make herself strong to survive them. The frontier was no place for womanly softness.

At midnight, with the moon shining through the square cannon portal and Jerusha asleep on her straw mattress, Rose pulled a pair of scissors from her sewing basket. Then, without a mirror and without lighting a candle, she took the scissors to her hair, so thick it was still damp from washing, and cropped it till it was short as a boy's, watching her hair fall like long satin ribbons to the puncheon floor.

# Chapter Three

Rose did not see much of Dixon after her recovery. Fevers, dysentery, and injuries to the men kept him and the assistant surgeons busy. Every evening she wrote to Mark, sending a packet of letters wrapped in red ribbon with each departing mail team. Anxious to join him, she asked to accompany one of the teams on its journey north, but Sedgwick's commanding officer refused even to consider it.

"Mrs. Reynolds, you don't know what you're asking," Captain Carter said. He was thin and tired-looking with stringy gray hair. "Do you imagine I would send a young woman out there with only a mail team to protect her? You'd last as long as a snowball on a beach."

His patronizing tone made her angry. "You exaggerate the danger, surely. I doubt General Sherman would have encouraged the officers to bring their families along if things were as bad as you say. Why, he said we would have a wonderful adventure. Those were his very words—I heard him!"

Carter shook his head. "Sherman is the best officer I ever knew, but he doesn't know the situation here. He underestimates the Indians and the difficulty of the country itself."

Carter was reluctant even to let Rose travel with the supply train when at last it arrived, three weeks overdue. In truth, it was hardly a train at all but a collection of five wagons under the leadership of Lieutenant Frank Anderson. He was accompanied by his wife, Clara, and infant son, Rollo.

"I suppose you must go, Mrs. Reynolds," Carter said with a sigh, "but it's against my better judgment. If it were up to me I'd send you back East on the next stage."

He said this forcefully and Rose's surprise showed on her face.

"You remind me of my daughter, you see," he said. "Caroline, she would be about your age now, if she had lived. . . ." He turned his head. "This country is hard on women, Mrs. Reynolds. Do be careful."

Rose said she would and impulsively kissed him on the cheek.

It took Anderson an entire day to get his wagons and livestock across the South Platte. Shifting beds of quicksand lay just inches below the river's deceptively calm yellow surface, and it was hard to know where it could be forded safely. A man might walk from bank to bank without wetting his trouser cuffs one day and sink to his shoulders the next.

They used a flatboat to cross the wagons, with one group of men on board poling the boat forward and another on shore pulling hand over hand on a double cable strung over the water. Rose took this time for a final visit to the post sutler.

Royal Spicer, Mark's striker, accompanied her. A tall Kentuckian with a square head and broad shoulders, Spicer seldom let Rose out of his sight and sometimes even did her laundry. The other men teased him for his slavish devotion but he didn't care.

"Lieutenant Reynolds told me to look out for you," he said, "and that's what I aim to do. Them boys don't bother me none. They're just jealous because the company I'm keepin' is a lot prettier than what they're lookin' at."

Rose welcomed his company especially when she had business with Mr. Adams, the post sutler, an oily fellow with suspicious eyes and a narrow, bullet-shaped head. His store was dark and smelled of smoke, herring, and cheese. On this hot June afternoon two Winnebago women stood at the long wooden counter while one of Adams's assistants poured flour and sugar into their upturned skirts. Half-naked children squatted at their feet, eating bits of cracker off the earthen floor. Rose found the Indian children, with their big, brown eyes and long curling lashes, quite beautiful. She chose two calico patterns and paid for them quickly, cutting short Adams's attempts at conversation. She and Spicer walked out into the bright sunlight to find a crowd on the street watching a soldier kicking an Indian curled at his feet. A jacket with a first sergeant's chevrons lay in the dirt beside him.

"Run, find an officer!" Rose said to Spicer. "Quick, before he kills him."

As she spoke a stocky man in faded civilian clothing and a sweat-stained black hat pushed his way through the crowd and stepped between the Indian and the red-faced soldier.

"This don't involve you, Gregory," the sergeant said. "I got no truck with you. That buck was stealing my coat. I caught him red-handed. Ha! I caught the redskin red-handed!" He looked around to see if any in the crowd caught his joke but no one was laughing.

Gregory reached down and pulled the Indian to his feet. He was just a boy, no more than fourteen, with blood running from his nose and mouth. Gregory spoke to him briefly in the boy's language then turned to the sergeant.

"He says different," Gregory said. "He says you left your coat on that wagon and he was returning it to you."

"And I guess you believe him," the soldier said.

"Fact is, I do. I know this boy. He's no thief."

But the sergeant's blood was up. "Step aside, harelip," he said. "I aim to teach that Injun a lesson."

He lunged but Gregory was faster, striking the soldier's chin, not with his fist but with the flat of his hand and then following up with a blow from the elbow, all part of one lightning movement. The sergeant's head snapped back and he dropped like a stone, lying motionless in the dirt. The boy turned and ran.

As Gregory searched the crowd to see if the sergeant had any supporters, Rose studied him with interest. His green eyes were pale against his sun-darkened skin and his features were strong and well-formed.

He would have been perfectly handsome, she thought, if not for the scar of a harelip, barely visible under his mustache.

Rose asked Spicer who he was.

"Jack Gregory, the scout. He'll be coming with us. Anderson hired him to guide us to the regiment."

Back at the river they discovered the water level had dropped more than a foot, making the flatboat unusable. Since only Rose's ambulance and the troops had yet to cross, Anderson ordered them to proceed on foot. The men waded through the knee-deep, fast-flowing water, holding on to the cable with one hand and their carbines with the other. Rose's ambulance followed. She chose to ride on the driver's bench beside a Mexican teamster who wore a black patch over one eye. Halfway across he turned to her and stuck out a hand.

"My name is Ignacio," he said with a smile. He had beautiful white teeth.

She noticed his middle finger ended at the knuckle in a red, bulbous knob with a sharp bit of darkened bone sticking from the puckered flesh. She did not want to take his hand but rudeness was never acceptable. That was one of her dead mother's lessons that stuck.

"Rose Reynolds," she said. "So nice to meet you."

Not far from their wagon, three men crossing on horseback pitched into a deep hole. Two managed to make the shore by holding on to their horses' tails but the third man panicked and tried to swim. His eyes, wide with terror, met Rose's as he fought the water. His friends tried to save him but the young soldier sank below the surface before they could reach him. His body was recovered downstream an hour later.

Rose had never seen a man die before and she was deeply shaken. She was a strong swimmer, having spent many childhood hours racing—and defeating—her brothers across the lake on their grandfather's farm, and she thought she could have saved him. It would have meant stripping down to her chemise, however, and she didn't do it though she thought she should have. The drowned man was buried that evening in an old gun box he had pulled from a refuse pile that morning saying, "This would make someone a good coffin."

They spent the first night on the river's north shore, still in sight of Fort Sedgwick. After dinner Rose settled into a camp chair, her portable desk on her knees, to write to her Uncle Randolph and her brother in St. Louis.

*The country is flat and so brown the eye aches for a spot of color but I'm told that the scenery will improve as we go north. Carrington's guide (the famous Jim Bridger!) says that once we cross the Powder River we will enter a beautiful land of rolling green hills and lush valleys watered by icy streams of snowmelt from the Bighorn Mountains. There will be fields of tall grasses, wildflowers and natural grains, berries of all sorts growing along the streams, and plenty of game—or so he tells us and I believe him.*

*I wish you all could see our little camp now, as I write these words. It is so pretty in the red twilight,*

*the wagons with their white canvas tops and freshly
painted blue beds and the men's A tents glowing like
Japanese lanterns in neat rows.*

Here she paused. Her brothers would like Mark
even less if they knew he had left her at Sedgwick.

*Mark sends his regards.*
*In all we are a party of thirty-one souls led by
Lieutenant Frank Anderson who travels with his
wife and infant son. Poor Anderson! His wife is a
tyrant who outweighs him by at least twenty pounds
though he seems quite devoted to her. Also with us is
paymaster Major Ranald Henry, carrying wages for
Carrington's troops and the men at Fort Reno,
Henry's four-man escort, and a contract surgeon
named Daniel Dixon.*

Again she stopped writing. She had learned very
little about him. He was from Kentucky—he told her
that much—and had attended medical school in Cin-
cinnati at the distinguished Medical College of Ohio.
Most army physicians had no such credentials. So
what was he doing here, when he could earn a more
comfortable living back East? Was he running from
something or someone? Did he have dark past he
wished to escape? No one seemed to know much
about him.

*Our little company also includes a number of
so-called "Galvanized Yankees"—that is, former
Confederate war prisoners who gained their freedom
by agreeing to fight for Uncle Sam on the western*

*frontier. There are many of these types out here
and they are, to a man, a glum and dispirited lot.
We've got seven Mexican teamsters driving our
wagons (mine is a piratical fellow with a black
eye patch) and our guide is a Missourian named
Jack Gregory.*

When it grew too dark to write Rose folded her desk
and climbed into the ambulance, where Jerusha was
already asleep. She changed into a white cotton night-
dress, fell into her bed, and was asleep within seconds.

Reveille sounded at four and the general one
hour later, starting the wagons. Rose tied the rear
door open so she could watch the sun rise in the eastern sky like a giant fireball. The morning air was cool
and smelled of sage. A gentle breeze played with her
newly cropped hair. That breeze was refreshing now
but later in the day it would become an enemy wind
that carried an alkaline dust, fine and choking as
talc, which burned the eyes, coated the teeth, and,
if she was not careful, ruined a woman's complexion.

The road was sandy but well graded and the
wagons made good time. The mules were sleek and
fully fleshed, with tails that were shaven except for a
rectangular tuft at the end for swatting flies. The
team pulling Rose's ambulance was especially well
kept with coyote tails dangling from their bridles.
*Ignacio must be softer than he looks,* Rose thought.

Her ambulance home was surprisingly comfortable.
Spicer had removed one bench to make room for her

favorite chair and she rode there in the mornings, reading or sewing when the rocking motion allowed it. In the evenings she lowered the leather back of the remaining bench and this, when covered with a thin mattress and soft cotton quilts, made a fine bed. Spicer also made two canvas pockets that he hung on hooks on either side of the door. One held Rose's travel box and shawl, the other her needlework and books. One of these was a tedious biography of Benjamin Franklin but the other was a wonderful new English novel about a young governess and her mysterious but compelling employer, a character who reminded Rose of Daniel Dixon. Titled *Jane Eyre*, it was a loan from Margaret Carrington and Rose liked it so much she allowed herself only ten pages a day to prolong the joy of reading it. The value of a good book was the only meaningful lesson she had learned during a long, lonely year at the Female Baptist Academy in Columbia, where she was sent as a girl to escape one of the cholera epidemics that swept St. Louis. Novels—*David Copperfield, The Count of Monte Cristo,* and *The Scarlet Letter*—were her only source of joy that terrible, sad year, the year her parents died.

Mornings were pleasant, but by noon the ambulance was an oven. Clouds of buffalo gnats and flies tortured man and beast with stinging bites. Clara Anderson's baby, Rollo, wailed constantly, and his piercing cries carried the length of the column. Clara stretched a piece of cheesecloth over his bed—a champagne basket padded with cotton blankets—but even so the insects found a way to get at him, raising welts on his plump, pink body.

To protect themselves the women wore gloves and veiled hats, despite the heat, and the men tied handkerchiefs over their faces. Ignacio waved a cottonwood switch over the mules' sweating backs to discourage the droning flies that hovered in clouds above them. Still, some managed to settle, biting till the blood flowed.

They would travel till sundown, when the strong evening winds came. Although these complicated the business of setting up tents and starting dinner fires, Rose welcomed them because they blew away the insects. After one particularly long day they camped along Lodge Pole Creek, a fast-moving stream that teemed with fish. As she unpacked the mess chest, Rose heard the men laughing and splashing each other in the cold, clear water and she wished she could shed her clothes and do the same as she and her brothers did when they were children. They spent many happy summer months on their grandfather's Boone County farm swimming in the lake, racing horses, and exploring the overgrown vestiges of a pioneer trace that marked the southern edge of his property. The road, forged by the Boone brothers, Nathan and Daniel M., sons of the famous frontiersman, at a time when Missouri west of St. Louis was still a brushy wilderness, was a gold mine of archeological treasures and relics of bygone days. They found bent spoons, skillets, and unidentifiable bits of rusting metal, a homemade doll with a rotting calico dress, gold-rimmed spectacles with lenses intact, thimbles, scissors, and a pair of boots big enough to fit a giant.

Her eyes fell on Dixon, buttoning his shirt as he returned from his swim. He was an attractive man, she thought. Any woman would think so. Not as handsome as Mark, certainly, but still . . .

Spicer joined the men with hooks and lines in the water and before long dozens of fish lay shining on the creek bank like bars of silver. Jerusha made a fine supper of Spicer's catch, dredging the firm, white fillets in salt and cornmeal, then frying them in a skillet of hot olive oil. The meat was sweet and delicious, a welcome change from the menu of beef, salt bacon, beans, and hard bread that sustained them along the way.

During the night the air was cool and a light rain pattered on the canvas roof of the ambulance. Rose woke to reveille feeling strong and refreshed. The rain settled the dust and the air smelled of cottonwood smoke and boiling coffee. She dressed quickly, grateful for her cropped hair and the freedom it gave her. Gone were the days when she would spend half an hour every morning brushing, braiding, coiling, and pinning. Now she could be out the door in ten minutes and without even lighting a candle.

They breakfasted on bacon, skillet bread warmed over from the night before, canned peaches, and coffee with sugar and condensed milk. As always, Spicer ate as if he had not seen food for a week. Jerusha scolded him, saying there would be nothing left for the midday meal, but Rose shushed her.

"Let him eat," she said. "We have plenty."

Just before the column started, Spicer came to her with a bundle wrapped in red cloth. She opened it to find a leather-covered canteen with her name expertly embroidered across its face in yellow saddler's silk.

"Cover it with a piece of wet blanket and hang it from the roof of the wagon," he said. "Be sure to leave the cork out, thataway it'll catch the air and the water will stay nice and cool all through the day."

Rose was touched by the gift and the amount of time he spent working on it. She had not imagined the Kentucky boy's thick, sausage-like fingers capable of such fine stitching.

"Thank you, Royal," she said. "It's beautiful. Who taught you to do this?"

Blushing, Spicer looked down at the curled toes of his Jefferson boots. His face was nearly as red as the cloth that wrapped the canteen. "Tera, my brother, back home in Bardstown, he taught me. He was going to be a saddle maker like Pa but he died in the war. Measles."

"I lost a brother too," she said. "In Missouri, at Wilson's Creek. His name was Tim." In all their hours together, this was the first confidence they had exchanged.

The bugle sounded, starting the first wagons. The Mexican teamsters cracked their blacksnake whips and urged the mules forward.

*"Mula! Mula! Vamos, mula!"*

As Spicer walked to his horse Rose noticed the sleeve had begun to separate from the body of his jacket. He had spent long hours on his gift for her when his own clothes were falling apart. She resolved to mend it for him when they reached Laramie.

# Chapter Four

Of all the officers in his father's command, Mark Reynolds was Harry Carrington's favorite. He was the best horseman, the best shot, the one all the women looked at when they thought no one was watching. He usually won at cards. But one thing about Reynolds troubled Harry. How could he leave his wife alone at a place like Fort Sedgwick? Especially a wife like that? Harry thought Rose Reynolds was beautiful, especially her eyes. Not just because they were clear and blue, but because the delicate skin below them was faintly blue also, or maybe faintly silver, and moist-looking or dewy. Harry wondered if this was natural, and even considered asking his mother if Rose used something, some kind of emollient, to achieve that. Whatever, the effect was stirring. Lieutenant Reynolds must be supremely devoted to duty, Harry thought, to leave eyes like that.

Some days they rode together alongside the column, with Reynolds on his big bay and Harry on

Calico, a spotted Indian pony Quartermaster Fred Brown had given to him and his brother, Jimmy, back in Nebraska. Harry loved the prairie, loved the endless blue skies, the tiny yellow flowers that bobbed in the wind, the giant herds of grazing buffalo. Some people complained of feeling lost and reduced to nothing by the vastness of it all, but Harry experienced just the opposite. He was at home with the emptiness. He felt a new and exhilarating sense of health and power, as if his own twelve-year-old body were an essential, growing thing. Maybe soon the rest of him would be equal to his size-thirteen feet. They were so big, Bill Kellogg and the other boys had given him the nickname "Foot."

Each day was exciting and new. He especially liked the dark and sunless ones when the wind blew from the west, chilled by its journey over the far purple mountains. On these magical days, the towering sandstone formations of the North Platte valley became medieval castles and he and his friend Bill Kellogg were D'Artagnan and Aramis, racing their horses over the plains on a secret mission for the king of France. On a whim they decided to find out how many steps it took to encircle Chimney Rock at its base. The answer: 10,040. This important discovery was wasted on his father. When Harry shared the information at dinner that evening, he had frowned and said, "My God, son, have you boys nothing better to do?"

By early June the column was nearing Fort Laramie, famed way station for trappers, traders, missionaries, Pony Express riders, California-bound gold hunters, and grim Mormons seeking Zion. Laramie—in Harry's mind the very name bespoke romance and danger, no place for weaklings or fools. As testament to the latter, Laramie was the last home of the infamous Lieutenant John Grattan, a blustering shavetail who had picked a fight with the Sioux in 1854 and got himself and twenty-nine soldiers killed for his trouble. Every schoolboy in America knew of Grattan.

Though the morning had been cool and pleasant, by noon it was oppressively hot. At two o'clock Harry noticed a distant line of clouds the color of a ripening bruise. Soon the wind kicked up, the temperature plunged, and a wall of solid gray appeared in the west, moving toward them with a roar that grew in intensity till it was like that of a waterfall.

Carrington stopped the column and corralled the wagons around the livestock.

"You might want to tie them wagons down, Colonel," Jim Bridger said, scanning the sky with faded gray eyes. "We're in for a blow."

Harry turned Calico toward the rear, where his mother's ambulance was pulling into the circle. The pony broke into a run as the howl of the storm grew louder. They flew by soldiers and teamsters driving tent stakes into the ground to anchor the wagons. The air tasted of copper pennies.

Margaret waved to Harry from the door, fighting to keep it open against the wind. Calico covered the remaining ground in an instant. Harry slid to the ground, tied the reins to the wheel of a heavy supply wagon, and dove through the door just as the sky unleashed a fusillade of hailstones the size of hens' eggs.

The wind blew with the strength of a hurricane, rocking the ambulance on its wheels like a toy in the hands of an enraged child. The noise was like nothing Harry had heard before, like a locomotive steaming through crashing surf. Flashes of lightning lit the canvas walls and air that was hot and suffocating just an hour before was now icy cold. Though only mid-afternoon, it was dark as Egypt. Jimmy huddled in a corner with his hands over his ears and Black George, Carrington's orderly, squatted beside him, eyes wide with fear.

Fierce though it was, the storm was short-lived. An eerie quiet replaced the cannonade. When Harry opened the door he found a landscape of winter white dotted with countless bits of brown. These proved to be the carcasses of prairie dogs, flooded from their holes and pummeled to death by hail-stones. Men caught out in the open were bloodied, three wagons were overturned, and terrified horses ran wild, dragging their picket pins. To Harry's relief, Calico was still tied to the supply wagon.

The few remaining hours of sunlight were spent righting the wagons and capturing escaped horses. Margaret was dismayed to discover the rain had penetrated the canvas to soak their bedding. She thrust empty feed sacks at Harry and Jimmy and told them to collect buffalo chips for a fire. Usually the undignified job was six-year-old Jimmy's, but Harry knew better than to argue with his mother when she was angry.

Before following his brother onto the prairie, Harry stopped at the rope line to check Calico for injuries. As he knelt to examine a foreleg he heard a group of officers talking.

"What a Tweedledum business that was!" Harry recognized Fred Brown's honking voice. Despite the gift of Calico, Harry had never liked the blustering, bald-headed quartermaster. "Carrington couldn't manage a flea circus. I told him we should stop the column a good twenty minutes before the storm hit. We're lucky we didn't lose the beef herd."

"Why didn't Sherman give the command to someone who knows what he's doing?" This was Lieutenant William Bisbee. "I can't understand it—Carrington has no experience in the field. Where was he during the war? I'll tell you where—the recruiting department, the logistics department, the transportation department—anywhere but the bullet department."

Harry's face burned as the men laughed.

"He got the command because of his political friends," Brown said, "but don't worry, he won't last. It won't take Bill Sherman long to figure out what Carrington's made of."

Harry remained hidden until they moved on, then went on about his dung-collection business, sick with shame. It was true, his father had never seen combat, never felt the wind from an enemy bullet or artillery shell. This was true, even though the Eighteenth Infantry suffered more casualties than any other regular army unit during four years of war. Until now, Harry had never wondered about his father's ability to command these battle-hardened veterans but suddenly everything changed. Would they recognize his authority? Could he control them?

When he arrived back at camp Margaret was hanging wet sheets and quilts on bushes to dry. "These might be ready by bedtime," she said. "If they aren't, Sallie Horton has things we can use."

Black George knelt on the ground struggling to get a fire going. The buffalo dung was wet and produced an acrid smoke. Harry breathed in the stink of it thinking life had lost its luster. He was no longer D'Artagnan, French adventurer. Instead he was Foot, the second-rate son of a second-rate father.

"Harry?" Margaret said. "What's wrong?"

He felt her keen eyes on him.

"Harry?"

He saw she would not let it go. "Is it true Father got this command because he has important friends? Because Governor Dennison was his law partner back in Ohio?"

Margaret frowned. "Who said that? Has someone been talking against him?"

Harry shook his head. Brown and Bisbee were asses but Harry was no tattlepig.

Margaret sighed and sat in a camp chair, motioning him to sit beside her. "Harry, your father is a brilliant man who built the Eighteenth Infantry from nothing when the war started. Yes, he has influential friends, but he got this command because he earned it—not on the battlefield maybe but in other ways. I'm proud of him, very proud, and so should you be. Don't let anyone make you feel otherwise."

He nodded, not meeting her eyes.

"Good. Now go help Jimmy gather more chips. We'll need them in the morning."

Harry's black mood only deepened that evening as he watched his father at his camp desk, reading the Bible in Hebrew by the light of a coal oil lamp. He was an intelligent, well-educated man, Harry knew, but a regimental commander should be tall and broad-shouldered, a man like Mark Reynolds. His father was frail and undersized with pale skin and the large, mournful eyes of a spaniel. Even his hands were wrong, small and ink-stained, not the strong, scarred hands of a warrior.

In bed, Harry read by candlelight. His book was Biddle's *The Expedition of Lewis and Clark,* a battered, dog-eared text drawn from the explorers' journals. Because it contained the only written description of their destination lands, all Carrington's officers had been ordered to read it. Now it was Harry's turn. Tonight's action was William Clark's confrontation with the Teton Sioux on Bad River, early in the journey. Harry fell asleep wondering what would have happened if Colonel Henry Beebe Carrington, and not captains Lewis and Clark, had been in charge of President Jefferson's enterprise. Would he have finessed the standoff with the Partisan and his scheming Sioux as Clark had done? Or would the Corps of Discovery have ended its journey there and then, ingloriously, on the banks of Bad River?

# Chapter Five

The following night the regiment stopped four miles east of Laramie next to a creek full of mountain pike. Mark Reynolds showed Harry and Jimmy how to make a net from stitched-together gunnysacks. The fish they caught were strong and slippery and cold as living ice.

They were close enough to Laramie to hear the boom of the evening gun. Some of the men wanted to visit the post but Carrington would not allow it. He called his officers to his tent for a council.

"As you know, peace talks are under way at the fort," he said. "Commissioners are negotiating rights to the Bozeman Road, trying to get the chiefs' assurance that emigrants will not be harmed on their way to Montana Territory. Hundreds—maybe thousands—of Indians are in the area. I'm sure I don't need to tell you the situation is delicate." He paused to look each officer in the eyes. "We must not disturb the balance. This is important, and some silly incident could be disastrous. The men are to have no contact with the Indians—none whatsoever. If an Indian approaches camp, for any reason, bring him directly to me. Understood?"

Just then a breathless orderly ran into the tent to say two of the regiment's most experienced sergeants were missing. "They went for a swim and they ain't been seen since!" he said. "Their clothes is still on the bank."

Carrington sent Reynolds out with a search party, and Harry took advantage of the commotion to saddle Calico and tag along. They found the two naked bodies in a rocky shallows a few miles downstream. Harry's heart thumped in his chest as Reynolds rolled the first one over. The gray face was bruised and bloated but otherwise undamaged. The second man was the same.

"Doesn't look like Indian business," Reynolds said. "They've still got their hair on."

They wrapped the bodies in blue army blankets, draped them over a horse, and returned to camp. After a brief examination, Surgeon Horton said the men indeed had drowned, apparently swept away by the stream's strong current. The deaths were the first since the regiment left Fort Stephen Kearney thirty-three days before and they cast a pall over the previously picnic-like atmosphere.

That evening, as the sergeants were being buried, a lone Indian rode into camp. With Bridger interpreting, he identified himself as Standing Elk, a chief of the Brule Sioux and participant in the Laramie talks. Carrington invited him to sit and smoke.

Harry could not take his eyes off the Indian sitting

cross-legged before the fire. Standing Elk looked very different from the Pawnees he had seen at Fort Kearney or the short, squat Winnebagos who hung around Fort Sedgwick. This man was tall and sinewy with good features. His black hair hung loose to his shoulders and he wore a single feather at the crown.

"Where is the Little White Chief going?" he asked.

Carrington frowned. "My name is Carrington. We are headed across the Powder River to the Bighorn Mountain country."

"Why do you go there?"

Carrington hesitated. "To protect emigrants on the Bozeman Road. We will build three forts."

Bridger paused before translating. "You sure you want to tell him all that, Colonel?"

"Why not? Surely it won't come as a surprise. Surely our mission has been discussed at the Laramie talks."

Bridger laughed. "Colonel, if them Injuns know anything about your so-called mission I'll eat this." He raised his sweat-stained hat above his head. "The only reason they're here in the first place is for the presents the army gives 'em just for showin' up. When a chief touches the pen, his people get even more. That's how it works. Them peace commissioners don't care if the Injuns understand, they just want 'em to sign so they can go back to Washington and talk up their big success. You can be sure no one's said, 'Oh, and by the way, our man Carrington's comin' through with his soldiers any day now to build a road and three forts right through your best huntin' grounds.'"

Bridger replaced his hat. "No, sir, and the Injuns won't be real happy when they find it out."

Carrington considered, stroking his silky beard. "Please proceed with the translation."

Standing Elk listened closely. "The Lakota people of Red Cloud and Young-Man-Afraid-Of-His-Horses who live up in the north country will not sell their hunting ground to the white man for his road and forts," he said. "You bluecoats will have to fight them for it."

Carrington smiled. "Red Cloud," he said. "Yes, I've heard of him. And what of you, Standing Elk? Will your people fight us too?"

The Indian shook his head. "The Brules want no war with the bluecoats. It is the fighting men of the north you should fear. Red Cloud and his Bad Face warriors will show you no mercy."

"We fear no one," Carrington said.

Standing Elk looked around the camp. "Is this all the soldiers you have?"

"The White Father in Washington has given me all the soldiers I will need," Carrington said.

Standing Elk smiled. "Then the White Father and the Little White Chief are fools."

# Chapter Six

Rose did not like riding in the stuffy ambulance and spent afternoons on horseback, despite Clara Anderson's warning.

"Lieutenant Reynolds won't be happy to find you brown as a squaw," she said, "and with your lovely hair all chopped off too. You'd be wise to think about such things, dear. A man's heart is a wayward thing."

Rose laughed as if this did not concern her. In fact, although she liked her boyish haircut and the freedom it gave her, she was a bit worried about Mark's reaction. "He would love me if I was bald and black as midnight."

She was careful to wear gloves and a wide-brimmed bonnet though she would have preferred to ride bareheaded and bareback and dressed in the loose white shirt and Turkish trousers she had worn as a girl exploring the Missouri countryside with her brothers. But even in those carefree, prewar days someone had been around to scold her. Then it was tall, unsmiling Grandmother Alice who complained

her only granddaughter was becoming "a wild hea-
then who would not be welcome in the stone mansions of St. Louis's North Garrison Street." But this
put no fear in Rose as she had no interest in stone
mansions or the people who lived in them.

On these hot summer afternoons Rose rode an
old cavalry horse, a claybank gelding named General
Rosecrans but that the men called Carl. Though her
leg and stomach muscles protested painfully at first,
soon she was comfortable as ever in the saddle and
the sweet prairie air was invigorating.

Often she rode beside Dixon, with Spicer close
behind whistling songs of glory. Although he was
from Lexington, Kentucky, he had split with his slave-
owning family—a rupture that pained him but, as he
said, "no human being has the right to own another"—
and fought with the Fifty-fifth Illinois at the battle of
Shiloh, where he formed a low opinion of generals
Grant and Sherman. Later in the war he was posted
to Smallpox Island, a prison hospital in the Mississippi River outside of Alton and a place Rose knew
well. St. Louis residents walking on the levees held
their breath when the wind blew from that direction.
Beyond this, Dixon offered no more information
and Rose, despite her curiosity, did not press.

To celebrate the Fourth of July, Jerusha made an
apple cake from molasses, raisins, flour, eggs, spices,
and dried apples soaked all day in whiskey water. She
served it warm from the cook-all with a drizzle of
simple syrup. After dinner, Rose sat with Dixon and
the Andersons at the fire drinking coffee and listening to the Mexican teamsters play guitars and sing

*corridos.* Gregory, just back from scouting the next day's route, joined them.

"The mules had a hard pull today," Anderson said. "Will tomorrow be more of the same?"

Gregory shook his head as he poured a mug of coffee. "No, the road is easier from here on. You'll make Mud Springs by noon. There's a telegraph there and a blacksmith's shop. Might be good to stop a day or so, rest the mules. That's the only good water you'll find till Pumpkin Creek, and from there the going gets hard sure enough."

They sat in silence, anticipating the road, listening to the pop of the fire and the Mexican guitars. After a time, Gregory spoke again.

"I came across a trench and breastworks on Rush Creek," he said. "Cartridge shells all over the ground. I'm guessing that's where Collins and his boys tangled with the Cheyenne last winter."

Anderson made a sound of disgust. "We wouldn't be having all this Indian trouble if it weren't for John Chivington and his Colorado yahoos," he said. "That's the problem with irregulars. They muck things up for the rest of us."

"Muck things up?" Dixon said. "Is that what you call it when women and children are slaughtered in their sleep?"

Anderson threw the contents of his cup into the fire, sending up a line of white smoke. "I grant you, that wasn't a pretty business," he said, "but—"

A shot rang out. Rose turned and saw a soldier's cap spinning in the air like something tossed at a wedding. Dixon jumped to his feet and ran toward the sound. She and the others followed to find a man lying facedown on the ground beside a supply wagon, his head a wet mush of blood and brains.

"I seen it happen, Doc," a white-faced soldier said to Dixon, kneeling beside the body. "He was climbin' up with his shotgun in his hand and it discharged on accident. Blew the top of his head clean off!"

Rose saw a tear in the dead man's jacket, separating shoulder and sleeve. Dixon rolled the body over and she looked down on the dead face of Royal Spicer, his features bloody but undamaged. She covered her mouth with her hands and ran to the nearest bushes, where her stomach emptied of all its contents.

"Well," Gregory said, "he's the first."

# Chapter Seven

The air smelled of animals, dust, and the sugar-loaf cactus now fully in bloom. Harry Carrington filled his lungs as he and Calico crested a hill. Laramie lay below. At last he would see the West's most famous fort.

He was disappointed. Sprawled across the plain, it looked more like a prairie village than a fortified garrison. There was no stockade with massive blockhouses at its corners, no armed sentries or wheeled artillery at the gates. Instead it was a collection of simple buildings, some frame but mostly of stone and adobe, squatting on a flat, treeless plateau at the confluence of the North Platte and Laramie rivers. Only Laramie Peak, six miles distant and snow-covered even in mid-June, gave the scene any grandeur.

But the closer he got, the more Fort Laramie came alive. The people were unlike any Harry had seen before. There was the usual collection of soldiers and scouts, Mexican teamsters and civilian freighters,

but even these were made of different stuff, leaner
and tough-looking. Along the riverbanks hard-
faced emigrant women with long wooden paddles
stirred kettles of boiling laundry while barefoot
children with dirty faces hung on to their skirts.
Their men sweated over charcoal pits, heating iron
tires to glowing red to refit them over wooden wheel
rims shrunken by the sun.

Indians on horseback tended herds of spotted
ponies scratching for forage on the overgrazed land
while others relaxed on blankets before their lodges,
puffing on long clay pipes that added to the smoky
haze. Blanketed squaws moved up and down the
rows of painted teepees, bracelets of tin or brass shining on their stout copper arms. Naked children
chased dogs from scaffolds hung with drying meat.
The colors were a feast to Harry's starved eyes, from
the vermillion-painted faces of the young girls to the
striped trade blankets and bits of calico the women
wore as shawls to the streamers of bright flannel
cloth the men and women tied in their hair. The
colors seemed unnaturally brilliant and beautiful
after the prolonged sameness of brown prairie and
blue sky.

"It ain't nothing like it was back in the thirties,"
Jim Bridger said, trotting his big mule at Harry's
side, "back when me and the boys owned it, me and
Broken Hand Fitzpatrick and Milt Sublette. Called it
Fort William. Back then it weren't so full of trail
trash."

The post commander, Colonel Henry Maynadier,
invited Carrington's party to his headquarters, where

an orderly served lemonade and gingersnaps still warm from the oven.

"So, how go the talks, Colonel?" Carrington said. "I've had no news."

Maynadier sat at the head of the table, tamping tobacco into the bowl of his pipe. "Well, Carrington, if you'd asked me a week ago I'd have said things were going well. Now I'm not so sure. We'll have no trouble with the Brule Sioux—Spotted Tail, Red Leaf, Standing Elk—those chiefs will sign the treaty. But the Oglala, well, that's a different story."

He lit his pipe, taking several deep draws before continuing. "Last Friday Red Cloud and another Oglala chief—Young-Man-Afraid-Of-His-Horses—took off in the night and all their people with them. I don't expect them back."

Carrington frowned. "This Red Cloud, is he head chief of the Sioux? Does he speak for all of them?"

Maynadier shook his head. "The Sioux don't have a head chief," he said. "None of the tribes do and that's part of the problem. They negotiate like they fight, on their own hook, every tribe for itself. Even so, Red Cloud would be a good man to have on our side. The Oglalas listen to him. Can't trust him, though. You can't trust any of them. Remember that, Carrington."

He drew on his pipe. "Do you remember that business at Platte Bridge Station last July?" he said. "When young Caspar Collins was killed? You ever meet him, Carrington? Bill Collins's boy? No? Well, he was a fine young man and a promising officer. Damnedest thing! He went out of his way to be friendly with the Indians, used to visit their camps, learned their language and hand signs and all that twaddle but they killed him anyhow. Even after he went to all that trouble. No, it just goes to show you, those red devils will turn on you like that."

He snapped his fingers in the air. "So there you have it. Red Cloud and Man-Afraid left but talks are continuing with lesser chiefs. Your arrival at this particular time presents a bit of a problem, Carrington, but we'll finesse it somehow."

Carrington and Bridger exchanged glances. "Do the Indians know of my mission?" Carrington said.

Maynadier shifted in his chair. "Well, not just yet. Didn't seem a good time to mention it, what with Red Cloud and Man-Afraid in high feather."

Carrington pulled on his beard. "We might have a problem," he said. "Earlier you mentioned an Indian by the name of Standing Elk."

"Yes, a Brule chief. Why?"

"He visited our camp last night. He asked our business and I told him we were on our way to make a road through the Powder River country. I said we would build three forts along the road to protect emigrants."

"And how did Mr. Standing Elk respond?"

"He suggested Red Cloud's people would put up a fight."

Maynadier took this in, then shrugged his shoulders. "Oh, well. What's done is done. Our commissioners would have preferred to reveal that later, after the treaty was signed, but never mind. Join us when the talks resume tomorrow. We'll smooth things over." Maynadier consulted his pocket watch, signaling an end to the discussion.

Carrington said, "When can I pick up the horses and ammunition I requisitioned? General Cooke said they'd be waiting here at Laramie."

Maynadier cleared his throat. "Yes, well, I've got twenty-six wagons of supplies loaded and ready for you. I can give you mules to pull them, but no drivers. Those you'll have to furnish yourself. As for ammunition, you can have one thousand rounds. No horses. I'm sorry, I can't do it."

"What!" Carrington's face went red. "Cooke promised one hundred thousand rounds of rifle ammunition and horses for all my mounted infantrymen!"

Maynadier shook his head. "I'm sorry, Carrington, but I can't give what I don't have. Things are different now, not like during the war. The frontier army is the redheaded stepchild, a woods colt. You'll learn. A good officer makes do with what he can get. Now, let's go to dinner." Maynadier got to his feet. "I've invited the commissioners to join us. You'll want to meet them before tomorrow."

The next day wives and children accompanied the officers to the fort. Margaret and Sallie Horton shopped at the store of Messrs. Bullock and Ward while Jimmy and Harry waited outside. Jimmy played with a set of tin soldiers in Revolutionary uniform while Harry listened to the treaty talks under way across the parade. Despite the distance he could hear the speakers clearly. A few Indians sat on the pine benches set up for the occasion but most squatted on their heels or stood.

When the commission chairman introduced Carrington an angry sound moved through the crowd, like the buzzing of ten thousand blue flies. The noise grew in pitch and volume, drowning Carrington's words, until an Indian seated on the platform stood and raised his arms. The man was tall and barrel-chested and his voice was powerful. He gestured toward Carrington as he spoke. An interpreter translated the Indian's words.

"The Great Father sends us presents and wants us to sell him the road, but the Little White Chief goes with soldiers to steal the road before the Indians say yes or no. Every year we are pushed farther north, where the living is hard and our women and children starve. I urge all Indian people to stop fighting each other—Loafers against the Angry Ones, Bear People against Smokes—and come together to fight as one against the *wasichus*!"

This brought cries of *"hou!"* and *"hoppo!"* The head commissioner tried to regain control but could not.

A second Indian, old and bent with wispy gray hair, got to his feet. Again the crowd quieted. In a thin voice he began listing the white man's offenses against his people and concluded with a prediction. "In two moons, the Little White Chief's command will not have another hoof left." Again the Indians responded with loud approval.

The head commissioner abruptly ended the conference. Carrington hurried across the parade ground and ordered the women and children back to camp immediately. He was worried, Harry saw that, but they made the trip without trouble.

When Carrington and his officers returned at sundown they brought two strangers with them. One was short and wiry, the other was a tall, black man dressed like an Indian.

"You know them?" Harry said to Bridger. He respected the old mountain man and spent as much time with him as he could.

"Oh, yeah, I know 'em. The little one's Jim Brannan—he's all right. But the other, Jim Beckwourth, he is a son of a bitch and the gaudiest liar this side of St. Louis."

"Jim Beckwourth!" Harry couldn't believe it. The Mulatto of the Plains was almost as famous as Bridger.

"Yep, Medicine Calf hisself. I'd like to buy him for what he's worth and sell him for what he thinks he's worth."

They made their way to the headquarters tent, where Carrington was introducing the new men, both scouts, to his officers. Beckwourth looked to be about sixty, with long gray hair worn plaited, Indianstyle. His quill shirt and leather leggings were dark with grease and sweat and he left a smell in his wake, like that of an animal.

"A treaty was signed today, but frankly, it won't be of use to us," Carrington was saying when Bridger entered. Harry, not allowed to enter when his father was with his officers, listened outside the tent door. "We're headed into a region the Northern tribes, Sioux and Cheyenne mostly, do not wish to surrender. Even so, I expect no serious difficulty. We will demonstrate patience, forbearance, and common sense in our dealings with these tribes and these qualities will go far to advance our cause."

Bridger laughed. "It may not be that simple, Colonel. This morning at Laramie I seen some bucks ridin' off with gunpowder kegs strapped on their ponies and I hear Arapahoes on the trail are beggin' for matches. They use the phosphorous to make percussion caps. Point is, things could be worse than you think. Mebbe you should hold out for that ammunition you was promised before movin' on."

Beckwourth spat on the tent floor. "Gettin' nervous in your old age, Big Throat?" He called Bridger by his Indian name, a reference to the goiter bulging from his collar. "Jumpy like a old prairie goat? You can't let a few Injuns beggin' for matches slow you down, Colonel. You want to get up north and build your forts 'fore winter sets in."

Carrington turned to his officers. "Any opinions?"

"I agree with Beckwourth," Mark Reynolds said. "We have no idea when—or if—that ammunition will get here. Besides, we need to consider appearances. To do as Bridger suggests would make us appear weak. We can't let the Indians think we're afraid of them."

Bridger said, "There's a difference between weakness and being careful, Reynolds. We got women and children along, remember. We got to consider them. But mebbe you don't think thataway."

"What do you mean by that?" Reynolds said.

"All right, all right," Carrington said. "We'll move on tomorrow, but cautiously, as Major Bridger suggests. I depend on his advice and knowledge. I want everyone here to know that." He looked at Reynolds.

"No need for that, Colonel," Bridger said. "I don't care what some puke lieutenant thinks of me anyhow. Some of your men want their hair lifted, that's fine by me. But don't let the Injuns git hold of your women and children, Carrington. Don't let that happen."

He turned and left the tent, walking right by Harry and disappearing into the red twilight.

# Chapter Eight

Royal Spicer was buried at sundown in a shallow grave by the side of the road. There was no wood for a coffin so he met his maker wrapped in a blue army blanket. Lieutenant Anderson read over his grave from the Book of Psalms and afterward he and Rose covered the mound with broken bottles and whatever bits of glass they could find to keep the wolves away.

That night she wrote to Spicer's parents, addressing the letter to the Spicer Family, Bardstown, Kentucky. She wrote of his kindness and assured them his death was painless. She was sad for the elderly couple, who'd already lost one son, knowing the pain her letter would bring them.

Even though she was bone-tired, sleep would not come. When finally she began to drift off she was overcome by a wave of hot panic that left her wide awake with a racing heart. Mark should be here, she thought. He should not have left her alone. She gave way to tears of self-pity.

"Cryin' don't do no good," Jerusha said from her pallet on the floor. "Lord knows I done my share and it ain't worked for me."

Rose was embarrassed. "I thought you were asleep," she said.

"Ain't nobody gonna help you 'cause you pretty or you sweet," Jerusha said. "You need to harden yourself. You need to prepare for the time of testin' that's comin'."

"Time of testing? What do you mean?"

"I mean we is all gonna be tried—you, me, Lieutenant Reynolds, all of us—and after that we'll know for sure what we is. You best be ready, 'cause there won't be no hidin' when it comes."

"And who will test us?" Rose said.

"You know who."

"Oh, what mumbo jumbo! Hard times may lie ahead but we have more to fear from man and nature than divine judgment."

"Think how you want," Jerusha said. "Way I see it, ain't nothing more fearful than His judgin'."

Rose was not a churchgoer, but Jerusha's words, and the confident way she said them, left her uneasy. She felt she had been warned, but of what? "I'm tired," Rose said. "I don't want to talk anymore."

At last she slept, waking to a gray, hazy morning. She had a headache, as if she had taken too much champagne the night before. As she dressed she wondered, for the first time since leaving Fort Sedgwick, if maybe she had made a mistake by following Mark into this desolate country. Maybe she shouldn't have married him in the first place. But then, how could she have done otherwise? Mark, with his hooded brown eyes and easy grin, could have had any girl in St. Louis. The daughters of the wealthy industrialists and bankers—the Blair girls, the Chouteau sisters, the Lebeaus—they all made eyes at him at the cotillions and soirées. But for some reason he had chosen her, Rose King, an orphan girl who, with two older brothers, had been foisted off on the charity of a well-off bachelor uncle. She grew up believing herself plain, too tall, with a flat chest and no talent for coquetry. "You're a pretty girl, Rose," her Grandmother Alice used to remind her, "but you'll never be as lovely as your mother, my poor, dear Rebecca. God rest her soul." When Mark made it clear he was interested in her and no one else, Rose could hardly believe it. How sweet it was to be envied by those rich girls in their fine silks and brocades. And how astonished her grandmother would have been, had she lived to see it. Of course Rose could not resist him. Still, maybe she should have waited just a bit, as her brother Joe suggested.

"He has a reputation, Rosie," he said. "They say he's had his hand up more skirts than a dressmaker."

"Please, don't be vulgar," she said. "Mark can't help it if women throw themselves at him. Anyhow, I don't care what he did before he knew me. I've changed him, he says. I've made him a better man."

Joe said, "I just don't want to see you hurt. That's all."

That conversation came back to her as they traveled an especially bumpy stretch of road. Her headache worsened and she worried she was getting sick again. When they finally met another train, a southbound line of freighters loaded with animal skins from the distant Black Hills, the wagons smelled like an abattoir. Rose held a handkerchief to her nose as they rolled by.

At midday she asked a soldier to put a ladies' saddle on Carl. Headache or no, she could not stand another hour in the ambulance. The soldier obliged with a smile that revealed a mouthful of broken teeth. Once the march resumed Carl hunted down Dixon's bay and fell into step alongside.

"I'm sorry," Rose said. "He's devoted."

"I'm not complaining," Dixon said.

The day was hot and sultry. As they clopped along, Rose found herself drowsing in the saddle. Would she find a letter from Mark at Fort Laramie? The regiment would be long gone—Anderson's late arrival at Sedgwick made a Laramie reunion impossible—but surely there would be a letter. She wondered if Mark had received hers, each painstakingly written. It would be easy to lose something so small in this endless ocean of land.

"I don't like the look of that cloud." Dixon's voice roused her from her waking dream. "Better go to your wagon, Mrs. Reynolds. That's a sandstorm coming."

Rose turned to see a steel-gray cloud hanging low on the horizon. It was oddly flat, as if pressed down from above by a giant hand. She turned Carl back toward the column, where the wagons were forming a corral, but as the wind rose the old horse got a different idea. For the first time in their association, he fought her, tossing his head and kicking his rear legs. Rose struggled with him, holding her hat with one hand and the reins in the other.

"It's all right, Carl," she said, as calmly as possible. "Don't be afraid." As she spoke they were hit by a blast of gritty wind that sent her hat flying and filled her skirt like a billowing sail. The white flash of petticoat was all it took to push Carl over the edge. His ears went flat, he gave two hard pulls on the bit, and he was off, running with the wind at his back like a Kentucky Thoroughbred.

Rose leaned forward, gripping the horn of her ladies' saddle with her right knee and pulling on the reins with all her strength, but the old cavalry horse was hardmouthed and terrified and she was powerless to stop him. The wind grew louder and more urgent, drowning out all other sound. She had no choice but to hold on and pray Carl did not tumble into a ravine or step in a prairie dog hole. She lowered her body Indian-fashion onto his sweating neck and grabbed hold of his mane, cursing the ridiculous sidesaddle. If only she could ride astride!

With a roar loud as a hunter's horn the storm struck in all its fury. The wind nearly blew Rose from the saddle and the air was so thick with dirt she could not even see Carl's ears. She choked on the dust and dirt that filled her nose and mouth.

All at once Dixon was beside her in the darkness, leaning in to grab Carl's bridle. His arrival had a calming effect on Carl, who sidled up next to Dixon's mare and gradually began to slow. In less than a minute Dixon managed to stop the horses altogether. Rose's only thought was to dismount, to get her feet on solid ground, but Dixon took her arm, preventing her. He shouted but she could not make out his words.

The storm chose that moment to do its worst. The wind struck them like a blow. Carl squatted in terror as a small tree tumbled by like a bit of sagebrush. Rose felt herself lifted from the saddle, suspended briefly in midair, then slammed to earth so violently she feared her back was broken. Above her the two horses, giant black shadows, wheeled in the swirling cloud of earth and debris, their iron-shod hooves striking the ground just inches from her head. Instinctively she curled into a ball, expecting at any moment to feel the crushing weight of the horses upon her. Instead it was Dixon who found her, taking her in his arms and covering her body with his own. He held her this way for what seemed a very long time, so close she could feel the beating of his heart, until finally the storm played itself out and the air began to clear.

Slowly Dixon released her and stood. The prairie, eerily silent, was awash in a strange greenish light. Rose rolled onto her back and looked up at him. His face was black with dirt with a streak of bright red blood running from a cut above his eye.

"Are you hurt?" he said.

"No, but you are. Your head is bleeding."

He touched his forehead then looked at the blood on his fingers. "Head wounds bleed a lot. I don't think it's bad." He helped her to her feet, careful to offer his unbloodied hand. Her dress was torn at the shoulder and her hip, which had taken the brunt of her fall, felt bruised and tender.

"Thank you," she said. "You seem always to be saving me."

He smiled, his teeth white against his dirt-blackened face.

"You seem worth saving. But then, I've been wrong about a woman before."

# Chapter Nine

The regiment left Fort Laramie at dawn, following the North Platte River. Harry said good-bye to his friend Bill Kellogg here. Bill's father would remain at Laramie. "Well, good-bye, Foot," Bill said. "Maybe I'll see you again sometime." Harry mumbled a few words of parting, trying not to cry. Bill was his closest friend.

For two days they moved through a flat, prairie-like bottomland. Scrubby pines and cedars clung to the bluffs and sand hills while box elders, quaking aspens, and willows lined the streams. On the third day the road descended a steep canyon with two rocky towers, like castle turrets, at its entrance. Tall cedars wound around the towers' sides in narrow rows that reminded Harry Carrington of the ropes of greenery his mother looped around the porch rail back home in Ohio at Christmastime.

The column halted at the canyon's mouth, stopping earlier than usual to rest before a final crossing of the North Platte the following day. After making

camp Harry and Mark Reynolds escorted Margaret
Carrington and Sallie Horton deeper into the canyon
so the women could hunt for moss agates. When cut
and polished, the colorful stones made rings and
brooches, gifts for friends and family back East.
Reynolds carried a feed sack filled with cans that
clanked as he walked.

"What's that?" Harry said.

Reynolds winked. "You'll see."

While the women searched the ground Reynolds
took three cans from the sack, balanced them on a
rock, and led Harry to a spot about thirty feet distant. "You've handled a gun before, haven't you,
Harry?" he said.

"Sure," Harry lied.

"Not one like this, I bet." Reynolds pulled from his
belt a .38-caliber Smith & Wesson cartridge revolver
with mother-of-pearl grips and filigree etching on
the breech and barrel. He offered it to Harry, who
accepted it gingerly, as if it were made of glass.
"Careful now—it's loaded," Reynolds said. "Beautiful, isn't she? I've got a pair."

Harry examined the gun closely, admiring the
exquisite craftsmanship. "They must've cost a for-
tune!" he said.

"Not a thing, actually. Spoils of war. Anyhow, try
her out. Aim for the can on the left."

Harry extended his right arm. The gun's weight
and balance felt perfect and he liked the way its polished barrel gleamed in the late afternoon light. He
closed his left eye, took aim, and squeezed the trigger.
There was an explosion of yellow corn as his bullet

found its mark. The shot reverberated through the steep canyon.

Reynolds slapped him on the back. "Well done, Harry. You're a natural. Go ahead—try the next one."

Harry was about to fire when Bridger galloped into view on his gray mule. "Stop!" he shouted. "Don't shoot!"

The old man dismounted stiffly and hobbled toward them with a face like thunder. "What the hell's the matter with you, Reynolds?" he said, gesturing at the canyon rim. "You afraid there's still some Injuns around who don't know we're here?"

Reynolds surveyed the high ground. "Calm down, Bridger. We haven't seen any Indians since Laramie."

Bridger spat on the ground at Reynolds's feet. "Dammit, Reynolds, you don't know shit. When you don't see 'em is the time to be most on the lookout. Another thing—you got no business taking these women so far from camp. Even a shavetail like you should know that."

Harry eyed the bluff tops nervously, imagining painted Indians lying on their bellies under wolf skins, watching and waiting for the right moment to ride down on them and sink a hatchet in their skulls. His skin rose in gooseflesh.

"Shavetail?" Reynolds smiled but not because something was funny. Harry saw that plainly enough. For the first time, he sensed Mark Reynolds could be a dangerous man. He took the gun from Harry and, for a moment, the boy thought he might use it on Bridger.

"That's what I said," Bridger said. "It's officers like

you git folks killed out here, Reynolds. Pukes who don't know shit from sherbet and don't have the sense to admit it."

"You've been out here too long, old man," Reynolds said. "You've forgotten your manners, if you ever had any. If you weren't so old I'd be pleased to remind you."

Bridger stepped forward, fists clenched under his grizzled chin. "Go ahead! You're from Missouri, ain't you? Show me what you got!"

"I'd like to, Bridger, but I can't hurt an old man. It's bad form."

Harry was relieved to see his mother and Sallie Horton hurrying toward them, moving slowly over the broken ground. "What's happening here?" Margaret said, out of breath. She looked from Bridger to Reynolds to Harry. "Is there some trouble?"

"No trouble, Mrs. Carrington." Reynolds spoke with an easy smile. "Major Bridger and I were just discussing my military experience, which he finds lacking. That and my Missouri heritage. Actually, Bridger, you're wrong about that too. I'm from Michigan."

Margaret looked skeptical. "Well, Sallie and I have all we need. We're ready to go back." She gave Harry a feed sack heavy with stones.

They walked back to camp, Bridger leading the way on his mule. More than once Harry paused to look over his shoulder, thinking he heard running, moccasin-clad feet close behind him.

That night the soldiers sang around their fires, mostly sentimental songs of home. Soon the wolves joined in with their own mournful cacophony, a frightening sound Harry could not get used to. The soldiers stopped at nine but the wolves were still howling at midnight when the sentries called, "All's well."

The next day the column arrived at Bridger's Ferry, a ranch and river crossing Bridger had built and sold for a modest profit ten years before. Here they would cross to the north side of the North Platte River, leaving the heavily traveled Oregon Road to follow John Bozeman's route to the Powder River and beyond.

Ferry owner Ben Mills met Carrington with news that Indians had raided his beef herd the previous morning.

"They was Sioux. I seen 'em, they was some of my wife's own relatives. That ain't never happened before, not in all the years I been out here. Don't know what to make of it."

Carrington frowned. "We must assume the raid was a hostile act," he said, "and proceed accordingly." That night he drafted, in great detail, five pages of directives outlining new security procedures. Watching him scratch away with his quill pen, Harry wondered if his father truly believed he could impose order on chaos with mere words on paper.

# Chapter Ten

French Pete squealed with delight when he saw Bridger dismounting his mule and ran over to embrace him.

"Lemme go, you old frog!" Bridger said as he struggled to free himself. "I thought I'd run into you out here. I see you still got your hair on. Guess you got your squaw and red babies to thank for that."

The diminutive trader beamed up at his friend. "Yes, yes. Life is good for French Pete. Me, I do not complain." Harry had never seen anyone like the little Frenchman. Pete Cazeau looked like a cannonball, small and round with black hair that gleamed with pomade. He had the smallest feet Harry had ever seen on a grown man.

French Pete and his partner, Henry Arrison, both from St. Louis, were the first white merchants to work the Bozeman Road, selling not only to miners and emigrants but to Indians as well. Their store was a rough, pine-plank shed that was easily taken apart and moved to wherever business beckoned. On this

June afternoon Cazeau and Arrison were set up along Sage Creek, at the spot where the road split in two. One fork, the Mormon Road, took those pilgrims westward to their land of Zion. Carrington's column would take the other, which led to Fort Reno on the Powder River.

Cazeau had an Oglala wife and five half-breed children. The oldest daughter, Jane, was a sixteen-year-old beauty, with black shining hair and delicate shell earrings dangling from her ears. Harry was not her only admirer. Every male eye in the regiment was turned her way. Jane helped her father and Arrison in the store, filling orders for cans of fruit and oysters, cornmeal and clothespins, catsup and soap. Ordinarily, Harry tried to get out of helping his mother with her shopping, but today he volunteered. Once, Jane caught him watching her and he quickly turned his head, feeling his face burn. When he dared look at her again she was selling a box of cigars to Mark Reynolds. Harry saw he had the same effect on Indian females as white ones. When Reynolds smiled at her, Jane blushed under her lovely copper skin.

Jimmy Carrington and French Pete's youngest son sat on the ground outside the store, petting the Indian boy's pet antelope. "My uncle found her on the prairie," the Indian boy said. His face was round as an Eskimo's and his black, uncombed hair fell in his eyes. "Her leg was broken. See?" He pointed to a tumor-like bulb on the fawn's slender foreleg. "My uncle made a splint. That's where it healed."

"Her ears are soft," Jimmy said. "Like velvet."

The Cazeau boy nodded. "I know it. Her name is Manishee and she comes when I call her. Watch." As he prepared to demonstrate, his older brother appeared. He pulled the younger boy roughly to his feet and led him away. The little antelope followed.

The column camped that night beside Cazeau's trading post. In his dreams Harry was visited by a beautiful woman who was partly Jane and partly Rose Reynolds. He woke in the moony darkness with his mind still full of the woman, so much so that when he walked to the river to relieve himself he was sure he heard her soft laughter coming from the darkness of the cottonwood trees.

In the morning as the train prepared to move out, Cazeau came forward carrying the little antelope. He stopped at the ambulance of Sallie Horton and lifted the animal to her. She had admired the fawn the night before.

"Here, doctor's wife, I make you the present," Cazeau said, beaming. "She give you good company in your wagon."

Cooing with pleasure, Mrs. Horton took the little animal in her arms and nuzzled it as if it were a child. Her inability to produce a baby was a grief to her. This was widely known.

"You can't take her!" Jimmy jumped out of their ambulance and ran to Mrs. Horton. "She belongs to him!" He pointed to Cazeau's young son, who stood in the door of his lodge, his round face wet with tears. "Her name is Manishee and she's his!" Jimmy said.

Mrs. Horton looked at Cazeau but the Frenchman waved his hand dismissively, as if shooing away an insect. "No matter," he said. "The prairie has many antelopes. We will find him another."

"Well, at least let me pay you for it," she said. "Let me give your boy some money. It's only fair."

Cazeau refused. "No, no. I do not accept. She is my gift."

As the column moved out, Harry saw Reynolds turn in the saddle and lift his hat in a parting gesture. Jane responded with a small wave of her hand. There was something intimate in the exchange, and Harry remembered the laughter from the cottonwoods the night before. Maybe he had not imagined it after all. This was a bad thought and he put it out of his head.

He opened his book to read when something drew his eye to Cazeau's lodge. The older son was talking to his father, his younger brother still crying at his side. Casually, as if it were something he had done many times before, Cazeau lashed out with his open hand, striking the older boy hard across the mouth. Harry looked away. He felt he had seen something ugly and indecent, the way he felt the night he saw a famous Union general fall drunkenly to his hands and knees to vomit in the snow.

# Chapter Eleven

"If I'd known you Yankees would send me to a place like this, I'd have stayed at Rock Island. Even prison was better than this hellhole." The thin man lowered himself carefully into a chair, letting his crutch fall to the ground. The left leg of his trousers was empty, pinned at the hip. "Sergeant Simon Trover," he said, leaning forward to shake hands with Anderson and his officers. "Company C, Fifth Volunteers. Welcome to Reno Redoubt."

In a slow Southern drawl Trover told them his troop was one of captured Confederates who were released from prison in exchange for fighting for Uncle Sam on the western frontier. "I've been a recipient of Yankee hospitality since my capture at Pittsburg Landing on the seventh of April, eighteen hundred and sixty-two, although I'm happy to say our long association will soon be coming to an end."

Rose listened as she unpacked the mess chest. She liked the aristocratic sound of his voice, and his hands, she noticed, were large and beautifully formed with long, slender fingers and clean nails. It was easy to imagine them moving deftly over ivory piano keys or holding a cut glass tumbler of Kentucky bourbon.

"This country takes top prize when it comes to sheer desolation," he said, squinting into the sun. "Why don't you Yankees save everyone a lot of trouble and just let the natives keep it?"

They sat in the shade of a ten-foot wall of sand-filled gunnysacks. This was the north bulwark of Reno Redoubt, a small fortress of sand and adobe on Antelope Creek that served as a way station for mail teams traveling between Fort Reno on the Powder River, 41 miles to the north, and Fort Laramie, 130 miles to the south. A low adobe stockade outside the walls enclosed a small hay yard and a rickety stable for mules and horses.

"How many men have you got here?" Ranald Henry said, eyeing Trover's troops as they went about their evening work, lashing down wagon covers, tending to hungry mules, struggling to start cook fires in the dry, sundown wind.

"There are twenty of us," Trover said, "including myself."

"Indians give you much trouble?" Gregory said.

"Not that much until lately," Trover said. "They've raided our mule herd twice in the past week. Two days ago they killed a man." He pointed to a rock-covered mound of earth on the far side of Antelope Creek. A grave, barely visible in the dying light. "I say man but really he was a boy, seventeen or eighteen, if that. Italian, barely spoke English. We called him Joe."

"What happened to him?" Anderson said.

Trover shrugged. "It was just before dawn—you'll learn that's when things tend to happen out here. Joe went off to answer a call of nature and wasn't missed till the detail was starting. We found him in that draw over there with his pants down around his ankles and a hatchet lodged in his spinal column. No one saw or heard a thing."

Rose shuddered.

"Sioux?" Gregory said.

"I can't say. One of my boys kept the weapon—you're welcome to examine it if you like."

Rose wanted to hear more but Clara Anderson was calling from her ambulance. She and Rollo had fallen ill that morning and Rose had looked in on them a few times that day, though not for several hours. As she climbed into their wagon, Rose nearly gagged on the stench.

"I'm sorry," Clara said, "but Rollo's napkin needs changing and I simply cannot manage it. Would you, please? His clean ones are there, in the pile by the chair."

Rose was disturbed by the change in Clara. In just a short time her skin had taken on a yellowish cast and her eyes were sunken. Rollo, asleep in his champagne basket, was flushed and breathing fast. "I'm going for Doctor Dixon," Rose said.

"No." Clara's voice was firm. "Do not bring him. That would worry Frank and he's got enough of that. We'll be better soon. I'm sure of it."

Rose hesitated, remembering her own illness at Sedgwick and understanding Clara's desire not to be a burden to her husband. But what about Rollo? As she looked down at him a fly crawled across his cheek toward his open mouth. Rose waved it away.

"Please, just bring us some water," Clara said. "And extra blankets. It's gotten cold." The ambulance was an oven.

Rose filled Clara's bucket from the water barrel strapped to a platform on the side of the wagon. When she returned Clara was asleep but Rollo was fussing. Rose damped a cloth, gently lifted the baby from his basket and removed his sodden pant. His stool was foul and curd-like. She cleaned his hot little body, pinned on a fresh napkin, and gave him a bottle of water which he sucked down greedily. He immediately soiled himself again.

"Poor baby," she whispered. "Poor little man." He needs a doctor, she thought, and soon. She changed him once more, returned him to his basket, and went in search of Dixon. She found him eating a plate of beans with Trover at his fireside. The surgeon stood when she approached and Trover moved to do the same, wincing in pain.

"Stay as you are," she said.

"That leg still bothers you," Dixon said. "When did you lose it?"

"I did not lose it, sir. You Yankees took it from me."

"Let me take a look," Dixon said.

"Here?" Trover glanced at Rose. "Now?"

"I've seen my share of war's work, Mr. Trover," she said but in fact, Rose had seen very little. She had joined the St. Louis Ladies' Aid Society, against her uncle's wishes, because she wanted to do something useful. She was inspired by newspaper accounts of "Mother" Mary Ann Bickerdyke, the Illinois widow and botanic physician who traveled with the Union army, venturing onto blood-soaked battlefields in her Shaker bonnet and calico dress to care for the dying and wounded. But when Rose presented herself to the Reverend Charles Peabody at the Soldier's Home, he sent her away.

"I told them to send me *plain* women," he said. "The men must maintain a Christian outlook and avoid all excitement. Their healing depends on it." When Rose insisted, he gave her light work folding bandages and linens in the aviary.

Trover unpinned his folded trouser leg and rolled back the cloth to reveal an ugly knob of puckered flesh where his knee used to be. A bit of bone, like the stamen of a poisonous flower, protruded from the angry red center. "The worst of it is I can no longer ride," he said. "I used to be an excellent horseman, the best in all of Alcorn County, Mississippi. Now they have to cart me about like an overgrown melon."

Dixon examined the stump. The flaps of flesh were swollen and brown in places, with blebs of yellow serum dotting the surface. Even from a distance Rose detected an odor, ripe and corrupt.

"This is infected," Dixon said. "You must know that. It should be treated."

Trover neatly repinned his trouser before reaching

for his crutch. "No disrespect to you, Dixon," he said, getting to his feet, "but I've had my fill of Yankee doctoring." He turned to Rose and smiled. "Mrs. Reynolds, I'd like to offer you and Jerusha my cabin for the evening." He pointed to a rough, one-room shack in the corner of the redoubt, the only fixed dwelling among the rows of small canvas tents. "Maybe Mrs. Anderson and her son would be more comfortable there as well?"

"Yes, I'm sure they would," Rose said. "Thank you. Dr. Dixon, would you look in on them after I get them settled? I'm worried."

"Of course." He and Trover watched her walk to Clara's wagon, where an anxious-looking Lieutenant Anderson met her at the door.

"Mrs. Reynolds is a fine-looking woman," Trover said, "and all the more attractive because she doesn't seem to realize it." When Dixon said nothing Trover continued. "Her husband was through here with Carrington's regiment several weeks ago. He left a letter for her. Why would a man leave a woman like that alone out here?"

"I've wondered about that myself."

"I'm sure you have." They were silent for a moment, then Trover said, "I suggested to Lieutenant Anderson that he wait until our replacements arrive before moving on. That way, my men and I could accompany you as far as Fort Reno. It would be safer for all involved but he refused, said he must adhere to schedule. Do you have influence with him?"

"Not much," Dixon said. They watched Anderson

carry his wife to Trover's cabin, Rose following with Rollo's basket.

"Well, ask him to reconsider," Trover said. "Tell him it's unwise to ignore advice from a man with one foot in the grave."

Dixon got to his feet. "I'll do it," he said, "but if his wife's illness is what I think it is, she may settle the question for us. She won't be able to travel for a while." He got his medical bag and went to the cabin where Clara lay on a narrow bed, Rollo cradled at her side. There was a smell in the room, one he knew well. It was the calling card of an old adversary. "What are your symptoms, Mrs. Anderson?" he said, pulling a chair to her bedside.

"Fever, diarrhea." Her voice was barely audible. "Baby too."

"How long has this been going on?"

"Since this morning."

Dixon measured her pulse, then pinched the flesh on her upper arm. It remained peaked when he released his fingers. He unbuttoned the top of her shirtwaist to reveal rose-colored patches on her neck and chest. When Dixon was done examining the child, Anderson pulled him aside.

"What's wrong with them?"

"I'm afraid it's typhoid."

The blood drained from Anderson's face. "No, it can't be. My God, man, do something! Give them calomel or an emetic. That's what our surgeons did during the war."

"Yes, and a good many men died because of it,"

Dixon said. "Your wife and child are dry as chips, the both of them. A purgative is the last thing they need. They've got to take water and keep it down. Tonight is critical."

Anderson went to his wife's bed and took her hand. "I'll stay. Of course I'll stay."

"I will too," Rose said. "Jerusha also."

"Good," Dixon said. "Clara will need at least a cupful of water every half hour and the boy as much as he will take. Let me know right away if anything changes or if they start having abdominal pain. And, Rose, be extremely careful with any fluids they pass, when you change Rollo's napkin, for example. Wash your hands with soap afterward. This is very important."

"I understand."

"Would you like me to stay?" Dixon said. "I could do that."

Rose shook her head. "No, we'd be crowded. I'll take care of them. Don't worry."

She had first vigil. Only when the others were asleep did she open Mark's letter. Dated June 26, it was four weeks old and obviously written in a hurry:

*Dearest Rose,*

 *We march in an hour so this will be brief. Fort Reno is only two days' travel from here and the scouts say we will look upon the Bighorn Mountains within the day.*

 *I haven't had a letter from you in some time but I put this to the errant nature of the mails and not to*

*fickleness on your part. I think of you often, my
darling, and with great pride. Not every woman
would have the steel to come on alone, as you have.
You are a true soldier's wife.*

*I hope Spicer and Jerusha have been of use.*

Mark didn't know of Royal's death so her letters
weren't reaching him. She posted them at every opportunity, even stopping northbound mail details as
they flew by on the road. What else could she do?

*Margaret Carrington sends warm regards. She
is very fond of you. I have become great friends with
her older son, Harry, an intelligent boy who will be
twice the man the father is. (Harry asks of you
often, I've noticed, and seems to welcome the mail
trains as eagerly as I do. I believe you've made a
conquest there.)*

*Morale among the men and officers is getting
worse every day. Carrington brings this on himself
with his dithering and obsession with minutiae.
Brown and Bisbee are especially critical. I sincerely
hope Sherman replaces him and soon. We must
succeed. Careers hang in the balance.*

*The Indians haven't made much mischief
beyond their usual pilfering and begging. Still
old Jim Bridger constantly sounds the alarm,
thus encouraging Carrington's natural timidity.
They are a fine pair.*

*I hear the boots and saddles—
I remain, your loving husband,*

*Mark Reynolds*

Rose closed her eyes, longing to feel Mark's arms around her, his breath warm on that spot where her neck met her shoulder. She sensed she was different this way from other wives, who spoke of the marriage bed as a thing to be endured. She enjoyed their time in bed together, looked forward to it, in fact, and felt no shame or guilt. After all, she reasoned, if there is a God, He gave man—and woman—a capacity for pleasure for a reason, did He not?

Clara moaned and Rose went to her, lifting her head as she drank a cup of water without fully waking. She tried to get Rollo to take some water also but he refused the nipple. His skin was dry and hot as a stone in the noontime sun.

The nighttime quiet was broken by the howl of a single wolf. Bridger once told her a real wolf's howl produced no echo but the cry of an Indian imitating a wolf did. Was there an echo? She listened, trying to hear, and fell asleep, dreaming she was alone in a darkened house with long hallways and many cavernous, high-ceilinged rooms. Something was in the house with her, something evil and deadly, silently moving closer. She waited, frozen with fear, powerless to escape. All at once a man was beside her in the darkness. He took her in his strong arms and told her not to be afraid. In an immediate, sweet rush of knowing, Rose understood she was safe. Only when the sentry's call woke her did she realize the man in her dream was not Mark but the surgeon, Daniel Dixon.

# Chapter Twelve

It was almost dawn when Anderson left his wife's bedside to relieve the watch. The air was hot and motionless and Rose's skin was damp under her clothing. She wondered if she should wake Clara and the boy to give them water but decided to let them sleep a while longer.

She stood and stretched. Her back muscles ached from a night on the floor. What she wouldn't give for a hot bath and freshly laundered clothing that smelled of soap and sunshine! At Fort Reno she would—

"Indians! Turn out! Turn out! Indians!"

The cry shattered the stillness like a rock through glass. Rose felt a blast of fear. She heard the crack of a carbine, another and another, followed by a shrill whistle. Shaking off her paralysis, she ran to the door. Half-dressed men in stocking feet burst from their tents to take positions on the sandbag parapets or at loopholes in the adobe walls. Already the air smelled of gunpowder.

"Lord a'mighty." Jerusha stood at Rose's shoulder. "Sweet Jesus, have mercy on us."

"Oh, God!" Clara reached down and pulled Rollo from his basket, holding him close.

Rose looked toward Antelope Creek, where a mist thick as smoke hung over the water. Barely visible in the haze, bare-breasted warriors on spotted ponies drove mules and horses, some dragging picket pins, away from the post. Two Indians rode along the flanks keeping the frightened animals together and moving in the right direction.

"They're stealing the livestock," Rose said. "They're not here for us—they're here for the horses and mules."

Trover stood in the center of the yard, leaning on his crutch and shouting instructions. Only when the shooting subsided did Major Henry poke his head from his tent. His face was white and sweaty.

"You can come out now, Major," Anderson said. "It's safe."

"I resent your implication, sir," Henry said, smoothing his thin, ginger-colored hair across his wet forehead. "I'll have you know I was guarding the payroll."

Anderson laughed. "Indians aren't interested in your payroll."

"They could've been road agents disguised as Indians. Such things happen, you know."

Anderson shook his head, then ordered his troops to saddle the remaining horses still tethered to a picket line just outside the walls. He went to his wife's bedside, lifting her hand to his lips.

"Oh, Frank," Clara whispered. "Are they gone? I was so frightened."

"Yes, they're gone." He stroked her hair. "Poor girl. You and Rollo are having the devil's own time of it." Anderson touched the baby's face. "The boy is cool. I believe his fever's broken."

"Oh, we're better today," Clara said. "Much better. I'm sure of it."

"Well, let Jerusha fix you a good breakfast," Anderson said. "Regain your strength. I'll be back before you know it."

"Back?" Clara tried to sit. "What do you mean? You can't mean to go after them!"

Anderson pushed her gently back on the pillow. "I have no choice. We need those animals, we are paralyzed without them. Be brave, Clara." He kissed her on the lips, Rollo on the forehead. "Take care of our boy. As I said, I'll be back in no time." He left without looking back, though Clara called his name. Rose followed him to the door, where she was surprised to see Dixon and Gregory waiting in the ragged line of horsemen.

"Mount up!" Anderson said as he swung into the saddle. "We'll teach those redskins to steal from the United States Army!" One of Trover's men, a strapping youth with hair the color of corn silk, stood frozen beside his horse.

"What's wrong with you?" Anderson said. "Mount your horse!"

Tears rolled down the boy's face. "I can't, Lieutenant," he said. "I'm scairt of Injuns, terrible scairt, ever since I seen what they did to Eyetalian Joe."

"What's your name, soldier?" Anderson said.

"Schubert, sir. Otis Schubert."

"Schubert, you get your sorry ass up on that horse or so help me God I'll drum you out of here with nothing but a toothpick and the clothes on your back!"

As he spoke three Indians appeared on the ridge across the creek, riding their ponies back and forth and shouting insults. One dismounted and turned his backside toward the watching soldiers, lifting his breechcloth to expose his buttocks. This taunting continued until Anderson's men, including the ashen Schubert, trotted from the redoubt in columns of two. Dixon broke away at the last minute and rode to Rose at the cabin door.

"Do you have a gun?" he said.

She reached into the pocket tied around her waist and withdrew a .44 caliber Colt with ivory handles. "My brother carried it through the war. He said it brought him luck."

"Do you know how to use it?" Dixon said.

She nodded, and their eyes met in a powerful exchange of feeling. Rose was unprepared for the emotion that welled inside her. She should turn away, she knew that, but she did not want to. She was sorry when the moment ended, when he turned his horse and joined the others.

Rose made sure all six of the revolver's chambers were filled and clicked the cylinder back into place. If the time came, could she send a bullet crashing into human—even Indian—flesh and bone? She returned the revolver to her pocket and reentered the cabin.

# Chapter Thirteen

Time passed slowly. Rose made oatmeal for breakfast and forced Clara to take a few swallows. Rollo could manage nothing more than a few feeble pulls on his water bottle. The child was dying, Rose felt certain of that.

Trover's little cabin was surprisingly comfortable and well-furnished. The earthen floor was carpeted with grain sacks sewn together and pegged down at the corners. Red woolen blankets hung on the chinked log walls provided color and warmth. A small stove stood against one wall and a sturdy bunk, occupied by Clara and Rollo, was built into another. There was a tin washbasin and pan of brown soap on a table by the door with a clean towel and shaving mirror hanging from nails above. Curtains of a sky-blue fabric hung at the cabin's lone window and the morning sun shining through them produced a pleasant, watery light.

Jerusha took Rollo from the bed and unpinned

his napkin. The child was so dry it scarcely needed changing.

"It's here," she said.

"What do you mean?" Rose sat beside Clara on the bed, sponging her head, neck and shoulders. Her breath was so foul Rose had to turn her head.

"That time I told you about," Jerusha said. "The time of testin'."

They had spent many hours together but Rose realized did not know Jerusha at all. At one time she had hoped the two could be companions, friends to one another but it had gradually become clear to her, for whatever reason, this would not happen.

"Jerusha," Rose said, "I've often wondered . . . my husband offered you freedom after the war. Why didn't you take it? Why are you here? Please, speak freely."

Jerusha smiled to herself but did not answer. Instead she lowered her head to the baby in her arms and rocked him gently. "This baby is about to meet our Lord."

Rose looked down at Clara, thinking his mother would soon follow. What a cruel world this is, she thought. Why did this woman and her son have to die while a man like Ranald Henry lives on? Maybe if she had faith, if she had attended church as her grandmother wanted, she could know the answer to these questions.

Suddenly she was desperate to escape the cabin's tomblike atmosphere. "I'm going for water," she said, picking up the empty bucket and walking out into the yard. The morning sun was dazzling. She shielded her eyes with her free hand and saw Trover on the sandbag parapet looking through field glasses. He seemed very intent.

Curious, Rose dropped the bucket and climbed onto the sentry walk. Two soldiers with coils of rope wound over their shoulders were splashing across Antelope Creek to collect the remains of the mule herd, the sorry few that were too old or infirm to run with the rest. An Indian's body lay on the slope of ground between the redoubt and the creek. He was on his back with his arms fully extended, like Jesus on the cross, his head turned at an unnatural angle. Trover turned to a tall, hard-faced man next to him. "Mike, get on out there, help Skinny and Pat with those mules. Take Reuben with you."

"Me?" The soldier, Reuben, had wiry red hair and a head several sizes too small for his body. "Why me?"

Mike jumped down and clapped a dirty hand on Reuben's shoulder. "C'mon, Rube," he said. "Me and you is gonna get us a scalp!" He slapped the sheathed knife hanging from his cartridge belt. "And we'll take some fingers too. Make us a necklace like them Cheyenne bucks wear."

Clara and Rollo temporarily forgotten, Rose stayed on the walk watching the soldiers. When they reached the Indian's body Mike kicked it with his square-toed boot then dropped to his knees beside the corpse. He unsheathed his knife, grabbed a fistful of the warrior's long, unbraided hair, and began to cut, beginning behind the left ear. Rose turned away. "You permit such things, Mr. Trover?" she said.

He responded without lowering his glasses. "Once I would not have, Mrs. Reynolds. Now it hardly seems to matter."

When the scalping was complete, Mike hopped around the body in an imitation of an Indian war dance, waving the bloody thing above his head for the benefit of spectators in the redoubt.

"Get on with it, dammit!" Trover shouted.

With a shrug, Mike tied the scalp to his belt, picked up his carbine, and waded into the shallow water of Antelope Creek. Reuben, who had not participated in the scalp dance, followed. Meanwhile, a sentry called Trover's attention to a cloud of dust rising above the brown hills to the north. Trover trained his field glasses on horsemen cresting the ridge. "It's Anderson," he said, "coming like the devil himself is on his heels."

Rose felt for the revolver at her waist as Trover swung his field glasses to a ravine east of the redoubt. Swearing, he dropped the glasses and called to Mike and Reuben, now halfway across the creek. "Come back!" he shouted, making wild windmilling motions with his arm. "Run for it!"

The two men turned and started back toward the redoubt, but the others, Pat and Skinny, were fixing a rope line in the cottonwood thicket on the far side of the creek and out of earshot.

Ellen heard the blast of a bugle and warriors sprang from the ravine to fire at the four soldiers caught outside the walls. Mike and Reuben splashed through the creek as bullets sent up fan-shaped sprays of water and gravel. They raced through the gates and immediately took up arms to help defend Skinny and Pat.

Now the Indians trained all their fire on these two, and the futility of their position was obvious. They burst from the scrub and floundered into the water. Pat flung aside his carbine as he ran but Skinny, tall and skeletal, paused in his flight to take a shot. Trover's men kept up a steady covering fire, with every man in the redoubt, even the Mexican teamsters, helping out. To the north, Anderson's men rode for the redoubt at top speed pursued by at least fifty warriors. They gained steadily on the soldiers, whose underfed horses were played out.

Trover called down to Rose. "Take cover in the cabin, Mrs. Reynolds. Now!"

Frightened though she was, Rose could not retreat like an animal to its hole. Somehow she had to participate in her own defense. "I have a gun," she said, showing her weapon, "and I can use it."

"Suit yourself," Trover said. "I warned you."

By now Pat had cleared the creek and was starting the final dash to the redoubt. Skinny still struggled through the water, a dark stain spreading on his thigh. He was nearing the bank when he threw up his arms and pitched forward, falling to his knees in the stream with an arrow protruding from his back. When he finally managed to get to his feet his coat was black with blood and water. "Pat!" he cried. "Come back. Don't leave me, you little shit!"

Pat turned and took one step in Skinny's direction, but an arrow grazed the front of his blouse, tearing the fabric. He broke and ran for the redoubt and through the gate without slowing. Skinny staggered forward out of the water before a bullet struck him in the leg. He fell again. "Help me!" he yelled. "Please, somebody help me!"

Now the Indians turned their fire on Anderson's

men, thundering forward in a white cloud of dust.
Pat stood beside Rose on the sentry walk, his eyes
fixed on Skinny, who was slowly dragging himself
forward. Rose heard a strangled sound and saw Pat
was crying. "Come on, Skinny," he whispered, "Please,
come on."

The first of Anderson's men reached the creek.
Jack Gregory rode at the head of the column but at
the last minute his Appaloosa stallion reared and refused to enter the water. Gregory applied his spurs to
the horse's flanks and at last the animal surged forward, plunging through the stream. Once across Gregory galloped to Skinny, dismounting before his horse
had fully stopped. He lifted the wounded man easily
as a sack of grain and tossed him across the saddle but
as he put a foot in the stirrup to remount, an arrow
brushed the stallion's shoulder, causing him to wheel
in circles with Gregory hopping alongside. Rose
gasped, sure the animal would fall, crushing both
men, or bolt and carry Skinny into enemy hands, but
somehow Gregory managed to gain his seat and control of the horse. The soldiers in the redoubt cheered
as he and Skinny rode through the gates.

"I was wrong about you, Jack," Skinny said as the
scout lowered him to the ground. "I'll never call you
harelip again, I swear it."

By now the rest of Anderson's men were fording
the creek. Rose found Dixon, with a Henry rifle, at
the rear of the column. As she watched he shot two
Indians off their horses. One of the first soldiers to
clear the water took an arrow in the back. He fell
from his horse, catching a boot in the stirrup. Terrified, the animal ran blindly, dragging the soldier

toward the Indians. Rose looked on in horror as he struggled unsuccessfully to free himself, each bounce along the rocky streambed driving the arrow deeper into his flesh.

Finally he worked his boot free. The horse, bleeding from wounds in the withers and flanks, continued running with the saddle turned under his belly. The soldier managed to gain his feet—Rose recognized the man with the yellow teeth who had saddled Carl for her the day of the sandstorm—but his leg was bent at an unnatural angle and would not support his weight. He fell to his hands and knees and tried to scuttle to the redoubt like a sand crab but before he made even ten yards a warrior was on him. The soldier screamed and raised an arm as the Indian lifted his heavy war club and, with one powerful swing, crushed the man's head, rotten teeth flying from his mouth like seeds.

Anderson's men, singly or in groups of two or three, ran their horses through the gates and into the yard. Dixon triaged the wounded as the others joined the defense, firing on the Indians who were now circling the redoubt on painted ponies.

Their horses careened through the redoubt, endangering the wounded. Trover ordered Pat, still beside Rose on the walk, to control them. Even as he spoke, a bullet hit Pat squarely between the eyes. He stiffened, then pitched forward into Rose's arms. She heard a woman screaming as Pat's body slid down hers, leaving a trail of blood and brains on her dress. Only when it stopped did Rose realize the screaming woman was she.

# Chapter Fourteen

The sun was a blister in the sky. By noon the thermometer had climbed to 107 degrees. Each person was allowed one-half dipper of water every hour and the suffering animals got none. Anderson posted a soldier at each of the three water barrels to prevent stealing.

The Indians surrounding the redoubt outnumbered the soldiers many times over. It was impossible to count them. Mid-afternoon they massed for a charge and galloped down on the little post in one wide, terrifying line. The attack was preceded by the bugle Rose had heard at dawn. All the men, even Anderson's troops, looked to Trover for direction. He was always in motion, vaulting around on his crutch, shouting orders and words of encouragement as calmly as if he were directing target practice. "Hold your fire, boys," he said. "Wait till you got something to hit. Aim low."

In the cabin with the other women, Rose crouched against a wall, her hands over her ears. Pat's death had changed her mind about participating in the redoubt's defense. The noise was deafening—a constant roar of gunfire, screaming men and horses, shrieking bone whistles. Rose had never heard it before, the sound of war.

No soldiers were injured during the assault, which Trover said may have been mostly a means of measuring the redoubt's strength. After, the Indian leader rode back and forth before his warriors, exhorting them in a powerful voice even the soldiers could hear. A giant on a big American horse, he wore no war paint other than vertical lines of red and black across his face. On his head he wore a feathered war bonnet with two short, black buffalo horns on either side.

"What's he saying?" Trover asked Gregory. "Do you know him?"

"I know him," Gregory said. "He's called Cloud-splitter, a Cheyenne war chief. He's telling his bucks they are many and we are few. He says, 'Tonight we will bring the bluecoats' scalps to our fires.'"

The war drums started. Rose found this the most frightening sound of all. They aroused in her a primal fear and a wild, irrational impulse to run. If only they would stop. The throbbing was unbearable, like pressure on a broken bone. She fled the stifling cabin, hoping to find a breeze, but there was none. Across the yard Anderson, Dixon, Gregory, and paymaster Henry were deep in conversation. She moved closer until she could hear them.

"What are you going to do, Anderson?" Henry

said. "We can't just sit here and wait for them to finish us off. You're in charge. What do you propose?"

Anderson, sitting on a cracker box, wiped the back of his neck with a handkerchief. "There's only one thing we can do," he said. "We have to send a rider for help. Tonight, after dark."

"Who've you got in mind?"

"I'll ask for volunteers."

Rose went back to the cabin and Anderson soon followed. He knelt by his wife's bed and took her hand but Clara was too far gone to acknowledge him. "They're dying," he said dully. "Both of them."

Rose said nothing. She would not offer false encouragement.


Anderson stayed with his wife and son until evening, sometimes dozing in his chair. With the darkness came clouds, sailing fast across the moon, and cool air that smelled of rain. Indian fires burned on the high ground across the water accompanied by the drums and wailing voices. Rose, standing alone in the yard, could not take her eyes off the black silhouettes moving before the fires' orange glow. She sensed she was witnessing something ancient, from a ghost world.

A light rain began to fall. Closing her eyes, she lifted her face to it. The cool wetness was refreshing and she stood this way for a long time, until she heard voices. She crossed the darkened yard and found Gregory and her driver, Ignacio, sitting on the ground tearing a blanket into strips and winding them around their feet.

"What are you doing?" she said. "What's going on?"

"Me and Ignacio, we're going for help," Gregory said. "If we make it by the Indians, this will disguise our footprints."

Footprints, Rose thought, would be the least of your problems. "You're very brave," she said.

Gregory kept his eyes on his work. "I don't know about that, Mrs. Reynolds, but somebody's got to go, that's clear. Anyhow we're lucky tonight on one count, there's good cloud cover. And we're gonna need all the luck we can get. *Verdad, amigo?*" Ignacio nodded.

The two men wore dark ponchos made of army blankets with holes for their heads. Their boots were tied around their necks. When his foot-wrapping was done Gregory walked over to Rose. "Mrs. Reynolds, if anything happens to me, will you see my mother gets this?" He handed her an envelope addressed to Widow Gregory, Pleasant Hill, Cass County, Missouri.

"Of course," she said, putting it with the revolver in her waist pocket.

He nodded his thanks and turned back to Anderson. "We'll follow the creek bed far as we can. Once we're clear of the Indians we'll head north. It'll take us at least fifteen hours to get to Reno. At least that."

Anderson nodded and offered Gregory his hand. "May God be with you." He extended his hand to Ignacio and said, *"Dios se lo pague."*

The Mexican smiled, his white teeth gleaming in the darkness. "I take my rewards on earth, Teniente," he said.

Each man carried a gun and a pack with water, dried beef, and hard bread. Soldiers had dug a narrow tunnel under one of the adobe walls, just big enough for Gregory and Ignacio to slide through. Every soul in the redoubt prayed for their success—some silently, some aloud—as the two men crawled away into the darkness.

The minutes that followed were agony. Anderson and Rose waited at the open door of the cabin, expecting any moment to hear the terrible sounds that meant discovery. Every incidental noise—Clara's labored breathing, the distant yip of a coyote—was magnified tenfold.

A man yelled. Rose felt her skin tighten in terror. Then she realized the shriek came from inside the redoubt. Major Henry was running across the yard carrying an open box. He stopped in front of Anderson, panting and red-faced.

"They stole it!" he said, flinging the empty lock box at Anderson's feet. "Gregory and that one-eyed greaser! The payroll money—every goddamn penny. Gone!"

# Chapter Fifteen

Harry was glad to see the last of Fort Reno, an ugly and sunbaked outpost filled with dispirited troops. Discipline was so poor men urinated against the stockade walls, an act that would result in court-martial back in the States. Still, he knew that in leaving this fort they were leaving the last civilized place on the Powder River Road. Between Fort Reno and Bozeman City lay 250 miles of undiscovered country inhabited by a wild, ferocious people. The men of his father's regiment were like sailors, Harry thought, setting out across a wide, roiling ocean with no friendly ports.

They left before dawn. By eight o'clock the sun was already blinding, by ten the mercury had climbed to 103. Heat-sick soldiers rode with women and children in the ambulances, fouling the air with their sweat and misery. Harry chose to ride, kicking Calico to the head of the column to escape the dust.

The Indians first appeared after midday break, lining the sandy hills in front of the train and along its flanks. They showed themselves in greater numbers as the column neared a flat plain strewn with white objects Harry initially took for rocks but, upon closer inspection, turned out to be bleached human bones. There were also a number of stone cairns flying flags of faded calico that snapped in the wind. Harry rode to Bridger to ask him what it was.

"A Sioux holy place," Bridger said, "where they fought a famous battle with the Mountain Crows."

Just then a dozen soldiers broke from the ranks to collect skull souvenirs. Bridger tried to stop them but they ignored him so he appealed to the nearest officer, Quartermaster Brown.

"Stop them," Bridger said. "Call them back to the column."

Brown snorted. "What's the damage? Let them have their fun."

Bridger was still angry that night when Harry and Jimmy joined him at his fire. Lit from below by the glowing orange coals, the old man's face looked ancient as an Egyptian mummy's, Harry thought.

"Are you still bothered by what happened today?" Harry said. "Is it really so important?"

"My bother don't signify," Bridger said, staring at the fire. "What signifies is the Sioux who was watchin'—and they was. Just because you don't see 'em don't mean they ain't there. These soldiers ain't got the sense of a pinecone and the officers neither. They're a danger to your father's enterprise."

To change the subject, Harry asked why the stream by their campsite was called Crazy Woman Creek.

Bridger always was glad to share his knowledge of the land.

"Well," he said, fishing through his bag of possibles for his pipe, "there's two ways of tellin' it and both come from the Injuns. One is it's named for a old squaw, a crone, who lived here alone in her wigwam a long, long time ago. She had big medicine, so big that when she opened her mouth a bright light shone out, brighter than the noonday sun and hotter too. You could see that light for miles around, even in the daytime, and if it shone direct on you, well, you was rendered down to a smokin' piece of charcoal. She could cast spells and shape-shift and whatnot and she used her gifts to make mischief. Though she ain't been round here for an age, the Injuns say her spirit remains. Can ye feel her, boys? Can ye?"

Jimmy edged a little closer to Harry. "What's the other story?" he said.

"So the others say it comes from the time Sioux warriors attacked a train of religious pilgrims followin' the Black Robe, De Smet. Happened here, where we be sittin' now. That big rock marks the spot." He pointed to a boulder with the bowl of his pipe.

"Right here?" Jimmy said.

"Yep, this very spot. The Injuns cut one of the pilgrims up into little pieces right in front of his wife and made her watch while they fed him to the dogs."

Jimmy gasped.

Bridger nodded. "What they say. Naturally, the poor woman lost her mind, why of course she did, watchin' the dogs eat them little pieces. After that folks tried to do for her but she was past help, just wandered around like she was asleep with her eyes open, talkin' nonsense to nobody but herself—kindy like that Lady Macbeth your ma read us about t'other night. Anyhow, one day the woman up and disappeared. Clean vanished. No bones, no nothin'. Some claim you can still hear her though, around here, cryin' for her man."

He leaned in toward Harry and Jimmy, till his face was just inches from theirs. "You boys hear anything tonight, you come git me, all right?"

That night Jimmy slept pressed up next to Harry. Ordinarily, Harry would not have tolerated such closeness but tonight—for Jimmy's sake only, he told himself—he made an exception.

The countryside improved dramatically the next day as they moved north. The flat, dry plain they had traveled since Fort Reno began to give way to a lush, green steppe thick with buffalo and gamma grasses. Wild strawberries and raspberries grew beside icy streams and the air was cool and sweet.

They also started seeing more signs of Indians. Pony droppings littered the ground and vast stretches of prairie were scoured by travois-drug lodge poles so they resembled plowed fields. At noon Bridger and his scouts returned to the column saying they had met up with a band of twenty Sioux braves a few miles up the road.

"They said they were hunting but they was spies," Bridger said to Carrington, "sent to size us up."

The column continued with a new sense of caution. Later that afternoon they came across a weathered bit of paper nailed to a stake addressed "to all passers-by." The author, captain of a train of civilian miners, reported an Indian raid on their beef herd and the wounding of one man. Not long after that they found a solitary grave marked with a rough wooden cross. Written in axle grease were the words:

*G Maupin*
*Callaway County Missouri June 26 1866,*
*killed by Indians*

That evening, after they made camp, a strange black cloud appeared in the clear northern sky. Men paused in their work, women stood up at their cook fires. One soldier nearly started a panic shouting the Indians had fired the grass. But soon it became apparent the fast-moving cloud was not smoke or storm but a legion of grasshopper-like creatures with bulging red eyes. Within minutes, the air thrummed with the beating of countless wings as insects covered every object in sight, moving and stationary, like a living blanket. Mules kicked and plunged and horses pulled their pins and bolted. Margaret and Harry freed their chickens and turkeys from their boxes in hope they would devour at least some of the winged invaders, but they were so many they darkened the sun and the confused poultry went to roost. Giving up, Margaret and Harry joined

Jimmy and Black George in the tent. The creatures covered the canvas, making the interior dark as night. George was certain the insects were the Devil's emissaries. "Their red eyes reflect the fires of Hell!" he cried.

Harry remembered Bridger's story of the evil old squaw and wondered if these were her messengers. Or maybe they had been sent by a malign god who lived high in the fog and snow of the Bighorn Mountains like Zeus on Mount Olympus.

Gradually the buzzing stopped and daylight returned. When he stepped outside, Harry found the ground covered with dead insects that crunched underfoot like peanut shells at a circus. Then another flying legion appeared, this one of black birds, which circled overhead before diving down to devour the remains. After an orgy of noisy, argumentative feasting, every crusty carcass was consumed and the birds, like the insects, vanished as abruptly as they had come.

# Chapter Sixteen

Rollo died at dawn on the second day of the siege and Clara followed him four hours later. Dixon worked tirelessly to save them, even when it was clear to Rose they would not recover. His devotion was so intense, she found herself wondering if perhaps he saw in Clara and Rollo another woman, another child.

A soldier made a coffin from boards stripped from the side of a wagon and they were buried together beside Pat inside the redoubt walls. It would not be their final resting place but because of the heat the dead could not remain unburied, even for a day. Trover read from the Bible over the grave as Lieutenant Anderson stood by, dry-eyed, stunned.

By noon of the third day the water barrels were empty. Thick saliva collected in the corners of Rose's mouth like a paste and her tongue grew until it was a rubbery, alien object in her mouth. By day four her thirst was like a knife stuck deep between her shoulder blades. She could think of nothing but water.

Even worse, her treasonous brain tortured her with images of crisp, sweet apples, heavy with juice that ran down her chin with each imagined bite.

She passed the hours lying on a blanket on the cabin floor, for she could not bring herself to take Clara's deathbed. Whenever she stood her head swam and her field of vision shrank as if she were looking through the wrong end of a telescope.

The white sun filled the sky, as if the distance separating it from Earth had been reduced by half. Though she was careful not to look at it, Rose was keenly aware of the soldier's body rotting on the banks of the creek while vultures circled overhead, eyeing their ripening meal. The boldest one flopped to earth beside the corpse and leaned in, thrusting its red head into the gore. A sentry shot at it, then swore when he missed and the vulture rejoined his comrades in the sky.

"Save your ammunition, Cy," Trover said. He sat on the ground with his back against the sandbag wall. "We may be needing it."

The soldier turned to him. "Dammit, Trover! Me and Hugh, we was like brothers. We been together since we was boys! Through all the war, Rock Island, all of it. Ain't it bad enough I got to stand here watchin' him rot out there, swole like a poisoned pup? Do I got to watch them things eat him too?"

"Reuben, go up there and relieve him," Trover said. "Cy, you come down. You need a rest."

Reuben groaned as he got to his feet. Rose pitied the sentries who stood for thirty-minute intervals in the biting sun, watching the Indians splash in the water and taunt them, all the while remaining out of range. She wondered if sentries were even necessary. Clearly Cloudsplitter planned to let the sun do his killing for him.

That night, as they sat at the fire, Rose started to believe she might actually die in this place. She thought it likely she would never see Mark again, or her brothers, never have a child, never have her own home with plenty of windows and white muslin curtains and window boxes brimming with red geraniums. She felt the hope bleeding out of her, like a spirit abandoning a lifeless body.

"Don't give up."

She looked up to see Dixon watching her from across the fire. He smiled. "They got through," he said, "Gregory and Ignacio. Help's on the way. I feel it."

Henry laughed. "Oh, you feel it. Put your worries aside, Mrs. Reynolds, because the good doctor feels it. Don't be a fool, Dixon. Even if those thieves, the harelip and the greaser, got past the Indians—which I doubt—they're halfway to Canada by now. They wouldn't go anywhere near Fort Reno."

Trover joined them at the fire, lowering himself slowly to the ground. "No, if the Indians caught them they'd want us to know it. Their bodies would be out there beside Hugh's. And even if they didn't go to Reno our relief detail is due in three days. Don't forget that."

"We can't go three days without water," Rose said. "Skinny will be dead by morning without it."

"He's dead now," Henry said, "or good as. Just look at him."

"She's right," Dixon said. "We've got to have water. I'm going to the creek tonight. Who's coming with me?"

There was a silence as men looked at each other across the flames.

"Me," Cy said. "Anything's better than this."

A young Mexican teamster also spoke up. "And me," he said. "I will go *también*."

"Good," said Dixon. "We'll leave right away before the clouds move off." He took up a handful of soot. "Blacken your face and hands, any bit of skin. Anderson, round up canteens and kettles." Anderson seemed not to hear. He had scarcely said a word since Clara and Rollo died.

"I'll do that," Rose said. She went about it, looking at the Cheyennes' fires on the hills across Antelope Creek. Cloudsplitter's camp was unusually quiet. Maybe the heat got to them too.

Soon they were ready to leave. Each man carried four canteens around his neck and a two-gallon kettle in either hand. Rose's heart thumped like a bat in a barrel as they walked to the gate. Dixon caught her eye and smiled, his teeth white against his soot-blackened face, and she remembered the day he'd saved her in the sandstorm. Had she thanked him properly? If not she might never have the chance, for in an instant he and the others were gone, crawling away through the same tunnel Gregory and Ignacio had used days before.

Almost sick with fear, Rose went to the cabin to

wait. Jerusha, knitting by candlelight, did not look up. The soldier Mike stood at the open window, the barrel of his carbine resting on the frame. "Well, at least it's plenty dark," he said. "You can't see nothin' out there."

Skinny murmured from the bed.

"I wish he'd shut up," Mike said. "He's giving me the willies."

Rose sat on the floor. The revolver in her waist pocket pressed uncomfortably against her hip. As she reached in to move it she felt Gregory's letter. She had forgotten about it. The envelope was unsealed. Did Gregory mention his plans to steal the payroll, perhaps try to justify the crime to his mother? Why did he do it? After a short debate with her conscience she opened it.

*Dear Neglected Mother,*

*I found the Yankee officer who brought those murdering Redlegs to the house that day, the ones who killed Pa. I know where he is and I will put him through if it takes all the devil that's in me I will do it and let you know when the job is done.*

*I have money left with Lieutenant Ewell Bell, quartermaster at Fort Sedgwick. He is a good man and if you write him and tell him who you are he will see you get it. I do not need the money. I want you and the girls to have it.*

*You may hear some hard things about me and you can be sure not all of them are true. I did shoot that wood contractor at Fort Fletcher but you can be sure Saint Peter will not turn me away on his account.*

*Give my love to Sarah and America Alice. I
do not know if I will return to Cass County or if
I will see you again but if not on this earth we
will meet again in Glory.*

*I am sorry I did not write to you more often.
I should have.*

*Your loving son, Jack Gregory*

Cass County. Rose knew it—one of those in the
Burnt District, a once-rich farmland reduced to a
ruin of scorched earth and crumbling chimneys. She
could guess what must have happened on the Gregory farm that day. Western Missouri was a rough
place, hostage to pro-Confederate guerillas like William Quantrill, George Todd, and Bloody Bill Anderson who roamed the countryside with scalps
swinging from their bridles. These bushwhackers
were opposed by irregular forces, Jayhawkers and
Redlegs, who had the support of the Federal government but who were cut from the same murderous
cloth.

What was Mark's role in all this? Often she wondered. As adjutant to General Thomas Ewing,
commander of the border district, he must have
been deeply involved. But he never spoke of those
days, and, because he wouldn't like it, Rose never
asked. When Ewing and his staff were transferred
to St. Louis, just before Christmas of '63, she'd
heard rumors of misconduct on Ewing's part, alle-
gations that Sherman arranged the move for his
brother-in-law's career and personal safety. To be
sure, Ewing was hated in western Missouri. The

people blamed him for turning their homeland into a haunted desert, forsaken by God and government.

"I see them!" Mike's cry shook her from her remembering. "They're coming back!"

Rose jumped up and immediately fell to her knees. When the blackness retreated and her head stopped spinning she joined Mike at the window. At first she saw nothing. Then, gradually, she could make out the shadow of a crouching man, scuttling across the sage-studded ground. Canteens hanging from his neck bumped together with a dull clunking sound.

The Indians heard this too. The quiet was split by a shrill whistle followed by shouts and the crack of a rifle, first one then many. The soldiers returned fire.

"Careful!" Trover shouted. "Don't hit our boys!"

Now all three men were visible, running as fast as their liquid cargo would allow, making no attempt at concealment. Cy was in the lead, identifiable because he was the smallest, followed by the Mexican with Dixon bringing up the rear. Though each man could have saved himself by dumping his liquid load, no one did. For the first time that night, the moon broke through the clouds and Rose saw three warriors urging their horses through the creek. One, ahead of the others, closed in on Dixon, raising an arm that was unnaturally long and skeletal. It was a war club he was preparing to bring down on Dixon's skull.

"Run!" she screamed. "Run, Dan! Drop the water and run!"

A thunderous boom shook the walls. The Indian's

pony tumbled to the ground on top of his rider, who lay motionless. Above, on the sentry walk, Rose saw Lieutenant Anderson lower his rifle as the men beside him cheered and clapped him on the back. At the same time Trover exploded a shell of spherical case over the heads of the other two warriors, turning them back. The water carriers ran through the open gate and were surrounded by a jubilant throng. Rose threw her arms around Dixon.

"Rose." He spoke her name softly, his mouth next to her ear, sending a chill down her spine.

The men insisted she get the first drink. Rose's hand shook as she raised the cup to her lips and filled her mouth with warm water that bathed her swollen tongue, her parched palate, the aching places at the back of her throat. The water was gritty with sand but to her it was sweeter than the finest French champagne. She forced herself to take it in measured amounts, as Dixon advised, instead of gulping it down as her body demanded. The water's healing effect was not immediate—it took a while for the fluid to saturate her depleted tissues—but gradually, blissfully, her thirst was satisfied and the sharp pain between her shoulder blades melted away.

She took a cup to the cabin for Skinny. His head was fallen to one side and his open eye shone like a wet grape. She bent to touch his face and found it cold. Would anyone, if they knew, mourn his passing?

"Life is cheap out here, isn't it?" Dixon stood beside her, wiping soot from his face with a handkerchief. "This country makes you see what's important in life," he said. "Water is important, loyalty and trust. Doing the right thing for people you care about, that's important. Rose, this may not be the best time to say this but—"

"Don't say anything," she said. "Whatever our feelings are, we haven't done anything wrong. I don't want to do anything wrong."

He shook his head. "Wrong? That word has a new meaning out here. All those rules and notions you learned back in Missouri don't hold in this country. Things are different. Don't you feel that?"

She turned to him. "One thing is the same no matter where I am. I'm a married woman. I love my husband."

He smiled, lifting his eyebrows. "Do you?"

"Yes."

"Rose, you can't will your feelings to be one thing or another. You can try, but it won't work. I know something about this." His hazel eyes held hers and she felt herself growing warm. She felt as if she had no clothes on.

"I've got to get out of here," she said. She ran from the cabin to her ambulance, where she closed the door and lay down on the hard bed. At once she was seized by an uncontrollable fit of shaking that lasted until exhaustion overcame her and at last she slept.

She woke to the sound of gunfire. It was fully daylight. The Cheyenne were attacking again. She opened the door, sick at heart. When would this nightmare end? But instead of Indians she saw a long line of mounted soldiers riding down the ridge on the far side of the creek. The Indians were gone.

The men in the redoubt were shooting in the air in celebration and running through the gate to meet their rescuers. Rose followed, first stopping at the creek to bathe her face in its cold, clean waters.

The reflection of a horseman appeared beside her on the water's surface. Something about the width of his shoulders and angle of his hat sent her heart to her throat.

"Rose?" he said. "Rose, is that you?"

Still on her knees, she looked up to see Mark's face framed by the morning sky.

# Chapter Seventeen

Jim Bridger did not like the site Carrington had chosen for the new post, a grassy plateau at the fork of Piney Creek in the center of a lush green valley. "It's a fine spot, Colonel, if your aim is to show us like fish in a barrel," he said, waving his pipe at the bluffs, black in the night sky, bordering them on three sides. "The Injuns will set up there and watch our every move."

Sparks from a collapsing log landed on Harry's trousers, eating brown holes in the denim. He and Jimmy sat by the fire with Carrington and his officers.

"I know this country, Colonel," Bridger said. "There's better places up north, along Goose Creek and Tongue River. Why not take a look, see for yourself if I ain't right?"

Fred Brown sat at Carrington's right. "There's no time for that, Colonel," he said, casually crossing his legs. "Anyhow, why look further when we've got everything we need right here? Water, pine for building, cottonwood for fuel, everything." He gestured toward the Bighorn Mountains, six miles to the west. Their snowy crests gleamed like silver in the moonlight and their slopes were black with pine. "Not only that, but the tall grass back by that lake will make fine hay when it ripens. So what if the Indians watch us? They couldn't fire on us from those hills. And we can watch them too, by posting sentries there and there." He pointed to a conical summit some two hundred yards to the east that commanded a wide view of the valley, then to a long narrow ridge to the northwest.

"I agree," said Bisbee. "We need to start building. It's mid-July. Winter comes early up here."

Bridger laughed. "Like you know anything about how things happen up here. I was trappin' in these mountains when you was still suckin' on your momma's tit and I tell you there's better places up north."

Bisbee started to respond but Carrington raised his hand. "Major Bridger is right. We'll reconnoiter the upper country tomorrow. We can spare a day."

That night Harry lay awake in the tent, listening to the creek rushing over the Big Piney cascades. He thought of Rose Reynolds, her blue eyes, freckled nose, and sweet smile. Was she all right? When would she join them?

The next morning his father took twenty-five men to explore the Tongue River valley to the north. Carrington's party consisted of his inner circle of officers—Captain Ten Eyck and lieutenants Brown and Frederick Phisterer—with Brannan and Jack Stead as scouts. Reynolds would have been included but he had been sent back to Fort Reno for additional supplies. Bridger, Harry noticed, was not invited.

After they left, it was discovered that nine men had deserted during the night. Lieutenant John Adair, officer of the day, sent Bisbee out after the "snowbirds" but the detail returned in an hour without the deserters. There was someone new with them however—a small man with a badly pock-marked face.

"A group of Sioux and Cheyenne stopped us a few miles up the road," Bisbee said. "They'd been trading with French Pete and Arrison. Donaldson, here, was with them. You remember Donaldson—one of the teamsters Brown released back at Reno. Anyhow, the Indians gave him a message for Colonel Carrington. Tell him, Donaldson."

"The message is from Black Horse, a Cheyenne chief," Donaldson said, puffed up with importance. "He asks the Little White Chief, 'Do you want peace or war?' He says to send his answer with the black white man."

The black white man meant interpreter Jack Stead, whose skin was brown as a nut and who had been married, at one time, to a Cheyenne woman.

"Stead's not here," Adair said. "He went with Colonel Carrington. They won't be back till sundown." As he spoke, a lone Indian on horseback appeared on the road. "He waiting for you, Donaldson?"

"I reckon," Donaldson said. "I know him, he's one of Black Horse's warriors."

Beads of sweat appeared on Adair's upper lip. He called to Bisbee and they stepped aside, out of Donaldson's hearing. "The Indians might take it wrong if I send Donaldson back without an answer but Carrington doesn't want anyone but him talking to the Indians. Also, I'm shorthanded here. In addition to the men with Carrington, another twenty went with Reynolds. I don't want that lazy troublemaker, Donaldson, telling the Indians this."

The two officers turned to Donaldson. "Go tell your Cheyenne friend he'll have to wait till tonight when Carrington gets back for his answer," Adair said.

"Oh, no, I ain't hanging around here all day." Donaldson started for his horse. "I'm going back to French Pete's. I'll come back tomorrow."

Adair waved at a sergeant. "Finley, hold Mr. Donaldson under guard until the colonel returns."

Donaldson struggled, and the sergeant had to wrestle him to the ground. The Indian wheeled his pony and vanished into the hills. His departure left everyone nervous. What would he tell Black Horse? How many warriors were out there? Margaret tried to work with Harry and Jimmy on their lessons, but no one could concentrate on mathematics or ancient Greek. The weather matched their mood. Dark clouds, like crouching bears, crept toward them from behind the mountains. Occasionally they heard a rumble of thunder.

Adair paced before the headquarters tent, pausing often to raise his field glasses and scan the hills for Carrington's party. Only Bridger was unconcerned. He spread his bedroll under a wagon and slept the afternoon away, waking when Carrington returned at sundown. After learning of the day's events, Carrington composed a letter to the Cheyenne chief and ordered Donaldson released so he could deliver it immediately. Harry, outside the tent, listened as his father dictated to his adjutant.

> *Headquarters Mountain District*
> *Piney Fork, July 14, 1866*
> *To the Great Chief of the Cheyennes:*
> *Friend,*
> *I have learned that you wish to come and have a talk with me. I shall be happy to have you come and tell me what you wish. The Great Father at Washington wishes to be your friend and so do I and all my soldiers.*
> *I tell all the white men who go on the road that if they hurt Indians or steal their ponies I will follow and catch them and punish them. I will not let white men do hurt to the Indians who wish peace.*
> *You may come and see me with two other chiefs and two of your big fighting men when the sun is over head after two sleeps.*
> *You may come and talk and no one shall hurt you and when you wish to go you may go in peace and no one shall hurt you.*
> *I will tell all my chiefs and soldiers that you are my friends and they will obey.*
> *Your white friend,*
>
> > *Henry B. Carrington*
> > *Col. 18th U.S. Infantry*
> > *Comd'g Mount. Dist.*

Not for the first time, Harry wondered why his father and his officers talked to Indians as if they were children.

Donaldson was in a black mood and ready to go when the letter was delivered to the guard tent. "I'll make sure Black Horse gets it," he said, "but I ain't happy about the way I was treated. I ain't a soldier no more. Adair had no call to hold me!" He jumped on his horse and galloped north on the Bozeman Road, disappearing in the red twilight.

Once Donaldson was gone, Carrington called Bridger and his officers to the headquarters tent to announce his decision about the new fort's location. "The Tongue River country is magnificent, just as Major Bridger said it was. We found plenty of game—buffalo, bear, elk, antelope—and the land is rich in fruits and natural grains. But it's too far from the tall pine we'll need for construction. Also, if we build in the north we'd be leaving the major Indian trails through the Powder River basin unguarded and, after all, isn't that our very reason for being here in the first place? Therefore, I've decided the new fort will be here, on the plateau, as originally planned. We'll start building in the morning."

Bridger, who had listened quietly to this point, shook his head. "You're makin' a mistake, Colonel. A big mistake."

# Chapter Eighteen

The surveyors set out in the first blue light of morning. The sun lit the Bighorns slowly, by degrees, touching first their white caps, then inching down the piney black slopes. Harry rode with them despite his mother's objections. He shivered as a wind, cold as ice water, blew down his collar.

Carrington carried a cardboard cylinder with plans he and Ten Eyck had drafted at Fort Stephen Kearney the previous spring. Once they reached the top of the plateau he dismounted and spread them on the ground, using stones to weight the rolled edges. "Here it is, gentleman," he said, "the Eighteenth Infantry's new home. Construction will be a challenge, but when we're done we will have the finest post on the western frontier."

He used his saber to point out its features. A stout stockade would surround the fort proper, including a parade ground, barracks for the men, and cabins for the officers. The southeast quadrant would house a powder magazine, sutler's store, bakery, and quarters for the band and regimental offices. An area west of the men's barracks would go to warehouses, horse stables, and quarters for the noncommissioned officers and laundresses.

A large trapezoidal quartermaster's yard would attach to the stockade's east wall. Extending all the way to the banks of the Little Piney, this would house stables for the mules, hay and wood yards, shops, and quarters for the teamsters and mechanics, blacksmiths, carpenters, saddlers, and armorers. The post's main gate would be on the east side, facing the Bozeman Road.

"The slope is too steep for the main gate, Colonel," Bisbee said. "We'd have to do a lot of grading before wagons could use it. Why not put the main gate here, in the west wall?"

Carrington shook his head. "No, it must front the road. A rear or side view would create a poor first impression."

"Is that so important?" Bisbee said.

"Of course," Carrington said. "Now, getting the stockade up will be our first order of business. Ten Eyck will assign work details, three shifts of each. I want the men working around the clock."

By mid-morning the heavy wagons and mowing machines had been pulled to the site. The grass, tall enough to brush a horse's belly, yielded to the crushing iron wheels and sharpened steel blades, releasing a fresh green aroma. Teamsters drove their wagons repeatedly around the perimeter of a parade ground and through its center, flattening the grass and packing the earth to form streets and avenues. By mid-afternoon a network of roped stakes showed the future location of the stockade walls and the positions of the post's major buildings.

The men, invigorated by the fine weather and the end of their grinding journey, worked with enthusiasm. By day's end the entire camp had moved from the banks of the Piney to the new site. Troops pitched their tents by companies in neat rows around the parade and rolled the twelve-pound howitzers into place. In the final hours of daylight wagon masters and teamsters pulled the horse-powered sawmill to its spot along the smaller branch of the Piney Creek, the so-called Little Piney.

That night the band played for the first time in days, beginning with the majestic "Grand Paris Entry." The band had never sounded better, Harry thought, than it did here, on this night, in this beautiful valley at the foot of the Bighorn Mountains. It seemed to him a whole new world. Ohio might as well be on a different planet. Bandmaster Sam Curry ended the evening's program with the Southern ballad "Barbara Allen." Many of the men sang along.

Harry went to bed with the ambulance door tied open—there were no mosquitoes at this altitude—so he could have an unobstructed view of the ebony sky. The moon looked close enough to touch. Despite the quiet beauty, a finger of fear tickled the back of Harry's neck when he thought of the Indians who would come the following day. Could they be trusted? Maybe they would pretend friendship, like the Sioux Lewis and Clark encountered on Bad River, while in fact they were just waiting for the right moment to fall on them with tomahawks and scalping knives. Or maybe they'd be like the gentle, helpful Mandans. He fell asleep praying for Mandans.

The Cheyenne arrived at noon. First, a few mounted braves appeared on the hilltops, with flags of white cloth tied to long lances. Jack Stead rode out alone to meet them, returning with the Indians following single file. The line kept coming from over the hills until Harry counted forty men, some accompanied by blanketed women.

The soldiers wore dress uniforms for the occasion, the men in frock coats so recently unpacked they still bore the creases of folding, the officers in epaulettes, plumed hats, and crimson sashes beneath their sword belts. The band played "Hail Columbia!" as the Indians' ponies splashed across the Big Piney.

The Indian men were bare to the waist, their narrow, hairless chests hung with necklaces of grizzly bear claws and seashells. Some had bands of shining metal around their upper arms and brass earrings as big around as Harry's wrist. The head chief was old and wrinkled with long white braids and a silver medallion round his neck. Harry recognized Thomas Jefferson's aristocratic profile on the medallion and wondered if it was a gift from Meriwether Lewis himself, given when the old man was a strapping young warrior. Behind him rode a long, lanky fellow carrying a bright red umbrella that was giving him trouble in the wind. Harry laughed, but Bridger gave him a poke in the ribs. "Injuns don't like to be laughed at," he said.

Stead led them to a white hospital tent. Inside, Carrington and his officers waited at Margaret's oak dining table, draped with the garrison's oversize American flag. Despite the wide smiles and hearty handshakes Harry felt an undercurrent of tension. Brown seemed especially nervous. Drops of sweat ran down his face and Indians who shook his hand wiped their own on their shirts afterward.

Carrington steered them to the cane-backed chairs set in rows before the table but the Indians chose instead to sit cross-legged on the ground. Their women stayed outside the tent, huddled together, stealing glances at the officers' wives and children watching from across the lawn.

Before any talking began, the old chief with the Jefferson medal produced a red sandstone pipe that was passed from hand to hand and often refilled. After each man had a turn Stead stood to introduce each Indian by name. The old chief, Black Horse, smiled when it was his turn, showing teeth that were stubby and brown as nuts. The subchiefs, Dull Knife and Two Moons, were more impressive-looking. Dull Knife was especially handsome, with chiseled features and a dignified bearing.

"He looks like a Philadelphia lawyer," Harry said to Bridger.

"Honest as one too," Bridger said.

After the introductions Black Horse raised his arms for quiet. He spoke, pausing for Stead's translation, in a singsong voice that rose to a shout then dropped to a whisper. All the while he gestured expansively, waving his matchstick arms and letting his buffalo robe fall from his bony shoulders. "I represent one hundred and seventy-six lodges of Cheyenne people who want peace with the whites," he said. "Our desire for peace has forced us to break with other bands of our own people—those who live east of Powder River beside the Black Hills and those who hunt south of the Republican River. These people will join with Mahpiya Luta, the one you bluecoats call Red Cloud.

"I spoke to Red Cloud four sleeps ago," Black Horse said, "while my young men were hunting on the Tongue River. He invited us to a sun dance. After, he said, we will fight together, Sioux and Cheyenne, to drive the bluecoat soldiers back across the Powder River. Even now his Bad Face warriors are attacking wagons on the white man's road. He will cut you off. You will be beyond help."

Carrington pulled on his beard. "And what did you say, Black Horse, when Red Cloud asked you to join him?"

The old man raised a bony finger with a long, yellow nail. "I said I want no part of his war with the white man. I knew this would make him angry but I said it anyhow. Now I must think about my women and children, left alone in my village with only old men to protect them. I will take my people away from this country. You will not see me again."

He waved a withered arm in a gesture that encompassed the entire soldier camp. "I tell the Little White Chief this as a friend. Red Cloud has more warriors than you. You cannot fight him. Take your people back across the Powder River before it is too late. You have women and children. Think of them."

Black Horse offered one hundred of his young men to fight with the soldiers against the Sioux in return for provisions but Carrington did not accept. "Thank you for your generosity, but I have all the men I need to fight the Sioux. But I will give you provisions regardless and, in return for your good faith, something even better."

He called for pen and paper and wrote a letter instructing all who read it to treat its Indian bearer kindly. At first Black Horse was puzzled by the paper with the strange markings but after Stead explained its meaning the old man smiled. Dull Knife and Two Moons requested papers too, and Carrington made copies as provisions were distributed. Each Cheyenne man received tobacco, flour, bacon, and coffee. Squaws got bits of old clothing, trousers, flannel shirts, and old shoes, and these delighted them.

After the gift-giving the Indians were anxious to leave. Black Horse wished Carrington luck before departing.

"Do you think that was wise?" Brown said as they rode away. "Giving them safe-pass papers? They could use them to make mischief."

"I don't think so," Carrington said. "Black Horse was sincere about not wanting war. I saw it in his eyes."

Brown shook his hairless head. "Colonel, an Indian will kiss your feet then stick a knife in you first chance he gets. I don't know what you think you saw in that old man's eyes, but don't bet our lives on it."

# Chapter Nineteen

Harry woke with a start, sweaty and tangled in his blankets. A light rain pattered on the tent canvas. It was just before dawn, that suspended moment between darkness and day. Something had woken him, but what? A few heartbeats later he heard the loud clanking of a bell followed by shots. He threw off the blankets and sprang to the door. There was a commotion in Captain Henry Haymond's camp across the Big Piney. It was hard to see in the soupy gray light but Harry could just make out a warrior astride the wagon master's bell mare, flogging her with his quirt and running her toward the hills. As they were trained to do, the rest of the herd followed.

Carrington stepped fully dressed from the tent he and Margaret shared. His officers joined him, in various states of undress. "It's those damn Cheyennes, Black Horse and his bucks," Brown said as he tucked his shirttails into his trousers. "I told you not to trust them, Colonel! I told you!"

"You don't know who it is, Mr. Brown," Carrington

said, raising his field glasses to his eyes. Rain was coming down heavily now. "It's too dark," he said, lowering the glasses. "I can't see anything. Brown, go over there. Bring Haymond to me."

Within minutes Brown was back. "Haymond's gone," he said breathlessly. "Took out after the Indians, left orders for a twenty-man detachment to follow." The men were riding out as Brown spoke. "I'd like permission to join them."

"Denied," Carrington said. "Haymond had no authority. He should've reported to me first. He lost his head."

"He may do just that," Bridger said. "Lookit how they're leavin', one or two at a time, all strung out in a line. That's just how the Injuns like it—makes 'em easier to pick off."

The morning routine went on with the usual chopping, hewing, hauling, and ditching, but everyone was on edge. All eyes returned to the place where the Bozeman Road disappeared over Lodge Trail Ridge, where Haymond's troops were seen last. Finally, just after seven, a single rider galloped over the rise. The trooper raced to Carrington's tent and dismounted. "Captain Haymond requests reinforcements, sir. He's engaged the Indians—they're everywhere, Colonel, hundreds of them. I've never seen so many!"

Carrington's voice broke as he issued orders. "Bisbee, organize a relief party, fifty mounted men and two companies of infantry. Brown, follow with two ambulances and a wagon of ammunition and rations. Private, you go with Bisbee. Take them to Haymond."

The messenger turned to follow the officers, but Carrington stopped him. "Just a minute, Private," he said. "What's your name?"

"Jacob Rosenburg, sir."

"Where's your hat, Rosenburg?"

"My hat?" He raised a hand to his head. "Why, I don't know. I must've lost it."

"A soldier in my regiment does not lose his hat, Rosenburg. You're out of uniform. Don't let it happen again. You're excused."

Harry saw the anger on Rosenburg's face as he hurried after Brown and Bisbee. Why did his father do those stupid things? Harry wondered. He would never earn the respect of his men. Never.

The camp prepared for attack. Men took up arms and primed the howitzers. Harry helped Ten Eyck distribute ammunition and smelled whiskey on his breath, though it was just half past seven.

As the minutes turned to hours, fear and idleness strained nerves to the snapping point. Two men started arguing and would have come to blows had Sergeant Timothy Garrett, a thick-necked Irishman and the regiment's star pugilist, not come between them. Finally, at mid-afternoon, Haymond's command and the relief parties appeared, moving slowly down the slope of Lodge Trail Ridge. Brown's supply wagon and the two ambulances brought up the rear, with only four stolen horses in tow. Two dead soldiers lay in the bed of the wagon, their bodies bristling with arrows.

Two Indian women and several children walked behind the column. When they got closer Harry recognized the lovely Jane and other members of French Pete's family. Cazeau himself and the eldest boy were missing. When Haymond reported to headquarters he brought Cazeau's wife with him, leading her roughly by the arm.

"I lost two men, Colonel," he said. "Livenberger and Callery, and two more wounded."

"What happened?" Carrington said.

"I pursued the Indians, leaving orders for twenty men to follow me. They were slow getting away and the Indians doubled back, hitting us where we were thin. I managed to get my boys together but the Indians kept on coming. There were hundreds of them, Colonel, too many to count. That's when I sent Rosenburg. They skedaddled when Bisbee showed up and we gave them a good running fight, but our horses played out. We couldn't catch them."

Haymond paused, wiping his hand across his sweating forehead. "We found the remains of French Pete's outfit on the way back, about six miles north of here on Peno Creek. They were dead, all of them—Cazeau, Arrison, Donaldson, and three others I didn't know—all butchered so bad I hardly recognized them. I found Pete's squaw here and her children, hiding in the bushes." He pushed the Indian woman forward. Despite the afternoon heat, she was visibly shaking under her trader's blanket.

Carrington spoke gently. "What is your name?"

"Mary."

"We've met before. Do you remember me, Mary?"

She nodded. "Yes, the Little White Chief."

He frowned. "My name is Colonel Carrington. Tell me what happened to your husband and the others."

She started talking in a patois of English, French, and Sioux, but Stead managed to make sense of it. French Pete had been trading with the Cheyenne band of Black Horse and Dull Knife. They sat up late, talking and smoking. At midnight twelve Bad Face warriors led by Mahpiya Luta himself rode into the camp.

"Red Cloud?" Carrington said. "Red Cloud himself came to your camp? Are you sure?"

"Yes, I know him," Mary said. "He and my father were boys together in Old Smoke's village. They were like brothers. My father was with Mahpiya Luta on the day he killed Smoke's rival, the Oglala chief Bull Bear, the day he became a big man and divided the Sioux people into two camps. He remembered me and called me by name." She said this with pride. "Mahpiya Luta asked Black Horse if he had passed his warning to the Little White Chief, if the soldiers would go back to the Powder River. He grew angry when Black Horse said the white soldiers ignored his warning and would build their forts along the White Man's Road." She paused, looking at the unfriendly male faces around her.

"Continue," Carrington said. "No one will harm you."

"The Bad Faces rode their ponies in circles around the Cheyennes, beating them with their bows and calling them women. Even after they were gone I was still afraid. Black Horse and his people were in a hurry to leave after that but first Black Horse said to my husband, 'The waters of the Powder River will run red with blood.' We were coming to you, to the soldier fort, for protection when we met the Sioux warriors again, driving your horses. The rest you know."

Brown spat a jet of tobacco juice at her feet. "Why did they spare her? I'll tell you why—because she's one of them! She's spying for Red Cloud, she's here to find out how many men we have, about our munitions. Throw her in the guardhouse, Colonel, and her nits too!"

Mary sank deeper into her blanket.

"That's enough, Brown," Carrington said. "I don't think she's a spy. She is a woman who just lost her husband. She may not be a Christian but she deserves Christian kindness. Stead, tell her she and her children have a home with the white soldiers as long as she wants one. Phisterer, see to it they have something to eat and a place to sleep."

"Shall I post a guard, sir?" Phisterer said.

"No. They're our guests, not our prisoners." When the Indians were gone, Carrington excused all the officers except Haymond. In a shrill voice that carried throughout the camp, Carrington berated him for chasing the Indians without orders. Harry heard grumbling about this later because Haymond was a man of action and popular with the men.

Later that evening Harry volunteered to help carry food to Mary and her children because he wanted to see Jane. He found her with her little brother who had been, temporarily, reunited with his fawn.

"He cried all night when Father gave it away," she said. "He won't miss Father. Neither will I."

"Where will you go?" Harry asked. "What will you do?"

Jane shrugged her shapely shoulders. "My mother is small but she is strong. She has relatives." She dropped her eyes. "I wonder, where is the tall officer? The one called Reynolds?"

Harry's stomach dropped. "My father sent him to Fort Reno for supplies. He'll be back in a day or so. What about your older brother? Where's he?" When she did not answer Harry knew the boy with the angry eyes had joined the warriors. "What is Red Cloud like?" he said.

Jane smiled. "My grandfather told me of a time when he and Mahpiya Luta were young men, fighting the Utes. An enemy warrior fell from his horse into a fast river and started to drown. None of his people moved to save him but Mahpiya Luta rode into the water and pulled the Ute to safety. The Ute clung to him and vowed to be his friend forever. As soon as they reached the shore, Mahpiya Luta plunged his knife into the Ute's heart and scalped him. He wears eighty scalps on his shirt, my grandfather said."

Harry was sorry he'd asked.

# Chapter Twenty

Mark was thinner than before and his hair so long it brushed his collar. Still, to Rose he had never looked more handsome. He dismounted, lifted her from the ground, and took her in his arms. She buried her face in his coat, breathing in his familiar scent of wood smoke and horse and leather. At that moment there was nothing, and no one, else in the world but the two of them.

"Rose." For the second time in twenty-four hours a man whispered her name into her ear. "I shouldn't have left you, you have no idea how I've regretted it. Is it . . . I mean, are you still. . . ."

She shook her head. "But I'm fine. Everything will be all right."

He held her close a few moments longer, then pushed her to arm's length. His brown eyes ran the length of her body, resting on her hair. "What happened?" he said, touching it.

She put her hand to her head, feeling her hair wet and stiff with dirt. How long had it been since she looked in a mirror? What must she look like? "I did it at Sedgwick," she said, "while I was sick. I hardly remember cutting it. Oh, I must look like the troll under the bridge."

He laughed and pulled her close again. "You're safe, that's all I care about. We're together again." He bent his head to kiss her, a moment she had dreamed of all her life, it seemed.

"Are you in charge of this detail, Lieutenant?"

Mark straightened up and saluted. "Yes, sir."

"I am Major Ranald Henry, paymaster for the Department of the Platte, and I wish to report the theft of thirty thousand dollars in greenbacks, stolen by Jack Gregory, our so-called scout, and a Mexican teamster—this woman's driver. Your wife?" Mark nodded. "Well, she can tell you his name, he wears a patch over one eye. They were together in this, Gregory and that greaser. You must pursue them at once. No doubt they're bound for the Canadian border."

Mark frowned. "Jack Gregory was alone when he showed up at Reno. No Mexican with him."

Rose gasped. "They really did go for help? They went to Fort Reno?"

"Gregory did," Mark said. "If it weren't for him, you'd still be up against it. We had no idea what was happening here."

Henry waved his hand dismissively. "Then the greaser has the money or they stashed it somewhere along the way. Where is Gregory now?"

"At Reno. He was going to rest up a day or so and join us later."

Henry groaned. "We'll never find him. Cooke will

have my commission. Send out a detail right away—
I demand it!"

"I'm sorry, Major," Mark said. "It would be folly to
divide our force in the presence of so many Sioux."

Henry turned to Lieutenant Anderson. "You're
senior here. Send a detail after those thieves."

Anderson looked at Mark. "Please handle this,
Reynolds. I am ill. I am not myself."

"A fine pair you are," Henry said. "Your superior
officer will hear about this, you can be sure of it."

They left for Fort Reno that very afternoon.
Trover traveled in the ambulance with Rose and
Jerusha. His leg stank like meat left in the sun. He
was embarrassed and apologized repeatedly.

"I don't notice anything," Rose said.

The day was dark and hazy, threatening rain that
never came. They traveled twenty miles and made
camp in darkness. Despite the hour, Rose asked
Jerusha to heat water for her bath but Jerusha said
she was ill so Rose did it herself, washing with lemon-
scented soap before joining Mark in his tent. He had
pushed two cots together and covered them with a
single mattress to form a large bed. Their lovemaking was all she remembered and more. He was
hungry but gentle and attentive to her needs—
indeed, more than before. In the morning she felt a
woman's pride at the sight of his broad shoulders,
browned by the sun, beside her in the bed. Even so,
Daniel Dixon was never completely absent from her
thoughts. She felt sad to think of him alone when she
was so happy.

When she stepped out of her tent, Rose was

surprised to see snow-covered mountains in the distance, a view obscured by the previous day's haze. They were beautiful, the air was fresh and clean, she was free of the stifling, foul-smelling redoubt and, best of all, she and Mark were together again. She breathed in deeply, filling her lungs with the sweet air, and stretched her arms over her head. She heard a noise and turned to see Dixon emerging from the conical Sibley tent next to hers, where Trover and other sick men had passed the night. Their eyes met and she felt her face redden.

She lowered her arms. "Good morning," she said. "How is Mr. Trover?"

The surgeon looked tired. "His leg is infected, but you know that. Bits of necrotic bone are working out of the stump."

She shuddered. "How awful."

"I can't clean it properly till we get to Reno. Will you and Jerusha keep him with you again today?"

"Of course."

"I gave him laudanum, so he should sleep most of the day. Make sure he takes plenty of water and don't cover the wound. It's better left open to the air. Don't worry if you see maggots—they only eat diseased tissue, actually clean the wound. Something we learned during the war."

He noticed her look of dismay. "Would you prefer I move him to the other ambulance?"

"No, it's too crowded already. We'll take care of him."

But the smell combined with the heat and rocking of the ambulance was too much. Rose tried to ride, but Carl had been weakened by the ordeal at the redoubt. Even without her weight he had difficulty keeping up with the remuda.

"You've got to get strong again." She leaned forward to stroke his neck. "If you don't, you'll go to the dead herd." He turned his head, as he always did at the sound of her voice. "You've got to, Carl. We've been through too much."

They traveled all day in a dry creek bed, seeing not another living thing until, hidden away in a shaded ravine, they came across an ancient buffalo, abandoned and waiting to die. Wolves lurked nearby. Over and over again the old bull tried to stand, his hooves scoring the ground around him, but again and again he failed. Once he must have ruled a harem of adoring cows, Rose thought, and now he was reduced to this, the wolves his only companions. When a trooper approached the old buffalo managed to stand, lowering his head in a pitiful show of fight, but his legs collapsed and he went down again. The soldier leveled his carbine and shot him in the head but the bull did not die. Instead he rolled onto his side, breathing wetly and noisily, regarding the shooter with an accusing eye. The trooper was about to finish him off when Mark stopped him.

"You idiot—do you want every Indian within fifty miles to know we're here?"

"Begging your pardon, sir, but we can't leave him like this. Those wolves will eat him alive."

"I said no shooting." Mark restarted the column. As they moved away the wolves closed in. Rose covered her ears but still she heard the buffalo's hoarse bellows as the predators began to tear him apart. Mark was right, of course, she thought, but couldn't they have done something, maybe cut the old thing's throat?

They arrived at Fort Reno at sundown under a fire-red sky and camped beside the Powder River. Instead of the mighty rushing torrent she expected, the famous river was only a muddy yellow stream, no wider in places than an irrigation ditch, flowing listlessly through the flat, sage-studded expanse.

The fort itself squatted on a bald plateau with a rickety cottonwood stockade enclosing only the warehouses and stables. Most of the post was open to the plain. The hospital, barracks, and officers' quarters, usually the pride of a post, were shabby structures with sod roofs and dirt floors. Would her new home—Camp Carrington, Mark called it—be like this? She hoped not.

Captain Joseph Proctor, the post commander, visited their camp that evening. He said the supplies Mark had been sent for were loaded and ready but they would have to wait before moving on. "No train with fewer than thirty armed men is allowed to travel the Bozeman Road beyond this point," Proctor said. "Colonel Carrington's orders. Here, read for yourself."

He gave Mark a paper covered in Carrington's spidery hand. "It's too dangerous," he said as Mark read. "Did you know Sioux wiped out French Pete Cazeau's outfit two days ago? It happened not far from Carrington's new fort."

Mark returned the paper to Proctor. "This applies to emigrant trains. Not military."

"Actually, Reynolds, that determination is left to the commanding officer and I say it applies to you. Yesterday I let Lieutenant George Templeton's party through six men short and I've been kicking myself ever since. He had women and children along, just like you. My God, if the Indians . . ." He glanced at Rose and left the sentence unfinished. "Thirty men. No exceptions." Mark protested but Proctor would not change his mind.

The night was very cold. Mark had guard duty so Rose went to bed alone, shivering under thin wool blankets. Sometime after midnight, unable to sleep, she stepped outside, wrapping a blanket around her shoulders. The stars were bright in the coal-black sky and ghostly fingers of fog reached out from the river.

Somewhere a bell rang, not the clank of a bell mare, but a tiny and tinkling sound, like a child's toy. She froze, a knot of fear tightening in her stomach. The sound came closer. At last a small, dark form tottered out of the mist. It was a dog, skeletally thin, with a piece of buffalo hide tied down firmly over its eyes. It limped toward them on shaking legs, drawn by the heat of the sentry's fire.

"Jesus, Mary, and Joseph!" the sentry said. "What the hell is that?"

"It's a dog, Private, some cruel person's idea of a prank," Rose said. "Give me your knife. I'll cut that blindfold off and we'll give the poor thing something to eat."

Major Henry stepped out of the gloom. "We don't have food to waste on the likes of that." He unsheathed a knife, reached down, and slit the dog's throat from ear to ear. The animal's hindquarters collapsed and slowly it rolled onto its side, dying without a sound.

"Damn savages," Henry said.

# Chapter Twenty-one

They did not have to wait long for the next train. A line of Tootle and Leach Co. freighters with a few emigrant wagons rolled into the fort before noon. After resting and watering his animals, wagon master Hugh Kirkendall moved out that very afternoon. Dixon was in the hospital, operating on Trover's leg, and could not leave with them.

"Maybe we should wait," Rose said to Mark. "Otherwise he may be held up for days."

Mark stopped buttoning his coat and looked at her. "What's that to you?"

"Well, it seems ungenerous after all he did for me at Sedgwick and then again at the redoubt." She chose to omit the sandstorm incident. "I should think you'd be grateful."

Mark smiled and kissed her. "Of course I'm grateful but we're on a tight schedule. The doctor can take care of himself. I've no doubt of that."

The road from Fort Reno was sandy and poorly graded and they made only seven miles by nightfall.

As she and Jerusha were preparing dinner, Rose spotted two hungry-looking men and a sweet-faced boy among the emigrants. On impulse, she invited them to join her. She wanted company, Mark was often called away, and they looked like they could use a good meal. The three accepted eagerly, introducing themselves as William Thomas, a farmer from Illinois, Charley, his seven-year-old son, and Joseph, their Canadian driver.

Dinner was a thick antelope stew served with fluffy yeast biscuits. The guests ate ravenously, using the biscuits to wipe their tin plates clean. For dessert Jerusha served apple dumplings sweetened with a drizzle of golden syrup. When Joseph excused himself to take his shift guarding the mule herd, William and Charley seemed reluctant to leave.

"Mrs. Reynolds, Miss Jerusha," William said, "it's been a long time since Charley and I enjoyed a meal prepared by a woman's hand. Maybe you'll let us thank you with some music? Yes? Son, fetch the instruments." William's eyes followed the boy as he ran to their wagon. "His mother died last spring," he said, "after bearing me twin daughters, two pretty babies. Lung fever took them, all three."

"I'm sorry," Rose said.

"Yes, it was a trial, for Charley especially. He grieved for his mother so—he looks just like her, with that flaming red hair. For a time he wouldn't eat. I feared I'd lose him too."

"Well," Rose said, "he appears to have regained his appetite."

William laughed. "He has at that, thanks be to

God. Anyhow, Charley, Joe, and I, we're seeking a fresh beginning. My brother, George, is prospecting on the Gallatin River and doing well. He wrote to say he could use some help and here we are."

Charley returned with a mouth organ and a well-worn fiddle.

"'Dan Tucker' to start," William said, sticking the fiddle under his chin, and at the count of three father and son launched into a well-practiced rendition of the rollicking tune. By the time they finished a handful of soldiers had gathered around. One called for "Blue Tail Fly" and they swung into that familiar melody, done equally well. A second fiddle player joined them at the fire, then a soldier with a guitar. Before long, they had a crowd of men, women, and children clapping their hands and moving their feet. A couple started dancing and within minutes more dancers joined them.

A sunburned young private bowed to Rose and offered his hand. At first she refused, but he looked so disappointed she laughed and relented. When that tune was finished she danced with another soldier and then another. She felt like a girl at cotillion again until she saw Mark coming toward her with a face like thunder.

"What are you doing?" He gripped her arm. Her dance partner melted away.

"Dancing," she said. "What of it?" She tried to free herself but his fingers dug deeper.

"An officer's wife does not dance with enlisted men. I thought you knew that. It is not done." His mouth had narrowed to a tight line.

The music stopped. Rose realized they were being watched but she didn't care. With a hard yank she freed her arm. "For heaven's sake, it was perfectly innocent," she said. She had never been this angry at him before. "Everyone else was dancing. Is it against regulations for an officer's wife to enjoy herself? Is that also not done?"

The blood drained from Mark's face and for one heart-stopping moment Rose thought he would hit her. Instead he forced a smile and leaned in to give her a kiss, she thought for the benefit of onlookers. "We'll discuss it later." He walked away.

"I'm sorry," William said as the dancers and musicians drifted back to their fires. "I didn't mean to cause trouble for you."

Embarrassed, Rose waved her hand dismissively. "It will soon be forgotten."

But Rose did not forget. She pretended to be sleep when Mark came in at midnight after his watch ended, and she did not speak to him in the morning.

They were under way before dawn. The cool morning gave way to a strong sun and a dirty wind. The road was sandy and steep, with the skeletal remains of cattle, so-called Mormon milestones, littering the countryside. They made thirteen miles before camping in a stand of trees along Crazy Woman Creek. When another train, guided by Jim Bridger, rolled into camp that evening, Rose looked for Dixon but he was not with them. This was a supply train, under Captain Thomas Burrowes, bound for Camp Carrington with several new officers. One of these, Lieutenant Alexander Wands, traveled with his wife, Jennie, and their young son. They and some of his fellow officers had left Fort Reno ahead of the train, hoping to reach Fort Carrington early, but were attacked by Sioux, right there at Crazy Woman Creek, just forty-eight hours before.

"It was worse than you could possibly imagine," Jennie told Rose. "Poor Lieutenant Daniels, poor, dear Napoleon, he was killed right before my eyes! I heard they did terrible things to his body, I feel quite ill just thinking of it." As she spoke she kneaded the sleeve of her dress so vigorously Rose thought she might tear the fabric. Jennie's hands were small-boned and white, meant to lift nothing heavier than a bone china teacup, Rose thought.

"They were riding point, Napoleon Daniels and Lieutenant Templeton," Jennie said, "when before you knew it the devils were upon us. Arrows zipping through the air—that's how they sound, zip! zip! zip!—and those awful shrieking whistles!" She closed her eyes and Rose reached for her hand. "They kept coming and coming, like Hell had thrown wide its doors. Then Napoleon's horse came back without him, the saddle turned under its belly, with George— Lieutenant Templeton—right behind, his face covered with blood. Thank God Captain Burrowes showed up when he did. Oh, my father was right— I shouldn't have come."

Rose tried to comfort her as she shook with sobs. Jennie Wands did not strike her as the kind of woman made for life in a frontier garrison. Rose hoped she would not make everyone's life miserable.

They left Crazy Woman Creek at dawn with Burrowes's

train in the lead. The signs of Indians were all
around them. A few miles north of the creek the trail
split in two and from this point forward the wagons
moved in parallel lines with passengers walking between for safety. Twice they passed fortifications
where earlier travelers had been forced to make a
stand.

When they stopped along Clear Creek at the end
of the day, Kirkendall's freighters, traveling at the
rear of the column, failed to arrive. Thomas Dillon,
master of the Tootle and Leach ox teams, took five
men and went back to look for them. They had not
gone far when they were attacked by Sioux warriors.
Dillon was shot in the stomach. Caught in the open,
without cover, Dillon's men fought their way toward
Kirkendall's train with two men carrying Dillon while
the other three walked backward, shooting as they
went. Finally Kirkendall heard the gunfire and rode
to their rescue. It was fully dark by the time both parties rejoined the main column.

Legions of wolves, drawn by the smell of blood,
circled the camp during the night. To Rose their
howls seemed to be the sound of Hell itself. She lay
beside Mark on their ambulance bed, staring at the
full moon hanging over the mountains like a giant
lantern, and wondered: could this possibly be the
same moon shining down even now on the stately
brick homes of St. Louis's Garrison Street? Surely
not, surely they had stumbled through some invisible
portal into another realm, a place apart from the
known world.

Thomas Dillon died at dawn. Mark and Burrowes

wanted to bury him on the spot, but Kirkendall
would not allow it. "Tom and me go way back," he
said, "been in more tight corners than a feather
duster. I won't leave him out here for the Indians
and wolves to dig up. How'd you like it if somebody
did you that way, Reynolds?"

"I'd be past caring."

"Maybe you would, maybe you wouldn't. It don't
matter anyhow. I'm taking him on to the new fort to
bury him proper and that's that."

That day's travel took them into a different country. The flat desert gave way to grassy fields and the
hot dusty air turned sweet and cool, smelling of
the blue pine forests that darkened the foothills. In
a thrilling way she could not explain, Rose felt she
had been here before, as if she were somehow
coming home.

At noon they stopped near a lake called De Smet
after the Jesuit priest. It was a large, still lake surrounded by waist-high grass and a bluff of brick red
earth on the north shore. Though blue and beautiful to look at, the water stank of sulfur. Charley
Thomas threw a stick for his dog but the hound
would not go in the water to fetch it.

That afternoon they entered a rich green valley.
Green-skinned hills, like ocean swells, rolled west to
the Bighorn Mountains. Their snowy crests gleamed
against a sky blue as the lapis lazuli in Rose's Egyptian cameo. When they stopped to water their horses
in a shallow stream, Rose lay on her stomach to drink
also. She could see every pebble in its bed, and the
water was so cold it made her teeth hurt. Lying there,

smelling the crushed grass beneath her, with her mouth full of clean, pure water, Rose felt an unexpected sympathy for the Indians who had lived on this land for generations and why they fought so savagely to defend it.

At last they crested the final ridge and Rose found herself looking down on Camp Carrington, nestled at the fork of a sparkling creek. Tidy rows of white tents lined the neatly mowed parade lawn, and one wall of a sturdy stockade was already in place. A steam-powered sawmill buzzed beside the water and she heard the bell-like rings of the blacksmith's hammer. On a hill to their left a soldier on horseback waved a white flag, signaling their arrival to the camp below.

Carl picked his way gingerly down the rocky hill. Then, as if he smelled the barn, he broke into a trot after they crossed the shallow creek. As they neared the gate another train, loaded with timber, also approached, and Mark stopped to let them enter. In the bed of the first wagon, Rose saw the naked body of a man. Feathered arrow shafts protruded from his white skin and muscle bulged from gashes in his thighs like sausage burst from its casing. Turning her head, Rose's eyes met those of a passing teamster.

"Welcome to Camp Carrington," he said with a wolfish smile.

# Chapter Twenty-two

Margaret kissed Rose on the cheek. "How I've missed you," the older woman said. "There's been no one to talk to!"

They were alone in one of the two tents that would serve as quarters for Rose and Mark until their cabin was finished. Margaret had prepared it for Rose's arrival, lining the canvas walls with blue army blankets to keep the interior cool on hot days and dry on wet ones. Buffalo skins carpeted the floor.

"I was worried about you at Sedgwick," Margaret said as Rose unpacked. "And just look at you—pretty as ever! I wish I had the courage to do that to my hair. It quite becomes you."

"Thank you. I like it too," Rose said, "but I'm not sure Mark does." She was starting to think she might keep it short anyhow.

"Henry tells me that nice-looking surgeon who took care of you there—Daniel Dixon—will be joining Sam Horton's medical staff, for a while at least."

"Yes, he mentioned that. He's an excellent doctor. He'll make a good addition."

"He seems very nice," Margaret said. "It's so sad about his wife and child."

Rose's heart jumped into her throat. "Wife and child?"

"Yes, apparently they died just after the child was born. Sam told me about it. He said Daniel took it hard. Don't you know anything about it?"

"No. Nothing." Rose's hands shook as she took her Nile-green silk from the bottom of the trunk. It was ruined. Water had penetrated the trunk's leather seams, leaving dark stains on the skirt and bodice. She threw it to the floor. She knew so little about him.

"Oh, no! Your silk!" Margaret picked it up. "You were so lovely in it the night I met you, remember? The night of Wessells's reception. Imagine—that was only weeks ago." She shook her head. "Doesn't it seem a lifetime? Well, don't throw it out. Maybe we can save it."

"I don't care," Rose said. "It doesn't matter now." She felt Margaret's eyes on her and changed the topic. "How are the boys? I saw Harry—he's grown so."

Margaret smiled. "He's already tall as Henry. It's all I can do to keep him in food and trousers—and shoes, of course. My poor sons, they look like street urchins with their too-small things and patches. I do my mending with bits of antelope skin and flour sacking, that's what we're reduced to." She paused.

"Rose, how does Henry seem to you? Please, speak frankly."

The question caught Rose off guard. "Well, he's thinner. I'd say he looks a little tired." In fact, she thought, Carrington looked as if he'd aged ten years since last she saw him.

"He's under a terrible strain," Margaret said. "He doesn't eat, cannot rest, he sleeps in his clothes. If only he'd share some responsibility, but he refuses to delegate. Take the building of this post. He is engineer, draftsman, and construction superintendent—this on top of everything else! Worst of all, he gets no support from Omaha. General Cooke does not understand our situation here. The Indians are so much more troublesome than anyone anticipated. On top of that, we're woefully undersupplied and understaffed, yet our last communication from Cooke included transfers for Haymond and Phisterer—two of Henry's most dependable officers. They're to leave next week, the first of August. It makes no sense."

Rose said, "What about the officers who arrived with us, lieutenants Templeton and Wands and the others? Won't they help?"

"They may, but Henry needs men with experience, men he can trust, and these are in short supply indeed. Please keep this to yourself, Rose, but he thinks one of the lieutenants is corresponding secretly with Cooke, trying to undermine him. He suspects Bisbee. I don't know what to think. Sometimes I fear he's losing his mind!"

Rose put her arm around Margaret's shoulder.

Clearly, the colonel wasn't the only one feeling stress. Rose thought Margaret was about to cry.

"And still Cooke insists on three Powder River posts," she said, pulling herself together. "How is Henry supposed to guarantee the Bozeman Road, build two new posts, and maintain the mails all with only eight companies and no supplies?"

"I agree, it's too much," Rose said, "Surely Colonel Carrington can make Cooke see this?"

Margaret laughed. "My dear, that's part of the problem. He's too proud to try. Henry believes— perhaps rightly—that complaints would be seen as failure. No, he's already decided to send Lieutenant Kirtland and F Company back to Fort Reno to shore up that horrible place while Kinney and Burrowes will take D and G companies north to the Bighorn River to build the third post. We're to be called Fort Philip Kearny here. Henry just received the order yesterday."

"But I thought this was to be Fort Carrington."

"Yes, we thought so too. Henry was so pleased— but no, he's denied even that small satisfaction." Margaret shook her head. "By the way, Mark has been a great help to Henry. His loyalty is much appreciated."

Rose nodded, feeling like a traitor. Mark constantly complained to her about Carrington's "timidity and incompetence." Just the night before, as they lay in bed, he said he was thinking about writing to Sherman. "Carrington's worthless as a commanding officer," he had said. "General Sherman should know."

"Why would you do that?" Rose said. From the beginning, Carrington had treated Mark with kindness and respect. "Are you hoping Sherman might promote a junior officer? You, for instance?"

Mark raised himself on one elbow and turned to her. She could not see his face but sensed his anger. "That's not my intention, but what if it were? I didn't work my ass off studying law and toadying to Tom Ewing so I could be a first lieutenant forever. Carrington will botch this and pull me down with him. Is that what you want? What's the matter with you, Rose?" She felt his anger growing. "Dancing like a laundress with enlisted men, inviting road trash to dinner. You don't even look like a proper officer's wife, with your freckles and your boy's haircut. In fact, you don't even look like a proper woman anymore. You're too thin—you have no breasts! If I wanted to bed down with a boy, I'd do it."

He threw back the blankets and dressed hurriedly, leaving with his shirt still unbuttoned. Rose felt as if she'd been kicked in the stomach. Mark used to say she was the most beautiful woman in the world, that no one could hold a candle to her. Now she disgusted him. Had she changed so much? Had she become one of those army wives who, in his words, used a hardship posting as an excuse to let themselves go?

She lay in bed, listening to the roar of the Big Piney cascades and the round-robin calls of the sentries. Things were not going as expected, true, but was that her fault alone? She was disappointed too. They had talked about what they would do after Mark's time in the service, after the territories had settled. They would start a family, buy some land— land out here would be cheap at first—and begin building their lives together. He was interested in a judicial or political career. They also talked about a ranch, or maybe a store. Whatever it was, they would make something valuable together, an opportunity they would never have in war-ruined Missouri, and pass it on to their children and their children's children. This was their dream—their shared dream— or so she thought. Now she wasn't so sure. Maybe she had changed some, in appearance and otherwise, but how could she not? Not every woman could endure what she had at the redoubt, and before at Fort Sedgwick, and come out a stronger person, as she had done. She was competent, healthy and determined. She had the qualities a woman needed to survive in this hard country. Did Mark appreciate none of this? Had she misjudged him, or had he changed?

She was still awake when the wood wagons rumbled through the gates for Piney Island, a logging camp six miles to the west. As she dressed, she wondered where Mark spent the night.

She and Jerusha passed the morning washing whites and bed linens. Rose considered asking Jerusha if she knew of Mark's whereabouts but did not. Jerusha wouldn't tell her anyway, Rose was sure of that. They worked without speaking though Rose found company in the sounds of industry that surrounded them. The sawmill hummed steadily, turning logs into posts and planks, studding and rafters, while scenting the air with the clean aroma of raw pine. Mules brayed for their morning grain and men called to one another over the ripping of handsaws and pounding of hammers.

That afternoon Dillon and the soldier from the wood train were buried, inaugurating the post cemetery at the base of Pilot Hill. Chaplain David White, a Methodist clergyman with gray hair and cold blue eyes, presided at the funerals. He was new to the regiment, arriving with Lieutenant Wands and party. Thunder rolled and a teasing wind played with the Bible's gilt-edged pages as he read from the Seventy-ninth Psalm. A poor choice, Rose thought, and one that did little to soothe the anxious mourners:

> *"O God, the heathen are come into thine inheritance.*
> *The dead bodies of thy servants*
> *they have given to be meat unto the fowls of heaven,*
> *the flesh of thy saints unto the beasts of the earth.*
> *Their blood have they shed like water around*
> *       Jerusalem;*
> *and there was none to bury them."*

Rose attended alone. She and Mark had not spoken since his outburst the night before. After the funerals, William Thomas invited her to the emigrant camp for coffee. They sat in folding chairs by the Big Piney as the thunder grew louder and more frequent.

"What did you think of Brother White's service?" Rose said.

He looked sheepish. "I wasn't listening, to tell you the truth. I was thinking about what's ahead for Charley and me." He looked to the mountains, their summits white against the darkening sky. "Kirkendall says we'll be moving on in a day or so and, I confess, I feel geese flying over my grave."

That was something Rose's grandfather used to when he sensed trouble coming. "Everyone feels that way occasionally," she said. "It doesn't mean anything."

"Oh, yes, of course. Still, I wonder if you would do something for me?" She nodded. "If I am killed, will you see to it that Charley finds his way to my brother, George, in Gallatin City? He shouldn't be hard to find. I've written down his name and particulars."

As she took the paper from him she remembered Jack Gregory's similar request. "I'm sure this won't be necessary," she said. "You and Charley will find George yourselves and I'll come visit you there when you're settled."

William smiled. "I'm sure you're right."

He offered to escort her back to the fort before the storm came but Rose wanted to be alone with her thoughts. Halfway up the hill she saw a man standing on the path. She recognized Fred Brown's shining bald head.

"You shouldn't go roaming around by yourself, Mrs. Reynolds," he said. "Something bad could happen to you."

She smelled whiskey on his breath. "Thank you for your concern, Lieutenant," she said without stopping.

He fell into step beside her. "I'll be Captain Brown soon. My commission will arrive any day."

"How nice for you."

Although Brown and his ribald humor were popular with the men, women tended to avoid him, especially when he was drinking, which was often. More than once Rose had caught him looking at her like a hungry dog eyeing a bit of meat.

"Why do you mix with those hayseeds anyway?" he said.

"They aren't hayseeds," she said. "They're my friends."

"Maybe you and I could be friends." He put his hand on her arm.

"Not likely," she said, shaking him off. "Besides, I don't think my husband would like that."

Brown laughed. "Lieutenant Reynolds has friends of his own. A man gets lonely when his woman isn't around. Sometimes even when she is."

Rose felt the ground shift beneath her. What was he telling her? "You're drunk," she said. "Leave me alone or I'll tell Mark about your ugly insinuations."

A flash of lightning split the sky followed by a crash of thunder.

"You never have liked me, have you?" he said. "Well, I suppose that's to be expected. After all, I'm just a shopkeeper's son from Toledo, not one of your St. Louis bluenoses. Why, I bet you've never met a man like me before." He smiled, swaying on his feet.

"You're wrong, Mr. Brown," she said in her sweetest voice. "St. Louis has its share of jackasses too."

He stopped smiling and she moved on, relieved he did not follow. The wind picked up and she lifted her skirts to run, hoping to beat the rain. Just as she reached the post she was startled by the report of a gun, a single shot. She saw men running to a tent on officers' row. She joined them. Inside she saw a man on his knees with his head on the ground before him, as if in prayer.

"Come away, Mrs. Reynolds," a soldier took her by the arm. "You don't want to see this." She recognized one of her dancing partners.

"What happened?" she said. "Has there been an accident?"

"No accident, ma'am. It's Lieutenant Anderson. He drank a bottle of whiskey and put his revolver in his mouth."

Rose covered her eyes with her hands. He had been strange since Clara and Rollo died but she had no idea he had sunk this far. Maybe if she hadn't been so wrapped up in her own problems she would have noticed the degree of his suffering. Maybe she could have done something to help.

She went to her tent, lit the lamp, and lay down on her cot without undressing. A solitary cricket chirped from a dark corner. How alone she was. How far from home and any sort of comfort. As if on cue, with a blue-white flash of lightning the storm finally broke. Fat drops of rain thumped on the canvas, just a few at first and then a barrage. Yellow lamplight bounced off the tent walls as they shook in the wind. A red wave of panic swept over her. Something monstrous was coming, slinking through the darkness, closer every minute, every second. Whatever it was, she would have to face it alone.

# Chapter Twenty-three

She was thinner and her hair was different but in Harry Carrington's eyes Rose Reynolds was still the most beautiful woman in the world, so beautiful his heart skipped a beat when she waved him over to her tent.

"Harry, come here. I've got something for you."

He obeyed with a studied casualness as she went inside, then returned with something behind her back.

"Close your eyes and put out your hands," she said. "Now open."

Harry looked down and saw *The Count of Monte Cristo*, the only book by Alexandre Dumas Harry had not read. "Ah!" he croaked with happiness.

"I bought it from a soldier at Fort Reno," she said.

"Thank you," he said when he got his voice under control. "Dumas is my favorite author."

"I knew that. Your mother told me. Now come." She sat in her rocker and motioned for him to sit beside her. "Tell me what you've been up to since Fort Sedgwick."

He started talking, haltingly at first but gaining confidence because she was an interested listener. He told her of their encounter with Black Horse's Cheyenne and the deaths of French Pete's party, about riding Calico with the woodcutters to the Pinery. He had her full attention until horsemen appeared on the Fort Reno Road.

"It's just the mail," Harry said, wanting to draw her focus back to him. He recognized Montgomery Van Valzah, a short, thick man with a bulbous nose and dark beard, who carried the locked mailbag between forts Phil Kearny and Laramie with stops at Bridger's Ferry and Reno. For this dangerous work he received the handsome pay of ten dollars a day. A civilian, Van Valzah usually traveled with a three-man military escort, but on this occasion there was a fourth rider.

Rose stood. Mail call was an exciting event. Already a crowd was gathering at the adjutant's office, but Harry sensed it was not the mail that aroused her interest.

"Excuse me, Harry," she said. "I see a friend. I must say hello."

"Oh, sure." Harry tried to hide his disappointment. "Thanks for the book." He watched as the fourth rider on the bay horse dismounted and walked forward to meet her. Harry did not know him but the tall man and Rose were in a hurry to reach each other, almost running. For one shocking moment Harry thought the stranger would pick her up and kiss her. But he didn't. Instead he took off his hat and gave her his hand. As Harry turned to go back to his tent, he noticed someone else watching them. For the second time, he thought Mark Reynolds could be a dangerous man.

By mid-August the main stockade was finished, with eight-foot walls of solid pine and an additional three feet buried in a gravel-filled trench. Each log was shaved to a point and there was a notch at every fifth joint for small-arms fire. A banquette, or sentry walk, circled the perimeter, with five open platforms a foot above to give the sentries a clear view. There were lookout towers on the north and south corners and blockhouses for the artillery under construction in the east and west. A third blockhouse would be built in the quartermaster's yard.

Three sides of the stockade had massive double gates, two planks in thickness, with sally wickets so pedestrians could come and go when the gates were closed. The fourth wall, behind officers' row, had a small sally port that only the officers and their families could use.

Cheered by the stockade's completion, Colonel Carrington suggested the officers and their families celebrate with a picnic in the mountains. Margaret questioned the wisdom of this, but Jim Bridger said it would be all right.

"The Injuns are busy huntin' now," he said, "stockin' up for winter. That's why we ain't seen none

lately. And if you're wantin' a day trip, best do it while
the weather obliges. That'll change in a few weeks."

The day they chose was sunny and crisp, with a
clear blue sky. They rode away from the post at mid-
morning with Bridger in the lead. Five armed men
leading two pack mules brought up the rear. Carl's
groomer, Private Pat Smith, had the old horse in top
form, his coat brushed and gleaming. No longer a
candidate for the dead herd, he trotted along with
eyes bright as a three-year-old's.

Bridger led them single file south along Little
Piney Creek till they came to an old Indian trail twist-
ing through meadows of wild wheat and oats. From
there the trail entered a dark fragrant forest of pine,
balsam, and hemlock. When they emerged again
into the daylight Rose was surprised to see they were
already halfway up the mountain. After the cool of
the forest, Rose felt the sun's bite on her neck, despite her wide-brimmed hat. She was grateful when
Dixon offered a red handkerchief, which she tied
around her throat.

They had to stop several times to rest the laboring
horses but when at last they reached the summit the
view was magnificent. The Pineys looked like ropes
of blue diamonds sparkling on a fabric of rich green
velvet and the fort tiny as a child's plaything.

On the far side of the ridge Bridger took them to
the ruins of an ancient Indian fort, its crumbling
stone walls hidden by stunted, wind-blasted trees. In
the middle were the remains of a recent campfire.

"I didn't see that when I was up here t'other day," Bridger said with a frown.

"What does that mean?" Sallie Horton said, her voice rising. "Maybe we should go back?"

"We're not going back," Carrington said. "We've come all this way for a picnic and that's what we're going to do. Thompson, start the fire."

He ordered other enlisted men to set up the canopy and tend to the horses. Rose sat on a sun-warmed boulder, feeling ghostly eyes upon her. Who built this fort and why? Was it a holy site, a place to thank the Everywhere Spirit for the gifts of nature, or did the Indians come here to watch the white soldiers and plan ways to kill them?

Mark sat down beside her and rolled a smoke. Even though he apologized for what he'd said in the tent—"I didn't mean those things, Rose darling. Please forgive me"—there was still tension between them.

"This is insane," he said, lighting his cigarette. "Usually Carrington's timid as my maiden aunt, now he insists on a garden party in Red Cloud's front yard. I'm surprised he didn't bring the band along."

He exhaled a blue cloud of smoke. She noticed he smoked more than he used to.

"Major Bridger doesn't seem worried," she said. "Anyhow, it's nice to get away from the post."

"Bridger. That old goat makes ten dollars a day. Did you know that?"

"Well, the colonel values his opinion."

Mark's eyes went to the kerchief at her neck.

"What's this?" He touched it with his cigarette hand, bringing the glowing ember close to her face.

"My neck was getting sunburned. Dr. Dixon gave it to me."

Mark gave a short laugh. "Of course—the good doctor. He's very attentive, isn't he? That poacher. Stay away from him, Rose. That's the last thing I need, gossip about my wife and some washed-up sawbones. Take it off."

"Don't be stupid," she said.

"I said take it off."

She started to loosen the knot but before she finished Mark yanked it free, burning her skin.

"Ow, that hurt!" she said, rubbing her neck. "What's the matter with you?" She felt her face grow warm. "And if you're worried about ugly gossip, you might want to talk to your friend Fred Brown!"

Mark's eyes cut to the other picnickers. If they heard their argument they were too polite to show it. "Has Brown said something to you?" he said quietly.

"Ask him yourself."

Mark ground his cigarette into the dirt. Then, to her surprise, he took her hands and smiled in the old way, the way that once made her heart flip in her chest. "You're right. I am being stupid. I'm sorry, Rose." He reached up to touch her cheek. "I don't want to hurt you. I'm just not myself lately, I know that. I think it's the strangeness of this place, the remoteness of it, knowing the Sioux and the Cheyenne are out there day and night, invisible, watching and waiting. Plus all the double duty we're pulling, and that's only going to get worse when Kinney and Burrowes go north in a few days."

Rose softened. "It has been hard," she said, "harder than we thought it would be. But reinforcements are coming. Things will be better then."

Mark shook his head. "Even if those cavalry companies show up—which I doubt—we're still in trouble. The real problem is Carrington. Just look at him." The colonel stood at the fire instructing the man on how to grill the elk steaks. "He's going to fall on his face," Mark said, "and every officer in the command will be tarnished by his failure. I've come too far, worked too hard to be ruined by the likes of him."

For the first time it occurred to Rose that maybe Mark, not Bisbee, was sending those poisonous letters to General Cooke. It was a bad thought, one she wanted to put out of her head. She was relieved when Margaret announced dinner.

The new sutler, clearly attempting to impress Carrington and his officers, had provided the lavish banquet now spread on blankets before them. In addition to the elk steaks, still hot from the sage-scented fire, there were jars of jellies chosen to complement elk's distinctive flavor, canned lobster, cove oysters, pineapples, tomatoes, sweet corn, fresh puddings, gingerbread, plum and jelly cakes and, to finish, three magnums of Madame Clicquot.

"I feel like I'm back in St. Louis at the Planter's House," Mark said, "only the view is better." This started a discussion of famous restaurants the officers had visited.

"How about you, Dixon?" Mark said. "Have you a favorite?"

The surgeon smiled. "The only meals I remember were home-cooked."

"Is that so?" Mark raised his eyebrows. "I'm surprised you're not married then." The two men looked at each other and Rose could see the dislike between them. She wondered if others saw it too.

"I was married," Dixon said, "but my wife and baby died. It was during the war." It was clear he did not want to say more.

Rose broke the silence by asking about Simon Trover. "I've been wondering about him," she said. "I think of him often."

Dixon nodded. "He should be on his way home to Mississippi by now. There's one story with a happy ending. I hope so anyway."

The sutler, John Fitch, was telling them about his years in Utah and the term he'd served in Congress when dark clouds appeared in the west and the wind developed an edge. They packed in a hurry and started for home. Halfway down the mountain, they found the skeletal remains of a man. Clumps of black hair clung to the crushed skull and the bones wore the remnants of jeans and a red shirt. Two arrows were buried half the length of their shafts in the corpse's chest, as if shot with super-human strength.

"Should we bury him?" Sallie Horton said.

"No," Carrington said, looking up the mountain into the dark woods. "We will proceed."

The storm broke when they were a half mile from the fort. They rode through the gates soaked through and, in Rose's case, shaking with cold.

# Chapter Twenty-four

Carrington finally gave Kirkendall's 110-wagon train permission to move on. After breakfast, Rose and Jimmy Carrington walked down to the emigrant camp to say good-bye to Charley and William Thomas.

"I'm counting on you to come see us, Rose, just as you promised," William said. "You too, Jimmy. It's not far, only two hundred and fifty miles or thereabouts. George has a flour mill on the river, next to the ferry. Like I said, he shouldn't be hard to find." He paused, then looked directly into her eyes. "Mrs. Reynolds, you do remember that other thing we talked about, don't you?"

Rose nodded, a stone growing in her throat. Partings seemed final in this country, not like in the States. "Take care of yourselves," she said, bending to kiss Charley on the cheek. She was about to wish them good luck but stopped because she did not want to suggest luck was needed.

The wagons started north at two o'clock under a

lowering sky, escorted by a detail under Lieutenant George Templeton, still recovering from the wounds he'd received the day Napoleon Daniels was killed. Charley rode in the arc-shaped opening in the rear of the clumsy prairie schooner, waving, his brilliant red hair shining, until it disappeared over the crest of a hill. Rose and Jimmy walked back to the post in low spirits and Rose sank even lower when she found Mark in their tent, lying on their bed. Though the sun was fully up the tent's interior was dark and cool. "Come here," he said, raising himself on one elbow. "I've got the morning free."

Rose looked at him, remembering the wild abandon of their early days together and the thrill she had felt at their lovemaking. She wished she could feel those things again but now she realized she did not. Something had changed within her. "I can't," she said. "Margaret and Sallie Horton are expecting me. We're going to play croquet."

He came to her, putting his hands on her shoulders. "The hens will wait."

He bent to kiss her but she turned her head. "I don't like it when you call them hens," she said. "It's patronizing."

He walked to his shaving stand. Their eyes met in the mirror. "Rose, is it my imagination, or am I losing you?"

She said nothing.

"I see," he said. His face darkened and he turned to face her. "Just remember this. You're my wife, Rose. That's what you are and that's all you are. That's the only reason you're here. Things may be rough right now but I'm going places. So don't do anything to interfere with that. If you do, you'll regret it. You know what I mean." He left the tent leaving her to wonder if the man she once loved was now someone to fear.

# Chapter Twenty-five

Captains Nathaniel Kinney and Thomas Burrowes went north on the third of August, taking two companies and Bridger and Beckwourth as guides. Carrington ordered Bridger to return as soon as Kinney chose a site for the new post, to be called Fort C. F. Smith in honor of the Mexican War hero. Beckwourth was to find his friends the Mountain Crows and learn what he could about Red Cloud's Sioux, reportedly camped along the Tongue River.

Their departure left Carrington with only 381 men and a handful of civilian employees to defend Fort Phil Kearny. Their stores were running low, with flour, lard, and sugar in especially short supply. Hunters would venture out for game but were rarely successful. People were hungry. One night Rose dreamed of her grandmother's Christmas cake, heavy with butter and cream, molasses, walnuts, spices, plump and floured raisins, and covered with a crusty, sugary glaze that crunched when she bit into a slice still warm from the oven.

The day Kinney and Burrowes left, Indians attacked the wood train returning from the Pinery. The gunfire was heard within the fort. As Carrington formed a rescue detail a civilian teamster rode through the gates on a lathered draft mule, still in harness, and went straight to the quartermaster to resign. He did not apologize for abandoning his comrades or for the dark stain on the front of his trousers.

"They sprang up out of nowhere, all painted and howling like banshees!" he told the men crowded around him. "Like nothing you ever saw! I tell you, I'm going back to Reno with the next mail detail and anyone with any sense will do the same. Stay here and you'll all be dead by Christmas—mark my words!"

The Indians quit the attack before rescuers arrived, and all the men returned safely. Still, the teamster's fear was infectious. The words "dead by Christmas" echoed throughout the post. That night, for the first time, Rose thought she heard wolves sharpening their claws against the stockade walls.

# Chapter Twenty-six

From that day on Indians appeared daily on the hills, flashing mirrors and waving flags as if mocking the sentries' signals. No one could leave the stockade without permission, and women and children could not leave at all. There would be no more picnics on Fort Ridge or horseback rides through the valleys and meadows. Morale, already low, declined even further. Some officers began to complain openly about Carrington's leadership.

"Bisbee calls him coward," Mark said one gray morning as he dressed. He and Rose had settled into a kind of uneasy truce. "He's the only one who has the balls to say it but we all know it's true. Carrington always comes up with some reason not to move against the Indians. If we don't strike soon the season will be over and we'll have nothing to show for it. Nothing. Only Ten Eyck defends him."

The tent was very cold, even with the little heat stove going full blast.

"What do you say?" Rose asked, shivering under the blankets.

"I keep my mouth shut. A man never knows when his words will come back to bite him."

If Carrington was unaware of the rising tide of resentment, his wife was not. Although officers' wives usually avoided political talk during their afternoon sewing circles and card games, Rose sensed Margaret's anxiety. The storm could break any moment, and Margaret Carrington was too keen not to know it.

The fort's inhabitants were afraid, and their fear grew day by day. No one expected an attack on the fort for it was well-known Indians never went after a well-defended, entrenched opponent. Still, the sight of painted warriors sitting on their ponies on top of the hills kept everyone on edge. Mark was anxious and irritable. The smallest incident—coffee not to his liking, or an undarned sock—set him off. Their lovemaking, which he insisted on, had become something Rose dreaded. She felt like his prisoner.

She saw Daniel Dixon only on those infrequent evenings when the weather was warm enough for a concert under the stars. The entire garrison turned out with blankets and folding chairs to listen as Sam Curry's musicians filled the valley with the sweet sounds of brass and flute, strings and drums. The music seemed magical in this place, even more so on those nights when bands of multicolored light waved across the sky, rippling and billowing like a celestial stage curtain. These were the famous northern

lights, a phenomenon Rose had heard others speak
of but never seen herself.

At the end of August, Colonel William B. Hazen
arrived with a train of government and emigrant
wagons. As acting inspector general for the Department of the Platte, Hazen was touring the Western
posts and compiling a report for Cooke. His party
included a topographical engineer named Ambrose
Bierce, a small man with a limp and glittering black
eyes, who found at Fort Phil Kearny a wartime friend.
This was Ridgway Glover, a photographer and special
correspondent for *Frank Leslie's Illustrated Newspaper,*
who had arrived with Templeton's group in late July.
A pale, thin aristocrat from Philadelphia, Glover
roamed about with his Roettger camera and a wheelbarrow full of developing chemicals, always working
to capture views of the frontier landscape and its natives. The soldiers made fun of him but Harry had
made friends with Glover and liked working with
him in the darkness of his "development" room,
bathing and rinsing negative plates and watching the
images magically appear.

In the evenings Bierce, Glover, and a few others
played poker in Bierce's tent. The winner took a pot
of wooden matches since Glover's Quaker beliefs
would not allow him to gamble for coin. Afterward,
sitting by the fire, Bierce would tell stories to anyone
who wanted to listen. His audience often included
Harry. Bierce's tales were of medical dissecting
rooms, morgues, lonely cemeteries, and ghosts, and
he appeared to make them up as he went along. His
dark eyes glittered in the red firelight as a devilish

new plot twist came to him. Harry's favorite was about a condemned soldier's miraculous escape from the noose and his long journey home to a wife who loved him. Just as they found each other, just at the blissful moment of their reunion, the soldier plunged to his death. The escape and journey had been only the dying man's last beautiful dream.

Hazen spent three days inspecting Fort Phil Kearny and the two logging camps that supplied it. Though he admired the post's design and construction, he questioned the need for the elaborate stockade.

"I'm not criticizing you, Carrington," Hazen said around a mouthful of elk steak, a napkin tucked in his collar. He was pink-faced and healthy-looking with an air of supreme self-satisfaction. This was Hazen's last night at Phil Kearny and he was eating dinner with Carrington's family and a few select officers in Carrington's quarters. In the morning Hazen and his group would head north for Fort C. F. Smith. "It's not easy to command a remote post and your case here is especially difficult, I grant you that," he said. "God knows how I'd have managed down in Texas if I'd had women and children along."

He raised his wineglass for George to refill. "No offense to you and the other ladies, Margaret, but Bill Sherman made a mistake when he allowed dependents to accompany the regiment. I thought so at the time. If it weren't for your women and children, Carrington, and your understandable concern for their safety, you'd be much further along by now. You wouldn't have spent so much time and manpower on a stockade that you don't need. As it stands, you'll be hard-pressed to get the men's barracks done in time. Some of your officers will winter in huts."

Officers traditionally waited until the men were housed before building their own quarters but Carrington's house was almost done. The regimental band was building the family a fine, two-story frame home with a shingled roof, two brick chimneys, and an attached kitchen. Though he did not mention it, Hazen had heard grumbling. The information would find its way into his report.

"In short," he said, "you overestimated the Indian threat and it's caused you to make questionable decisions regarding your distribution of manpower." He pulled the napkin from his collar, wiped his fleshy lips, and dropped it on his plate. "You have enough men to take on the Indians, Carrington, and you should do so. My report to Cooke will reflect this."

Carrington's face reddened. Why would Hazen humiliate him like this in front of his family and top officers? His voice shook when he spoke. "Colonel Hazen, with all respect, I disagree. These northern tribes are hostile. True, they've been quiet during your stay, but I assure you their intentions are warlike. I need more men to take them on—trained cavalry especially—and I need them now. Escorting the mail, wood and supply trains, delivering messages to forts Reno and Smith, riding picket, outpost duty—all this is dangerous, taxing work. My officers are pulling double—even triple—duty and I am woefully undersupplied. I need munitions and grain for the animals. They can't get by on hay alone."

Hazen looked at Carrington as if he were a whining child. "I believe you are selling your men short," he said. Bisbee and Brown exchanged satisfied smiles. "Your officers are capable—take the upper hand. Be aggressive. This defensive posture you've taken, this eight-foot stockade, it's the wrong way to deal with Indians, Carrington. Sends the wrong message. If there's anything I learned fighting Comanches and Apaches in Texas it's that you've got to show them you mean business. Get busy, man, show the red devils who you are."

"May I remind you that my orders are—"

"Yes, yes, I know." Hazen waved his hand dismissively. "Avoid all-out war, try to make allegiances, so forth and so on. Well, Bill Sherman is a hell of a soldier but he doesn't know jack about fighting Indians and I'm not afraid to say it. Neither does Pope, Grant, none of them. It makes your job more difficult, Carrington, I know that, but you've got to make do with what you've got, dammit."

He banged his fist on the table, making the plates jump. "They respond to fear. Harass their villages, use your howitzers when they swarm on the hilltops. If they respond in a hostile manner, you've got every right to defend your people and your post. I'm sure Sherman would be the first to agree." He settled back in his seat and reached for his pipe. "Now, about tomorrow. I'll need a guide and an escort of at least twenty-six men. Horses too, of course."

Carrington's mouth fell open. "You can't be serious!

That would reduce my mounted force by one-third.
It would leave me with only forty horses. I can't do it.
I won't do it."

Hazen appeared not to have heard. He stood,
brushing crumbs from his trousers, and the other
officers rose also. Only Carrington remained seated.
"I don't know why those cavalry companies didn't
meet me at Reno as planned," Hazen said, "but
they'll be along any day with plenty of horses. You'll
see. Chin up, Carrington. Chin up!"

After he and the others had gone Harry helped
George clear the table where his father sat alone, his
head in his hands.

# Chapter Twenty-seven

August gave way to September. The tall grass turned to gold and the cottonwood canopy shading the Pineys to lemon yellow, persimmon orange, blood red. Afternoons were still sunny and warm but mornings and nights grew bitter. Jack Stead told Harry he had never seen snow so low on the mountains this early in the season.

"Is that bad?" Harry said.

"It ain't good."

Harry had grown two inches since they left Nebraska and Margaret had to make most of his clothes. Although his added height made him less sensitive about the size of his feet, he felt like a clown in his homemade trousers, which were too big in the waist and puckered under his belt like a girl's dirndl skirt. He was grateful when Daniel Dixon gave him a pair of his denim jeans. They fit pretty well in the waist and hips and he cuffed the too-long legs.

He worked alongside the men, a day that began before daylight and continued on till tattoo and sometimes longer if Quartermaster Brown ordered an all-night shingling bee. The officers were pushing hard to finish the barracks, storehouses, offices, and commissary buildings before the snows came. The work was backbreaking—blood, sweat, and tears work, Brown said—but made a little easier by the fine quality of the pine timber which grew tall and straight, without knot or blemish, making planks that fit together so snugly no chinking was needed. But lumber and water were their only abundant commodities. Food and medical supplies were low and getting lower. The physicians were beginning to worry about scurvy.

"How will you know if it comes?" Harry asked.

"We'll know," Dixon said grimly. "When men start showing up with stiff legs, bleeding gums, and breath that'll strip paint, we'll know."

By the second week of September traffic on the Bozeman Road had slowed to a trickle, so everyone got excited one gray afternoon when the sentries signaled wagons were approaching. But it was not a supply train or reinforcements but a group of civilian hay cutters, the last of the season, looking for work. Brown hired them to harvest the fields near Lake De Smet and Goose Creek. On their first day of work Sioux warriors attacked, killing three of the cutters and wounding five. When rescuers arrived they found the mowers and wagons burning and the Indians riding away with the mules that pulled them.

Later that afternoon Indians stampeded buffalo through the post's beef herd. When the dust cleared two hundred animals were gone, more than half the regiment's winter meat supply. Another group of raiders stole dozens of horses and mules grazing outside the stockade, wounding two soldiers in the process. Ten Eyck pursued them but the soldiers' grain-starved horses played out and they returned empty-handed.

At the end of this long day, Dixon went to headquarters, where Carrington was finishing his weekly report to Cooke. The day's events, the colonel knew, would not make him look good.

"What is it, Dixon?" Carrington said, not looking up.

"Sam Curry is dead, Colonel."

Carrington fell back in his chair. "Sam, dead? How can that be? I just saw him this morning! I know he'd been sick but he was recovering. . . . When did he die?"

"About thirty minutes ago. It was very sudden. He had a seizure and then he was gone. Maybe his heart, or some sort of hemorrhage or aneurysm."

Carrington stared sightlessly at the canvas wall. "Sam was scoring new pieces," he said. "'Overture to Poet and Peasant' and several waltzes. It was coming along well. I was looking forward to it."

This was the least of their problems, Dixon thought with annoyance. "Curry's wife is distraught," he said. "I thought Mrs. Carrington might sit with her tonight, maybe help with the youngsters."

Carrington did not respond. Dixon wondered if he'd heard him. Several moments passed.

Finally the colonel looked up. "What? Oh, yes. I'll

just finish here. Please, go to the house and tell Margaret what's happened. I'll be along directly."

Dixon crossed the yard to Carrington's quarters, where twin columns of white smoke rose from two brick chimneys. George answered the door and led him to the warm front room, where Rose Reynolds was reading aloud from Dickens's *Tale of Two Cities* as Margaret sewed in a chair by the fire. Rose's face flushed when Dixon walked in.

"Ladies," he said, removing his hat, "I'm sorry to be the one to tell you this but Sam Curry died tonight. Mrs. Carrington, the colonel and I thought you might keep his wife company."

Margaret stood, letting her needlework fall to the floor. "Poor Elizabeth. Of course I'll go to her. Just let me get my shawl." She went upstairs to her room, leaving Rose and Dixon alone for the first time since their escape from the redoubt. Despite the sad news, she was happy to see him. She got to her feet and walked toward him.

"What happened to Sam?" she said.

"I can't say. It was fast, he didn't suffer."

"Poor Beth," she said. "How will she manage with two babies?"

"She'll go back East," Dixon said, "and you should go with her. You've got to get away from here, Rose. You, all the women and children have got to get out of here before it's too late. I hope it's not too late already."

"Does Sam's death make you say this?"

"No, it's not that, it's everything. We don't have

enough food. Winter's coming and it won't be like any winter we knew back in the States. We aren't equipped for it. But most of all it's the Indians. There are thousands of them out there in the hills, Rose, and they're all bent on one thing: getting rid of us. You've got to get out of here." He seemed to be pleading. She jumped when a log fell in the fireplace, creating a shower of sparks.

"But I don't want to leave," she said. "I don't want to go back to the States. I don't want to go back to Missouri." Not until she spoke them did she fully realize the truth of those words. She could not bear the thought of returning to St. Louis, with its crowded streets, dirty air, and tired people.

"You don't have to go back to Missouri," he said, taking her hands. "Just go to Fort Reno, stay there until spring. You'll be safe there."

They heard Margaret descending the stairs and Rose turned from him, taking her plaid shawl from a peg on the wall.

"I'll come with you," she said to Margaret. "You'll need help with the children."

The cold had deepened in the last hour. The frozen grass crunched beneath their feet as they crossed the parade ground to the bandmaster's cabin. Rose did not look at Dixon again, not even when he said good night.

That night wolves gathered in unusual numbers outside the stockade, drawn by the offal of the cattle slaughtered during the day. Their howls and growls grew in pitch and fury as they fought among themselves for some bloody bit. Rose listened to the violence from her bed and wondered if Daniel was right. Maybe the creatures, man and beast, who were here before them had finally decided to reclaim what was theirs, and to fight to the death for it.

# Chapter Twenty-eight

Two days after Sam Curry's funeral, Indians captured Private Peter Johnson alive. This was the worst fate imaginable, the thing every man, woman, and child at the post feared most. He was among those guarding the heavy hay wagons returning from Lake De Smet. A dim boy with his head in the clouds, Johnson let his horse get too far ahead of the others. His bunk mate, John Ryan, had just called him back when a warrior on horseback flew up out of a gully separating Johnson from the column.

"He panicked," Ryan said later. "He should've tried to get back to us—he might've made it—but when he saw that Injun gaining on him, he plumb lost his head. He jumped off his horse and made for a washout by the road and for some reason he threw his carbine down. That buck didn't have no trouble taking him."

"Who was in charge of the hay detail?" Carrington said.

"I was, sir." Sergeant Garrett, the thick-necked Irishman, stepped forward.

"Why was no effort made to save Private Johnson?"

"Well, Colonel, it was him or us." Garrett's tone was matter-of-fact, as if explaining why there was no toast at breakfast. "First there was just the one, then there was Injuns everywhere. Lieutenant Brown knows what it's like." He did not have to say Carrington didn't, his meaning was clear. "My boys had but three rounds of ammo to the man. We couldn't fight 'em, we had to come back. If they'd got between us and the fort we'd all have been done for."

Ridgway Glover said, "You might have shot him. It would have been the merciful thing."

"Who asked you, Quaker?" Garrett said. "Who cares what you think? I hear Quakers sit down to piss. Is that right, Glover? Do you sit down to piss?"

A few of the men snickered. Glover looked down at his feet.

"No, he's right," Ryan said, his lower lip trembling. "I wish we had shot him. It was awful the way Pete was screaming. I keep hearing it in my head."

Garrett laughed. "Well, boyo," he said, "you didn't let that concern slow you down none, did you? You wasted no time gittin' back to the fort."

Ryan volunteered to ride with a rescue detail, but they returned without seeing any sign of Johnson or the Indians.

Rose did not know him but she could not stop

thinking about what must be happening to the young soldier. Jim Bridger once told her of watching a group of Crows torture a Sioux warrior to death. "The squaws do most of the work," he said. "First they stuff hot coals in his ears, then they start taking him apart, finger by finger, toe by toe, with their husbands and children cheerin' 'em on. When he's finally dead, they turn him over to their men. They drag the body behind their ponies till it falls to pieces."

Rose did not pray often, but that night she sent one up for Private Peter Johnson. The next morning, when Glover started out for a day of picture-taking, Rose tried to talk him out of it. "Don't go, Ridgway. Please, it's far too dangerous. Your editor will understand."

Glover shook his head as he tightened the surcingle under a pack mule's belly. Besides his camera equipment, he carried a butcher knife, sketch pad, and pen but no firearm. "*Frank Leslie's* didn't send me all the way up here to make pictures of stockade walls," he said. "Besides, I don't fear the Indians. They understand I mean them no harm. Why, you should see how they marvel at my medicine every time I make their likeness with my shadow box. Soon they'll be welcoming me into their lodges. I'll be the first to photograph wild Indians in their natural, uncorrupted state. Think of that."

His eyes shone with excitement as he described two Indian men he had seen near the timber-cutters' camp the week before. "I didn't reveal myself because I didn't have my camera but I sketched them.

Here, take a look." He took his sketchbook from his saddlebags and showed her a fine charcoal drawing of two Sioux on horseback. One was a giant whose feet nearly touched the ground. The other was slight in build with wavy, unbound hair.

"I call them David and Goliath," Glover said. "This one"—he placed a long finger on the giant—"must be seven feet tall with shoulders wide as a barn. The other was much smaller, as you can see, and unusually fair. His hair was lighter too. A white man, I thought, maybe taken as a child. Even though he's smaller, I sensed he was in command. I shall ask them to sit for me. What a photograph that will be!"

Rose looked at him and shook her head. "Ridgway, they will kill you. Think of poor Private Johnson."

Glover smiled. "I am not afraid, Mrs. Reynolds. I have faith in natural man's inherent goodness, no matter his skin color, and so should you."

She watched him walk down the wood road, leading his pack mule. Because Glover was a civilian and a journalist, Carrington let him come and go as he chose, though he told him he was foolish. Glover turned once to wave and Rose waved back, sensing it would be the last time she would see him alive.

That afternoon five mounted warriors made a run on the Pilot Hill sentries. Carrington personally loaded and fired the howitzer. The exploding shell knocked one Indian off his horse and scattered the others. An hour later a larger group cut fifty animals from the post's dwindling beef herd. Brown led a company in pursuit and Bisbee followed with extra ammunition and an ambulance.

The day was cool and overcast with occasional rolls of thunder. To keep busy, Rose carried armloads of firewood from the quartermaster's yard to her tent. The exercise felt good and she liked being in the yard. She found peace in the ring of the blacksmith's hammer and the munching of mules in their corrals, and was refreshed by the clean smells of the hay and the hot soap billowing from the cabins of laundresses' row.

After this she tended to their dinner, salted venison and army beans that had been cooking since dawn over a low fire. Beans required twice the usual cooking time at this altitude, something she and the other wives had been slow to discover.

There was great joy late that afternoon when the long-awaited commissary train finally arrived. Everyone stopped to cheer as the wagons rolled in with barrels of hams and bacon, lard, sacks of flour, sugar, coffee, corn, and oats for the grain-starved animals and sixty thousand rounds of Springfield rifle ammunition.

While these were being unloaded, the Pilot Hill sentry signaled more visitors. The mail train was coming from the east and a lone vehicle, the ambulance that went with Bisbee, approached on the wood road. The ambulance entered first with Private Ryan driving.

Carrington met him. "Where's Bisbee?" he said. "Did you engage the Indians? Do you have wounded?"

"No, sir. Lieutenant Bisbee sent me back with a body we found on the road. It's the *Frank Leslie's* man. Indians got him."

Carrington walked to the rear of the vehicle and opened the door. From where she stood Rose could see Glover's body lying faceup on the bench. He had been disemboweled, his midsection stuffed with dry grass and set aflame, his face mutilated. The photographer was almost unrecognizable.

A woman traveling with the mail train saw the body also. She stood in the wagon and screamed so shrilly the horses were frightened. When an officer tried to calm her she pushed him away. "Let me in!" she cried. "Get me in the gate at once!"

Rose did not know it then, but Frances Grummond and her swaggering husband would change their lives forever.

# Chapter Twenty-nine

Margaret and Rose helped the distraught woman to Carrington's quarters. Harry followed with her bags. She walked with a strange hobbling gait and leaned heavily on his mother's arm. Once inside the house she sank into a chair and heaved a sigh. "Oh, that dreadful thing in the wagon! I wish to God I hadn't seen it! What a land of horrors this is!"

She took off her hat and fanned her plump, perspiring face. "Dear Lord in heaven, what have I gotten myself into? As you can see I'm in a delicate condition. This trip has worn me to the bone."

Harry understood "delicate condition" meant a woman was in the family way.

"Did you have an accident?" Margaret said.

Frances snorted. "Accident! That stupid Mexican driver went off and left me while I was attending to a call of nature. I had to run nearly a mile—in cloth slippers—to catch up. Can you imagine it? I was yelling to him the whole time and he never even turned his filthy Mexican head. Why, I ran through a bed of cactus, I've been pulling spines from my feet for two days. Just look at them." She kicked off her slippers to reveal swollen feet that looked like little red pillows. Harry had to bite his lip to keep from laughing. When he looked up Rose gave him a wink.

"Those so-called surgeons did nothing for me," Frances said. "I told George—my husband, Lieutenant George Grummond—I told him it would serve them right if I developed a raging infection. Can I lie down somewhere please? I am spent."

Margaret helped her to stand. "Of course. Come upstairs and stretch out on my bed. Harry, bring Mrs. Grummond's things to my room. Rose, will you make tea?"

As Harry bent for her bags Frances put a hand on his arm. "Young man, run fetch the post surgeon first. Someone competent—if there is such a thing in this wilderness. And do hurry, I am in great need of medical attention."

Harry found Dixon with Ten Eyck's crew building a permanent hospital. "Cactus spines?" Dixon said, throwing a shovelful of dirt. "I can't do anything she couldn't do herself with a pair of tweezers."

"Well, she wants a surgeon," Harry said. "And she's expecting a child."

Dixon stopped shoveling and wiped his forehead. "All right then. I'll get my bags and wash up. What did you say her name was?"

"Frances Grummond."

Ten Eyck froze. "Did you catch her husband's name?"

"I think she called him George."

Ten Eyck turned to the sutler's store, where the officers were welcoming the new arrivals. He focused his one working eye on a short, strong-looking man with a mustache and well-trimmed beard. His hair was carefully parted.

"You know him?" Dixon said.

"I know him," Ten Eyck said. "And I can't say I'm happy to see him."

At sundown on this busy day a southbound party of miners stopped to ask Carrington's permission to camp on the Big Piney. "The Indians have deviled us all the way from Virginia City," said their leader, a man named Bailey. "They killed two of my boys when we was crossing Tongue River."

A courier from Fort C. F. Smith traveling with the miners brought a letter from Captain Burrowes describing the fate of an emigrant party. After reading it Carrington searched for Rose, finding her in Curry's quarters where she was helping the widow pack. The cabin smelled of the rosemary leaves women packed in their trunks to keep clothing fresh.

"I thought you should see this," Carrington said. "I believe you knew them."

Rose took the letter, knowing what it would say.

*Their bodies were found on the Yellowstone River. The father and boy were beside the wagon, scalped and shot full of arrows. Schultz, the driver, was*

*found in the river where he was fishing. His body
not mutilated. Jim Bridger advises me it is likely
they were killed by Blackfeet since those Indians will
not molest a body in the water. The three were buried
beside the river in a single grave.*

Rose closed her eyes, remembering William's face as he spoke of geese flying over his grave. She saw Charley, waving from the rear of the wagon. "Why did he leave the train?" she said. "Why would he do that?"

"They were in Crow country," Carrington said. "I suppose he thought it was safe."

"He had a brother in the Gallatin Valley. He should be notified."

"Yes," the colonel said, "it's being seen to. William's diary was found on his body. That will be sent to the brother as well. My son Jimmy will be upset by this. He and the Thomas boy were friends."

"Then don't tell him," Rose said. "At least not now. He doesn't have to know."

Carrington smiled as he reached for the letter. "One mustn't shield a child from the pain of life, Mrs. Reynolds, especially a boy. It makes him soft. You'll want to remember that when you and Lieutenant Reynolds have children of your own."

For the first time, Rose thought maybe Mark was right. Carrington was an ass. "Surely Jimmy could be spared just a bit of life's pain, Colonel," she said. "He's only six."

Carrington patted her shoulder. "You're upset,"

he said. "I'll leave you now, let you ladies get back to your work." Rose and Beth Curry watched him cross the twilit parade yard.

"Could he possibly be more patronizing?" Rose said with a frown.

"The colonel means well," Beth said, "but he doesn't understand people, he doesn't know what to say. Sam said it was like a kind of tone-deafness."

The night was very cold and the wind had teeth. Rose piled on every blanket they owned but still she could not get warm. How nice it would be, she thought, to have a man beside her, and she wished not for Mark, who had guard duty, but for Daniel Dixon. What was he doing now? Was he at the hospital or was he alone too, thinking of her?

The temperature dropped and the wind intensified. At midnight she heard the snap and boom of a tent collapsing, followed by loud curses. She pulled her blankets tighter, pitying those poor souls and praying her own tent would hold. Gradually she felt herself growing warmer and at last she slept. When she woke after daylight, there were four inches of fluffy snow on the ground. It was the snow, she realized, banking up around the base of her tent and blocking the wind, which finally made sleep possible.

It was gone by noon, melted by the hot September sun, but the snow inspired the men to work harder. Of the officers, only Carrington's and the bandmaster's quarters were finished. The enlisted men were in barracks, but these were crude shelters with dirt floors. One company, tired of living in mud, pooled their wages to buy lumber and nails from the quartermaster and laid a plank floor in one day.

The morning after the snow, Indians rode down on the miners who were still camped by the Big Piney. The soldiers, watching from the banquette, cheered as the miners fought them off, killing six. The attack occurred during guard mount and the band continued playing throughout, lending the bloody scene an air of unreality. It was like a dream, Rose thought, or a theater play.

George Grummond offered to lead a detachment in the miners' defense, but Carrington refused. "You'll have plenty of opportunities to fight Indians, Grummond," he said. "Best to learn the ropes first." Grummond was clearly disappointed but did not argue.

"He could be trouble, Colonel," Ten Eyck said.

"Why do you say that?"

"He has a reputation. He drinks."

Carrington looked at Ten Eyck with raised eyebrows and a slight smile. "And you, Tenodor? Isn't this a case of the pot accusing the kettle?"

Ten Eyck did not return the colonel's smile. "He borrows money from enlisted men."

"Does he? I'll look into that. If true, I'll put a stop to it."

After a pause, Ten Eyck said, "Colonel, did you know of Grummond's court-martial during the war—that he was found guilty of drunkenness while on duty and in the presence of the enemy?"

Carrington stroked his beard. This news reinforced his growing suspicions that Omaha had no real interest in his campaign. Was Cooke getting rid of troublemakers by sending them to him? Grummond came with a strong letter of recommendation but an officer often sang the praises of a subordinate he wanted shed of. "How do you know all this, Tenodor?" he said.

"My nephew served under Grummond in the Fourteenth Michigan for one year," Ten Eyck said. "At first, Rob admired him. George Grummond is no coward, no question of that, but he's also a hothead and a drunk. He once—while drunk—shot at a fellow officer."

"Your nephew witnessed this?"

"He did. He also saw Grummond pistol-whip a noncommissioned officer and shoot an unarmed civilian, an old man. When one of our surgeons tried to help the old fellow Grummond had the surgeon arrested."

"Is there more?" Carrington asked.

"At Kennesaw Mountain Grummond, drunk again, ordered his men to storm an entrenched enemy position. Our boys would've been massacred but Rob convinced him to withdraw his order. Grummond was court-martialed and found unfit to command. Rob had to testify."

"I wonder his career wasn't ended," Carrington said.

"Well, as I said, no one ever accused him of cowardice. And he performed well against Joe Johnston in North Carolina. That must be said."

"Have you mentioned these things to anyone?"

"No, sir, though he was publicly reprimanded. His history must be known."

"Maybe not. I didn't know of it. Keep all this to yourself for now, Tenodor. I need every officer I've got. Let's give him a chance to prove himself anew."

"Oh, he'll prove himself," Ten Eyck said. "Of that I have no doubt."

# Chapter Thirty

The Indians accelerated their campaign of terror attacking wood trains and logging camps almost daily. One morning four Sioux warriors surprised a six-man crew felling trees on Piney Island. The loggers raced for the safety of the blockhouse as the Indians flew out of the forest on their painted ponies but three men, working farther out, were caught in the open.

Two ran for the trees but Private Pat Smith tried for the blockhouse. Halfway there he was shot down by arrows, falling in the tall grass. A warrior ran to him, unsheathing his scalping knife. The men in the blockhouse fired at the Indian but did not hit him. They were forced to listen in horror to Smith's hoarse screams. At last they stopped and his comrades gave him up for dead.

The loggers were well armed and the Indians quit the attack. The two men who hid in the forest came out cautiously and ran to the blockhouse. They waited, quiet and afraid, expecting the Indians to return. After about twenty minutes they saw movement in the waist-high grass. One of the men raised his carbine.

"Wait," the corporal said, lowering his arm. "Don't shoot. I think it's Smith." Even as he spoke, the wounded soldier pulled himself into the clearing, inching forward on his side with arrows protruding from his chest and thigh. His head and face were black with blood.

"My God," the corporal said. He ran to Smith and dragged him back to the blockhouse, laying him on the dirt floor. His scalp was gone, leaving the top of his head raw and meaty, showing white patches of exposed skull. A flap of skin hung forward over one eye. "We've got to get him to the post."

"Hell, I don't want to try it, corporal, not with them Injuns around," a soldier said. "I say we wait for our relief. Smith's gonna die anyway. Just look at him."

Smith moaned, turning his bloody head from side to side.

"I said we're taking him back," the corporal said. "Ty, put him in the little wagon."

The corporal and two others drove the six miles to Fort Phil Kearny with Smith grinding his teeth and shaking under a woolen blanket. Dixon and assistant surgeon Edwin Reid met them at the gate.

As Dixon lifted Smith's head to give him water, he thought how young he was. Probably didn't shave but twice a week. How many boys and men had left this world with their eyes on his face, he wondered. Would this boy be next?

The surgeons carried Smith to the operating table. Oil lamps burned on either side and the window flaps were open to admit as much natural light as possible. Dixon examined the chest wound, tapping his fingers on Smith's bony chest. A frothy mixture of blood and air oozed from the hole. He unlocked the medicine cabinet and reached for a full bottle of whiskey. That was all he had to dull the boy's pain, no opium or laudanum. Someone had pilfered the supply.

"Drink all you can keep down," he said, "but take it slow." Smith nodded and, in a few deep gulps, downed about one-fourth of the bottle. The liquor worked quickly. Within minutes, Smith's trembling stopped and his body seemed to relax.

"I'm going to clean and dress your wounds now," Dixon said. "Try to keep still. It won't be easy, but it's important you try." Smith nodded, eyes closed.

He started with the chest wound. Blood had softened the sinew twine that bound the iron point so the shaft slid out easily but the barbed point held fast. The wound began to hemorrhage. Dixon probed with his finger to find the arrowhead's location, then widened the track with a long thin knife. As Reid threaded a needle with catgut, Dixon inserted a wire snare, encircled the loop around the iron point at its base and, with one strong pull, yanked it free. He dropped it in a tin basin where it landed with a cheerful clink. The arrowhead was a short blade, sharpened on both edges with hooked rear shoulders. It was surprisingly heavy, as if it had been made from an emigrant's fry pan. The small iron point in

Smith's thigh came out easily. Reid sutured this wound while Dixon turned his attention to the boy's head, grimacing as he unwound the dirty, blood-soaked bandage. He cleaned and irrigated the wound with a solution of zinc chloride before tucking the raw strip of loose flesh into place.

"I ain't gonna die, Doc," Smith said, startling Dixon, who had thought the boy asleep. "God spoke to me out there, after that Injun finished with me. He told me I was goin' home." Smith tried to open his eyes but they were buried in bruised and swollen flesh.

"Good," Dixon said. "Here, take more whiskey." He gave the boy the bottle and, after it took effect, reattached the flap of skin quickly, using a clean, continuous stitch. At the same time, Reid used tweezers to remove bits of splintered bone from the oozing hole in Smith's chest. When the suturing was done and the wounds were freshly bandaged, the surgeons moved the boy to the rear tent, a sort-of ward room, while an orderly spread piney sawdust under the operating table to absorb Smith's blood.

Dixon untied his bloody apron and stepped outside, where the young soldier's friends waited. He was surprised to see Rose among them, then he remembered Smith was Carl's groom and caretaker.

"Will he live?" the corporal said.

"Coin's still in the air," Dixon said. "We did all we could for him."

The men drifted away until only Rose remained. They faced each other in the fading light. "Rose," he said, "have you thought about what I said? Doesn't what happened to Smith today tell you anything? It's not too late."

"It is too late," she said. "Beth Curry and the boys left with the mail this morning. So even if I wanted to leave, I couldn't. Colonel Carrington doesn't have the men for another escort. But I don't want to go, so it doesn't matter."

A gust of wind blew a lock of hair into his eyes and Rose fought the impulse to lift her hand and push it back in place. He needs a haircut, she thought. He has no one to do these things for him. They stood looking at each other, not speaking, when Reid called to him. Dixon shook his head and went back in the tent.

Late that afternoon Brown returned from a patrol with nine Indians in tow. Among them was Two Moons, one of the Cheyenne chiefs who visited with Black Horse just after the regiment's arrival. He was so changed, so dirty and bedraggled, no one recognized him until he showed the identity papers Carrington had given him. Two Moons said Black Horse was dying in their camp in the mountains, where many others also were sick. The young men had joined Red Cloud's Sioux.

"We've come to ask the Little White Chief's permission to hunt in the valley of the Tongue River so we can bring food back to the sick and starving," Two Moons said. "Then I will take our people south and you will never see us again."

Carrington gave his approval and, over the objections of his officers, let the Indians camp overnight on the Big Piney. After dinner, he walked to the quartermaster's office where Brown and Grummond were playing cards. Brown had his boots up on his desk and did not lower them when his commanding officer entered.

"I want you to take bacon and coffee to the Indian camp tonight," Carrington said. "A bag of flour also."

Brown glanced at Grummond, who kept his eyes on his cards. "Are you sure, Colonel?" Brown said, finally lowering his feet. "Are you sure you want to be so hospitable after what happened to Smith this morning?"

"Those people had nothing to do with that," Carrington said irritably. "They are starving. It's an opportunity to show the White Father's generosity and compassion. Besides, it's the Christian thing to do."

Grummond spoke for the first time. "Our boys are looking for an opportunity too, sir, an opportunity to nail some red scalps to their doors."

Captain Ten Eyck knocked, then entered the office. "Pardon the interruption, sir, but Private Smith just died. I thought you should know. The men are—"

"Goddamn savages!" Grummond jumped to his feet. "Do you still want to give them bacon and coffee, Colonel? Maybe our wives could bake them a cake?"

Carrington paled though he spoke with a tone of finality. "I'm sorry about Smith, of course I am, but his death doesn't change anything. I say again, Two Moons and his people had nothing to do with it."

Ten Eyck cleared his throat. "I'm afraid our boys

think differently, sir. I saw some of them going over the wall as I was walking over here."

"What?" Carrington shouted. "Ten Eyck, get fifty men and meet me at the water gate. Brown, go with him. I'll get my sidearm and join you."

"I'll go with Brown," Grummond said.

"No, you will not," Carrington said. "You keep order here."

Grummond shrugged and took his coat from the wall. "Colonel," he said, "what makes you so sure those Indians weren't in on that raid this morning? They all look alike. Those papers could have been stolen."

"They are who they claim to be." Carrington's voice was becoming shrill. "And even if they weren't, what do you suggest? That I stand by and allow those Indians—the women and children—to be massacred? That I let my men dishonor themselves and the regiment? I am not John Chivington, Mr. Grummond, and this is not Sand Creek." Grummond gave him an exaggerated salute and went out the door, slamming it behind him.

Carrington ran to his house for his gun and joined Brown and Ten Eyck in the quartermaster's yard. Soon the officers and fifty armed men were marching down the grassy slope toward Little Piney Creek. A single fire burned on the small island where the Indians made their camp. The cold night air smelled of wood and tobacco smoke. As they neared the water a voice from the cottonwood scrub called out a warning.

"It's the colonel. Run for it!" Dozens of shadowy figures sprang from the brush and ran for the fort, some stumbling and falling in the darkness.

"Stop!" Ten Eyck shouted, without effect. Carrington repeated the command but still, no one stopped. Finally he raised his revolver and fired twice into the air. Only then did the runners halt. Ten Eyck, holding a torch, ordered them to attention and gradually ninety men stood in a ragged line. Carrington walked slowly before them, looking each in the eye. The orange torchlight lit the faces of some of his best men, including several band members. Carrington stopped at the center, with his hands clasped behind his back.

"I'm shocked and disappointed by what almost happened here," he said. "Were you prepared to murder innocent women and children? Is this the kind of men you are? Do you realize the disgrace such an action would have brought to this post and the Eighteenth Infantry?"

A silence followed broken only by the crackling of the Indians' campfire. They watched silently, wrapped in their blankets.

"It was because of Smith, sir," one of the men said. "Because of what they did to Pat. We can't let them get away with that!"

Carrington shook his head. "Ten Eyck, take these men to their barracks and see to it they remain there until morning." As they trudged up the hill Carrington returned to his quarters. Margaret met him at the door.

"Were any officers among the mob?" she said.

"No."

"Thank God." Her shoulders sank with relief. She was afraid the mutiny had come. "Come to bed, Henry," she said in a gentle voice. "You look exhausted."

In the morning Two Moon's Indians were gone, leaving only a cold fire. Cazeau's widow and her children, including the beautiful Jane, left with them. Rose found a small deerskin pouch outside their tent. Inside was one of Jane's delicate shell earrings.

# Chapter Thirty-one

The October mornings were so cold Rose had to break a film of ice on the water bucket before washing. There was no traffic on the Bozeman Road, no birds in the air, no fish flashing in the streams. Other than the busy soldiers, all life seemed to have come to a standstill, as if saving strength for the ordeal to come.

Tension mounted along with the cold. Although the men were in barracks, most of the officers still were living in tents. Some essential structures, including the hospital, were barely started. To make things worse, lurid accounts of Indian depredations regularly appeared in the eastern press, delivered in the mails weeks after publication. Newspapers printed false reports of women snatched from the arms of their men and tortured. Cooke complained of these stories in a letter to Carrington.

"It is time—indeed, well past time!—to strike a blow against the red man!" Cooke wrote. "Are you capable of this, Carrington, or should I find another commanding officer?"

In his response, Carrington said he was willing and eager to punish the Indians but lacked the tools to do so. "I must have more men. Where are the two companies of cavalry promised me? I will not endanger the lives of my troops."

Shortly after this angry exchange of letters, a cloud of gray dust appeared in the southern sky. Carrington and Ten Eyck rode out to explore. Instead of reinforcements, they found an immense cattle herd driven by a sunburned, trail-hardened man who introduced himself as Nelson Story. A successful gold miner, Story was returning to his Virginia City home with one thousand Texas longhorns he bought in Fort Worth to sell to the beef-hungry miners of the Gallatin Valley.

"We'd like to camp by your fort tonight, Colonel," he said. "We had Sioux trouble just south of Reno on the Dry Fork of the Powder. They shot two of my boys—wounded, not killed—and made off with twenty head. We went after 'em and got the steers back, all but the one they were eatin'."

"How many Indians were there?" Carrington said.

"Six, and we killed them all. It was them or us. You know, I been up here three years and I never killed an Indian before. Never even shot at one, before this trip."

Carrington shifted his eyes from Story to his beef herd. "I'm sorry to hear it. Things are bad enough already. That won't help."

Story shrugged. "I did what I had to."

"I'm afraid you'll find the trip from here to Virginia City even more difficult," Carrington said. "You'd be wise to sell your beeves to our quartermaster, Captain Brown."

The last mail brought news of Brown's promotion and reassignment to Fort Laramie. Despite his shortage of officers, Carrington would not be sorry to see him go.

"Thanks, Colonel," Story said, "but I know what the army will pay and I also know I can get four or five times that in Bozeman City. Anyhow, we'll make it. My men have new rifles, Remington breechloaders. Just let us stay the night by your fort and we'll move on in the morning."

Carrington stroked his beard. "How many men do you have?"

"Twenty-five. I left my two wounded back at Reno."

"Well, I'm sorry, Mr. Story, but I can't let you pass without at least forty armed men." He raised his hand when Story started to protest. "Army regulations. You'll have to wait for another train before moving on."

Story studied Carrington with cool blue eyes. "October's half gone, Colonel Carrington. You and I both know there probably won't be another train this season. We'll be snowed in."

Carrington raised his hands, palms up. "As I said, there's nothing I can do. Of course, you could lessen your risk by selling to my quartermaster today. As to your other request, bad news there too, I'm afraid. I can't let you camp by the fort. Forage is thin enough, our animals need what little remains. You'll have to move off a few miles. Captain Ten Eyck will direct you to a place where you'll find water and grazing."

Story gave a short laugh. "And plenty of Sioux too."

Carrington smiled. "Your men have their Remingtons, don't they?"

Story slapped his hat against his leg producing a cloud of dust. "Colonel, I believe you are trying to strong-arm me into selling my beeves."

"Think what you like."

"I'm not liking it."

Carrington said nothing.

"I'm a fair man, Colonel," Story said, putting his hat on, "and generally a law-abiding one. I'll wait a day or two, but I've got ten thousand dollars invested in those longhorns, I drove them all the way from Texas, and I'll be damned if I'm going to let the Sioux or the U.S. Army stop me from getting them to Bozeman City."

Carrington kept close tabs on the cow camp, sending Ten Eyck to check on them twice a day. During one of these visits Story requested a surgeon for his men. Dixon accompanied Ten Eyck on his next trip and lanced a boil, cleaned several lacerations, and pulled a rotten tooth. After the men were seen to, Dixon and Story spent more than an hour drinking coffee sweetened with a bit of whiskey and talking. When it came time to leave, Dixon would not accept any pay.

"You're a good man," Story said, as they shook hands. "I hope you'll think about my offer, Dixon. I believe you'll find a golden chance up in Bozeman. Reflect on it."

The next morning Ten Eyck found Story and his outfit vanished, leaving only a note on a wooden stake:

*October 22, 1866. Carrington, I waited long enough. No hard feelings on my part. Nelson Story.*

Carrington crumpled the paper and threw it in the fire. Within the hour he drafted new orders requiring all civilian travelers be quartered inside the stockade while waiting to move on. *All gates and wickets will be locked at retreat,* he wrote, *except that at the quartermaster's gate which will be closed at tattoo and then only will be opened by the officer of the day or sergeant of the guard in their line of duty or for good cause.* Any soldier absent from his quarters after tattoo would be arrested, confined, and possibly court-martialed.

The new regulations were not well received by the men or the officers. "I'm beginning to feel more like a prisoner than a cavalryman," Grummond said to Brown in front of the men.

By the end of October most living quarters were complete. With its wooden floors and plastered log walls, Rose's three-room cabin felt like a palace after six months of living under canvas. Mark bought her a bolt of turkey-red fabric from which she made curtains and coverings for their trunks and folding table. For the bed and chairs she used a pale yellow cretonne patterned with tiny white flowers. The effect was cheerful and bright and pleased her very much. Although Mark complained about the "womanish" look of the place, Rose sensed that he too was happy with it.

She waited a few days for the green pine floor-boards to dry before unpacking her prized possession, a thick woolen Brussels rug left her by Grandmother Alice. Since childhood, she had loved its intricately woven floral patterns in deep jewel tones of ruby, lapis, and jade. She spread it on the floor of the front room, stood back and considered, then rolled it up and returned it to its former place under her bed. Its elegant beauty was out of place in a home where corn and grain sacks made more practical and effective carpeting. Muddy boots would ruin it anyhow. No, Rose felt it luxury enough to have a full-size bed to sleep in, glass in the windows, and the carpenter's promise of window boxes in the spring. She looked forward to buying geraniums from Judge Fitch and coaxing them along till the boxes were brimming with fat, gaudy blossoms of pink and red. Her eye ached for color. What she wouldn't give for a vase of fresh flowers on her kitchen table.

At the end of the month Lieutenant James Bradley returned from escorting Colonel Hazen to Fort Smith and points north. Bradley looked years older than when he left two months before. Four of the twenty-six men who went with him did not come back. Three deserted just days after they left Phil Kearny and Jim Brannan had been killed by Indians, probably Blackfoot.

Bradley also brought bad news about Jim Beckwourth. The Mulatto of the Plains left Fort Smith in September and struck out for the Crow villages where he hoped to learn about Red Cloud's activities. But just days after his arrival, Beckwourth died in the lodge of Iron Bull, a trusted Crow chieftain who carried messages between forts Smith and Phil Kearny.

"Some say he was poisoned by a jealous husband," Bradley said, "but Iron Bull denies it and I don't believe it either. Beckwourth was a horn, true enough, but he was already sick when he left Fort Smith, bleeding every day from the nose. My guess is years of hard living finally caught up with him."

Carrington had expected Bridger to return with Bradley but the old mountain man's rheumatism was bad and he was unable to make the trip. Despite this, and the deaths of Brannan and Beckwourth, Carrington's spirits were buoyed by Bradley's return and the twenty-two men he brought with him. Each one of them would be needed for what was coming.

The Indians were a constant presence on the hilltops, flashing mirrors by day and burning signal fires at night. To relieve the tension, Carrington declared a two-day holiday at the end of October to celebrate the raising of the post's giant flag. With a thirty-six-foot fly and twenty-foot hoist, it would be the first full-size flag to fly in the Dakota Territory. Two carpenters, both former seamen, built a flagpole that stood 124 feet when the two pieces, top mast and main, were joined together. They painted the pole black, planted it in the middle of the parade, then built a bandstand around it. To make sure things would come off without a hitch, the two spent most of the day before the ceremony reeving and testing the halyards.

Everyone welcomed the change in routine and the dancing and feasting that would follow the ceremony. Each officer's wife polished her husband's saber and epaulettes, adjusted the ostrich plumes on his dress hat, and smoothed the creases from his crimson sash before seeing to her own dress. Then there was food to prepare. The women of Fort Phil Kearny were proud and competitive cooks. Mrs. Bisbee made three "Phil Kearny mince pies," a recipe of her own invention using beef hearts, dried apples, raisins, and sweetened vinegar. Sallie Horton baked puddings and sauces while Captain Ten Eyck's serving woman, Susan, prepared her specialty, venison and buffalo sausage.

Rose volunteered to make a three-layer stack cake, then immediately regretted it when Jerusha took sick and was unable to help. An inexperienced and uninterested cook, Rose was counting on Jerusha's expertise with the wood-fired stove. Pine kindling burned hot and needed constant adjusting. More than once it had reduced Rose's breads and cakes to bits of smoking charcoal. She was determined, however, to succeed this time.

She was already at work when reveille sounded. After starting the fire she set about improving the salty butter Judge Fitch sold in his store, which had to be tempered with hot water before it would suit. The flour also was of very poor quality, cakey and old and peppered with mouse droppings. She had to sift it three times before it was usable, then carefully measured and added the remaining ingredients to make a batter; sugar, salt, two rare and precious eggs, a cup of equally rare and precious milk from the post's only remaining milch cow, baking soda, and a splash of vanilla. After putting the three pans in the oven she made a paste of dried apples, molasses, brandy water, and raisins to spread on the top and between the layers.

Her careful attention to the difficult oven paid off. The layers came out even and fully risen, baked to a fine golden brown. Gingerly, as if they were made of glass, she put them on iron trivets and stood back from the table to admire her work, wishing for a female relative—a mother, grandmother, or, best of all, daughter—to share her triumph.

The autumn day was sunny and warm. At noon the men, in full dress uniforms, marched in companies to the parade ground and stood at attention before the platform where the officers, their families, and a select few civilian employees were seated. Colonel Carrington walked to the edge of the platform.

"Order arms!" The men swung their muzzle-loading rifles onto their shoulders with a loud rattle. "Parade rest!" Quiet fell as Carrington took sheets of folded paper from the inner pocket of his jacket and adjusted his reading glasses. He cleared his throat:

"Officers and men! Three and one-half months ago stakes were driven for the now-perfected outlines of Fort Philip Kearny. Aggressive Indians threatened to exterminate the command. Our advent cost us blood. Men have died to redeem our pledge to never yield one foot of advance, but to guarantee a safe passage for all who seek a home in the lands beyond.

"Fifteen weeks have passed, varied by many skirmishes and by both day and night alarms, but that pledge holds good. In the pine tracts or in the hay fields, on picket or general guard duty, no one has failed to find a constant exposure to some hostile shaft and to feel that a cunning adversary was watching every chance to harass and kill. And yet, that pledge holds good . . ."

Rose's mind drifted. Where was he? She looked again and this time found Daniel smoking a cigarette by the hospital tent.

By now several officers on the platform were dozing in the midday sun. Carrington droned on but Rose, sitting on the platform between Mark and Harry Carrington, found it impossible to listen. The Colonel was a good man, Yale-educated, with a broad knowledge of military history. Why was he so ineffective? Why was he so easy to ignore while another man took charge of a room the moment he walked in? Was Mark that kind of man? Once, she thought so, now she was unsure. And Dixon? Yes, in his own quiet way, he was.

A mirror flashed on the ridge across the Big Piney and there was an answering flash from the Sullivant Hills. What did the Indians make of this strange blue-coat ceremony? Rose wondered.

Carrington's speech was already too long but he went on for another twenty minutes before asking Chaplain White to conclude with a prayer. Finally the drums rolled, the band broke into "The Star Spangled Banner," and the garrison flag went up the flagpole. There was no wind and it hung limp on the pole's black surface. Still, a lump formed in Rose's throat as she thought of the men—Royal Spicer, William and Charley Thomas, Patrick Smith, Ridgway Glover, all the others—who died to bring it here. Did they give their lives for a just cause? What was a flag, after all, but a symbol of ownership, and what right had they to claim ownership of this land? She wished she shared Chaplain White's confidence that the Lord preferred his white children to his red ones.

Back in her cabin, Rose dressed for the evening's gala. She'd decided on a two-piece silk traveling suit, trim and well cut, midnight blue in color with a black silk braid on the cuffs and mandarin collar. Finally, she took from her trunk a maroon velvet pouch that was tucked away under her linen underthings. Inside was the rope of pearls her Uncle Randolph had given her as a wedding gift, a string of large, perfectly matched pearls with a silver, mirror-like luster. The necklace was long enough to twice encircle her slender neck. She had not worn the pearls since leaving St. Louis, and she had forgotten how beautiful they were. Opening her collar, she studied her reflection in Mark's shaving mirror, feeling the pearls' cool smoothness against her skin. She was too thin and had too many freckles, but still, she was pleased with the way she looked. Her hair was almost shoulder length now, and the paleness of the pearls enhanced her complexion, even though it was darker than it should be. A glance down at her feet, however, brought Rose firmly back to earth. She wore the same worn-out kid shoes with curled toes she had worn every day since leaving Nebraska Territory. They were the only pair she had.

It was dusk when she and Mark left the cabin. The post was bathed in soft red light. Couples greeted each other as they crossed the parade ground to Carrington's quarters and, for this one evening, all fear and thoughts of Indians dissolved and Rose could almost believe she was back in St. Louis, walking by the mansions of Portland Place. Margaret and her sons had decorated their home with wreaths and ropes of fragrant pine. Inside, garlands with red berries framed the doors and windows and the walls were draped with swags of colorful ribbon. Margaret's best embroidered white cloth covered the food table, which was laden with delicacies. Rose's tall stack cake finished even better than she dared hope. In the center of the table Margaret's cut glass bowl, filled with red wine punch, sparkled like a giant ruby in the candlelight. The band's string musicians played softly in a corner.

Rose and Mark joined a group that included Frances Grummond. She looked like an overstuffed French confection, Rose thought, in a dress of pink silk and white netting caught up at the waist and shoulders with artificial pink roses. She gave Mark a dimpled smile and Rose understood that Frances would happily take Rose's place in bed that night.

Many women felt that way, she was sure, but Rose no longer cared. It would do no good to lie to herself. Had this happened because of Daniel Dixon or would her feelings for Mark have eroded anyway? Was this permanent or would her love for Mark return? She wished she had some way of knowing.

Mark excused himself to join the men smoking cigars by an open window. Grummond and Brown, she noticed, appeared to be already in their cups. Dixon was on the far side of the room talking to Carrington and Sam Horton. Rose thought Carrington looked angry.

"You look lovely tonight." Startled, she turned to see Harry Carrington offering her a glass of punch.

"Thank you, Harry," she said. "You read my mind." The wine and brandy punch was syrupy but she drank it down at once anyway, feeling its warming effect immediately. "Delicious," she said, smiling at him.

"That's a pretty dress you're wearing," Harry said. He was unusually bold, having helped himself to a large glass of punch when no one was looking.

"Thank you," she said, trying not to smile at the cherry redness of his face, "but it isn't right for evening. I wish I had something fancier."

"Oh, it doesn't matter." Harry soldiered on. "You're by far the prettiest woman in the room."

"I agree." Daniel Dixon stood behind her. She had not heard him approach. "By far the prettiest," he said with a smile.

Rose laughed. "You two will give me a big head."

Her heart was thumping wildly as she tried to think of something charming and witty to say. It had been so long since she'd talked to him, there was much she wanted to tell him, but circumstances weren't right. They were never right. "Did you enjoy the ceremony?" It was lame, she knew, but nothing else came to her. "The colonel worked very hard on his speech, Margaret said."

"I'm afraid I didn't hear it," Dixon said.

"It was too long," Harry said. His words came out in a punch-fueled rush. "And it was boring. No one was listening."

Rose looked at him with amused surprise, then changed the subject. "So, what were you and the colonel talking about just now, Dr. Dixon? He looked upset."

Dixon fixed his hazel eyes on her. He was not smiling now.

"I gave Sam Horton my resignation today. When my contract's up next month I'm going north, to the Gallatin Valley. I've been thinking about it for a while."

"You did what?" Rose felt as if she'd been kicked in the stomach. "You can't mean it."

"Do you remember Nelson Story, the cattleman who came through a few weeks ago? He wants me to go halves in a dry goods store up in Bozeman City. He thinks I should open a medical practice there too, and I've decided to do it. Bozeman sounds like a good place to start over. Sometimes a person has to do that, Rose, admit a mistake and start over. There's no sin in it."

She could not believe he would leave her. He couldn't, not now. She heard a woman's loud laughter. Rose looked across the room, seeing Frances Grummond lean toward Mark, touching his arm with her gloved hand.

"Life is short, Rose," Dixon said, calling her back. "Too short to postpone happiness. If there's anything these last five years have taught me, it's that. You and I could be happy together and you know I'm right. Come with me to Bozeman. You won't be sorry."

Harry stood as if nailed to the floor. He felt sick, and not because he had drunk too much punch. His two favorite people, the people he most admired in all the world, were considering something unthinkable. It would ruin them, certainly it would ruin her! He looked at Rose, and she also appeared stunned. She and Dixon were in their own separate world. They had forgotten about him.

A woman screamed. On the far side of the room George Grummond drunkenly grabbed his wife by the arm, spilling red punch down the front of her pink dress. He said something to Mark and though Harry could not make out his words their meaning was obvious. The room went silent; even the musicians stopped playing.

Mark smiled and spoke to Grummond in a low voice. Grummond hesitated, then threw back his head with a surprised shout of laughter. The tension broke and the musicians struck up a waltz. Dixon took Rose in his arms and led her onto the dance floor, moving her about the room with an easy grace. He was a fine dancer, another of his many talents. As Harry watched them, and just for that moment, he hated the surgeon with a passion that was equaled in intensity only by his love for Rose.

# Chapter Thirty-two

Jerusha died one November morning following the miscarriage of a child. No one, not even Rose, knew of the pregnancy. Jerusha went to her grave without naming the father, despite questioning from Sam Horton and even Colonel Carrington himself.

"Might it have been our George?" Carrington wondered as the family sat at the dinner table. "He denies it, of course, but he lies."

"No, it wasn't George," Margaret said. "I'm quite sure of it."

Harry was too. He remembered the day George went calling on Jerusha with a bouquet of wild-flowers and how she laughed at him and sent him away. Harry and Jimmy, watching secretly, were embarrassed for him.

"Well, who then?" Carrington said. "Reynolds's striker? What's his name—Timson?"

"No, I can't imagine that either," Margaret said. Despite the sad circumstances, she could not suppress a smile at the thought of "Timid" Timson trying to woo the ferocious Jerusha.

"Do you boys have any idea?" Carrington said, looking at Harry. "Have you seen anything? Heard any gossip?"

"No, sir." In fact, however, Harry did remember a night, some weeks before, when, on his way to the sinks, he saw a man leaving Jerusha's tent. He thought he recognized him but did not want to believe it and therefore said nothing.

Brown, officer of the day, ordered that Jerusha be buried next to the post cemetery in a burial ground set aside for Negroes, Indians, and Chinamen. When he learned of his, Mark flew into a rage.

"That woman was with me during the meanest days of the war," he said. "She cooked meals for me and my men with bullets flying around her like bees and never complained. Not once. I won't let her be cast aside."

Brown tried to calm him. "I understand your feelings, Reynolds. I'd probably feel the same way if I were you. She was a fine woman, I'm sure, and handsome too, for her kind. But I can't do what you ask. The men wouldn't stand for it."

Mark took the matter directly to Carrington, whose abolitionist views were well-known. He overruled Brown, demanding that Jerusha be buried in the post cemetery at the base of Pilot Hill. Despite Brown's claims, not one of the men objected, though few mourners attended the service. Halfway through it started to rain. Droplets driven by a mean wind cut into the skin like shards of glass. Chaplain White read from his Bible a little faster.

Throughout the service Harry stole glances at Rose, even when he was supposed to be praying. Her face was pale and expressionless though Mark wept openly. Toward the end of the ceremony, a spontaneous cheer erupted from the stockade as the Pilot Hill sentry signaled the approach of a long train. Soon a column of uniformed horsemen appeared on the Fort Reno Road. At last, the cavalry companies had arrived. White hurried through the last of the service so Jerusha's mourners could join the throng gathering at the quartermaster's gate.

The newcomers were sixty-three men of the Second Cavalry, Company C, under the command of Captain William Judd Fetterman. Three additional officers came with him: Lieutenant Horatio S. Bingham, a round-faced farmer's son from Minnesota; Major Henry Almstedt, the officer who replaced the disgraced Ranald Henry as paymaster for the Department of the Platte; and Captain James Powell, a well-respected veteran who carried two rifle balls in his body, a souvenir of his service with Sherman in Georgia.

Fetterman was warmly welcomed by his fellow officers, especially Bisbee, who embraced him like a long-lost brother. They fought together in Tennessee and later with Sherman in Georgia and the Carolinas. Even the enlisted men lined up to shake Fetterman's hand for they knew him as a humane officer, one who was concerned with the needs of his men.

Harry remembered Fetterman too. He met him in

Columbus at the start of the war when Fetterman was an ambitious young officer learning the ropes at Colonel Carrington's School for Instruction for regimental officers. Harry was only eight years old at the time and did not expect the distinguished officer to remember him.

"Harry Carrington!" Fetterman said, clasping his hand. "My God, son, you've become a man." Despite the cold rain, Fetterman's hand was warm and dry, his smile genuine. "Why, you're almost as tall as I am," he said. "Finally growing into those feet of yours. So, how old are you now? Seventeen? Eighteen?" He winked at Captain Powell.

Harry was pleased though he knew he was being humbugged. "Thirteen, sir. Just turned."

"You don't say! Well, you look older. Still planning to become an army man, I hope?"

"Well, actually I'm thinking about training as a surgeon." This was true but Harry had never said it before.

"A sawbones?'" Fetterman shuddered. "No glory in that, lad, standing up to your knees in gore all day. No, Harry, I see you at the head of a company of cavalry, waving your saber over your head while your enemy turns tail and skedaddles."

Powell laughed. "Sounds like Custer."

"Bah," Fetterman said, "Custer's a rooster with his nose up Phil Sheridan's ass. No, sir, our man Harry, here, will be the real thing. Tell you what—tomorrow morning we'll go riding. You can show me around. What do you say?"

"I'd like that, sir." Harry was not about to tell

Captain Fetterman his parents wouldn't allow him outside the stockade. Surely they would make an exception in this case and if not, he might go anyway. After all, he was thirteen now and too old to be pushed around.

As it turned out, Fetterman did not come for him in the morning. Harry was disappointed but he knew the new captain had many demands on his time. The officers sought him out and the enlisted men seemed to regard him as a kind of savior. Within days of his arrival, Harry started hearing talk that Fetterman would take command of Fort Phil Kearny and Powell would go north to replace Kinney at Fort C. F. Smith.

"Is it true?" Harry said. He and Margaret sat in the kitchen eating a midday meal of venison stew. She hesitated.

"Well, it's true the War Department plans to create a new regiment of infantry," she said. "General Cooke wrote to your father about this some time ago. All the units here at Phil Kearny will be part of that new regiment but whether Captain Fetterman commands remains to be seen. It seems he expects to."

Harry was surprised and angry. "What about Father?" he said. "Where will we go? Why is Cooke doing this?" Harry did not want to leave Fort Phil Kearny, especially now that Dixon was leaving. Rose might need him—for what he wasn't sure—but she might. Not only that, he could not bear the thought of going back to gray and gloomy Columbus. Not after living here, in this open country with its towering mountains and endless skies. True, he was confined to the fort now but that was only temporary. The Indian threat wouldn't last forever, he was sure of that, and then he and Rose could ride for miles, over the hills and through the forests.

"We'll go wherever we're sent," Margaret said. "We are army. Still, I must say one would think Sherman and Cooke could show a bit more gratitude."

Her mouth compressed into a fine line and Harry knew the conversation was over. After dinner he helped the men spread red gravel on the walkways around and through the parade ground. Mined from the sandstone bluffs near Lake De Smet, the rock got its brick-red color from iron oxides in the soil and brought a cheery bit of color to the garrison.

His mood improved as he worked in the cold November sun. Already he was stronger than some of the soldiers and growing stronger every day. Sometimes he thought the happiest men in the regiment were the carpenters, laborers, and smiths, the fellows who worked in the fresh air and sunshine from dawn until dusk and then slept like the dead. They didn't worry about politics, promotions, and the stupid stories newspapermen wrote. They weren't at the mercy of ungrateful generals.

Despite the cold, Harry was sweating and his mouth was dry as cotton. He dropped his shovel and walked to the water barrel by the headquarters building. The water was sweet and cold and he filled his cup again. As he drank he heard Fetterman's voice from his father's open office window.

"After dark we'll hobble eight or ten mules between the Big Piney and the main gate. Then Brown,

Grummond, and I will take fifty men and hide in the scrub. When the Indians come for the bait, we'll open up on them. Simple as that. I'm surprised it hasn't been done before."

Harry peered in the window to see Fetterman and Brown standing before his father's desk.

"No disrespect, Captain Fetterman," Carrington said, "but you've been here what, two days? The Indians don't fight like Confederates. They don't behave as you'd expect them to. What you propose is dangerous. I won't allow it."

Fetterman answered impatiently. "I may be new to the frontier, Colonel, but I know combat." He did not say, "Unlike you," but he may as well have, Harry thought. "Moreover, I know the men of the Eighteenth Infantry and what they can do. A single company of regulars could whip a thousand Indians and a full regiment could whip the entire array of hostile tribes. Why, with eighty men I could ride through the whole Sioux nation!"

"He's right," Brown said. "It's high time we show them something."

A long quiet followed. Harry sensed his father was backing down and his next words confirmed it. "If I permit this, Fetterman, you must promise to exercise the utmost caution. If the Indians flee, do not pursue them over the ridge. This is important. I'm short men already. You must do nothing to diminish my forces even further."

"Agreed," Fetterman said. "If—that is, *when*—the Indians run we won't go after them."

"Very well," Carrington said. "I will prepare the

howitzers personally. This fight—if it comes and I'm not convinced it will—must take place within range of our cannon. Again, do not, under any circumstances, pursue them. Is that clear?"

"Yes, sir," Fetterman said. "Completely."

Within an hour, every man, woman, and child in the post knew of Fetterman's plan and most, including Harry, planned to watch the action. He passed the early evening hours playing solitaire with a sticky, worn deck. At midnight he climbed to the observation deck on top of the headquarters building where his father and Ten Eyck were waiting, field glasses in hand. Fetterman and his men already were hidden in the cottonwood thicket next to the Big Piney and the hobbled mules grazed nearby. It was a cloudless night with a bright moon that flashed on polished gunmetal and, occasionally, the flat lenses of a soldier's eyeglasses.

"I believe Captain Fetterman underestimates our opponent," Carrington said. Ten Eyck grunted in agreement.

The temperature dropped as the hours passed. Harry froze, even in his thick woolen coat and buffalo mittens with the fur on the inside. He pitied the poor men in the thicket so close to the water where surely it was even colder. The hours passed without incident. After what seemed an eternity, pale blue fingers of light reached across the horizon. If the Indians were going to strike they would do it now, in that half-formed moment between darkness and daylight when man and beast begin to let down after an anxious, watchful night. But the dawn came cold and gray and quiet. No Indians appeared. After another thirty minutes, Fetterman's men straggled out of the scrub and headed back to the fort.

"I told him it wouldn't work," Carrington said with a small smile. "He should have listened to me." The Colonel and Ten Eyck climbed down the stairs, leaving Harry alone on the platform. Suddenly he felt an anticipatory tingle, as if he were standing in the wind that runs before a storm. Harry was first to spot the Sioux horsemen, led by two warriors—a slight, fair-haired warrior and a giant—as they swooped down from the Sullivant Hills to stampede the cattle herd of civilian James Wheatley. They made off with all his animals as the hobbled mules grazed peacefully beside the Big Piney.

# Chapter Thirty-three

Jim Bridger returned from Fort Smith with Yellow Face, an English-speaking Crow warrior, and sobering news about the growing number of hostiles in the Tongue River Valley.

"The village is so big it takes half the day to ride through it," Yellow Face told Carrington and his officers. "Red Cloud has called in all his Sioux brothers—the Sissetons, Oglalas, Hunkpapas—and also his friends the Arapaho and Cheyenne. He even asked my people to put aside our bad feelings for the Sioux and join him, but we would not. 'No matter,' Red Cloud said. 'I have enough fighting men to shut down the white man's road and starve the fort soldiers. Then when the bluecoats are weak with hunger my warriors will descend on them like locusts and wipe them all out.' That's what he told to my relatives."

"Which post is he talking about?" Carrington said. "This or Fort Smith?"

"Both."

Brown laughed. "I just hope he tries it soon. I leave for Laramie next month and I don't want to go without a scalp—Red Cloud's, I hope."

Carrington, seated at his desk, tented his fingers before his mouth.

"I doubt the Indians could close the Bozeman Road," he said, "but even if they did, we've got supplies enough to last us through the winter."

Fetterman jumped to his feet, knocking over his chair. "For God's sake, Colonel, why are we here?" He looked around at his fellow officers, as if seeking their support. "Did we come all this way to build a fort and hide in it? We must go after them. We must act!"

The room went quiet but for the tick of the grandfather clock and the clang of an orderly's shovel as he emptied stove cinders in a bucket. Carrington and Fetterman looked at each other, Fetterman beside his fallen chair and Carrington still seated at his desk. Bridger watched with a glint of amusement while Yellow Face kept his eyes on the floor.

Mark Reynolds broke the silence. "I agree with Captain Fetterman, Colonel. We must strike a blow but not immediately. First, we need to start drilling the men regularly and practicing battalion formations. Simple target practice—they've had none. Ammunition was too short at one time but now we have plenty. We must begin."

Carrington got up and walked around to the front

of his desk until he and Fetterman were only inches apart. Fetterman was the taller man and Carrington had to look up at him. "Of course I will engage the Indians," he said, "but on my terms and only when the time is right. As commanding officer, I alone will determine that. And I tell every man in this room that my first priority is to ensure that this post is secure and that every man, woman, and child is provided with comfortable winter quarters. I am fully aware of the need for drill and target practice, Mr. Reynolds, and I will order it when appropriate. This meeting is over. You are excused. All of you, return to your duty. Bridger, you and Yellow Face stay with me. I want to hear more about this village."

Fetterman left without righting his chair, Grummond at his heels.

The next morning Sioux attacked the wood train on its way to Piney Island. Escorting officers Fetterman, Bisbee, and Ten Eyck were surprised as they watered their horses. They ordered their frightened men to take shelter in the brush and return fire. An eighteen-year-old bugler at the rear of the column heard the shooting and turned his horse back to the fort. He galloped through the gates shouting that every man in the wood train had been killed.

Mrs. Bisbee, hearing this news, collapsed on the parade lawn. She was a heavy woman and her companions, Rose and Margaret Carrington, struggled to lift and carry her to her cabin. Margaret sent Jimmy for a surgeon. He returned with Sam Horton, who took the distraught woman's pulse, prescribed tea and comfort, then hurried back to the hospital tent for the wounded he expected to begin arriving any minute.

Rose made tea. Mrs. Bisbee was not a tidy housekeeper. Breakfast dishes sat unwashed on the table and oatmeal had turned to glue in a pan on the stove. Rose tossed kindling onto the coals, put a kettle of water on to boil, and searched for a few clean mugs. She went about these tasks automatically, as if sleepwalking. Was this the day it all came to smash? Had the Indians finally decided to overrun the hated soldier fort? If so, then she'd made sorry use of her short time on Earth. She'd leave no children to mourn her, no lasting accomplishments, no record to show she had ever drawn breath. She was disappointed in herself, disgusted she had wasted so much time and energy on things that did not matter. If she lived, she would do things differently. And if it was indeed her time to die, she prayed it would not be painful.

She heard the thunder of running horses and pushed aside the dingy muslin curtain. Rescue riders were racing through the quartermaster's gates. Mark was on Carl, digging his spurs in the old gelding's sides and vigorously applying the crop. Rose knew Carl would not be able to keep up with the other horses, though he could well die trying. How dare Mark use Carl in that way? He was her horse—the men had given Carl to her. She threw open the door and started running to the quartermaster's yard, thinking she would call him back. But after a few steps she stopped. What was she thinking? Men's lives were at stake and there were precious few horses left. Of course Carl must go. And what kind of woman worried more for her horse than her husband? She turned and went back into Mrs. Bisbee's dingy kitchen.

The kettle was boiling. Rose made the tea, then carried a tray to the back room, where Mrs. Bisbee lay sobbing on the bed. Her toddler son, Gene, played quietly in a corner, undisturbed by his mother's condition. Margaret sat beside her, holding her hand. After pouring the tea, Rose took a chair by the window. She looked to the empty quartermaster's yard where the corporal of the guard was closing the gate. What if Mark did not come back? she thought. Is that what she wanted?

She looked toward the hospital tent where she saw Daniel Dixon tying on a surgeon's apron. How sick he must be of blood, pain, and death, she thought. He'd seen little else the past five years. She wanted to run to him, kiss him full on the mouth, and say yes, she would go to Bozeman. Yes, she would be his lover and companion, maybe someday his wife. Yes, they would invent fresh lives for themselves and perhaps, God willing, create new lives as well. Yes to all of it. Was it too late?

After more than an hour's wait, the rescue riders appeared on the wood road followed by the logging party. Despite the bugler's frenzied alarm, no one had been killed in the attack or even wounded. Fetterman grinned as he rode through the gate, pointing with a gloved hand to the garrison flag, which Carrington had lowered to half-mast.

"Hello, Alex!" Fetterman called to Lieutenant

Wands. "Sorry, there's no captaincy open after all. I guess you'll have to wait a while longer for your second bar!"

Mark came in riding double behind Bisbee. His face was bloody and his clothes were muddy and torn. Rose, watching from the Bisbee's cabin door, went to him.

"Where's Carl?" she said.

Mark slid to the ground, brushing dried mud from his jacket. "Lying in the Big Piney with my bullet in his brain!" he said. "Dammit to hell! How are we supposed to fight Indians with horses like that!"

"What happened?" Rose said. She felt sick.

"That miserable bone rack broke a leg climbing out of the creek and fell on me. Nearly broke my leg too!" Mark touched his forehead, then examined his fingers, sticky with blood. "He must've kicked me, dammit. I put him out of his misery. Should have done it long ago."

Rose pictured Carl lying by the water, alone, food for the wolves and carrion birds. He was a great old soul, loyal and capable of strong feeling. Her eyes filled when she remembered the way he would lift his head at the sound of her voice, then daintily pick his way across the muddy corral to nuzzle her and let her stroke his neck.

Mark laughed. "Are you crying? Oh, that's rich. Here we are, forgotten by the world, surrounded by savages, and you're crying about a broken-down old horse. It could've been me lying out there—did you think of that?"

"Yes," she said, hating him. "I thought of that."

He looked at her, his face full of anger. She expected hard words, she braced herself for them, but abruptly, Mark's expression changed.

"Rose," he said, "what's happened to us? This isn't how we're meant to be. Remember how we were back in St. Louis, when we started? How did we let this happen?"

Rose felt her heart twist, wrung like a towel.

"Let's go home," he said. "Let's talk, let's make things right." He took her arm and she let him guide her to their cabin, though his touch no longer had the power to move her.

# Chapter Thirty-four

A thick fog lay over the post and the Piney bottoms, hiding the mountains from view. Harry Carrington woke with a sore throat and throbbing head and would have given twenty dollars to stay in bed but his father insisted on church attendance for all officers not on duty and their families. Even enlisted men, Christian or not, were expected to observe the Sabbath. Because the chapel was still unfinished, Chaplain White exhorted for the Lord from behind the long counter of Judge Fitch's store.

Harry wore his Sunday clothes, a black serge coat with sleeves ending two inches above his wrists and black trousers that stopped above his ankles. He followed Jimmy and his parents across the parade, his wool overcoat buttoned to his chin, but even so his bones ached in the damp cold. What he wouldn't give for one of the heavy buffalo coats the soldiers had made for themselves.

Fetterman sat on his horse watching his company form for guard mount while the band played listlessly.

Maybe it was his illness, but to Harry's eyes everything seemed gray and drained of life. Even Sally Horton's little fawn, lying on the cold ground in front of a barracks, was still. She did not stir, even when Private Thomas Burke, late for formation, almost stepped on her as he stumbled through the door and took his place in line. Because he was still buttoning his coat, Burke did not see Sergeant Garrett coming at him and was unprepared for the shove that sent him sprawling.

"That'll teach you to be late!" Garrett shouted. He then let fly with a string of profanity.

Though shorter than Garrett and at least sixty pounds lighter, Burke jumped up and lunged at the sergeant, lowering his head to butt him in the stomach. But Garrett was too fast. He lashed out with the butt of his musket and hit Burke full in the face, knocking out a tooth. Burke fell again. Garrett drew back his boot and kicked him in the ribs.

Margaret grabbed the colonel's arm. "Henry, for God's sake do something. Garrett will kill that boy!"

Carrington looked at Fetterman. Garrett was his sergeant, it was Fetterman's place to discipline him, but he watched the beating without expression and did not intervene. Carrington called to Bisbee, who was also en route to church with his wife and child. "Arrest that man!" he said, pointing at Garrett. "Put him in the guardhouse."

Bisbee obeyed, with obvious reluctance, while two of Burke's bunkmates carried their unconscious friend to the hospital, blood dripping from his mouth.

After the service Carrington drafted Order 38. Clearly a reprimand of Fetterman for not halting Garrett's attack, it labeled swearing, verbal abuse, kicks, and blows a "perversion of authority" and instructed his officers to adopt a more humane and principled approach to discipline. Bully 38, as the officers called it, deepened the growing rift between them and Carrington and solidified the lines of battle. Fetterman became the leader of Carrington's opponents, a group that included Powell, Brown, Bisbee, Grummond, sutler Fitch, and contract surgeon C. M. Hines. Ten Eyck, Wands, Horton, Bridger, Reid, and Dixon supported Carrington.

Mark walked a tightrope, outwardly remaining loyal to Carrington but in private conversations with Fetterman's group suggesting his true allegiance lay with them. Much as he despised Carrington, Rose knew Mark was too ambitious to throw in with the malcontents before knowing which way the wind would blow. Complicity in a failed mutiny would be fatal to a military career.

Meanwhile, letters from an anonymous officer stationed at Fort Phil Kearny began appearing in the *Army and Navy Journal*. Although the journal was weeks old by the time it arrived in the mails, each letter, signed "Dacotah," caused a stir. One complained about an officer's meager pay, which was many times less than the wages earned by the government's civilian employees.

There is not an officer in the army but will testify that it is next to an impossibility to live like an officer and a gentleman on his pay. Pay of a second lieutenant amounts to $110.80 for a thirty-one-day month, tax off. On this one must live, clothe ourselves, and appear like a gentleman. What is left to pay board and bills and where and how are we to obtain a cigar if we desire to smoke after our scanty meals?

The writer blamed Carrington for this imbalance, even though he must have known an officer's pay was beyond the colonel's control.

The mysterious Dacotah became a celebrity. Captains Powell and Brown were considered the most likely candidates and neither denied it. Brown started talking about the book he would write when he got back to the States.

"I'll tell the true and honest story of Fort Phil Kearny," he said, "then we'll see who holds the whip hand!"

Only Rose knew Mark was Dacotah, having found a half-written letter in his jacket pocket. She was ashamed and did not speak of it to anyone, not even Mark. He was short-tempered and irritable. Sometimes she wondered if she was afraid of him.

Carrington's troubles only deepened as November wore on. General Cooke kept up a steady stream of letters and telegrams—carried by courier from Fort Laramie, a 236-mile trip over roads often blocked with snowdrifts—scolding Carrington for his failure to punish the Indians for the "large arrear of murderous and insulting attacks by the savages on emigrant trains and troops."

At the end of the month Captain N. C. Kinney and fifty men arrived from Fort C. F. Smith, ninety-one miles to the north on the banks of the Bighorn River. It would be their last trip until spring as snow soon would make travel between the two posts impossible.

"Things are bad up there, Colonel Carrington," Kinney said. "I'm not going to lie to you. Indians have killed five of my men in the last two weeks. Ammunition is low, I've got only ten rounds per man."

Only this last problem was Carrington able to solve. "As for the rest, I can't help you," he said. "I'm shorthanded myself. Cooke knows this. All we can do is wait." He did not tell Kinney that Cooke was talking about closing Fort Smith altogether. In a rare act of defiance, Carrington refused to do so. In a letter to Cooke, he said closing the fort would leave emigrants bound for Virginia City at the mercy of the Indians. "And isn't this why the regiment is here in the first place?"

Kinney stayed at Fort Phil Kearny for a week, re-supplying and clarifying with Carrington his winter objectives. The day they left, snow was falling and an iron wind blew down from the mountains. Harry, his father, and Jim Bridger watched from the observation deck as Kinney's short column forded the Big Piney, slowly climbed the stony road, and disappeared over the crest of Lodge Trail Ridge.

"What will happen to them when winter closes in?" Carrington said. "If the Indians attack, how will they survive?"

Bridger rubbed his jaw with a gnarled, arthritic hand. "You could ask the same question about all of us, Colonel."

# Chapter Thirty-five

The cold deepened. Temperatures regularly reached ten below zero, sometimes twenty below. Supply trains were stopped by the snow and forced to turn back to Fort Laramie. The men lived mostly on beans, lard, and hard bread. Occasionally scouts ventured out for game but they were rarely successful.

One morning a soldier's bunkmates carried him to the hospital with legs stiff as fence posts and gums so swollen he could not close his mouth. "He stinks so bad we thought he was already dead," one said.

After a short examination, Dixon diagnosed scurvy.

"I'm surprised we haven't seen it before now," he said to Sam Horton. "We need antiscorbutics, things like potatoes and vinegar. Someone will have to go to Bozeman or we'll have big trouble."

Horton pinched the bridge of his nose. "That's a dangerous trip. Who'll go?"

Dixon volunteered without hesitation. Traveling

through two hundred miles of Indian country and sleeping rough in subzero weather was better than remaining at Fort Phil Kearny, knowing the woman he loved slept every night with another man. He did not know if she was thinking about leaving with him in January but he did know if he didn't get away from the post, at least for a while, he would lose his mind.

"Are you sure about this, Dixon?" Carrington said when the two surgeons announced their plan. "I don't have enough men to give you a proper escort."

"Colonel, if I don't go you won't have a man standing. I'd like to leave tomorrow."

Carrington sighed. "I suppose I can free up Bridger and ten men to take you as far as Fort Smith, but from there to Bozeman City, you'll be on your own unless Kinney can help you out, which I doubt. Bridger and the others will have to come back right away—I simply can't spare them and the horses. I'll ask Kinney to give you an escort for the return trip, but again, no guarantees."

"I don't expect any."

Dixon left at four the next morning, with Lieutenant Bingham leading the escort. No one other than Horton and Carrington knew of their mission. Dixon and Bridger rode shoulder to shoulder in the supply wagon, with Dixon's bay and Bridger's mule tied to ringbolts in the rear. Dixon drove the team. As they crunched through the thin ice of the Big Piney, he looked over his shoulder toward her darkened cabin.

"She's a fine-lookin' woman," Bridger said. "That's a fact."

"Who?" Dixon said.

Bridger laughed. "You know who. Me, I prefer a female with more flesh on her bones, but Rose Reynolds is easy on the eyes, no question. A good woman too, far as I can tell—too good for that horse's ass she's married to. Question is, what do you aim to do about it?"

Dixon kept his eyes on the road and said nothing.

"Yessir, I been in your shoes one or twice," Bridger said. "Course, in my case the ladies concerned was squaws. They got a simple way of dealin' with such things, the Injuns. They let the lady choose which buck she wants and that's an end to it, usually. Now, your situation is more prickly. Me, I'd like to see you win out—like I said, that Reynolds is a real turd in the kettle, you might say."

"I didn't know you were such a talker," Dixon said. "Are you planning to keep this up all the way to Fort Smith?"

Bridger shrugged. "He's smart, though, Reynolds, I'll give him that. Determined, got that bent-on-one-thing look about him. I'd watch my back if I was you, and that's all I've got to say on the matter."

A pack of gray wolves joined them at Goose Creek and followed at a distance until they made camp. Bridger figured they had come forty miles, almost half the distance to Fort Smith. Other than the wolves, they saw not another living creature.

Bingham and the troops pitched tents while Dixon and Bridger, wrapped in heavy robes, slept in the bed of the wagon under a canvas tarpaulin tied down at the rails. Despite an angry wind, the howling of the wolves, and Bridger's open-mouthed snoring, Dixon slept like a dead man. At dawn they breakfasted on hard bread, jerked venison, and water. Dixon would have given fifty dollars for a cup of hot coffee but they could not risk a fire. By half past five they were again under way. An icy snow started mid-morning, tiny, wind-driven pellets that stung the flesh like heated shot. Dixon's back ached and his face burned from the cold and wind. He hunched his shoulders deeper into his buffalo coat and pitied the poor mules leaning into their collars, pulling against the storm.

The snow stopped but the wind did not. The cold grew worse by the hour. The sun was no match for it, giving no warmth and only a feeble light. Ice crystals formed on the men's whiskers and the mules' furry rumps. When Dixon opened his mouth, the cold hit his teeth like the flat of a knife. Neither he nor Bridger did much talking.

Bingham wanted to make camp at sundown but Bridger insisted Fort Smith was close so they pressed on. Dark fell quickly. Stars twinkled in the black sky, as if the heavens were mocking them. Fool! Dixon cursed himself. He should have stayed at Phil Kearny, scurvy or no scurvy, Rose or no Rose. Anything would be better than slowly freezing to death. He looked at Bridger beside him on the bench, eyes closed and whiskers ice-covered, and prayed the old man knew what he was talking about when he said they were close.

At last the yellow lights of Fort Smith came into view. The suffering animals smelled the barn and quickened their pace. Dixon's hands felt like wood inside his wolf-hide mittens and he struggled to control the team. When finally they rolled through the gates he was so relieved he could have jumped down and kissed Lieutenant Templeton.

"Bit chilly tonight, eh, Doc?" Templeton said with a grin.

Fort C. F. Smith was smaller than Fort Phil Kearny but neat and well maintained. The enlisted men's barracks were clean and warm and the stables sturdy. Templeton managed to come up with a bit of grain for their animals. After seeing to them, he took Dixon, Bingham, and Bridger to a squat, two-room cabin of logs and adobe with an earth floor and pole-and-dirt roof. "Guest officers' quarters," he said as he opened the door.

The front room was clean and warm, with a fire burning in the heating stove. Flames dancing behind the isinglass window threw an orange light on the whitewashed plaster walls. The only furniture was a shaving stand, a small table, and two cane-bottom chairs. A coal-oil lamp hung from a wall peg.

"You'll find your bedding back there." Templeton pointed to a windowless back room where straw-tick mattresses, wolf and buffalo robes, and woolen blankets were heaped in a pile. "Should be plenty for the three of you."

Templeton removed his hat and for the first time Dixon got a good look at him. His face was swollen and he had lost a lot of weight since Dixon treated him for the injury he received when Lieutenant Daniels was killed. A long laceration on the left side of his face was puckered and angry-looking, still partially open.

"That should have healed by now," Dixon said. "Let me take a look."

The wound was infected. Templeton must have been in considerable pain, but there was no surgeon at Fort C. F. Smith. Dixon cleaned the wound with hot water and a solution of zinc chloride he carried in his saddlebags. After this, he covered the leaking flesh with lint and an adhesive plaster.

By the time Templeton left, Dixon's two companions were already asleep on the floor. He collected his robes and blankets, pulled off his boots, and stretched out on the straw mattress, which smelled of woodsmoke and damp earth. Finally, Dixon let himself relax, feeling the warming muscles of his back, neck, and shoulders loosen and slowly unknot. He closed his eyes and pictured Rose's face, the freckles on the bridge of her nose and cheekbones, her clear blue eyes, her habit of tucking her hair behind her ears. He liked the way her right ear stuck out a bit.

"Dr. Dixon? Are you awake?" The voice was Bingham's. Dixon did not answer. He wanted to sleep.

"Doc?" Bingham pushed himself up on an elbow. His round, clean-shaven face was half lit by the fire's glow.

"What is it, Bingham?" Dixon said. "Can't it wait till morning?"

"Please, Doc, I need to talk to you. I've got this bad feeling, peculiar, like something's wrong with me.

I'm tired all the time but I can't sleep. And when I do, I keep having this dream, the same terrible dream, over and over, every night. I really do think something's wrong."

"It's nerves, Bingham. Everybody has them out here at first. This country takes some getting used to. You'll be all right after awhile."

"No, it's more than that. It sounds crazy, I know, but it's like I'm seeing my own future, like I'm watching myself from someplace else. Do you know what I'm talking about?" Bridger grumbled and turned over in his blankets but Bingham went on.

"In this dream I'm riding with Grummond and Gid Bowers. We're out on the ridge, Lodge Trail Ridge, and it's sunny and cold and we're talking about Christmas. I'm telling Bowers about a plum pudding Mother makes, and we're laughing and feeling good and then, all of a sudden, there's Indians everywhere, all around us, hundreds of them, screaming and waving hatchets and axes, their faces painted red and black. God—it's so real. I see it clear as day!" His voice cracked.

"Don't get worked up," Dixon said. "We'll talk about it tomorrow."

Bingham was breathing hard, as if he'd been running. "Grummond's up ahead, fighting on his own hook, slashing away with his saber. Bowers rides back for me, and his face is red, and he's yelling, 'Run, Bingham, run for your life!' And I try to run—I'm on foot now because my horse is gone—but I can't because I'm floating above the ground with my legs churning in the air. Then this big Sioux buck rides up behind Bowers and sinks a hatchet in his head. It goes in real easy, like a hot knife in cheese, and the whole time Bowers is looking at me and yelling 'Run!' Then the Indian turns to me, waving that hatchet with Bowers's brains dripping off, and I try to run, but I can't, so I yell for Grummond, but he's too far away and I know he wouldn't help me anyhow. Then that Indian starts coming at me and . . . I wake up."

Now Dixon was listening. He had heard a similar story, remarkably similar, years before. "It's just a dream, Bingham," he said. "You can't put stock in it. Everybody has strange dreams." This was inadequate, he knew, but it was all he had.

"I have a sister, Stella, in St. Charles, Minnesota," Bingham said. "If anything happens to me, will you write to her? Would you—you know—tell her things a sister would like to hear?"

"I will," Dixon said, knowing someday soon he would be writing that letter.

# Chapter Thirty-six

Carrington was alone in his office, sitting at his desk. It was a warm evening, more like spring than early December, a welcome break from the bitter cold that for days had held the post in its grip. The oil lamp on his desk flickered in the breeze from the open window. With a sigh, Carrington dipped his pen and began to write:

*December 6, 1866*
*Fort Philip Kearny, Dakota Territory*
*General Philip St. George Cooke*
*Commanding, Department of the Platte*
*Omaha*

*Sir,*
*With deep regret I report the death of Lieutenant Horatio Bingham, Second U.S. Cavalry, an officer endeared to us all by his manly qualities and professional spirit. He was killed when he became separated from his command. I cannot account for*

*this, and his action defeated the success of the*
*movement as planned. Still, Bingham paid the*
*penalty of his life and, whatever the circumstances,*
*he died a soldier.*

Carrington listed the day's casualties in order of
rank: Lieutenant Mark Reynolds, Second U.S. Cavalry, wounded; Sergeant Gideon Bowers, Eighteenth
U.S. Infantry, killed; Sergeant Aldridge, Second U.S.
Cavalry, wounded; four privates, Eighteenth Infantry,
wounded. Three horses killed, five wounded.

He dropped his pen and walked to the window.
How to explain it? The command's first, large-scale
engagement with the Indians had been a disaster.
There was no other word for it. With the exception
of Fetterman and Reynolds, who was wounded early
in the fight, Carrington's officers performed badly,
very badly indeed. And the enlisted men, well, what
could one expect when their leaders behaved in such
an undisciplined and, in the case of Bingham, cow-
ardly fashion? Were it not for his, Carrington's, own
actions the casualty list would be longer. But Cooke
would not see it that way, of this Carrington was certain. Cooke would look for a way to blame him, as
always.

He returned to his desk and took up his pen.

*The skirmish involved a body of Indians*
*numbering, in the aggregate, not less than three*
*hundred warriors. Our force was fewer than sixty*
*men, all the mounted men I could move. The*
*occasion was an attack on our wood train.*

Carrington removed his reading glasses and rubbed ink-stained fingers across his eyes. In his mind he was back on the sere brown slope of Lodge Trail Ridge, in the cold hard sunlight. This was when things started to go bad. How, exactly? What went wrong?

He and his men were descending the ridge. They moved at a trot, fast as the jaded horses could manage. Their labored breathing produced white clouds of vapor in the cold, dry air. Carrington's heart sped up as he anticipated his first taste of combat. *At last,* he thought, *an opportunity to prove myself and put the lie to those whispers of cowardice.* Oh, yes, he had heard them. He turned in the saddle to urge his men forward. They would have to be quick if they were to intercept the Indians fleeing before Fetterman and strike a blow. Again and again, Carrington told his men to stay together, but Grummond defiantly galloped ahead.

> *Upon descending the ridge, I found, to my surprise, fifteen cavalry dismounted and without an officer. I passed through them, ordering them to mount and follow upon the gallop.*
>
> *Upon turning the point marked A upon the map (enclosed) I was confronted by a large force of Indians who, retiring before Captain Fetterman's command, attempted to cut off my detachment or stop its advance.*

Looking over his shoulder Carrington was shocked and dismayed to see only six of the cavalry troops, including bugler Adolph Metzger, were behind him. Ahead were the Indians, yelling and waving their weapons.

"Where is Bingham?" Carrington shouted. Metzger answered, saying he didn't know, that he had been with Bingham earlier when they were cut off by Indians and Bingham ordered a retreat. They were withdrawing toward the post, Metzger said, when Bingham, well in advance of his outfit, disappeared around the shoulder of a hill. Metzger pointed out the place. A few men, the bugler did not know how many, followed Bingham and had not been seen since. He thought Grummond was one of them.

"Sound the recall," Carrington said. "Call them back." Metzger blew his horn but Bingham and the others did not appear. Carrington had no choice but to fall back to the main body of his disordered troops and form a skirmish line. He hoped they did not notice how his hand trembled as he directed them toward their positions.

The Indians charged. The soldiers' terrified horses plunged and reared and Private James McGuire fell, his horse on top of him. A warrior raced his pony toward the downed cavalryman and raised his war club. Carrington went to McGuire's aid. He would tell Cooke of his heroic action, for he doubted anyone else would.

*I succeeded in saving the man and held the position until joined by Fetterman, twenty minutes after. The Indians, circling around and yelling, numbered nearly one hundred with one saddle*

*emptied by a single shot fired by myself. The Indians
did not venture to close in.*

*Upon the appearance of Fetterman's force, the
Indians broke in every direction. I moved to the
right toward Lieutenant Bingham's reported
movement and soon met Lieutenant Grummond
with three men, hotly pursued by Indians.*

At the sight of Carrington's force, the Indians
chasing Grummond wheeled their ponies and
veered away. Grummond spurred his lathered horse
to Carrington's side.

"What's wrong with you, Carrington?" he said.
"Are you a fool or a coward? Which is it?" In full view
and hearing of the troops, Grummond accused his
commanding officer of abandoning Bingham and
the men with him.

"Mr. Grummond!" Carrington was shaking with
rage. "How can I ride to the aid of men if I don't
know where they are? Officers who act on their own
hook endanger all of us, the whole enterprise. You
are at fault, Grummond, you and Bingham!"

Now, hours later, Carrington tried to be temper-
ate in his report. He repeated what Grummond told
him, that he and Bingham were chasing an Indian,
slashing at him with their sabers, when they found
themselves surrounded. Bingham was cut off.

*After an hour's search we found Lieutenant
Bingham's body and that of Sergeant Bowers. The
latter was still living and not scalped. He died*

*before an ambulance arrived from the fort, having
been cleft to the brain.*

Bingham had been scalped, stripped, and bent
over a rotted tree stump. His buttocks had been used
for target practice with more than fifty arrows piercing the white flesh. This, Carrington knew, was a sign
of disrespect. Bowers had a head wound that exposed his brain above the eyes. He lived for almost
an hour in agony, producing guttural, animal sounds
that were terrible to hear.

*Severe weather and coming night prevented
further pursuit, the Indians breaking for the
mountains and Tongue River valley.*
*The Indians' loss was not less than ten killed,
besides many wounded. Several of their ponies and
Indians on foot were seen after dark, working down
the valley or over the hills.*
*Reference is made to Captain Fetterman's report
also.*

This concerned him. How would Fetterman describe the day's events, particularly Carrington's
performance? Fetterman had handled himself well,
particularly when he confronted Bingham's panicked
troops and checked their retreat by threatening to
shoot any man who did not stop.

*All clue is lost as to the reasons for Bingham's
actions. His sergeant says his horse ran away with
him. This may be the case.*

*Much was done. The loss of Lieutenant
Bingham makes all seem lost but the winter
campaign is fairly open and will be met.*

*I do, however, most urgently ask for officers. As
Lieutenant Bisbee leaves, Captain Brown also, I am
to be left again with six officers for six companies
including adjutant and commissary.*

*This is all wrong. There is much at stake. I will
take my full share but this is small allowance with
the mercury at zero and active operations on hand.*

*I am, very respectfully*

> *Henry B. Carrington
> Colonel, Eighteenth U.S. Infantry
> Commanding Post*

He blotted the three pages, folded them, and put
them in a sealed envelope. A special mail detail
would leave in the morning for Fort Reno. "God
help us," he said as he put out the light.

# Chapter Thirty-seven

Bingham and Bowers were buried in tin-lined wooden coffins in the growing post cemetery. Some of the men wept, mostly for Bowers, who had served with the Eighteenth Infantry through its bloodiest fighting. Tears ran down Fred Brown's face as he placed his Army of the Cumberland badge on Bowers's chest. Along with the sadness, an undercurrent of anger, directed at Carrington, ran like a static charge through the mourners. Harry saw it in Bisbee's red face, in Grummond's clenched jaw. His father appeared to be unaware of the resentment building against him.

After the funeral, Fetterman came to Carrington's quarters to submit his official report. He was not his usual ebullient self, Harry noticed, but pale and subdued. At the door he paused and turned. "You were right about one thing, Colonel," he said.

"And what would that one thing be?" Carrington said dryly.

"This has become a hand-to-hand fight," Fetterman said, "a question of survival."

Carrington nodded. "Maybe a tragedy like this was necessary to help us all understand that, Captain Fetterman."

After he left, Carrington read Fetterman's report. He was relieved to learn that Fetterman also blamed the disaster on Bingham's actions and the cavalry's lack of discipline. He put the two reports in the mailbag and walked it over to Bisbee's cabin, where the officers and their families were gathered. Bisbee had been reassigned to department headquarters and Carrington, despite his shortage of officers, was glad to ship him off to Omaha. Though he was unable to prove it, he suspected Bisbee of writing critical letters to Cooke.

Harry was examining the ambulance Mrs. Bisbee and little Gene would travel in. It had been winterized with a double thickness of board and canvas and equipped with a tiny, sheet-iron heating stove. Even so, Harry thought mother and son were in for a miserable journey. Once that pitiless cold came for them, he knew it would take more than a little stove and two layers of board and canvas to keep it at bay.

Mrs. Bisbee had bequeathed her black-and-white milch cow to Frances Grummond, whose pregnancy seemed to become more visible each day. The prized cow was the only milk-producer left, Indians and wolves having claimed the rest. "Keep an eye on

Sallie's fawn," Mrs. Bisbee whispered to Frances before she and Gene boarded the ambulance. "The filthy creature drinks from the milk bucket!"

The women waved handkerchiefs and the band played the Bisbees away. The mail team traveled with them for protection. Harry watched the small group move slowly up the Fort Reno Road and disappear from view. Though he did not particularly like the Bisbees, their departure depressed him. His world was shrinking, both in size and population. He was tired of being confined to the stockade day after day, and starting to wonder if his magical western world was ever going to open up the way he thought it would.

Most days he hung around the hospital hoping for something to do. Horton and Hines rarely gave him work and when they did it was something uninteresting like sweeping up wood shavings or sanding bloodstains off the floor. It was much better when Daniel Dixon was on duty, as he taught Harry how to mix medicines and prepare plasters with oleoresin. Once Dixon showed him how to clean a wound with calomel, the sweet-smelling balsam of the South American copaiba tree. Another time he let Harry ply the sponges while he amputated a soldier's gangrenous hand. As he operated, he explained the initial injury had not been serious but the flesh mortified because a well-meaning friend had bound the wound too tightly.

Though he avoided the hospital when Dixon was not there, boredom drove him to it one cold morning. He was about to enter the surgery when he heard voices and stopped at the door. Hines and Horton were talking about Dixon, who was overdue returning from Bozeman.

"Maybe he's not coming back," Hines said. "He's leaving the service, you know."

Harry thought Hines had the features of a rodent and the personality to match.

"Oh, he'll come back if he's able to," Horton said. "He knows we're counting on him. Yes, I know he's leaving and I hate to lose him. He's the best man I've got—no disrespect to you, Hines, but he's more experienced. I'm trying to convince him to stay on, if only for another year, but I don't have much hope."

"Well, it may be for the best," Hines said. "He and Reynolds are headed for trouble. That's plain enough."

Horton did not pick up on the invitation to gossip. "Speaking of Reynolds," he said, "have you looked in on him today? He was—"

A woman screamed. Harry turned to see Sallie Horton kneeling on the ground, rocking her fawn in her arms. The animal was limp and her muzzle and distended tongue were strangely white.

Sam Horton ran out the door, almost colliding with Harry, and went to his wife. She wept on his shoulder, then raised her face to the growing crowd.

"Who did this?" She pointed to an overturned bucket beside the fawn's body. "Who filled the milk pail with paint? Why, why did you?"

Horton tried to calm her. "It was an accident, Sallie," Horton said. "No one would want to hurt Billie."

Harry scanned the crowd, his eyes resting on Grummond. A small smile pulled at the corners of the officer's full red lips.

# Chapter Thirty-eight

Dixon wiped the last of the gravy from his plate with a yeast biscuit.

"You want more?" the woman said. "I've got plenty."

"Thank you, ma'am, but I'm saving room for a piece of that." He nodded at a layer cake, dark with molasses and dusted with confectioner's sugar, on the sideboard. "You certainly are a fine cook, Mrs. Story. I never tasted a better stew or a lighter biscuit."

The woman beamed at the compliment. "Call me Ellen," she said, taking his plate, then those of his fellow diners. Ellen Story was a tall, handsome woman with dark hair, brown eyes, and a quick smile. Her baby boy slept in a cradle in a corner of the warm kitchen. Dixon looked around the clean, comfortable room and imagined the woman cutting cake as Rose, the infant in the cradle his son.

"You're a lucky man," he said to Nelson Story at the head of the table. "Luckier than you deserve to be."

Story chuckled. "Don't I know it. Say, I've often

wondered, how did Carrington feel about me giving him the slip last June?"

"He wasn't happy but it's forgotten now," Dixon said. "He's got bigger problems."

The door flew open and Story's half-breed hired man stomped into the cabin, brushing snow from his sleeves. He sat at the table and Ellen brought him a full plate and a steaming mug of coffee. After a few bites he said, "My Crow relatives say there was fighting down south. At the soldier fort on the Piney."

Alarm bells rang in Dixon's head. "At Fort Phil Kearny?" he said.

The half-breed nodded. "Some soldiers were killed, but my relatives do not know how many. The bluecoats fought badly, they say. They were not brave and could not control their horses. The Sioux are celebrating and fixing to fight them again."

Dixon's first thought was of Rose. "I've got to go back," he said. "I'll leave first thing in the morning." He turned to the silent fourth man at the table. The quiet man met Dixon's eyes reluctantly, anticipating his question.

"What about it, Gregory?" he said. "Come with me. You'll be paid—I'll pay you out of my own pocket if I have to."

Jack Gregory shook his head. "Carrington thinks I stole that payroll. You told me that yourself. I don't fancy wearing Uncle Sam's watch and chain for the next five years."

"I'll vouch for you," Dixon said.

Gregory laughed. "No disrespect, Doc, but that won't do it."

"Like I said before, Carrington's got bigger problems. You and Ignacio risked your lives to save all those people at the redoubt. He knows it, everyone knows it. That's what matters. The colonel will recognize that."

Gregory raked his hand through his sun-bleached hair. "I'm not so sure. I'd like to help, Dixon, I really would. There's a lot of good people at Phil Kearny and I don't want to see them hurt, but going back don't seem like a good idea. Not from where I sit."

Dixon stood up.

"Think of the women and children, Gregory. Please, I'm asking you to help me."

Gregory hesitated. "Mrs. Reynolds and her husband, that officer, the one who left her at Sedgwick. They still there?" he said.

"They are."

Gregory looked down at the table, then at Story. "Well, boss? Can you spare me for a bit?"

"You do as you please, Jack," Story said. "Ain't much going on here now anyhow. Come spring, though, I'll need you at the cow camp, so keep your hair on. And you too, Dixon. I'm expecting to have that mercantile a going concern by late spring. Not only that, but folks in Bozeman are looking forward to having a doctor in town. They're counting on it."

"I'll be back," Dixon said. To himself, he added, and I hope not alone.


They left at first light with Dixon driving the wagon, his bay tied to the back, his seven-shot

Spencer in the rifle stand at his side. Story loaned him four fresh mules to replace his exhausted animals. They would need them for the 130-mile trip to Fort Phil Kearny because the wagon was heavy with grain, medical supplies, and food including scurvy remedies such as potatoes, pickled cabbage, sauerkraut, and casks of vinegar.

Gregory rode ahead on his Appaloosa stallion. The weather held sunny and mild for the first two days and they made good time, pausing only to take short meals and rest the animals. They made no fires. At night they took turns sleeping two-hour stretches while the other kept watch. The nighttime sky was a living thing, full of glowing color and motion.

"Sun dogs by day and the northern lights by night," Gregory said, as they shared a meal of jerked elk, biscuit, and water. "Signs of change, both. Means something's coming."

Dixon bit off a piece of jerky. "How long did you ride with Quantrill?" he said.

Gregory stopped chewing. "Why you say that?"

"Couple things, that saddle for one." It lay on the ground by the wagon. The name Charley Hart was etched on the leather, barely visible due to heavy and hard use and someone's attempt to scratch it off. "Wasn't that a name Quantrill used sometimes?"

Gregory nodded. "I was hoping no one would see that. Me and Bill traded horses last time I saw him. He was in a hurry and his horse was done. That was just before he went to Kentucky, which he shouldn't have done and I told him so at the time." He resumed his chewing and raised his eyes to the moving sky. "Yep, I rode with Bill Quantrill and I'm proud to say it. He was the best officer I ever knew and the smartest too. Can't say the same for some who rode with him—Bill Anderson, Arch Clement, Frank James, that lot—but Quantrill was a man. I'd ride with him again tomorrow."

"Did you have any part in that Lawrence business?"

Gregory shook his head. "I didn't hook up with him till after that, after Tom Ewing unleashed those murdering Jayhawkers on my people."

"I spent some time in Missouri," Dixon said. "The war was bad there, worse than most places."

Gregory swallowed his jerky with a sip of water. "Yes, it was, largely due to Doc Jennison and his cutthroat band of Kansas scum. They came to our farm, looking for Quantrill and his boys. It was summer of sixty-three, right after Lawrence. Pa didn't know nothing about Quantrill's whereabouts, but Jennison didn't believe him. They hung Pa from a tree, right there by the house, with Ma and the girls looking on. When he was near dead they cut him down, asked him again, strung him up again. Three times they did this, finally he just said 'hell with it' and put Pa in the barn and set a match to it. Burned it down with him inside, alive. They burned everything, the house, the barn, till there was only the chimney sticking up from the ashes. Ma and the girls had nothing but the clothes on their backs and a wheelbarrow of what they could pull from the flames." He paused and shook his head, momentarily unable to speak. "There was a Union officer with Jennison that day.

That son of a bitch wouldn't lift a finger to help, not even when Ma told him we were Union people, which we were at the time. That changed."

"Where were you when this happened?" Dixon said.

Gregory laughed. "That's the good part. I was over to Fort Scott, a soldier in Mr. Lincoln's army. After they killed Pa, I took the bounce and joined Quantrill at his camp in the Sni Hills. I wasn't with him long, but long enough to know what he was made of."

"Do you know who that Union officer was?" Dixon said.

Gregory smoothed his mustache with his thumb and first finger. "I do. My sister pointed him out to me later, in Kansas City. He was riding in a big, fancy carriage with a couple of generals, all high and mighty like he was the pharaoh of Egypt. The bastard will pay for what he did. I will put him through."

They sat silently, each man following the drumbeats of his past.

"How about you, Dixon?" Gregory said. "What's your story?"

Dixon looked down at his hands. "I lost my wife and daughter," he said finally. "Laura and Mary. My Kentucky family disowned me when I went to fight with the Union. They were all I had—Laura and Mary—and I killed them."

Gregory said nothing, waiting.

"I didn't put a gun to their heads but I killed them just the same."

He hesitated and the silence grew long.

"You don't have to talk about it," Gregory said. "Not if you don't want to."

"No, it's not that." Dixon cleared his throat. "It's just that I haven't really spoken of this before. It's . . . well, it was near the end of the war. I was attending at a prison hospital. It was on an island in the Mississippi, just outside Alton, Illinois. Smallpox Island, they called it."

Gregory nodded. "I heard of it."

"The prisoners were very sick. Boys the army sent there to die. I felt bad for them, some I even managed to save. They came to trust me, started calling me the Saint of Smallpox Island. I started thinking of myself that way, like some kind of healer hero." He shook his head. "I stayed longer than I needed to. Longer than I should have."

"Weren't you scared of getting sick yourself?"

"I immunized myself," Dixon said. "Most physicians did. I wasn't sick a day, but I carried the disease on me, carried it back to Laura and Mary when I finally went home. A surgeon knows how to prevent contagion. I should've protected them—scrubbed head to toe with lye soap, burned all my old clothes and brought only new ones—but I was in a hurry. I had a letter saying this fellow was hanging around, a rich farmer from Lexington who courted Laura before me." He took off his hat, ran his hands through his dark hair. "I was wrong to doubt her, but that letter put a poison in me. I knew I'd stayed away too long."

He paused and his voice was husky when he spoke again.

"I couldn't believe it when I first saw the signs in them. I tried to tell myself it wasn't true but I knew it was. They died quickly, Laura first, then the baby girl. She wasn't even two."

Gregory looked away. It was not polite to gawk at a man when he was overcome. The northern lights were fading and the icy world was still but for the munching of the horses and mules in their nose bags.

"People die, Dixon. You know that more than anybody. It's no good beating yourself up." Gregory spoke clumsily, unfamiliar with the vocabulary of comfort. "What I'm saying is, you ought not blame yourself." Gregory wrapped himself in his buffalo robe and stretched out under the wagon. In less than two minutes he was snoring.

They made Fort Smith at sundown on the third day. Kinney could not tell them more than they knew about the fight at Fort Phil Kearny. After five hours of warm, uninterrupted sleep they were ready to move on. Jim Bridger, his face gray with pain, could not leave with them. "The rheumatism ain't never been this bad before," he said. "Tell the colonel I won't see him till spring."

Kinney gave Dixon and Gregory a five-man escort in return for two kegs of vinegar and three barrels of pickled cabbage. "You'll be glad of these when the scurvy comes," Dixon said, "and it will."

Soon after they started out the weather took a turn for the worse. The thermometer mounted on the wagon never topped twenty degrees and the wind was keen as a knife edge. It blew all day, died at night, and returned with new vigor in the morning. They saw no Indians until dusk on the second day after leaving Fort Smith. As they neared Fort Phil Kearny, eight Sioux warriors appeared, riding on the hills parallel to their short column. They made no move to attack.

"Why don't they attack?" Dixon said.

"Saving themselves for something bigger, probably," Gregory said, "or maybe they don't like the odds."

He gestured toward the south where Dixon was relieved to see twelve soldiers riding toward them. When they got close enough Dixon recognized Captain James Powell in the lead.

"Hello, Dixon," Powell said with his usual sideways grin. "I wasn't sure I'd ever see you again. You were born under a lucky star, doctor. Who's your friend?"

Dixon introduced Jack Gregory and if the name meant anything to him Powell did not show it. They continued on to the fort.

"No Indian trouble then?" Powell said.

"Those are the first we've seen," Dixon said. As he spoke, the Indians turned their ponies and vanished over the crest of the hill.

"Like I said, doctor, a lucky star. You hear about Bingham and Bowers? Indians killed them."

"I heard there was trouble but no names." Dixon was not surprised to learn Bingham had been killed.

"Five others wounded," Powell said. "Reynolds for one."

Dixon did not ask how serious Reynolds's injuries were—he'd find out soon enough. "What happened?" he said.

Powell shrugged. "The usual. Sioux hit the wood train, the colonel sent Fetterman out with the mounted infantry, Bingham had the cavalry. He was supposed to drive the Indians back over Lodge Trail Ridge but—I don't know what happened. Bingham lost his head, I guess, abandoned his men, then found himself surrounded. Could be his horse ran away with him, no one can say. Anyhow, the colonel finally saw action. Didn't piss down his leg like everyone expected him to."

"Any trouble since?" Gregory said.

"No, but there will be. There's more Indians around than ever, always signaling with flags and mirrors. It makes your skin crawl."

Dixon scanned the shadowy hills. "That's why we didn't see any Indians," he said. "They're here."

"At least we're finally drilling the men," Powell said. "I've got the cavalry and Fetterman has the infantry. If anybody can make soldiers of them, he can. Now that Reynolds is down, Grummond's got the mounted infantry and I don't envy him. Micks and Eye-tyes the lot, they ride like pumpkins."

Dixon wasn't listening. If Reynolds was badly hurt, how would it affect Rose? And what about Gregory? How was he going to finesse his return with Carrington? Dixon didn't know if Gregory stole the payroll money and he didn't care. He risked his life to help get these supplies to Fort Phil Kearny. There was no way he would let Jack Gregory be jailed.

It was fully dark when the lights of the fort came into view. It looked like a walled city from medieval times, Dixon thought, a village lost in time. Patches of snow dotted the ground and clung to trees on the sloping hillsides. As they neared the post he breathed in the familiar smells of cut pine, woodsmoke, and manure.

A crowd met them at the quartermaster's gate. Gregory was welcomed as a hero by the men who had been at Reno Redoubt. No one mentioned his alleged crime. Dixon searched for Rose but she was not there. Just as well, he thought, rubbing his jaw, rough with four days' growth of beard. He'd have time to wash up and shave before seeing her.

"Dixon!" Sam Horton came toward him, carefully picking his way through muck and animal droppings. "Am I glad to see you." He had lost a lot of weight, something Dixon hadn't noticed when he saw Horton every day. "What have you brought us?" Horton said.

"Everything on the list," Dixon said, "minus a few items I left at Fort Smith. How goes it here?"

Horton shook his head. "Not well. We have ten men in the hospital, three with scurvy and the rest wounded in that trouble on the sixth. I guess you heard about Bingham and Bowers?"

"I heard."

"Most of the wounded aren't too bad, except for Reynolds. I want you to look in on him right away."

Dixon climbed down and started untying the tarpaulin covering the wagon bed.

"He was shot in the arm," Horton said, "fracture of the left humerus. Hines got the bullet out, but the wound mortified. I was forced to amputate at the junction of the middle and superior third." He touched his arm to demonstrate the place. "The operation was uncomplicated, the usual double flap with no excessive bleeding. I thought he was recovering well but this morning he started hemorrhaging. He doesn't look good. Please go look at him."

Mark Reynolds was the last person Dixon wanted to see. His back ached, his legs were stiff, his eyelids felt as if they were lined with sand. All he wanted was a razor and a hot bath. "All right," he said. "I'll wash up first, meet you at the hospital."

"He's not there," Horton said. "He insisted we take him to his cabin. His wife is with him."

Christ, Dixon thought, this would not be the reunion he'd been looking forward to. "Can Reynolds be moved?" he said.

"I should think so."

"Then get him to the hospital—I don't care what he says. I can't operate in that cabin. I'll be along in a few minutes." He walked to his cold quarters, lit the lamp, and got a fire going in the stove. After putting on a kettle of water, he lay down on his cot and covered his eyes with his forearm. A thought slid through his brain like a snake down a prairie dog hole. He would have to operate on Reynolds. He'd seen enough of Horton's handiwork to know that. It would be easy to let the knife slip, to sever an artery. He could leave something behind. No one would know if he overlooked a sliver of diseased bone, a tiny bit that would poison Reynolds from within until first the limb and then the entire body began to rot. Yes, he could do that. Who was to stop him?

The kettle whistled. Dixon rose slowly and poured the steaming water into a basin on his shaving stand, then tempered it with cold water from the barrel by the door. He lathered his hands, face, and neck with strong brown soap. As he shaved, the face looking back at him from the mirror was that of an aged stranger, with hollows under the eyes and cheekbones. In his mind's eye, he saw himself as he had been before, sitting in a rocker by an open window on a warm summer evening, baby Mary asleep in the crook of his arm, then later, lying beside the child's sleeping mother in the moony darkness and thanking heaven for his happiness. Gone now, all of it, the woman and child, because of something he did.

He dried his face with a coarse muslin towel. He had one thing left. Through it all, the war and Smallpox Island, the deaths of Laura and Mary, through all of that horror he had remained true to his calling. "First, do no harm," he said. He had not betrayed that.

He changed into clean clothes, picked up his bag, and put out the lamp. He left a low fire burning in the stove so the cabin would be warm when he returned. As he crossed the yard he saw yellow lights burning in the surgery window although the back room that served as the inpatient ward was still unfinished. He shook his head. With only a canvas roof and newspapers covering the windows, it would be miserably cold in there, even with a stove going

full blast. The hospital should be finished by now—
Carrington should have seen to that.

When he entered the surgery he saw Hines in a
linen apron. Good, he thought. If he had to operate
tonight Hines would assist. With his sharp features
and pronounced overbite, Hines looked like a rat,
but he was a fine surgeon. Better than Horton or
Reid.

Rose was standing by the window. "It's good to see
you," she said. "You were gone a long time, we were
worried. And you didn't even say good-bye. You
should've told your friends you were leaving."

Dixon thought he had never seen her so beautiful.
Not trusting his voice, he turned to hang up his coat.

"I knew they'd try to talk me out of it," he said. "It
wouldn't have been hard."

"It's a good thing they didn't," Sam Horton said,
appearing at the door to the inpatient ward. "I just
gave our scurvy patients a tisane of barley and
vinegar. It works wonders, and quickly too."

A hoarse voice said, "Let's hope the good doctor
can work wonders for me." Mark Reynolds sat in a
chair, wrapped in a woolen blanket. His face was
gaunt and his eyes glittered with fever.

"Let me see your arm," Dixon said.

Reynolds dropped the blanket. He was shirtless
and Dixon was shocked by the change in him. His
ribs looked as if they would pierce his skin. "Funny
how things work out, isn't it?" he said as Dixon unwound the bloody bandages.

"Funny?"

"Well," Reynolds said, "what would you call it when a man's surgeon is the one who most wants him dead?"

"Mark!" Rose covered her face with her hands as Dixon removed the last of the bandages. The stump was red and covered with blobs of gray pus. It smelled of infection.

"This needs to be opened," Dixon said. "Maybe you'd rather someone else took care of it."

Reynolds shrugged, wincing at the pain that even simple movement caused. "What the hell," he said. "You're the best we've got, or so they say. Anyhow, you won't kill me. You haven't got the sand for that. But I bet you've thought about it. Haven't you, Dixon?" Their eyes met and Reynolds grinned. "I thought so."

Dixon turned to Hines and said, "I want you to assist me. Everyone else must leave."

Horton took Rose by the arm. "Come, dear," he said. "Come wait in our cabin. Sallie will fix a pot of tea."

Rose walked to Mark and kissed him lightly on the lips. Then she stood, brushed her hair from her face, and looked at Dixon. "Do your best for him," she said.

"I will." The snake stirred in its hole. Their eyes held for a moment and she left on Horton's arm.

Blood dripped from Reynolds's arm as Hines helped him from the chair onto the operating table. Dixon heard each drop hit the floor, distinctly as a heartbeat, as he unlocked the medicine cabinet and removed a brown glass bottle.

"I don't blame you, Dixon," Reynolds said. "She's

not the most beautiful woman, but there's something about her. But then, maybe you already know that. Maybe you already know things only a husband should know."

"Reynolds, shut the fuck up." Dixon gave the bottle to Hines, who uncorked it and wet a handkerchief with its contents. The room filled with the scent of ripe apples.

Reynolds smiled, his eyes on Dixon standing at the foot of the operating table. His gaze did not waver, even as Hines stepped in and covered his nose with the chloroform-soaked cloth. Within seconds, Reynolds's eyes closed and he was still.

Horton had amputated the left arm just below the elbow. Instead of signs of healing, Dixon found three sinuses boring through the soft tissue of the stump, each draining a foul yellow fluid. He picked up the knife and cut into the red flesh, opening the flaps. Membranes that should have been smooth, thin, and tough were a soft, gelatinous mass. The wound was filled with pus and large abscesses separated the muscles. No wonder Reynolds looked so bad, Dixon thought. The pain must be tremendous.

As he suspected, a fragment of dead bone about an inch long protruded like a bit of broken pottery from the ulcerated cartilage. He removed it with a gouge, then probed for more with his finger, finding three more slivers and pulling them out with tweezers. The ends of the long bones were eroded and covered with a dark, fleshy growth. Dixon removed the diseased tissue, sawing at a beveled angle till he reached healthy bone. Blood leaked

from the brachial artery, which was improperly
secured by ligature—more of Horton's handiwork.
Hines applied finger pressure to stanch the bleeding as Dixon drew out the artery with a hooked
tenaculum, a long handled device with a claw like a
witch's grasping fingers at the business end, and
quickly retied it. He irrigated and disinfected the
wound with a solution of soda chlorinate, closed
the flaps with widely spaced sutures to permit drainage,
and washed the stump with soap and cold water.
The last step was to paint the skin with a surgeon's
brush soaked in ferric persulfate, a styptic, to check
the oozing.

The operation lasted for about forty-five minutes.
Hines bandaged the arm while Dixon washed his
hands and instruments in a porcelain basin, watching the water turn red with Reynolds's blood. Now
that it was over, Dixon felt dead on his feet.

"Hines, I'm going to get some sleep," he said.
"When he wakes up give him morphine sulfate,
one-half dram, then laudanum and beef tea, every
two hours."

"There is no laudanum," Hines said. "The little we
had left disappeared during your absence. I suspect
Ten Eyck and so informed Doctor Horton."

Dixon thought Hines probably was right. Ten Eyck
was a heavy drinker who suffered chronic health
problems, including the loss of an eye, following two
years in a Rebel prison camp. Often he sought anal-
gesics from members of the medical staff. Still, Dixon
thought him one of Carrington's best officers. "Then
alternate the beef tea with porter or champagne," he

said. "Keep him still and comfortable. You know what to do."

"Is he going to make it?" Hines said. Reynolds's breathing was fast and shallow and his rapid pulse was visible in his neck.

Dixon shook his head. "Infection is the greatest danger. We'll know soon enough."

Hines cleared his throat. "Uh, Dixon, those things he said about you and Mrs. Reynolds, you know . . . no one could have done a better job tonight. I'll vouch for you, if it comes to that."

"Thank you, Hines." Dixon shrugged his shoulders into his coat. "Let's hope that won't be necessary."

"Oh, I almost forgot. Colonel Carrington wants to see you in his office, soon as you're finished here."

Dixon took an envelope from his coat pocket and gave it to Hines. "Will you see that he gets this? It's from Jim Bridger, it's important. As for me, I need sleep. There's only one thing in this world that would stop me and Colonel Carrington doesn't have it." He left the surgery, letting the door slam behind him.

# Chapter Thirty-nine

Rose sipped tea as Sallie Horton described the latest Butterick patterns from *Godey's Ladies Book*. It seemed she had been talking for hours. She looked at Sam, sipping a glass of whiskey, and wished she could have one too. Why couldn't a woman have a glass of whiskey now and then without causing a scandal? she wondered. She turned to the window to see bright lights burning in the surgery. What was going on in there? More important, what result did she hope for?

She realized the room had gone quiet. Sallie had asked her a question. "I'm sorry," Rose said. "I'm afraid my thoughts were elsewhere."

"Mark will be fine, dear," Sam said, with a smile. "Daniel Dixon is the best surgeon I've ever known."

Rose returned his smile, wondering what Sam Horton would think if he knew her true feelings. What would Sam say if he knew how she longed to be free of Mark and why?

Rose had come to accept the knowledge she was

not what she was supposed to be. Back in St. Louis, she tried to be a proper woman, but the truth was she was not pious, not devoted, she did not often put her needs second to those of everyone else. Maybe she should have pretended to enjoy needlework, maybe she should have spent more time painting flowers on glass vases and jars. Maybe then things would have turned out differently. But at the same time she thought she was exactly what she was meant to be. For whatever reason, whether it was growing up with three brothers, or without a mother's example, a woman's life had never appealed to her. Always she had longed for something different, for a life as big as a man's. In Mark she thought she had found a partner who would help her achieve that dream, but she was wrong. Should she pay for that mistake all her life? How bleak, to be stuck in the worst kind of prison, to be chained for life to a man she no longer loved or respected.

She looked out the window to see Dixon leaving the hospital. "I'm sorry," she said, jumping to her feet. "I left something in my cabin. I'll just be a minute."

She grabbed her shawl and was out the door before Sam could offer to come with her. The night air was very cold and the sky was brilliant with stars. Gravel crunched beneath her feet as she ran to Dixon. They met on the walk in front of her cabin. He was smoking a cigarette.

"He came through the operation pretty well," he said, before she asked. "That's all I can tell you at this point."

He smelled of tobacco and soap. She wanted to touch him but instead pulled her plaid shawl more tightly around her shoulders. "Should I go to him?" she said.

Dixon shook his head and dropped his cigarette, grinding the glowing ember into the gravel with his boot. "He won't know you're there. Hines is with him. It'll be a few hours before he comes around."

Laughter and cheers drifted across the parade. They turned to see Fetterman, Grummond, and Brown walking into Judge Fitch's store, where men gathered to drink and play cards. The three officers spent most evenings there.

"I'm recommending Reynolds be sent east to recover," Dixon said, "soon as he's fit to travel, if all goes well maybe in a week or so. You'll have to go with him." She started to object but he was right. She would have to go, if for no other reason than to take care of Mark. "This place is about to explode. Since my trip north I'm more convinced of that than ever. The Crows have tried to warn us, but no one's listening."

"Surely it's not bad as all that," Rose said. "Omaha would've sent reinforcements if it were."

Dixon shook his head. "Rose, are you really so naïve? No one in Omaha gives a damn about what happens here. Carrington—all of us—we're sacrificial lambs. We were sent here to distract the Indians, so the railroads can be built through Kansas and Nebraska. That's what Washington and Omaha care about, the regiment's great friend General William Sherman most of all."

This was not the conversation Rose wanted or expected. "You saw Major Bridger at Fort Smith," she said. "What does he say?"

"The same thing I'm saying. He wrote a letter to the colonel telling him thousands of warriors are gathering in the Tongue Valley, waiting for Red Cloud to lead them against the soldier forts. It is going to happen, Rose, and soon."

A blast of arctic wind blew her hair across her face. Dixon raised his hand and pushed it away. He traced the curve of her cheek with his finger. "I've almost forgotten what a woman's skin feels like," he said.

Lamplight from the windows of officers' row lit her face, softened her features. He thought she'd never looked lovelier.

"I don't want to leave you," she said, putting her hand on top of his.

He smiled. "I want you so much it hurts just to look at you," he said. "We'll work this out somehow, in a way we can both live with. Meantime, I'm going to convince Carrington to free up a train to Fort Reno. And if Mark won't—or can't—leave, promise me you'll go without him."

"I can't promise now. I have to think—I need time."

"That's one thing I can't give you," he said.

# Chapter Forty

Harry leaned against the porch rail and lifted his face to the warm morning sun. It felt more like spring than Christmastime. The wind ruffled the pages of the six-week-old *New York Times* spread across his knees. President Johnson's report to Congress called the Fort Laramie treaty an unqualified success. The Indians, Johnson said, "have unconditionally submitted to our authority and manifested an earnest desire for a renewal of friendly relations."

A previous reader had underlined this section and in the margin drawn Johnson's head with an arrow through it. Did the president really believe the Indians have submitted, Harry wondered? Did none of his father's reports reach Washington? He shook his head and turned the page. *Crime and Punishment*, a new novel by Russian author Fyodor Mikhaylovich Dostoyevsky, was drawing great reviews. On another page, Harry found accounts of society balls in Washington and Philadelphia, advertisements for hair and liver tonics, headache powders, kid gloves, and toboggans. The paper may as well describe events on the silvery moon for all the relevance they had to his life.

"It's hard to believe that world still exists, isn't it?"

Margaret stood before him on the steps, her hand resting on the rail. Harry noticed how thin and old-looking she was. Wearily, she sank into a chair.

"They've forgotten us it seems," she said, nodding at the newspaper. "Did you see where twelve companies of regulars have been posted to Fort Laramie, where there is no trouble, while here, with trouble all around us, we get only four?" She coughed, covering her mouth with a handkerchief.

"Are you sick?" Harry said.

She waved her hand. "Nothing a decent meal wouldn't cure. Oh, how I long for a crisp, cold apple or a baked potato, smothered in fresh, sweet butter. I'll never take those things for granted again."

They watched as the men began forming in companies for afternoon drill.

"I know you miss the world, Harry," Margaret said, "food, books, the company of people your own age—girls, for heaven's sake—the stimulation that comes with a good education. Already you're well beyond what I can teach you."

Harry thought he did not like the turn this conversation was taking.

"Your father and I have decided to send you east in the spring," Margaret said. "We're considering a preparatory school in Philadelphia. After that, we're thinking you can study for your West Point entrance examinations at Bragdon School in New York. Highland Falls, it's lovely there. Your father will have no trouble arranging this. He's already written some letters."

"I don't want to go to prep school in Philadelphia," Harry said. "I don't want to go to West Point."

Margaret looked at him with raised eyebrows. "What's this?" she said. "That's the plan. That's always been the plan."

"It's always been *his* plan," Harry said. He felt his blood rising. "Father wants me to go to West Point because he couldn't get in himself. But I don't want to be a soldier. I want to be a surgeon, or an engineer. I want to build things, try to make the world better. I don't want to spend my life killing Indians."

He had never spoken like this to his mother before, never openly opposed his parents' plans for him. But the violence he had seen on this journey, coupled with the months of watching his father struggle to please superior officers who ignored or scolded him, plus his inability to manage disrespectful subordinates and sullen troops, all these things had convinced Harry the military life was not for him. Most of all, he knew he did not want to spend his time on Earth oppressing other people be they red, black, or yellow. Racial injustice had a face now, the face of French Pete Cazeau's children.

"Do you honestly believe that's what your father is about?" Margaret said with a frown. "Killing Indians?"

Harry dropped his eyes. He had gone too far.

"We expect you to respect the family tradition of service to the country," Margaret said. "Consider what it would do to your father if you, his eldest son, turned away from that. It would be the same as turning away from him. Is that what you want, Harry? Do you really want to hurt him that way?"

Harry shook his head, keeping his eyes lowered. He did not want to see the disappointment on his mother's face.

"The truth is, I'm starting to think all three of us should go home—you, Jimmy, and I," Margaret said. "We made a mistake bringing you boys out here. It's more difficult, and so much more dangerous, than anyone anticipated. I'm worried, Harry. I'm very worried."

To Harry's horror she started to cry. He got up and put his arm around her shaking shoulders. Her bones felt sharp and breakable as twigs beneath her shawl. "Don't cry, Mother," he said. "Please, don't. I'll do it, I'll do what you and Father want, just please don't cry." Even as he said these things he was thinking spring was a long way off. A lot could happen before then.

"You're a good boy, Harry." Margaret wiped her tears away with the back of her hand. "You've always been a good boy."

The family spent the afternoon together in their quarters. Harry and his father played chess, Margaret wrote to friends in Columbus, and Jimmy played with his tin soldiers. The peaceful quiet was broken when Fetterman and Brown knocked on the door. Carrington asked them in, though he usually discouraged officers from interrupting his family time. They were careful to clean their muddy boots on a jack before entering.

"Colonel," Fetterman said, "Captain Brown and I propose an attack on the Indian villages along the Tongue River. He and I will lead it. Give us fifty mounted men and fifty civilians and we'll clean them out, once and for all."

Carrington frowned. He had passed the morning writing dispatches to Omaha, seeking troops and supplies. "Couldn't this wait until I'm in the office?" he said. "I have little enough time with my family as it is."

"No, Colonel," Fetterman said. "It can't wait. The men are sick to death of waiting."

Carrington moved a pawn before answering. Harry saw his ink-stained hand tremble. "Gentlemen, we mustn't let ambition override prudence in these matters." He kept his eyes on the chessboard. "By all accounts, the villages along the Tongue are huge, harboring thousands of warriors. One hundred men—no matter how brave or well led—are simply too few to take them on. Furthermore, the terrain in those parts is difficult and the men do not know it. Only Brown, Ten Eyck, and I have been there."

He raised his eyes to Fetterman. "The other officers, including yourself, Captain Fetterman, if you'll forgive me, are ignorant of the challenges it presents. Must I remind you of what happened earlier this month? The men are unschooled in the tactics of Indian warfare."

Fetterman's face darkened.

"And, if *you'll* forgive me, Colonel, do you include yourself among the unschooled? Since you mention the previous action, how do you defend your behavior that day? Why did you hang back on the ridge instead of closing in when we had the Indians flanked between us?"

Carrington's eyes blazed. *Do it!* Harry said to himself. *Take him down. Don't let him talk to you like that, in your own home and in front of your family.* But his father's response, when at last it came, was tepid.

"I concede we all have much to learn," he said. "But this is irrelevant. I couldn't agree to what you propose even if I wanted to." He went to his desk and picked up some papers, then handed them to Fetterman. "Morning report," he said. "As you see, I don't have horses for fifty men. Even if I were to abandon the mails and pickets, which I will not do, I would still be eight animals short."

They were interrupted by the shrill blast of the sawmill's steam whistle. Harry jumped up, knocking the chessboard to the floor, and ran to the window. The Pilot Hill sentry was waving a white flag above his head. Indians were attacking the wood train. Fetterman and Brown rushed out the door as the bugler sounded assembly.

The day was still warm with full sun and a strong wind from the west. Harry heard scattered gunfire as he followed his father to headquarters and up the stairs to the lookout platform. Private Archie Sample, Carrington's orderly, Ten Eyck, and Grummond were already there. Carrington trained his field glasses to the northwest, where the wood road skirted the base of the Sullivant Hills. He leaned over the waist-high rail and called down to Captain Powell, on the parade lawn below.

"Take C Company and the mounted infantry. Relieve the train and escort it back to the post. Heed the lessons of the sixth! Do not pursue the Indians across Lodge Trail Ridge!" Powell saluted with his usual grin.

Ten Eyck looked at Carrington in surprise. "Are you sure you want to send Powell, sir?" he said. "Do you trust him?"

On the day Bingham and Bowers were killed, Carrington sent a messenger to the post with orders for Powell to join him with troops and an ambulance. But Powell, complaining of a toothache, had stayed in his quarters with a heated, flannel-wrapped stone to his jaw, sending a junior officer in his place.

"It must be Powell," Carrington said. "He used to be a competent officer. I need to know if he's to be any use to me."

Within minutes Powell and his troops were riding toward the sound of the gunfire, now thin and sporadic. Even without field glasses, Harry could see the Sioux retreating over Lodge Trail Ridge with one Indian, on a spotted pony, trailing the others. The warrior flogged the pony with his quirt until it rebelled, rearing up on its hind legs and throwing the rider to the ground.

Harry studied this fallen Indian more closely. He was slight with fair skin and light, unbound hair. He was naked except for a breechcloth and moccasins, and his entire body was covered with spots of white paint. His headpiece was of a kind Harry had never seen before. It appeared to be a bird, bound to the warrior's head with a strap under his chin. He remembered a sketch Glover had shown him shortly before his death, a drawing of a slight, fair-skinned Indian who traveled with a giant companion. Was this the same man?

Four troopers broke from Powell's column to pursue the warrior, who had remounted and was now kicking his pony forward in a seemingly desperate attempt to rejoin the others on the far side of the ridge. Powell called his men back, then stopped his column and rode alone to the top of the ridge to survey the valley below. Immediately he wheeled his horse and ordered his troops back to the wood train. Soon they were all riding back to the post at a brisk pace. When he reported to Carrington, Powell was red-faced and sweating.

"The valley is swarming with Indians, Colonel. Thousands of them—I've never seen anything like it. That one Indian was a decoy, meant to draw us over the ridge and into the valley. Clearly, that was their intention."

"Thousands, you say?"

"No question, Colonel. Two thousand at least."

Carrington walked to the window. The sun was sinking, bathing the post in a salmon light. "We have one building left to finish," he said, "and sufficient fuel to last us till spring." A giant pile of sawmill slab and scrap lumber towered above the stockade walls. "One or two more trips to the Pinery should provide us enough lumber to finish the hospital. Then I will shut down the wood camps and devote the command full-time to drill and battle preparation. We will attack the Tongue River villages. We will make the Powder River Road safe again for civilian traffic in the spring."

He turned from the window. "Tomorrow I will lead the wood train personally. Ten Eyck, I want eighty men—sixty infantry, twenty cavalry. We'll build a bridge across the Big Piney, there at the place where the Indians attack the loaded wagons returning to the post."

"What's the point, Colonel?" Powell said, "if one more wood train is all we need?"

"I want to test them," Carrington said. "And we need a bridge there regardless. It's something I should have done months ago. Powell, you'll come with me."

A dry, powdery snow fell during the night but the sun was bright and the snow gone by the time the wood train and Carrington's bridge-builders rode away from the post. Harry watched, wishing he could go with them, Indians or no Indians. He had not been outside the stockade for weeks. Instead, he went to the stables, where Calico greeted him as he did every morning.

"Not today," Harry said, stroking the pinto's muscular neck. "We'll go for a run soon, but not today."

After grooming the pony, Harry joined the men splitting slab wood in the quartermaster's yard. Full of frustrated energy, Harry swung a heavy ax, sweating in the warm winter sun and singing along as the soldiers worked their way through their favorite working songs: "Babah of the Regiment," "Tenting

Tonight," and the cavalryman's standard, "Bucking and Gagging":

> Come all Yankee soldiers give ear to my song;
> It is a short ditty, t'will not keep you long;
> It's of no use to fret on account of your luck,
> We can laugh, drink, and sing yet in spite of the
>     buck.
> Dary down, dary down, dary down, down, down,
>     down.

> Sergeant, buck him and gag him, our officers cry,
> For such trifling offenses they happen to spy;
> Till with bucking and gagging of Dick, Tom,
>     and Bill,
> Faith! The Mexican ranks they have so helped to
>     fill.
> Dary down, dary down, dary down, down, down,
>     down.

> The treatment they give us as all of us know
> is bucking and gagging for whipping the foe;
> They buck us and they gag us for malice or for spite,
> But they are glad to release us when going to fight.
> Dary down, dary down, dary down, down, down,
>     down.

> A poor soldier's tied up in the sun or the rain
> With a gag in his mouth till he's tortured with
>     pain;
> Why I'm blest! If the eagle we wear on our flag
> In its claws shouldn't carry a buck and a gag.
> Dary down, dary down, dary down, down, down,
>     down.

The wood train and Carrington's team returned at six o'clock in high spirits, having completed the bridge in one day. They had seen not a single Indian. That night after tattoo, Captain Brown called on Carrington at his home. The colonel sat in Margaret's cushioned rocker before the brick fireplace, reading his Hebrew Bible as he did most evenings. Margaret and Jimmy played dominoes and Harry, sunburned and muscle-sore, lay on the floor watching the flames.

Brown brought a strong animal smell into the room, as if he had come directly from the stables. His greatcoat was open, his spurs fastened through the buttonholes. Although Carrington expected his officers to remove their guns before entering his home, Brown wore two revolvers at his waist and forgot, or neglected, to wipe his boots. Margaret frowned as Brown tracked red mud onto her floor.

"I've got Wands squared away, Colonel," Brown said. Wands would succeed Brown as regimental quartermaster. "He knows the stock and properties and he's up to date on the paperwork."

"Good," Carrington said. "So when do you leave for Fort Laramie?"

"The day after Christmas, sir. Six days from now."

"Well, our loss is their gain," Carrington said. Harry knew his father would be glad to see Brown's backside. Once Brown had been an efficient quartermaster, but since coming to Fort Phil Kearny his desire to hunt and kill Indians had trumped all other concerns. Even worse, the cabal he had formed with Fetterman and Grummond had been a serious threat to his father's authority.

"Thank you, sir," Brown said. "Though I wish I could stay until spring. Oh, what I wouldn't give for one more chance at those murdering sons of Satan, for one more chance at Red Cloud himself." He balled his fist. "I'd give anything to leave his bleeding scalp on Gid Bowers's grave—a remembrance from Baldy Brown."

Carrington cleared his throat. "Captain, my wife is present."

Brown inclined his head toward Margaret. "I apologize, Mrs. Carrington. I was carried away."

The room was quiet but for the loud tick of the Federal clock on the mantel and the pop of the fire. Brown turned to go, touching his hand to his head in a casual salute. "I'm just sorry to miss the fun," he said. His animal smell lingered long after he was gone.

# Chapter Forty-one

Harry's orders were to keep Jimmy away from the house for at least two hours while Margaret and Private O'Reilly set up the Christmas tree. O'Reilly had chopped down a small Douglas fir on the wood train's last run and kept it hidden in the quartermaster's warehouse, standing in a bucket of water. For weeks, Margaret had been secretly stringing ropes of dried red berries late at night while George made dozens of tiny tallow candles.

"We'll need time to trim the tree and decorate the house," Margaret said quietly. "Keep him away even longer, if you can." Her eyes softened as they fell on her younger son squatting on his heels and digging in the soft wet earth of the parade lawn. "He deserves a nice Christmas, poor fellow. He's unhappy here, not like you. Does he ever say anything about wanting to go home?"

"No," Harry said. In fact, Jimmy had said just that many times since learning of the death of his friend, Charley Thomas.

"The carpenter is building him a wagon," Margaret said, "and I'm making a pair of corduroy trousers with hide patches in the seat and the knees, like those cattle drovers wore. Jimmy was quite taken with them."

Harry nodded, feeling glum. He tried to get out of nursemaid duty when he learned Rose Reynolds would be coming to help his mother decorate. He rarely saw her now that she was cloistered away with her ailing husband and soon she would be gone. His father was sending Lieutenant Reynolds east to recover and she was going with him. But Margaret would not let Harry off the hook.

"Keep him busy," she said, raising a warning finger. "I'll be angry if Christmas is spoiled for him!"

Harry sighed and walked over to Jimmy, who was scratching around in the dirt. "Get up," Harry said. "We're going to the stables." Jimmy kept on digging. "What are you doing?" Harry said.

Jimmy had buried five tin soldiers up to their necks. "It's what Indians do to white people when they catch them. They bury them and leave them to die."

"Who told you that?"

"Mr. Grummond. He said they stand by and wait for birds and ants to come eat out their eyes."

Nice thing to tell a six-year-old boy, Harry thought. "Well, it's not true," he said. "Now get up. We're going to go see Calico."

"I don't want to."

Harry grabbed Jimmy's arm and jerked him to his feet. "You're coming whether you want to or not!"

Jimmy wore a sour expression as Harry led him by the arm toward the stables. It was a sunny morning, another warm day for late December. As they passed the quartermaster's warehouse, a great slab of snow slid from the steeply pitched roof and landed on the ground with a thud. Jimmy pulled his arm free and ran to the snow. Harry watched absently as his brother packed a handful into an icy ball. Jimmy stood, turned quickly, and threw it, catching Harry smack on the ear.

"You little shit!" Harry yelled.

Jimmy took off running but Harry easily chased him down, grabbed him by the collar and drove his head into a dirty pile of banked snow. Jimmy kicked and hollered but his muffled screams were barely audible.

"That's hardly a fair fight."

Harry looked up to see William Fetterman standing behind him on the walkway. "He hit me in the ear with a snowball," Harry said. "It hurt." He released his hold and Jimmy emerged red-faced and spluttering. He lunged at Harry, head-butting him in the stomach and knocking him down. He was about to kick him but Fetterman caught Jimmy up in his arms and held him tightly.

"Calm down," Fetterman said, winking at Harry while Jimmy thrashed in his arms. "You've got your blood up, I can see that, but a man must learn to master his feelings. Can you do that, Jimmy? Can I set you free?"

Jimmy kicked a few more times, then nodded. Fetterman put him down. "Anyhow, it's too nice a day for fighting," he said. "Say, look there." He pointed to a flat stretch of ground outside the stockade where a group of children were playing ball. "The Wheatley boys are getting up a game. Why don't you join them?"

The children of enlisted men and civilian employees were allowed more freedom than the children of officers. Lately, the two Wheatley brothers had been organizing games of dare ball outside the main gate. The towheaded twins were the sons of James Wheatley, a quartermaster's employee from Nebraska. Jimmy had not been allowed to join the ballplayers, partly for safety reasons but also because officers' children weren't supposed to associate with those of enlisted men. But before Harry could stop him, Jimmy took off running. Harry followed, catching up just as Jimmy was starting through the heavy, double-plank doors of the main gate. He grabbed Jimmy's arm. "You can't go out there," he said.

"Please, Harry," Jimmy pleaded. "You heard Captain Fetterman—it was his idea. Just this once, just for a little while. I want to play ball. Mother won't even know."

Harry ran a hand through his hair. It would be an easy way to keep Jimmy occupied for the required two hours. "Well," he said, "you'll come in when I say, right?"

Jimmy agreed with a happy nod and they slipped out of the post, not through the main gate but the sally gate on the west side. Once outside, they crept around to the north face, holding close to the wall. If the guards noticed their escape they took no action. Why should they, Harry thought. They weren't responsible for the commanding officer's sons.

As Jimmy joined the ballplayers, Harry found a place in the sun next to Wheatley's cabin. He leaned back against the bark-covered logs and pulled *The Count of Monte Cristo* from his coat pocket. Within seconds he was sewn up in a dead man's bag alongside Edmond Dantès, trying to escape the jailers at the Château d'If.

At ten o'clock he heard the mill gates swing open and the rumble of wagons leaving for the Pinery. They were getting a late start for this, the last wood run of the season. Harry glanced up from his reading as the train moved slowly past the buzzing sawmills. It was accompanied by an unusually large guard, he noticed, almost one hundred men by his estimate. He returned to his book.

The sun was warm on his face and the thrumming of the steam-powered saws was hypnotic. He dozed, letting his book fall open, only to be jolted awake by the blast of the sawmill whistle. Indians! Panicked, Harry jumped to his feet and searched for Jimmy. He was not among the throng of boys running pell-mell for the gates. Inside the fort, men were rushing to take positions on the banquette as the Pilot Hill sentry signaled an attack on the wood train. Harry heard gunfire.

"Jimmy!" he called, turning full circle in his search. "Where are you!"

"Harry—over here!" Jimmy's white, frightened face appeared in the cave-like opening of a civilian's dugout near the Big Piney. He burst out like a

frightened quail running toward Harry at top speed.
At the same time two Sioux warriors rode out of the
cottonwoods on the far side of the creek. They were
barely fifty yards away, close enough for Harry to see
black and yellow war paint on their faces and red
handprints on their ponies. One of the Indians
waved a rifle above his head taunting the soldiers in
the fort.

"Sons of bitches!" he shouted, his pony dancing
beneath him. "Come out and fight us, sons of
bitches!" The other sat motionless, his eyes trained
on Jimmy. Even from a distance, Harry could see the
calculation in his black eyes. Could he reach the boy
without risking a soldier's bullet? Harry raced toward
his brother. Frightened as he was, Harry knew he
could never live with himself if anything happened
to Jimmy.

Jimmy tripped and fell headlong. The watching
Indian saw this and kicked his pony in the ribs,
urging him into the icy waters of the Big Piney. Harry
was chilled to see his smile, his teeth white against
the black face paint. Jimmy got up and hobbled forward, blood flowing from his mouth.

"My ankle!" he said when at last Harry reached
him. "I hurt my ankle."

Harry turned and gave Jimmy his back. "Hop up!"
Jimmy threw his arms around Harry's neck and
wrapped his legs around his waist. Harry ran for all
he was worth, turning once to look over his shoulder.
He wished he hadn't. The warrior was more than
halfway across the Big Piney and coming fast. "Faster,
Harry!" Jimmy's breath was hot in Harry's ear. The

sentries on the banquette fired at the Indian but their shots went high.

"He's coming, Harry!" Jimmy screamed. "Faster!"

By now the Indian had cleared the water. Harry heard the pounding of the pony's unshod hoofs on the hard ground. Desperate with fear, he saw James Wheatley, down on one knee by the gate, squinting down the barrel of his sixteen-shot Henry rifle. He fired. Harry heard one boom, then another, followed by the scream of the warrior's charging pony. Harry looked back to see the horse lying motionless on the ground and his rider scrambling to his feet. The Indian turned and ran back toward the creek, where his companion was riding to his aid. Wheatley did not press his advantage, allowing the rescuer to pull the other up behind him onto his pony's back. They recrossed the Big Piney and retreated into the safety of the cottonwoods. Harry staggered through the gate and collapsed beside Jimmy on the ground.

"Are you boys all right?" Wheatley said. "What's wrong with your mouth, son?"

Jimmy stuck out his tongue to reveal a deep gash. He had bitten it when he fell. "And my ankle too," he said, his teeth red with blood.

"Thank you, Mr. Wheatley," Harry said. "He would've caught us if not for you."

Wheatley was a handsome man with white-blond hair like his twin sons and pale blue eyes. "You did all right too, Harry," he said.

Harry saw his mother running toward them. She kneeled beside Jimmy and covered her ears as the howitzer boomed, sending a shell into the cottonwoods. Harry looked across the creek to see twenty Indians, including the two who had threatened him and Jimmy, fly from the thicket on horseback.

"Take your brother to the house then fetch a surgeon," Margaret said when she finished examining Jimmy's injuries. "Then you can explain to me what you two were doing out there."

She followed as Harry carried Jimmy across the parade where men were preparing to ride in support of the wood train. Carrington had given command of the detachment to Powell but Fetterman stepped forward.

"As senior officer, I request permission to lead the party," he said. "As you see, my men are ready." Harry saw the men of Fetterman's A Company standing in neat formation.

Carrington looked at Powell, who shrugged. "Very well, Captain Fetterman," Carrington said. "Take any additional men you think you may need. And study this before you leave." He gave Fetterman a painstakingly prepared map of Lodge Trail Ridge and the Peno Valley beyond. The colonel had drawn it himself after the disastrous action of December sixth. It showed every stand of trees, each ravine and swale. "I'll send the cavalry out fifteen minutes after you leave," he said. "They should catch up to you before you reach the wood train."

Fetterman saluted and turned toward his men.

"Wait." Carrington placed his hand on Fetterman's right arm. "Support the train, Captain, and return to the post. Nothing more. Engage the Indians only as needed to defend yourselves and the train.

Do not, under any circumstances, pursue them over Lodge Trail Ridge. Do you understand?"

The two men stood face-to-face in the hard morning sun.

"I understand, Colonel," Fetterman said. With a crisp salute he joined his waiting company.

Harry continued on to the house carrying Jimmy. A half-decorated Christmas tree stood in the parlor and swags of pine hung from the windows. He thanked his lucky stars again for Wheatley's marksmanship. Some Christmas this would have been if Jimmy had been killed or, worse, captured. He carried his brother up the stairs and into the bedroom with Margaret close behind. He put Jimmy on the bed and, before his mother could scold him, ran down the stairs and out of the house in search of a surgeon. At the hospital, he found Hines, who agreed to come with him.

As Hines packed his case, Harry stood at the window, watching as Fetterman marched his foot soldiers through the mill gates. To Harry's surprise they did not take the wood road to the west, but headed north toward Big Piney Creek. Meanwhile, Grummond had prepared the cavalry and mounted infantry for inspection. As Harry and Hines crossed the parade, they saw Carrington walking down the line examining weapons and ammunition supplies. Three soldiers were dismissed but the rest passed muster. As they neared the house, Harry heard someone call his name. He turned to see Captain Brown, running toward him.

"Harry," he said, out of breath. "I need a favor."

His face was beaded with sweat though the temperature was dropping.

"A favor from me?" Harry said.

Brown looked at Hines. "Get on with your business, Hines. This is between me and the boy." When they were alone Brown said, "I need to borrow your horse."

"Calico?" Harry said. "You can't ride Calico."

Brown stepped in close. His breath was sour and tobacco-tainted. "The cavalry is leaving in a few minutes and I've got to go with them," he said. "That pinto is the only horse left."

Harry took a step back and shook his head. "You're too heavy," he said. "I don't think—"

Brown gripped Harry's arm. "This is important, Harry. I'm bound for Laramie in a few days—this could be my last go at the devils. Don't deny Baldy Brown a last chance to revenge Gid Bowers." His eyes gleamed in a way that seemed to Harry somehow indecent.

"Take him," Harry said, pulling his arm free. "But don't let anything happen to him."

Brown grinned and slapped Harry on the back. "That's my boy!" he said. "And don't you worry. I'll bring him back with a couple of Sioux scalps swinging from his bridle!"

Icy fingers tickled the back of Harry's neck as he watched Brown jog toward the stables. He did not follow Hines inside the house but went instead to the quartermaster's yard where the cavalry was preparing to leave. He heard Wands relaying his father's orders to Grummond.

"You're to join Fetterman. Together you will relieve the wood train and bring it back here, or, if Fetterman thinks it's safe, escort it on to the Pinery. The colonel says do not—under any circumstances—cross the ridge in pursuit of the Indians. Make sure Fetterman understands that."

As the corporal unlocked the mill gates, Wands added a caution of his own: "And dammit, Grummond, be careful. Remember, you've got a child on the way."

Grummond smiled, looking to Lodge Trail Ridge, where a group of fifteen Indians observed the feverish activity inside the soldier fort. With a wave of his gloved hand, Grummond moved his men through the gates. They had gone about two hundred yards when Carrington called from the observation platform.

"Halt!"

Grummond stopped the column and an unnatural stillness fell over the post. Even the mules were quiet.

"Report to Fetterman and relieve the train," Carrington shouted. "Do not pursue the Indians over Lodge Trail Ridge. Is this clear?"

Grummond stood in his stirrups and gave Carrington an exaggerated salute. "It is, Colonel." He gave the command and his troop rode through the gate following Fetterman's path, with civilians Wheatley and Isaac Fisher bringing up the rear. Just before the corporal of the guard closed the gates, Brown galloped through on Calico, racing to Grummond's side at the head of the column. Harry instantly regretted giving Brown permission to take the pony. Jimmy could not know of it.

After the men were gone, those remaining in the post went about their normal routines. Laundresses brought the wash indoors for folding, carpenters picked up their handsaws and hammers, teamsters went back to greasing axles and tightening bolts. But there was a charge in the air, a sense of fear and anticipation.

Harry joined his father and Ten Eyck on the lookout platform. The weather was deteriorating rapidly, with gray storm clouds moving in from the north. They heard gunfire from the direction of the wood train. Carrington fixed his field glasses on Fetterman's infantry.

"It looks like he plans to march up the creek and along the south slope of the ridge to cut off the Indians' retreat," he said. To Harry's unaided eye they looked like fat black ants moving slowly up the brown slope.

"I thought you told him to take the wood road directly to the train," Ten Eyck said.

Carrington responded, not lowering his glasses. "I did say that but I suppose this will be all right. He'll be in a good position to cut them off or save the train, should the Indians press the attack."

Soon Grummond's cavalry caught up with Fetterman's foot soldiers. The combined detachment, with the horsemen flanking the infantry, pushed north and west along the Bighorn Road until it disappeared behind the Sullivant Hills. Only then did Carrington realize he had not sent a surgeon out with either troop. "Find Dixon," he said to Harry. "Tell him to take an ambulance to the wood train."

"Sir," Ten Eyck said, "one of the men sawed most of a finger off. Dixon's busy with him."

Carrington shook his head impatiently. "Well, find Hines then. Tell my orderly, Private Sample, and Phillips, that foreign fellow—what's his name?"

"Portugee," Harry said.

"Yes, that's the one. Tell Sample he and Portugee Phillips are to escort Hines. If they're not needed at the train, the three of them are to press on and hook up with Fetterman."

Harry found Hines at his house, where he had just finished wrapping Jimmy's ankle. The surgeon did not receive the colonel's orders happily and he climbed the platform to complain. "You're sending me out there with two men? Colonel, I won't go, not without a larger escort."

Carrington did not try to conceal his anger. "I can't spare them, Hines," he said. "I am under-manned here—dangerously so."

"Well, sir, I will not go with only two men," Hines said flatly. "It's simple as that. You can throw me in the guardhouse, court-martial me, whatever you want, I will not do it."

"Dammit, man!" Carrington said. "Get started with Sample and Phillips and I'll send two more men after you—but no more."

Hines agreed with obvious reluctance. Soon after they left the stockade, the Pilot Hill sentry signaled the Indians had quit their attack. His waving flags meant the wood train was breaking corral and moving on toward Piney Island. Carrington pulled out his pocket watch and flipped open the lid.

"Twelve fifteen. Make note of the time, Tenodor." He stepped to the edge of the platform and called down to an officer, telling him to select a mounted infantryman and follow Hines's party. "It may not be necessary, now that the Indians are withdrawing," he said to Ten Eyck, "but I promised and I'm a man of my word, though Hines's manner was quite out of line."

Carrington put a hand on Harry's shoulder. "It's almost dinnertime, son. Let's go to the house and see what George and your mother have for us. Today I believe it's a saddle of mutton with mint jelly, yellow squash, and beets. For dessert, a custard blancmange with cream. How does that sound?"

Harry smiled. Now that the danger was past, his father was in a playful mood. The midday meal would be the usual, bread, soup made of reconstituted dried vegetables with maybe, if they were lucky, a bit of venison, perhaps some floury cake. "Great," Harry said. "I love mutton." He hoped his father's good mood would hold when he learned of Jimmy's near-disaster. They started down the stairs when Ten Eyck spoke.

"Colonel, hold up. It's Hines—they're coming back."

They looked to the wood road where Sample and Phillips were racing their horses around the shoulder of the Sullivant Hills. Hines was close behind in the ambulance. Again they heard gunfire.

"What's that?" Carrington said. "Is the wood train

under attack again?" The Pilot Hill sentry gave no signal.

"Sir, those shots are coming from the northwest," Ten Eyck said, "from the far side of the ridge. That would be Fetterman and Grummond."

Carrington pounded his fist on the platform rail. "Damn—they've crossed over! How many times did I tell them not to?"

They were struck by an icy blast of wind, so violent it took Harry's breath away. At the same time they heard a volley of gunfire, then another, another, and another, followed by rapid, random shots. Lieutenant Wands ran up the steps to join them on the lookout.

"What is it, Colonel?" he said breathlessly. "What's happening?"

Carrington swept the ridge with his field glasses. "I don't see anything."

The volley fire brought all activity at the post to a standstill. Harry saw his mother at the door of their quarters, looking anxiously up at the platform. In the quartermaster's yard the corporal of the guard unlocked the water gates for Hines, Sample, and Phillips, who flew through without slowing. Hines jumped down from the ambulance and ran toward headquarters with Sample right behind him. Men called out to them, seeking information, but they did not stop. They climbed to the platform, their boots pounding on the stairs like war drums.

"Colonel," Hines was breathless, "we couldn't reach Fetterman. The western slope is swarming with Indians. We couldn't get through. There was no way."

"Did you see Fetterman or the cavalry?" Carrington asked.

"No, but the shooting was coming from the far side of the ridge, from the Peno Valley."

All color drained from Carrington's face. He stepped to the rail and called to a man below. "Soldier, tell the quartermaster to ready three wagons and an ambulance. On the double." To Ten Eyck he said, "Assemble every man fit for duty, including those under guard. You will lead them. Take the most direct route to Fetterman and join him at all hazards. Hines, go with Ten Eyck. Sample, take my horse, bring communications back to me as Ten Eyck directs."

Wands started to follow them down the stairs but Carrington stopped him. "Lieutenant, stay here on the lookout, monitor the action. Harry, remain with Wands, run messages to me as needed."

Carrington and the others clattered down the stairs, leaving Harry and Wands alone on the platform. The wind had teeth and they had no protection from its bite. The warm morning sun was a distant memory. "I've got a bad feeling, Harry," Wands said. Harry nodded.

Ten Eyck assembled a relief party quickly. Carrington inspected their arms and ammunition, then ordered the corporal of the guard to open the mill gates. Harry counted seventy-five men marching away on the double-quick, following the route taken earlier by Fetterman and Grummond. Only Ten Eyck and Sample were on horseback. The others advanced on foot, clumsy in greatcoats and buffalo boots.

Once across the Big Piney the men took to the

road, as Fetterman and Grummond had done, moving toward the sound of the shooting, which had tapered off to a few scattered shots. What did that mean, Harry wondered. Had the Indians retreated or was it something else? His skin crawled as he watched Ten Eyck's men labor up the road toward the top of Lodge Trail Ridge, ragged and spiny as the backbone of a starving horse. What would they find on the far side?

A third party of forty men, mostly civilian employees of the post quartermaster, were preparing to follow them. Harry saw Daniel Dixon and Jack Gregory with this group, which also included an ambulance and three wagons loaded with ammunition. They left hurriedly, with Dixon driving the ambulance and Gregory beside him on the bench, his Spencer rifle across his knees and his Appaloosa stallion tied to the rear.

The post was still. There were no men's voices, no braying mules, no buzzing sawmills or ringing hammers, just the wind and the crack of the garrison flag. Though it was only half past noon, the sky was dark as dusk with a low ceiling of slate-colored clouds. Lamps were lit in the cabins of officers' row where the women and children were waiting.

"With all those men gone how many are left here?" Harry said.

Wands shook his head, surveying the vacant post. "I've been trying to work that out," he said. "Seventy, maybe."

Harry did not respond. If Red Cloud's warriors struck the post, how would they defend it?

# Chapter Forty-two

Dixon's ambulance led the ragtag column. Only a few of the men had horses; most rode in the wagons sitting on boxes of ammunition. The silence from the far side of the ridge made every quotidian noise that much louder; the creak of the wagon wheels, the leathery rattle of the harness, the *clop, clop, clop* of hooves on the rocky road.

"It's worse than the shooting, ain't it?" Gregory said. "Leaves more to imagine."

Dixon said nothing but urged the mules forward, sensing death's bony hand just over his shoulder.

"Look there." Gregory pointed to the east, about a mile distant, where a lone horseman raced toward the post. Dixon stopped the team and raised his field glasses. The rider was Carrington's orderly, Private Sample, on the colonel's horse, a large, powerful gray.

"He's carrying a message from Ten Eyck," Gregory said, "and by the way he's pushing that horse, it ain't good."

Dixon restarted the team, hunching his shoulders

deeper into his overcoat and cursing the idiots in the Quartermaster's Department who fussed over frog buttons and black silk braid instead of a fabric's practicality and warmth. The north wind penetrated the worsted wool like water through cheesecloth. He cursed an army that would deploy its soldiers on worn-out horses and expect them to fight the finest light cavalry the world had ever known, an army that equipped its men with clumsy, square-toed boots that blistered the feet, with obsolete, muzzle-loading weapons that discharged one bullet for every ten arrows fired by skilled Indian archers. He thought of Rose and wished for a daguerreotype or other mechanical likeness of her face, something to look at in his final moments, should they come. He tried not to think about what would happen if Indians doubled back to attack the fort in their absence. Before leaving, he had put the question to Carrington.

"Can you defend the post?" he said.

Carrington nodded. "I've got seventy-five men and I've recalled the wood train. That should be sufficient. But if it isn't, if it appears the day is lost, the savages will not take our women and children alive. You may rely on it."

Dixon did not need to ask what Carrington meant.

Following Ten Eyck's route, they kept to the road, which was free of ice and snow though muddy and deeply scored by the feet of men and horses. Near the top of Lodge Trail Ridge, Ten Eyck's trail veered off the road toward a peak that commanded a view of the Peno Valley. Dixon would have followed Ten Eyck's trail but his heavily loaded wagons made this impossible. He had no choice but to follow the road over the crest of the ridge, even though it would take them through a defile that presented a perfect spot for an ambush. This, he knew, was why Ten Eyck had altered his route. Dixon's nerves were tight as fiddle strings as they topped the ridge. The scene below confirmed his worst fears.

"Jesus, Joseph, and Mary," Gregory said.

The Peno Valley was alive with Indians in full war paint, mounted and on foot, swarming over the road and up the hillsides on the valley's far side. It was a nightmarish sight, as if every warrior north of the Powder River had joined Red Cloud to fight on this day. Frightening though it was, Dixon also felt relief. The presence of so many Indians meant they were not at the nearly defenseless fort.

Ten Eyck's men were to the east on a high point along the ridge but he saw no sign of Fetterman's infantry and Grummond's cavalry. Directly ahead, a group of about one hundred warriors blocked the road that led down into the valley. Some were on horseback, others were climbing over an outcrop of broken rock. Two Indians bared their buttocks at the soldiers and shouted insults in English.

"Sons of bitches!" they shouted. "Come fight us! Come fight, sons of bitches!"

Dixon's eye was drawn to one small, slender warrior sitting on his pony apart from the others. His complexion was so fair he could almost be taken for a white man. Despite the cold he was nude but for a breechcloth and leggings. His body and that of his pony were covered with spots of white paint. A marksman from Ten Eyck's command fired at him but he did not flinch. The bullet fell short.

By now the rest of the wagons were cresting the ridge behind Dixon, the mules staggering with exhaustion. The Indians blocking the road saw their arrival and began to withdraw.

Gregory gave a short laugh. "They think we've got artillery in the wagons," he said. "That may save us."

The warriors blocking the road moved down the slope to join those in the valley below. Only when they left could Dixon see what had occupied them: the naked bodies of soldiers lay on the rocks and along the road, their legs and torsos white as alabaster in stark contrast to their sun-darkened forearms, necks, and faces. The bodies were too many and too tumbled together to count. Dixon thought he was looking at twenty-five to thirty men. All were completely still. The only moving thing on the rocky ridge was a wounded cavalry horse, struggling to get to its feet.

Ten Eyck rode alone along the ridge to join them. His face fell when he saw the boxes of ammunition in the wagon beds. Like the Indians, he thought they held something else. "Where's the howitzer I requested?" he said. "Didn't Colonel Carrington get my message?"

"I don't know anything about a howitzer," Dixon said. "What we've got is ammunition, three thousand rounds. Where are the others?"

Ten Eyck shook his head. "I don't know. I wish I did. We've been here nearly an hour and I haven't seen anyone other than those poor fellows. They were finishing them off when we got here."

They looked at the bodies, stiffening in the cold.

"I'll tell you where the others are," Gregory said. "They're down the road a piece and in the same condition as these."

An angry wind raked over them, as if affirming Gregory's prediction. Below, Indians raced their ponies across the bottomlands, urging the white soldiers to come down into the valley and fight. Hundreds of additional warriors watched from the far slopes and hilltops.

"How many, would you say?" Ten Eyck said.

Gregory answered: "Fifteen hundred, maybe two thousand."

"We should go to them." Dixon gestured toward the bodies on the rocks and road. "Someone might be alive."

Ten Eyck looked at him, his good eye opened wide. "No one's alive in there—just look at them. No, I'm in command here and I forbid you or anyone else to go forward. We'll wait for the howitzer."

"It's not coming," Dixon said. "There's not a fit mule left to pull it."

Ten Eyck shook his head. "I sent Sample to the post with a report. The colonel knows my circumstances here—he wouldn't leave me in this position. No, we wait. Meantime, we'll join forces. Move your wagons along the ridge. We'll meet you halfway."

Dixon could do nothing but follow Ten Eyck's command. The cold and wind were merciless and time seemed to stand still. They waited for what seemed an eternity. When at last a rider from the fort appeared, it was Sample, alone, with a note for Ten Eyck. Despite the cold, the paper was damp with Sample's sweat. Ten Eyck read aloud:

"'Captain, forty well-armed men with three thousand rounds, ambulances, etc. left before your courier came in.' That would be you, Dixon. 'You must unite with Fetterman; fire slowly and keep men in hand; you would have saved two miles toward the scene of action if you had taken Lodge Trail Ridge. I order the wood train in, which will give fifty more men to spare.'"

Ten Eyck turned to Sample. "What about the artillery I requested?"

"There aren't any animals to pull the wagon," Sample said, still breathless. "Besides, the colonel said no one with your outfit knows how to handle the piece anyhow."

Ten Eyck made a sound of indignation. "How dare he criticize—"

"Forget it," Dixon said. "Look, we've been freezing our butts off up here long enough. We've got to get back to the post and I'm taking those men with me. I'll need help loading them."

"What about the Indians?" Ten Eyck said.

"If they were going to attack us they'd have done it by now," Dixon said. "I'm more worried about them striking the fort. We need to take care of business here and get back there."

Ten Eyck considered briefly, then raised his arm to move his shivering, frightened men forward. They kept to the road, advancing warily, watching the Indians for the first sign of attack. When finally they reached the bodies, not even the most battle-hardened veteran was prepared for the horror that met him. Some of the men were sick, producing steaming pools of vomit that froze quickly on the ground.

"My God," Ten Eyck said. "It's a scene from Dante."

Dixon walked silently through the field of corpses. Never had he seen such a violent display of hatred. Faces were unrecognizable, smashed by heavy Sioux war clubs to a meaty mix of brains, bone, and hair. The ground was slippery with frozen entrails. One man's guts encircled his neck like the devil's twine. A pair of eyeballs watched Dixon from a rock; beside them was a severed nose. Several bodies were sliced open from thorax to pubis, the empty cavity stuffed with dry grass and set aflame. Deep gashes scored marble-white thighs.

"Let's go back, Captain Ten Eyck," a young soldier shouted, his face contorted with fear. "We can't do nothin' for them—they're past caring what happens to them now. Let's go back before the Injuns kill us all."

Others voiced support for this idea, but Ten Eyck shook his head. "We won't leave them," he said. "Put the bodies in the wagons."

Dixon stopped at one particularly muscular corpse and found himself looking down on the remains of Fred Brown. His penis and testicles had been severed and stuffed in his mouth. A frozen trickle of black blood ran from a bullet hole in his left temple.

Fetterman's body was close by. Dixon studied it,
trying to make sense of what he saw. Then he understood: his throat was cut from ear to ear and his
tongue pulled through the slit. His broken jaw hung
open in a lopsided grin. Dixon was stunned by such
inventive cruelty, awed by the hatred that inspired it.

"Dixon! Ten Eyck!" Gregory stood on the driver's
bench of the ambulance. "The Indians—they're
leaving."

Down in the valley the warriors were moving en
masse toward the southeast. Were they returning to
their lodges, Dixon wondered, sated with killing and
eager to celebrate their victory? Or were they headed
to the fort, knowing that most of its defenders were
here, on this wind-blasted ridge?

Ten Eyck had the same thought. "Hurry, men!" he
shouted.

Some bodies were frozen to the ground in pools
of blood and had to be pried loose with rifle barrels.
Once free, they were stacked without dignity, head to
heels, in the wagon beds.

"What about the bits and pieces, Captain?" one
man said, lifting a muscular arm.

"Throw it in," Ten Eyck said.

In a gesture of respect to fellow officers, Ten Eyck
ordered that Fetterman and Brown be placed not in
the open wagon but the ambulance.

At last the hellish work was done and the freezing
men started the four-mile trek back to Fort Phil
Kearny. Along the way, Indian pickets on the hilltops
monitored their progress but offered no resistance.
Dixon's anxiety mounted with each step until, as they

neared the post, it was almost unbearable. He thought of Rose, saw her face, heard her voice. Did a new, unimaginable horror await him? He shook his head, trying to keep the terrible images at bay.

Finally the advance riders crested the ridge, gaining a view of the post. They cheered and raised their hats. It was secure. Dixon released a long sigh and realized he had been holding his breath. When the struggling mules pulled the ambulance to the top, Dixon looked down on the fort and, for the first time, thought it beautiful. Cheery yellow lights shone in the windows of officers' row and in the regimental offices. The wind was less now. Gray plumes of smoke rose heavenward from the chimneys of the barracks and cabins. The quartermaster's gates swung open and Ten Eyck's advance riders entered.

"Thank God," Dixon said.

"The night's not over," Gregory said.

# Chapter Forty-three

Dixon climbed down from the ambulance and almost fell. His legs were wooden with cold and he could not feel his feet. All around him, bundled men shuffled silently through the gray half light, lifting the stiffened remains of friends and bunkmates from the wagons and carrying them to a makeshift morgue in the hospital. Occasionally the stillness was broken by a curse or a cry as a man recognized a face or, if the face was unknowable, a tattoo. Dixon looked to the distant black hills, lit from behind by a rising moon, and felt the presence of an enemy, ancient and primordial, rallying his forces against them. On this occasion, the Indians and the elements seemed to be allies. Was survival against such a combination of foes possible?

"Doctor Dixon?" A small man approached. "It's Fessenden, sir. They say you've got Captain Fetterman in there."

Frank Fessenden was a young musician whose wife had given birth to a daughter at Fort Sedgwick.

Fetterman was charmed by the fat, happy baby and was often seen holding her in his arms, smiling down at her and talking nonsense.

"Yes," Dixon said. "Captain Brown too."

Fessenden removed his hat, as if he had entered a church. "I'd be honored if you'd let me help you with the remains. Captain Fetterman was a good friend to me and my family."

"Are you sure?" Dixon said. "Wouldn't you rather remember him as he was?"

"Thank you, sir, but I'd like to help."

"All right then."

Dixon led him to the rear of the ambulance, where Hines was waiting with a lantern. The door groaned on its leather hinges as Dixon pulled it open. The lamplight fell on two bodies. Fetterman lay on the bench nearest the door. Only the soles of his square-toed boots were visible, the left turned inward toward its mate at an unnatural angle. Dixon and Fessenden climbed in. The young man gasped but did not falter when he saw Fetterman's ghastly, grinning wound. The protruding tongue was beginning to blacken.

They put the body on a stretcher and carried it to the hospital. Hines and Gregory followed with Brown. Sam Horton directed the arrangement of corpses on the earthen floor of the ward room, with its open windows and canvas roof. Maybe it was a good thing the hospital was unfinished after all, Dixon thought. At least the bodies wouldn't rot as fast.

"My God," Horton said, his face haggard in the guttering candlelight. "Is that Fetterman?"

"It is," Dixon said. "Where do you want him?"

Horton waved them to a dark corner where four planed boards lay across a pair of sawhorses. "Our officers won't lie on the ground," he said. Only when the two men were lying side by side did Dixon notice the powder-singed flesh on Brown's left temple. "Are more coming?" Horton said.

"These are the last," Dixon said, "for tonight anyhow."

"Forty-nine men," Horton said, glassy-eyed. "I can't believe it. Most were bludgeoned to death, did you notice?"

"Most," Dixon said. "I believe some killed themselves. Brown, for example."

"Brown took his own life?" Carrington had entered the room unnoticed.

"It looks that way," Dixon said. He walked to the captain's body and pointed to the wound on his temple. "He died of a single shot to the head fired at close range."

Carrington stared down at the officers' bodies. "Tell me where you found them," he said. "Tell me exactly where Fetterman was in relation to Brown and the others."

"Didn't Ten Eyck give you that?" Dixon said.

"I'd like to hear it from you."

Dixon hesitated, wanting to be sure he remembered correctly. If they lived through this, such observations would be important. He described what he and Gregory saw as they crested the ridge, the locations of the Indians and Ten Eyck's troops, the mound of broken rock beside the road where most of the bodies were found.

"There were only a few cavalrymen—Brown and one or two others—with Fetterman's infantry. The horses were lying with their heads toward the post, as if the cavalry was retreating when they fell."

Carrington looked into Dixon's eyes. "What do you think happened?" he said. "I'd like your sense of it."

The room went quiet. "I'd say the cavalry got too far ahead of Fetterman. The Indians decoyed Grummond over the ridge and into a trap. Fetterman saw—or heard—what was happening and went in to save them."

Carrington's large eyes glittered in the lamplight. "Fetterman was in command," he said. "I ordered him not to cross the ridge but—for whatever reason—he chose to disobey. I also blame Ten Eyck. He might've arrived in time to save the whole outfit if he'd taken the road as I directed."

Dixon felt a red anger surge inside him. He understood how Carrington's brain was working, that he was forming a self-serving report to Omaha even as the bodies of his men stiffened around him. Until this point, Dixon had felt mostly sympathy for Carrington, but now he felt something very different.

"What should Fetterman have done, Colonel?" he said. "How could he hang back and let the Indians wipe out all those men? Once Grummond went over the ridge, Fetterman had no choice. As for Ten Eyck, he did what any competent, experienced officer would do. He was right to leave the road, to avoid the defile. He feared ambush, and rightly so. He was thinking of his men."

Carrington's eyes narrowed but before he could respond Sample appeared at the door to announce the return of the wood train.

"Thank God," Carrington said. "I was beginning to fear they'd gone up too." He raised his voice, addressing the room. "When you men are finished here report to your barracks and await further orders. Horton, you and your stewards remain with our valiant dead. Dixon, come with me."

He saw a light burning in the window of Rose's cabin as he and the colonel crossed the parade toward headquarters. He ached to see her, but it would have to wait. Signal fires burned on the hills surrounding the post and shadows moved before the flames. Dixon prayed the Indians had not taken captives, and had the unwelcome image of a bound man turning and roasting on a spit like a side of venison.

They entered the office to find Powell, Ten Eyck, Wands, and Hines waiting. Without a word, Carrington sat at his desk and swept his arm across its surface, clearing it of everything but a smoking lamp in a glass chimney. Dixon and the officers stood in a semicircle before him.

"Wands, how many men are available to defend the post?" Carrington said.

"One hundred nineteen, sir, including the civilians."

"Ten Eyck, station three men at each sentry stand and one at each loophole along the banquette and in the quartermaster's yard. Board all the cabin doors and windows, with loopholes for shooting. I want at least one armed man in each cabin. Dixon and Hines, see to the hospital—I want it boarded too. Then we must barricade the magazine. Take the wagon beds off the gears and position them on their sides, so." He placed his hand perpendicular to his desk and moved it in a clockwise, circular fashion along the surface. "Encircle the magazine at least three times."

He raised his head and looked each man in the eye. "When—that is, *if*—the Indians attack, all women and children will take shelter in the magazine. In advance, I will position the ammunition and cut and adjust the fuses in such a way that the whole can be ignited with a single match. If it appears the day is lost, I will send up the magazine and everyone in it. Our women and children will not be taken alive."

A blast of wind shook the door and rattled the windows. Fine hail pelted the glass.

"Of course, they must not be told," Carrington continued. "A mother may be unwilling to . . ." He bowed his head, unable to finish.

The men left headquarters without speaking. The cold had deepened, hard and dry, making each breath painful. "Go on to the hospital, Hines," Dixon said. "I'll be along soon. There's someone I need to see."

# Chapter Forty-four

Harry carried bedding from the cabins to Lieutenant Wands's quarters where the women and children would wait out the night. Rose was there, helping the frightened families settle in. She saw him and waved him over.

"James Wheatley told me what you did today," she said, "how you saved Jimmy. He said you were very brave."

Harry blushed and looked down at his muddy shoes. "I didn't have a choice," he said. "I couldn't leave him."

"You had a choice. We always have a choice."

Outside a sentry called out the hour: "Station six! Seven o'clock and all's well!" The cry was picked up by the guard at station seven, starting the round robin that moved through the post on the quarter-hour. As he listened to the familiar sound, Harry wondered if this would be the last night he heard them, his last night on Earth. His thoughts were interrupted by the crack of a gun, a single shot.

"Indians!" A woman screamed. "They've come!"

But no, Harry thought, the shot was close. It came from inside the post, from officers' row. From Rose's cabin. She thought the same. Her face went pale as her eyes met Harry's.

"Mark!" she said. She picked up her skirts and ran, with Harry close behind. Timson, Mark's striker, and a few others were already at her cabin. A pierced tin lantern in Timson's hand swung back and forth, throwing crazy patterns on the walls and frightened faces.

"Wait, Mrs. Reynolds!" Timson said, unholstering his sidearm. "Let me go in first!" But Rose pushed by him and ran through the door. Harry followed. Despite the fire in the heating stove, the cabin's interior was frigid. Harry saw that the window in the back room was open wide, its turkey-red curtains flapping in the wind.

They entered the room to find Reynolds lying motionless on the bed. Timson raised his lantern to reveal Mark's lifeless eyes staring blankly at the ceiling. A thin black line of blood ran from a bullet hole in the center of his forehead.

Rose dropped to her knees beside the bed and covered her face with her hands. She did not react when Dixon and Wands entered the room.

"What happened?" Wands said as Harry closed the window. "Did anyone see anything?"

"No," Timson said. "We heard the shot and found him like this. The window was open."

Dixon walked to the bed, lightly touching Rose's hair. She did not respond, keeping her face hidden.

"I was just here," Dixon said, "not five minutes ago. I came to see . . . I knocked, but there was no answer." He leaned in to examine the wound, then Reynolds's hands. One lay across his chest, the other hung over the side of the bed just above a .38-caliber Smith & Wesson revolver with mother-of-pearl grips and filigree etching on the breech and barrel. Harry recognized the gun—it was the one Reynolds showed him that day in the canyon. It seemed a lifetime ago. Dixon picked it up and opened the cylinder.

Colonel Carrington pushed through the crowded room. "Great God in heaven," he said, "what now?" He looked at Reynolds. "Did he do this to himself?"

"No," Dixon said.

"And how do you know that?"

Dixon showed him the cylinder. "This gun is fully loaded. My guess is Reynolds went for it, tried to defend himself, but ran out of time. This was an execution."

# Chapter Forty-five

Rose refused to join the women and children in Wands's quarters.

"I should stay here," she said to Carrington, avoiding Dixon's eyes. "It doesn't seem right to just leave him like this."

But Carrington insisted. "The women and children must be together tonight, my dear. I order it."

Margaret took her by the arm. "There's nothing you can do here," she said. "Henry will find out who did this. But for tonight, please come with me."

Rose nodded and the two women walked out into the bone-breaking cold. The sky was cloudless and disordered with stars. In her mind's eye Rose saw Mark's face, not gaunt and gray as it was at the end, but perfect, as when they met. Who had done this and why? She felt a crushing guilt, as if she had pulled the trigger.

Frances Grummond glared at Rose as they entered Wands's stuffy cabin. Rose took a chair by the window, boarded from the outside, and turned her face to the glass. In it she saw Frances's reflection.

"I hope you're satisfied." Frances fairly spat out the words. "You got what you wanted, didn't you? Mark Reynolds is dead—a fine man is dead—and you don't care. You may have even had something to do with it. It wouldn't surprise me."

"Frances," Margaret said, "please stop."

Frances's words had no impact on Rose. Already she blamed herself and she didn't care what Frances Grummond thought anyhow. She kept her eyes on the window where, in the gaps between boards, she saw men feverishly dismantling the quartermaster's wagons. It occurred to Rose that Frances cared for Mark more than she, Rose, realized. Her lack of reaction fueled the flames of Frances's rage.

"Jezebel! You never fooled me, not for one minute. Oh, yes, I've seen—"

Margaret stepped in front of her.

"Stop it." She spoke with authority. "You are not yourself, Frances. You are distraught and worried for your husband—we are all distraught—but this is no time for foul accusations. Our men need us to be strong, as they are. We face a desperate trial tonight, and in the days to come. Now, I ask everyone in the room to join me in prayer. We will bow our heads and petition the Lord for protection and guidance." Before she could begin, the sergeant stationed outside knocked and opened the door.

"Excuse me, Mrs. Carrington. Someone is asking for Mrs. Grummond. Shall I let him in?"

"Asking for me?" Frances said. "Who is it?"

"Phillips, ma'am. The civilian."

Frances frowned. "Phillips? I don't know anyone by that name."

Margaret said, "Show him in."

The visitor was small, with dark curling hair, a well-trimmed beard, and bright black eyes. He carried his hat in one hand and a robe in the other.

"Oh, Portugee," Frances said, coloring. "It's you."

Rose recognized him, a miner who arrived at the fort late in the season and took winter work for the quartermaster. He often delivered water and firewood to the Grummonds' cabin.

He walked to Frances's chair. "Tonight I ride for help," he said, in heavily accented English. "I go with dispatches, as special messenger from Colonel Carrington, if it costs me my life. I go for your sake!" He extended the robe. "I brought my wolf robe to keep you warm and to remember me by, if you never see me again."

Frances's color deepened. "Thank you, Portugee," she said, taking the robe. "It's very kind of you. I'm sure George will thank you too, when he returns."

Phillips's eyes glistened with tears. "Yes, sure, when he returns." He bowed from the waist, like a knight genuflecting before his queen. Rose idly wondered what Frances had done to inspire such devotion. She was a casual flirt. Maybe she said something in passing that struck a chord of longing in the lonely foreigner. Poor Phillips, she thought. A journey of unimaginable misery lay ahead of him. She wondered if he would survive it.

# Chapter Forty-six

Harry ran across the parade ground. It was the coldest night he had ever known. Each breath was torture, an icy assault on the throat and lungs, despite the woolen scarf he wore over his mouth and nose. He pitied the poor sentries huddled on platforms or pacing the banquette. Because of the cold, their shifts had been shortened to fifteen minutes.

At last he reached his father's office. Sample was stoking the fire in the heating stove while Carrington wrote furiously at his desk. The warmth was blissful.

"What are you doing here?" Carrington said, not looking up. "You should be with your mother."

"She doesn't need me right now," Harry said. "Besides, I'd rather be with you and the men. I want to help."

Carrington continued writing, his nib scratching across the paper. Finally he put down his pen and looked up at his son. "You can be a help to me at that." He stood and put on his coat. "Copy this letter. It is vital that I have a record of all my correspondence to Omaha from this moment forward. When you're done, bring the original to me at the stables. Write legibly."

He left, taking Sample with him. Alone in the office, disappointed with his seemingly unimportant assignment, Harry took up his father's pen, still warm from his hand, and started to write. The letter was addressed to General Cooke.

> *Fort Philip Kearny, D.T.*
> *December 21, 1866*
>
> *. . . Do send me reinforcements forthwith. Expedition now with my force is impossible. I risk everything but the post and its stores. I venture as much as anyone can, I have had but today a fight unexampled in Indian warfare; my loss is ninety-four killed.*
>
> *I have received forty-nine bodies and thirty-five more are to be brought in in the morning. Among the killed are Brevet Lieutenant Colonel Fetterman, Captain F. H. Brown, and Lieutenant Grummond.*

Harry copied word for word, even though the letter seemed at places incoherent. Why did his father say all were dead when Grummond's men were still out?

> *The Indians engaged were nearly three thousand, being apparently the force reported as on Tongue River in my dispatches of 5 November and subsequent thereto. This line, so important, can and must be held. It will take four times the force*

*in the spring to reopen it if it be broken up this
winter. The additional cavalry ordered to join me
has not reported; their arrival would have saved
us much loss today.*

*The Indians lost beyond all precedent. I need
prompt reinforcements and repeating arms. I am
sure to have, as before reported, an active winter
and must have men and arms. Every officer of the
battalion should join it. Today I had every teamster
on duty and but 119 men left at post. I hardly need
urge this matter, it speaks for itself. Give me two
companies of cavalry at least, forthwith, well
armed, or four companies of infantry exclusive of
what is needed at Reno and Fort Smith.*

*Promptness will save this line but our killed
shows that any remissness will result in mutilation
and butchery beyond precedent. No such mutilation
as that today is on record. Depend upon it that the
post will be held so long as a round or a man is left.
Promptness is the vital thing. Give me officers and
men. Only the new Spencer arms should be sent.
The Indians are desperate. I spare none and they
spare none.*

> *Henry B. Carrington*
> *Col. 18th U.S. Inf.*
> *Comd'g Post*

Harry blotted the pages, folded the original, and
put it in an envelope. He knew this letter would do
his father no good with Cooke, if they survived the
night, or his legacy, if they did not.

The walk to the stables was especially punishing

after the warmth of the office. Clouds rolling in from the west obscured the moon and stars. A storm was coming. Harry looked to the hills and saw the Indians' fires still burning. Were there drums? He thought he heard them but he wasn't sure. The throbbing could be his own blood, pounding in his head.

In the dimly lit stables he found his father, Sample, and a third man in a buffalo coat putting a bridle on Jack Gregory's Appaloosa. Only when he got closer did he see the third man was Daniel Dixon.

"What's going on?" Harry said. No one answered.

A guard called from the far end of the stable. "He's asking for Beau, Colonel."

Deep in the shadows Harry saw the guard and the foreigner, Portugee Phillips, standing by the stallion's stall. Beau was Carrington's special pride, a strong black Thoroughbred given to him during the war by an admiring horse breeder from the bluegrass region of Kentucky. No one but the colonel was allowed to ride him.

"He must have him then," Carrington said. "He's the strongest animal left to us. Guard, saddle Beau and bring him round to the sally gate. Sample, pack two kits with crackers, jerky, and grain for the horses. Each man gets a Spencer rifle and one hundred rounds of ammunition. Double quick!"

"Bring blankets too, Sample," Dixon said as he threw a saddle on the Appaloosa's back. With a shock, Harry understood that Dixon meant to ride with Phillips tonight.

"I don't understand why you insist on doing this, Dixon, when Gregory should be the one to go with Phillips," Carrington said. "I need you here. Where is Gregory anyway?"

"Gone," Dixon said.

"Gone?" Carrington said. "What do you mean?"

"Just that."

"Did you see him leave?"

"No, but his gear is missing."

"How can this be? You've got his horse."

Dixon bent down to cinch the girth. "He left the Appaloosa for us," Dixon said. "He knew we'd need him. My horse wouldn't make it halfway to Horseshoe Station."

Carrington made a sound of disgust. "The man is a common criminal. I should have thrown him in the guardhouse when you brought him back from Bozeman. Why would he disappear like this? I suppose he killed Reynolds."

Dixon walked to the Appaloosa's head and lifted his hairy lip to check the bit. "Whatever he did, Jack Gregory has risked his neck to help us—more than once—and now he's left us his horse. Anyhow, we've got bigger problems."

He stepped around Carrington, leading Gregory's Appaloosa out of the stables. Carrington and Harry followed with Phillips and Beau. News of the rescue riders had spread. As they walked to the sally gate, men came forward to shake hands with Phillips and Dixon and wish them luck.

A nervous sentry on the banquette challenged them

as they neared the gate. "Halt!" he cried, swinging his carbine in their direction. "Who goes there?"

"It's your commanding officer, you idiot," Carrington said. "Stay as you are."

They waited in the bitter darkness, each alone with his thoughts. The Thoroughbred was dancing. Carrington spoke to him softly, stroking his neck. His voice had a calming effect.

At last Sample arrived with the food and supplies. Dixon cut the blankets into strips, which he and Phillips used to wrap the heavy ammunition to their ankles. Harry had seen scouts do this before setting out on an especially difficult journey. The weight would help keep their feet in the stirrups. When they were finished Carrington told the sergeant of the guard to open the gates. The wood groaned as he slid the heavy bar from its brackets.

"Harry, give me the letter," Carrington said. He checked the envelope's contents, then sealed it and gave it to Phillips. "Deliver this to the telegrapher at Horseshoe Station." They shook hands. "May the Lord ride with you. Our life is in your hands."

He took hold of the bridle and steadied Beau as Phillips swung into the saddle. Harry heard sadness in his father's voice as he said good-bye to the horse. Then Phillips applied his spurs and they flew away into the darkness at a gallop. Carrington closed his eyes, listening to the diminishing hoofbeats.

"Good," he said. "He has taken the softer ground at the side of the road."

Dixon mounted the Appaloosa and said, "Colonel, you said we'd be paid for this."

Carrington raised his eyebrows. Dixon was not a man known to be concerned with money. "Yes. Three hundred dollars for both of you."

"And if we don't make it the money will go to our beneficiaries?"

"Yes. You have my word."

Dixon shook Carrington's hand, then turned to Harry. "So long, Harry." They too shook hands. "I've got a favor to ask of you. If I don't come back I want her to have it. You know who I mean. The three hundred dollars and everything else I've got. I've left a letter in my cabin. See to it, will you?"

Harry nodded, a stone in his throat. "I will," he said.

Dixon kicked the Appaloosa's sides and then they too were gone. For a brief time Harry heard the rhythmic beat of the horse's shod hoofs on the frozen road, then nothing.

"God be with them," Carrington said as the guard barred the door.

# Chapter Forty-seven

The boom of the sunrise gun shook her from a fitful sleep. For an instant Rose was buoyed by a fragile hope. Maybe she had only dreamed Mark's death and all the rest. But no, she woke to her surroundings and the truth came crashing down. She felt as a soldier must feel, she thought, waking in a trench on the day of battle.

Slowly she got to her feet. The muscles of her back were stiff and sore from sleeping on the floor and her head ached.

"I'm glad you slept." Margaret sat beside a small table. A lamp was lit and a book lay open in her lap. "You needed it."

"Have you been up all night?" Rose spoke quietly so as not to wake the other women and children.

"Most of it." Margaret looked down at Jimmy curled up in a pile of blankets at her feet.

"Has there been any change?"

"No," Margaret said. "Nothing."

Rose stepped gingerly around the bundled bodies

on the floor and cracked the door, breathing in the cold morning air. The eastern sky was beginning to lighten. Carrington had doubled the guard. Two men stood on every sentry stand and the banquette was lined with watchful gunmen. If the Indians were going to come, it would be soon.

Looking at her own cabin she saw it was dark, its windows boarded. Was Mark still there or had they moved him to the hospital to take his place with the other corpses? Poor Mark, she thought, to keep such ghastly company.

Dixon's cabin also was dark. Where was he? She wanted so very much to see him. She didn't care what Frances Grummond thought. Her opinion did not matter. Only one person's opinion truly mattered to her now. She closed the door and went to the kitchen where Margaret was stoking the fire in the cook stove.

"Fill the pot, will you?" Margaret said. "I'll make coffee."

Rose filled the tin coffeepot with water from the barrel by the door while Margaret ground the roasted beans. After putting it on to boil, she sat at the table and motioned for Rose to sit across from her.

"I hope Frances didn't hurt you last night," Margaret said. "She was upset."

"I don't care what she thinks. Truly, I don't."

Margaret smiled. "I believe you. That's something I've always admired about you, Rose, your honesty and independence. When all this is over you two should stay here, in the West. Helena, maybe. Henry says Helena will be a fine city someday."

"We two?"

"You and Dr. Dixon, of course. You belong together. I've thought so for some time. Tell me, did Mark know you were with child when he left you at Fort Sedgwick?"

Rose was stunned. "How did you know?"

Margaret shrugged. "When a woman wants to have a child—as I do—she is sensitive to signs in others. How far along were you? Ten or twelve weeks?"

"Ten weeks at most," Rose said. "And yes, Mark knew."

"Henry encouraged him to remain with you, you know, but Mark insisted he stay with the regiment. Lieutenant Reynolds was very keen to prove himself."

Rose nodded. She suspected as much. After Fort Sedgwick, she knew her well-being and that of her child always would be second to Mark's ambition.

"I'm glad the child was not born," Rose said. It was the first time she had admitted this, even to herself. "At the time I wanted it very much, but now I'm glad. Is that evil?"

Margaret shook her head. "I don't think so. But if the baby had come, I'm sure you would have loved him or her as much as I love my boys. You'll be a fine mother one day, I'm sure of it."

Her admission and Margaret's forgiveness made Rose feel as if a heavy load had been lifted from her shoulders.

"I'm not sure Mark loved me," she said. "Not really, not the way Daniel does." She stood, feeling light as a feather. "I'm going to see him—right now. Where is he, do you know? In the hospital?"

"Sit down," Margaret said. "Dr. Dixon isn't here. He rode with Phillips last night. He's gone to Horseshoe Station for help."

"What?" Rose felt the familiar heaviness returning. "Why didn't he tell me?" Did he mistake her tears of guilt at Mark's bedside for something else? Why hadn't she gone to him last night? Why, when confronted with the specter of death, had she let any meaningless sense of decorum stop her?

Margaret walked to the stove and returned with a steaming mug of coffee. "Drink it," she said. "You'll feel better."

Rose looked down at the black coffee, her mind racing. She remembered the last time she saw him, in the quartermaster's yard, with Jack Gregory, after their return from the ridge. Now, in her mind's eye, she saw him beside Phillips, dead on the frozen ground. Rose closed her eyes and sent up a prayer, just as the bugler outside sounded assembly. The notes sounded full of portent and mournful as a dirge. Please, she prayed, let him return to me.

The front door swung open and Carrington and Harry entered the cabin. They came first to the kitchen, moving awkwardly in their heavy coats and overshoes, stepping carefully around the small children still sleeping on the floor. Carrington took his wife's hands and kissed her on the lips.

"Did anyone come in last night?" Margaret said.

Carrington shook his head. "No. We must assume that Grummond and the thirty men with him are dead."

His words were met with a moan from the daybed where Frances Grummond had passed the night. Jennie Wands went to her, holding her as she sobbed. All eyes turned to Carrington.

A bead of sweat rolled down his face as he addressed the crowded room. "Last night I dispatched two brave men, Portugee Phillips and surgeon Daniel Dixon, to the telegraph office at Horseshoe Station. Our lives are in their hands."

Harry saw the pain on Rose's face.

"Captain Ten Eyck is forming a recovery detail," Carrington said. "I will lead it personally. I promise you"—here he looked at Frances Grummond—"we will not return until every man has been found and his remains brought to safety."

He walked to the daybed and removed his hat. His hair was wet with sweat and plastered across his pale forehead. "Mrs. Grummond," he said, "I am very sorry for your loss. I shall bring Lieutenant Grummond back to you."

Frances raised her wet, swollen face. "George and the others are beyond suffering now," she said. "You ought not risk other precious lives and make other women as miserable as myself."

Carrington looked at her with admiration. "Your selflessness does you credit," he said, "but my reasons are not wholly sentimental. If we cannot rescue our dead, as the Indians do at whatever risk, how can I send details out for any purpose? They will think us weak. It may stimulate them to risk an assault."

This served as a reminder the fort was still at risk. Ripples of fear went through the room. Margaret walked to her husband's side and took his arm.

"Yes," she said. "It is your duty. God will care for us. Go rescue the dead, Henry."

After he left the women busied themselves packing away the blankets and bed rolls. Outside they heard the relief column preparing to depart. Rose opened the door to cool the overheated room. Only Carrington, his two officers, and about a dozen men were mounted. The others were on foot or in the open wagons that would hold corpses on the return. Before leaving, Carrington handed Captain Powell two pieces of paper.

"What are those orders?" Rose said to Harry, beside her at the open door.

"I don't know." He lied. He watched his father write them.

"I don't believe you." She fixed her blue eyes on him in a way that demanded truth.

"One is a means of communicating with the troops in the field. If all is well, Powell is supposed to fire the sunset gun as usual and run a white lamp up the flagstaff. If Indians appear, he's supposed to fire three guns from the twelve-pounder at one-minute intervals and run up a red lantern."

"And the second?"

Harry remembered that document very well:

*If in my absence Indians in overwhelming
numbers attack, put the women and children in the
magazine with supplies of water, bread, crackers,
and other supplies that seem best, and, in the event
of a last desperate struggle, destroy all together
rather than have any captured alive.*

He could not, however, repeat it.

"Never mind," Rose said. "I believe I know." She
raised her eyes to the sky, gray and pregnant with
snow. "I don't think the Indians mean to attack the
fort. If they did they'd have done it by now. I suppose
Red Cloud means to starve us out." She spoke
matter-of-factly, Harry noticed, as another woman
might say, "I believe I will bake a cake this morning."
He admired her calmness.

Snow began falling mid-afternoon, driven by a
lashing, snake-tongue of a wind. By three o'clock it
was dark as night. The women prepared beans and
coffee for the post's defenders, a force of only forty
men. Harry carried a basket to the hospital.

The front room was empty but a fire burned in the
heating stove. Light showed under the sheet of
canvas that separated the surgery from the back
ward, which now served as a morgue. In there, Harry
knew, the surgeons were cataloguing injuries, a list of
horrors, for his father's report. Heart thumping,
Harry crossed the room and pushed the canvas to
one side. A ghoulish sight, reminiscent of something
conjured by Ambrose Bierce at the fireside, met his
eyes. Horton, wearing an overcoat and a cheery red

muffler, leaned over a nude body stretched out on a wooden stand while a steward held a lantern. The dead man's head and face were crushed, his features slid to one side like a partly melted waxen mask.

"Hello, Harry," Horton said, glancing up. "What have you brought us?"

Harry cleared his throat, hoping his voice would not fail him. "Beans and bread. Hot coffee."

"Thank you, son. Put them over there by the window. Carter, more light here." As the steward adjusted the lamp Harry saw a crude tattoo on the dead man's arm, a mermaid with full breasts and flowing hair, and knew he was looking at Purves, a Scotsman who used to entertain his fellow soldiers with stories, told in a thick burr, about his days aboard a Nantucket whaler.

As Harry unpacked the basket Powell stomped into the room, brushing snow from his shoulders.

"Horton!" he called. "Colonel Carrington is back. You're needed in the quartermaster's yard."

Horton came to the canvas door. "Was anyone found alive?" he said.

Powell shook his head.

Horton removed his bloody apron and tossed it onto a growing pile of dirty linens in the corner. "Did they find everyone?"

"To a man," Powell replied, "and they're in the same condition as those you've got. Worse, if anything. Grummond was nearly decapitated. Strange, they even butchered that pinto of yours, Harry. That did surprise me. You'd think they'd take that Injun pony with them."

Calico! With a stab of pure pain, Harry realized he had not given a thought to the sweet pony who had been so much part of his life since leaving Nebraska. Tears stung his eyes. How could he have forgotten about Calico?

"I'm sorry, son." Horton finished buttoning his greatcoat and walked to Harry, putting a hand on his shoulder. "I know how much that pony meant to you boys." He shook his head as he wrapped the red muffler round his head and face till only his eyes were showing. Harry watched Horton and Powell cross the parade yard. The new fall of snow lay white and perfect on the ground, reflecting the light of the full moon that hung over the Bighorns as if balanced on its highest peak. How peaceful everything looks, Harry thought, and what a liar Mother Nature is.

Suddenly he saw a glimmer, a glint, from a distant ridge. They had not seen any signal fires since the previous evening but surely the Indians were still out there, red men of steel, impervious to cold and wind. Harry squeezed his eyes shut, then looked again. The entire ridge had vanished behind a veil of blowing snow.

# Chapter Forty-eight

It snowed all night and all the next day. On December 22, the day after the massacre, the thermometer outside the quartermaster's warehouse plunged to twenty degrees below zero. Drifts piled so high against the stockade's west wall that a man could walk over the top. Carrington ordered the men to dig a ten-foot trench in front of the wall but within three hours it too filled with snow. The trench was dug a second time and then a third, but finally Carrington gave up and posted an extra guard.

A funereal silence gripped the post. The only sounds were the sentries' calls every quarter hour and the hammers of the coffin-makers. The dead officers— Reynolds, Grummond, Brown, and Fetterman—were buried on Christmas Eve in the cemetery below Pilot Hill. The ground was frozen hard as iron and the cold was so intense grave diggers worked in twenty-minute intervals.

Chaplain White kept the ceremony short. It began at one o'clock in a driving snow. No one wept. Even the widows' tears were spent. Although no Indians or signal fires had been seen since the night of the massacre, still the fear of attack hung over the post. Eyes that should have been closed in prayer scanned the hilltops for the first telltale sign of a lance or feathered headdress.

The seventy-six enlisted men and civilians Wheatley and Fisher were buried the day after Christmas, in a long trench. Gravediggers labored round the clock, again in shifts. To save time and timber, the dead were interred two to a coffin. Each man met his maker well-dressed, as survivors donated their best uniforms to clothe their dead friends.

No one spoke of Phillips and Dixon during the long and terrible time of waiting, as if saying their names aloud might somehow bring a curse down upon them. Rose managed to keep busy during the days but nights were torture. Alone in the cabin she once shared with Mark, she lay in the rope bed where he died and stared at the canvas ceiling as hellish images played out in her mind. One hundred and ninety miles separated Fort Phil Kearny from Horseshoe Station on the North Platte, a hard ride during ordinary circumstances. The mercury had not topped zero since the day of the massacre and often it was far below. Even if Daniel managed to avoid the Indians, how could he endure the brutal cold without a fire? Sometimes she thought of Mark, which kindled a roiling mix of emotions. She punished herself with feelings of guilt, believing she owed Mark at least that. But sometimes she let herself imagine a new life in the West, a life free of the smallness of society and its expectations. It wouldn't be easy, but it would be a life she chose and not one chosen for her.

In these waking dreams she shared her days and nights with Daniel Dixon, as his companion and the mother of his children—tall, strong boys who favored him and blue-eyed girls for her. Dan could practice medicine if he wanted to; if not, they would be ranchers or merchants or farmers. They would live in a big white frame house, two stories, with gable windows and a covered porch with a view of the mountains. She saw window boxes with showy red geraniums. Each child would have a pony and there would be a big yellow dog with a sweet face and floppy ears. Pleasurable though it was, she indulged in this dream infrequently because it made a return to reality all the more miserable.

The day after the mass burial, six days after the massacre, a line of soldiers appeared on the Fort Reno Road. Cheers and huzzahs rang through the post but these faded when it became clear the column was too short to be a regiment of rescuers from Laramie. Instead it was Captain George Dandy, Brown's official replacement as quartermaster, and his twenty-five man escort. He brought good news. Dixon and Phillips had made it to Fort Reno, arriving the day after Dandy's company. After learning of the disaster, Dandy had insisted on coming to Fort Phil Kearny at once, unlike Reno's commanding officer, who refused to move until the weather improved. They had seen no Indians on their journey.

Rose's spirits took off like a rocket. He had made it to Fort Reno! She felt hope, like the first warming rays of sun after a long, dark winter. Dandy's arrival had a healing effect on Fort Phil Kearny's anxious residents. A West Point graduate and experienced Indian fighter who campaigned against the Yakimas in Washington Territory in the 1850s, Dandy projected an air of competence and authority. The night of his arrival, alone in quarters that once were Brown's, he recorded his impressions of Fort Phil Kearny in his journal:

> *I found the garrison shut up in the stockade in a demoralized condition from fear and half frozen for want of proper fuel. The extreme severity of winter had been allowed to approach and little or no provision had been made for supplies.*

After touring the post the next morning, Dandy's perception of mismanagement and lack of discipline deepened. He found sawmills in poor repair, neglected wagons, shoddy construction. The warehouses, he noted, were not nearly big enough to hold the stores required for a garrison of its size. Many of the supplies listed in the account books were missing—stolen, Dandy suspected—despite round-the-clock sentinels.

He concluded that the post's materials and manpower had been misspent. Reluctantly, knowing his comments might later be used against Carrington, whom he liked personally, he noted:

*There are no records and the business has been*
*managed without system. The machinery, material,*
*and labor of the post seem to have been confined*
*mainly to two objects, viz—building the stockade*
*and erecting the quarters of the commanding officer.*

The snow stopped on New Year's Day but the cold
only deepened. Minutes turned to hours, hours to
days, days to weeks, and still no sign of reinforcements from Laramie, no word of Phillips and Dixon.
Food supplies, already short, were strained even
more by the addition of Dandy's men. Privation
became a great equalizer. Everyone, regardless of
rank or station, existed on the same diet of beans,
hard bread, and coffee. Starving mules and horses
chewed the bark off the logs of their stables and de-
voured their leather harnesses.

Fear hung over the post like a lowering storm
cloud. The Indians were felt though not seen. The
tension was too much for some. Harry Carrington
woke one morning to hear a rhythmic banging
coming from the kitchen. He went to investigate and
found Black George squatting by the kitchen stove
hitting his gray head against the wall hard enough to
rattle the windows. He kept it up until the colonel
put a revolver to his head and said he would shoot
him if he did not stop.

People passed the time reading or playing games,
chess, checkers, cards. One of Dandy's men had
brought a book, Richard Henry Dana Jr.'s sea adventure, *Two Years Before the Mast*. Harry read it in two
days and passed it along to Rose. She was captivated

by the beautiful but terrifying water world Dana described and imagined herself alongside the author on the California coast curing hides on a beach in moony darkness. She copied down a passage in which Dana urged his readers to "come down from our heights and leave our straight paths for the byways and low places of life." Only by doing this, he said, will we "learn truths . . . and see what has been wrought upon our fellow creatures by accident, hardship, or vice."

If she survived, Rose vowed to learn all she could about the world and the people who inhabit it. She would explore all aspects of life, the "byways and low places" as well as the grand and uplifting ones; she would discover other cultures, learn from them, improve herself with the knowledge they gave her. Above all, she would never reenter one of society's cages. She would not become one of its captive women, would never return to the East with its corsets and parlor talk. Even if it meant living alone for the rest of her life like the solitary squaw at Crazy Woman Creek, she would remain in the West with all its beauty and terror, with all its heart and cruelty.

On the afternoon of January 16, Rose was on her hands and knees scrubbing her cabin floor when she heard the bugle and long roll of drums that meant arriving troops. She opened the door to see men running to the quartermaster's yard. With a thudding heart, she pulled on her coat and buffalo boots and ran with them. Their rescuers had arrived! Companies of men, infantry and cavalry, approached the open gates with General Wessells himself leading the column. Rose surrendered to the hugs of a laughing soldier.

"We're saved!" he cried.

She searched the parade of tired, unshaven faces for Daniel but did not find him. Her joy turned to dread. Had something happened to him? Would she be denied this last chance at happiness after all?

The last horseman entered the yard. He wore a beard and an unfamiliar gray coat, and she did not know him until their eyes met. He slid from the saddle and started toward her and she began to run, not caring who saw. When they met he wrapped her in his arms and lifted her off the ground and they spun together in a delirious circle. When he kissed her the press of his mouth on hers was the most thrilling, the most intimate, feeling she had ever known.

"I'll never leave you again," he said.

"I won't let you," she whispered.

After a time he put her down but he kept his hands on her shoulders. "Rose, we'll have a good life in Bozeman. It will take time and hard work, but you'll never regret it. I promise."

"If you're there I couldn't be anywhere else," she said. For the first time in months, the future unrolled before her as something to look forward to and not simply days on a calendar to fill. They went to her cabin, where she prepared a meal of army beans and cornbread. As he ate, he told her of his ride.

"The first stretch, the sixty-five miles to Reno, were the worst. We traveled at night and hid during the day in bushes or ravines, wherever we found cover for the horses. We tied their heads together to keep them quiet but the cold was a greater danger than Indians. That first night it was so bad I thought we'd die. There were times I would've welcomed it. It was the thought of you that kept me going."

She reached across the table to touch his face, brushing the hair from his eyes. It was a small gesture, but one she had wanted to do so many times. Now at last she had the freedom and the right to do it. He took her hand and held it to his lips.

"Only you," he said. "My greatest fear was never seeing you again. I thought we'd never make Fort Reno, but finally, there it was. God, what a beautiful sight. We rested and warmed up for a couple of hours, then pressed on. We made Horseshoe Station on Christmas day, about ten that morning. The telegraph operator wired the news on to Omaha. I stayed there—my horse was played out. Phillips went on alone to Laramie, with a letter from Wessells and Carrington's dispatches."

"But why?" Rose said. "Why didn't the operator just wire them on?"

"He couldn't guarantee they'd go through, long as they were, and with the weather as it was, he thought the lines might be down. It was too great a risk, so Phillips went on alone. He's a brave man."

Rose said, "I believe he's in love with Frances Grummond. He came to see her before he left."

Dixon nodded. "I suspect the widow Grummond will set her sights a bit higher."

The room was warm, lit only by the glow from the heating stove. Rose got up to pour him a cup of coffee. Her hand shook. She was thrilled, but nervous, at the thought of sharing a bed with him that evening. They would go to his cabin, where there would be fewer ghosts.

"Rose, I've got to tell you something," he said. "Something you might not want to hear."

Her heart sank. *Please,* she thought, *please don't say anything to ruin my happiness.*

"It's about Mark," he said. "About what happened to him. I want you to know before, well, before things go farther."

She remained at the stove with her back to him. If she was about to be shocked, or disappointed, she did not want him to see it.

"Jack Gregory showed up at Horseshoe Station," he said, "just after Phillips left. He was riding a mule. He said he'd been following us. Rose, Jack killed Mark. He wants you to know why he did it."

Rose had suspected Jack had something to do with Mark's death, but she did not want to hear about it. Not now.

"Come," he said. "Sit down." She obeyed numbly. "What do you know of Mark's time as Ewing's adjutant in Kansas City?"

"He rarely spoke of it," she said. "He said he helped General Ewing clean out the trash. Those were his words—'clean out the trash.'" She had noticed Mark seemed bitter the few times he mentioned those days. She never questioned him, but she sensed he expected greater reward for his service than he had received. After all, Tom Ewing was

Sherman's brother-in-law. Certainly he could have advanced a junior officer's career if he chose to.

"Well, if Gregory was telling the truth, and I believe he was, Mark did more than clean up for Ewing. Doc Jennison and his Jayhawkers came to Jack's farm after the Lawrence raid. They tortured his father because they thought he knew where Quantrill and the boys were hiding. Jack wasn't there, but his mother and sisters begged a Federal officer with Jennison that day to stop. The officer said Missouri was full of pukes and trash and he didn't give a damn what happened to any of them. Finally, when it became clear the old man didn't know anything, he told Jennison to put Jack's father in the barn and burn it down. He burned alive."

Rose closed her eyes. "That officer was Mark."

"Yes."

"How did Jack know?" she asked.

"His sister pointed Mark out to Jack after the war, in Kansas City. She said he was easy to remember because he was so beautiful to look at. She said she couldn't believe that anyone so graced by God could be so evil. Jack got his name, vowed to get even. He thought he'd get his chance at Fort Sedgwick but Reynolds left early."

"Is that why he came back from Bozeman City with you?" Rose asked. "To settle the score with Mark?"

"Partly, I guess, but he had another reason. Turns out Jack did steal that payroll back at the redoubt. He and your driver, Ignacio. Do you remember the body we saw on the mountain last summer, on our way back from the Indian ruin?"

Rose nodded.

"That was Ignacio. Indians found them while he and Jack were burying the money at the old fort. They killed the Mexican but Jack got away."

"Did he go back for it? After leaving here?"

"I don't know. He didn't say and I didn't ask." He reached across the table and took her hand. "This is hard for you. Would you like to be alone?"

That was the last thing Rose wanted. She shook her head.

"It was over for Mark and me a long time ago," she said. "I think it ended when he left me at Fort Sedgwick. Did you know I was carrying his child?"

"I'd be a pretty sorry physician if I didn't."

"Do you think I'll ever be able to have children?"

He smiled and stood up from the table, still holding her hand. "There's only one way to find out."

# Chapter Forty-nine

Wessells had brought orders from Cooke relieving Carrington of command of Fort Phil Kearny. Wessells himself was to be Carrington's replacement. Carrington told his officers and his family he expected this, that his reassignment to Fort Casper was in the works even before the massacre, but Harry did not believe him. He knew the men blamed his father for the deaths of eighty-one brothers. No one wanted to serve under him.

Though he did not blame him for the deaths on Massacre Ridge, as Lodge Trail Ridge was now known, Harry understood his father was not a good officer. He saw trees instead of forest, he was too insecure to delegate, he wasted time and money on secondary goals. Worst of all, the men did not respect him. While they would overlook almost any failing in an officer they loved, where Carrington was concerned no shortcoming would be forgiven. Harry saw this clearly.

They would be leaving Fort Phil Kearny soon.

Harry felt a growing sadness as the time drew near. The Powder River country was frightening and cruel, he had lost people who mattered to him, he had often been hungry and cold, but even so he did not want to leave. He loved the rolling green valleys, the sparkling streams, and the towering Bighorns against an endless sky. He loved the mystery of the dark woods on the mountainsides and frozen snowfields on their crests, he loved the people he had known here. He was especially sad that Old Jim Bridger was still at Fort Smith and he would not have a chance to say good-bye.

They would leave in a driving snowstorm. Harry, Jimmy, and their mother would travel in a winterized ambulance, which was fitted out with double boarding and canvas just as the Bisbees' had been weeks before. Dan Dixon and Rose Reynolds came to see them off.

"I'll miss you," Margaret said as she hugged Rose. "But I'm so happy for you and Daniel. Write to me, promise?"

"I will," Rose said. "Of course I will. And you do the same."

Margaret nodded and wiped away tears, then looked slowly about the post that had been her home for the past seven months.

"It turned out badly here," she said. "For so many, including my Henry." She turned to Dixon. "Give my regards to Major Bridger when he returns." She cleared her throat. "Well, good-bye then. I wish you the best."

She climbed into the ambulance, where Jimmy

was making himself a nest with blankets and buffalo skins close to the little stove. Then she shut the door, leaving Harry alone with Rose and Dixon.

Harry kept his eyes on the ground, his throat too tight for speech. Dixon put his hand on his shoulder.

"Harry," he said, "this doesn't have to be good-bye forever. We'll be settled in Bozeman City by summer. Come stay with us when you can. You're welcome anytime."

Harry nodded, still unable to speak. Rose stepped in close and put her arms around him, something he had dreamed of many times but in his dreams he had not felt such pain.

"I'll miss you most of all," she whispered. He saw she was crying.

He cleared his throat, trying not to do the same. "Maybe I'll see you at Fort Casper or back East somewhere."

She shook her head. "No, you must return to us."

"I will." But even as he said it he knew he was looking at her for the last time. There was so much he had never told her. He'd never told her of his love—though he thought she knew—never told her of seeing Mark leaving Jerusha's tent that night, but maybe she knew that too. These things would never be said now, and maybe it was better that way.

"Good-bye," he said. He turned his head, unable to hold back his tears, and climbed into the ambulance. The column was starting. He pressed his face to the window, watching until Rose and Dixon were shadows and finally disappeared altogether in the swirling snow. In the roar of the wind Harry heard the voices of the dead and the lost, of Fetterman and Grummond, Bingham and Bowers, Glover and Reynolds, of Indian warriors and their women and black-eyed babies, of bullwhackers and freighters, scouts and hunters, of cattlemen and emigrants and gold-hungry miners.

The snow was falling faster and thicker now, dry and granular as sand. Eventually all was obscured, the black flagpole, the cabins and warehouses, the sawmill, the stockade walls, until all was lost in an impenetrable fog of snow.

# Afterward

*July 2, 1908*

The two men sat in wicker chairs on the porch of a large, two-story ranch house. One was portly and expensively dressed in woolen trousers and a silk waistcoat, the other tall and rawboned, wearing jeans and a faded cotton shirt.

"Thank you, George, for giving the old folks a place to stay," the stout man said. "It's an inconvenience, I know, but it'll only be for the two nights. You know, this has turned out huge for us. We've got press from New York and Chicago and St. Louis. Of course, it's a headache for me, as mayor." He picked a piece of lint from his trousers. "But it'll be worth it. This will put Sheridan, Wyoming, on the map."

He took a pack of cigarettes from his waistcoat pocket and offered one to his companion, rancher George Gier, who shook his head. They watched Gier's hired man wrestle the elderly couple's bags from the automobile, a Hewitt Landaulet, provided by the Chamber of Commerce. Gier's wife had already taken their guests to their rooms.

"Bound to be an emotional time for them," the mayor said. He struck a match on the sole of his boot and lit a cigarette. "They haven't been back here since it happened. Almost forty-two years."

Gier gazed out over the field of alfalfa growing thick on the plateau at the fork of the creeks. "We still find things," he said, "not like at first, when we first went to ranching, but every now and then. Up on the ridge, too—cartridges, buttons, lance points. Found a ball and chain over yonder. And this." He reached into his worn jeans pocket and produced a tiny tin soldier in Revolutionary costume, its red, white, and blue colors still bright. "I found it buried out there in the alfalfa field. Carry it around for luck. Say, you think the colonel and his wife would like to see any of this old stuff? We kept most of those things, out in the barn."

The mayor pulled on his cigarette, his face thoughtful. "I don't know, George," he said. "The old man is strung pretty tight, if you know what I mean. He looks sickly. It wouldn't do to upset him, right before the ceremony. Maybe after."

He discovered a stain on his waistcoat and worked on it with a wettened finger. "Hard to believe all the things went on back then," he said. "I was just a boy, but I remember reading about it in the Denver newspaper. Looking back, I guess you might say what happened here started it all—you know, the Indian wars. You don't hear much about Fort Phil

Kearny nowadays but it was big news back then, I'll tell you that."

Gier nodded. "I remember. Stories about how those eighty-one men were killed, pounding on the gates, because the soldiers inside the fort were too scared to open them up and let them in. Didn't matter that none of that stuff was true, the colonel got blamed anyhow."

Inside the house they heard Gier's wife asking their guests if they wanted to wash up before dinner. The old man thanked her but said they were tired and would go straight to bed. Perhaps she would be kind enough to bring tea and sandwiches?

"Yes, it ruined him, you know," the mayor said, lowering his voice. "His career never recovered. Poor Carrington. Spent his whole life writing letters, petitioning Congress, trying to get his good name back, but he never found any satisfaction. Sad, really."

Gier said, "What about his wife? Was she here too, back then?"

"Yes, she was here. But the colonel was married to another woman at the time. The first wife—Margaret, I think her name was—died back in seventy. Tuberculosis. They had two sons who were here too. One of them, Jim, is a writer for *Scribner's* in New York. The older boy, Harry, died in ninety-two or ninety-three down in Mexico, trying to get cured of consumption. He was a railroad engineer, lived in Chicago. Fine man, by all accounts. Frances, the current Mrs. Carrington, was married to one of the colonel's officers at the time. Grummond, one of them killed up there."

The men sat in silence, looking at Lodge Trail Ridge. The lush lower slopes were in shadow but the rocky, wind-blasted crest was lit by the setting sun. Just over the crest, at a site not visible from the Gier porch, stood a new monument, a stone obelisk, erected at the urging of a Wyoming congressman in memory of the eighty-one victims of Fetterman's Massacre. It would be officially dedicated the following day, with the eighty-four-year-old Henry Carrington delivering the memorial address.

Gier rocked in his chair, thinking of the aged soldier in his guest room. "He lost everything, pretty near," he said. "That explains his eyes. There's a lot of sadness in them."

The mayor nodded, then got to his feet. "Your place will be crawling with people tomorrow, George," he said. "Hundreds, I'd say. A lot of old-timers coming back for the dedication. I appreciate your cooperation, my friend. Damn good for the community."

"What about Doc Dixon?" Gier said. "Will he and Rose be here?"

The mayor shook his head. "No, they didn't seem interested. Anyhow, he and Rose are in California this month. Harry, their oldest boy, lives in San Francisco, you know. He practices medicine out there, makes a lot of money too, or so I hear. Doc and Rose, they're mighty proud of him. They're proud of all those kids, and so they should be."

He consulted his pocket watch then stuck out his hand. "Well, I'll be getting along. See you in the morning, George. Ceremony starts at ten but I'll be here at nine or so to pick up the colonel and the missus and drive them up to the site. Thanks again for being a sport about all this. It's a lot easier on them, you know, staying here, close to the action. Not so much back-and-forth."

The mayor climbed into the Chamber of Commerce car and with a wave of his arm began the twenty-seven-mile drive back to Sheridan.

The rancher stood alone on his porch. Inside the parlor someone began to play the piano. He smiled. That would be Mary, his youngest, showing off for the visitors.

A cool wind blew down from the mountains. Gier turned to go inside but something, distinct as a tug on his sleeve, compelled him to pause and look back, over the plateau where Fort Phil Kearny once stood, toward Piney Creek where silvery grasses rippled in the breeze, and finally to Lodge Trail Ridge where so many men, red and white, had lost their lives forty-two years before. He stood for a full minute, eyes closed, face to the wind, listening to the drumbeats of the past. Then he turned and entered his house, hungry for his dinner. The screen door closed behind him, reverberating like a pistol shot throughout the darkening valley.